D0610138

# DANCING ON CORAL

# DANCING ON CORAL

## GLENDA ADAMS

SIRIUS

*Creative writing programme assisted by the
Literature Board of the Australia Council,
the Federal Government's arts funding
and advisory body.*

*ANGUS & ROBERTSON PUBLISHERS*

*Unit 4, Eden Park, 31 Waterloo Road,
North Ryde, NSW, Australia 2113, and
16 Golden Square, London W1R 4BN,
United Kingdom*

*First published in Australia
by Angus & Robertson Publishers in 1987
This New Sirius edition 1988*

*Copyright © Glenda Adams 1987*

*Portions of this novel, in different form, have appeared in*
Meanjin, TriQuarterly, The Hottest Night of the Century,
*and* Lies and Stories.

*The maths riddle on pages 79-80 is from* Mindbenders,
*published by Midwest Publications, Pacific Grove,
California. Reprinted by permission.*

*National Library of Australia
Cataloguing-in-publication data.*

*Adams, Glenda, 1940- .
  Dancing on coral.
  ISBN 0 207 16103 8.
  I. Title.
A823'.3*

*Printed in Australia by Renwick Pride Pty Ltd, Thurgoona, NSW*

# ACKNOWLEDGMENTS

The author gratefully acknowledges the support of the National Endowment for the Arts and the Literature Board of the Australia Council, and of the MacDowell Colony, The Virginia Center for the Creative Arts, and the Yaddo Corporation, where parts of this novel were written.

Thanks to A. M. Barrett, who remembered the stops on the air route from Sydney to London, and to Barbie MacKenzie, who called her sheep Wooliam, Woolfred, and Woolbur.

# DANCING ON CORAL

# I

The rooster was crowing, at two in the afternoon, and the cicadas had started up again after their lunchtime quiet.

"It's a case of too much noise," said Henry Watter, the father of Lark. "Far too much noise." He was in the basement working on his project. He seized the hammer and rushed into the backyard. He thrust the rooster into the small wooden crate that rested under the gum tree within the circle of chicken wire that formed its coop and hammered it shut, the sun glinting on the hammerhead and on the lenses of his metal-rimmed glasses. The Bakers' dog next door started barking. The rooster continued crowing. From farther off came the buzz of a lawnmower.

Lark watched the hammering, then went back to looking through the old seventy-eights and the sheet music stacked near the pianola—Caruso singing *"Vesti la giubba,"* a silly song called "I Lift Up My Finger and I Say Tweet, Tweet," and polonaises and rhapsodies played by Ignaz Friedman. She had already saved a hundred pounds, almost enough for a one-way passage to somewhere, Singapore or Ceylon perhaps, and she had arranged for an interview with Qantas to be an air hostess, after her exams. That was one way to get away.

Lark's father rushed into the house, then returned to the backyard with several army blankets and a tattered French flag, which he draped over the crate, layer on layer, creating night for the confused bird.

"Sits there like a stunned mullet," said Henry Watter.

"Do you think that's wise, Henry?" asked Lark's mother from under her pink cloth sunhat. Her hands, in white gloves, were pegging clothes on the line with such alacrity that she could have been playing a scherzo on the pianola. The gloves protected her hands from the sun. The sunhat, in addition to performing its intended function, protected her head from the kookaburras and magpies, which liked to swoop down to take strands of hair for their nests.

"Like bombers," said Henry Watter. "It's a case of World War Two in our own backyard. This country's a joke. One big joke."

The crowing continued, muted, while he lobbed stones at the yelping dog next door. Every now and then he threw a stone into the trees to silence the cicadas. And he stood in the ankle-high grass waiting for the next noise, in his undershirt and khaki shorts, which were held up by a piece of rope tied around his waist in a reef knot. With the grass obscuring his feet in their black nylon ankle socks and lace-up shoes, he looked as if he had been planted and had sprouted from those white legs now trembling with rage.

"I do wish he would mow the grass," said Mrs. Watter, whipping a row of pillow cases onto the clothesline. "The paspalum gets on everything." She flicked at her skirt.

The lorikeets, fifty or sixty of them, started lining up on the veranda rail, jostling and squawking, peering in the window, arranged a multicolored *tableau vivant*, waiting for the daily bread that Lark's mother put out for them. Preserving Australia's natural heritage, Mrs. Watter called it, and when she collected colored river pebbles and sat turning the handle of the little barrel to polish them, she also felt she was preserving something Australian and natural.

Lark's father took a mop and waved it at the birds on the veranda rail. "Heritage be damned," he said. "In this flaming country it's a case of too much nature. Far too much nature."

"Henry, please, no language." Lark's mother tended to whisper whenever possible, even outdoors, among the noisy insects.

"Where's that cat when it's needed?" Henry Watter muttered. He swung at the birds. "William the First," he said and swung again. "William the Second," and he swung again. "Henry the First, Stephen."

"Watch my windows," called Lark's mother from under her hat. "They'll cost the earth to replace."

"Henry the Second, Richard Lionheart, John." Lark's father threw the mop down beside the back steps and stamped inside.

"Mind my parsley and my mint," Lark's mother called after him.

"William and Mary," said Lark's father. He threw himself onto the lounge and placed his hands over his face. "Far, far too much nature."

Lark had always planned to run away. When she was four, she had packed her cardboard sewing case with her supplies for the journey—a swimsuit, a cardigan, her money box, an aspirin bottle filled with water in case there was no water to drink, and another aspirin bottle of methylated spirits, and matches, in case she needed to make a fire. She kept it all under the bed, next to a large black umbrella that could also be used as a walking stick or a club. She planned to wander around the world, until she found some kind of island to settle on, where it would be peaceful.

"I'm going now," she often said, taking the suitcase and the umbrella, standing at the front door.

"She's going now," said Henry Watter if he said anything at all. Or, "It's a tricky place, the world. You've got to be sharp to manage it."

"Leave her be. She'll be back," said Mrs. Watter. "This is her home. She knows that."

And sometimes Lark went along the cliff road, above the Pacific Ocean, past the school, as far as the corner.

· · ·

In that house on Park Avenue on the cliff in Sydney, Henry Watter sat memorizing *Bartlett's Familiar Quotations*.

Lark was sorting through the records, as usual.

"Hold it," cried Henry Watter. "Let's do 'No News.' I'll be the servant." He had caught sight of the old Frank Crumit seventy-eight called "No News," a comic dialogue between a man and his servant.

Lark sighed. "Why don't you do some more work on your project?"

"You be the master," said Henry Watter, undeterred.

"Any news?" said Lark reluctantly, paraphrasing the record, trying to get it over and done with.

"'No sir. Everything's just about the same as when you went away.'" Henry Watter threw himself into the part, scraping and bowing in front of Lark. "'Nothing happened.'"

"'I'm dying for some news from home,'" droned Lark.

"Put some feeling into it, Larkie," said Henry, then, bowing and scraping again, "'Nothing to tell you at all, except for one thing. Since you've been away, your dog died, sir.'"

"'What killed the dog?'" Lark stared out the window.

"'It seems that the dog ate some burnt horseflesh and, er, dat's what killed the dog.'"

"Please don't say 'dat,'" said Lark. And she hated the way the information had to be elicited, step by step, rather than simply volunteered.

"Come on, Larkie, don't interrupt the dialogue."

"'Where did the dog get the burnt horseflesh?'"

"'Well, sir, your barn burnt down, and after the fire cooled down, the dog went in and ate some of the burnt horseflesh, and dat's what killed the dog.'"

"Don't say 'dat,'" said Lark, "or I won't play. I can't stand it. It's racist."

"Nonsense," said Henry Watter. "What nonsense." Then, in his servant's whining voice, "'The sparks from the house flew over and burnt down the barn and burnt up all the cows and horses, and after the fire cooled down the dog went in and ate up some of the burnt horseflesh, and, er, dat's what killed the dog.'"

Lark stood up and turned away from him. She put the records back in their pile.

Henry Watter was cringing before her, plucking at her sleeve. "'You see, there were candles in the house, and the flame from the candle crept up the curtain and onto the roof and the sparks flew over to the barn, burnt it down and burnt up all the cows and horses, and when the fire cooled down, the dog went in and ate up some of the burnt horseflesh and dat's what killed the dog.'"

Lark tried to push past him.

Henry Watter blocked her way. "'They had candles burning all round the coffin. Dat's another little thing I forgot to tell you all about. Your mother-in-law died. Don't know exactly what killed her, but everyone says it was from the shock of your wife running away with the chauffeur.'" He raised his voice. "'But outside dat, sir, dere ain't no news.'" Henry Watter slapped his thigh, cackling at the joke, at having forced her to listen.

Lark was staring out the window. Then she started dumping her books in a canvas bag.

"Test me," Lark's father said.

The lorikeets were at the window, nudging the glass, tapping it with their beaks, chattering.

"I was just going down to the beach to study," said Lark.

"Test me first," said her father. He, too, had been preparing to run away for years.

Lark sighed. "Kings of England? Shakespeare? Definitions?"

Henry Watter pointed at the street map of London pinned across the bookshelves.

"Streets of London, then," said Lark.

The muffled cries of the rooster still reached them.

"God love a duck," said Henry Watter. And then, "God stiffen the crows." And against her will, Lark saw God embracing a duck, in front of a line of crows standing at attention.

The Bakers' dog was still yelping.

"How do you get from Regent's Park Zoo to," Lark searched for somewhere for him to go, "to the Tower of London?"

When Lark was young, Henry Watter had taken her to the zoo, the Taronga Park Zoo on the north shore of the harbor, and at the end of the day had said, "Let's catch the ferry now and go home." Lark thought he had said he was going to catch a fairy, and she was in some state of excitement as they walked down the path to the wharf. When he asked, "Is this the ferry to the Quay?", the boat hand nodded and they boarded. "Where's the fairy?" Lark asked, and her father said, "You're on it." It felt like a cruel joke. Lark ran onto the wharf and refused to get back on. Her father had to get off, too, and the ferry left without them. That particular ferry caught fire in the middle of the harbor and the passengers had to take to the lifeboats. Several of them drowned. At home they said it was Lark's sense of impending doom that had saved them.

After that, every week, when she had her boiled egg, Henry Watter drew a face on the shell, and then, when she had finished her egg, he turned the empty shell upside down in the egg cup so that the face looked up at her, and let her smash it.

"That's Hitler," said Henry Watter. "You're saving us from Hitler with that strength of yours."

"Eat up all your egg, so that you can smash Hitler," they said.

Henry Watter settled in his chair, turning his back on the map. He pushed his glasses on top of his head. His voice became soft and slow. "Turn left on Marylebone Road, then south on Tottenham Court Road, which turns into Charing Cross Road, to Trafalgar Square. Then turn left on The Strand. Keep going." And he kept going, until he ended up at the Tower. "Of course," he added, "you could go out the northern end of the park, near Primrose Hill, and walk along the footpath beside the canal to Camden Town, then take the tube." He took care to explode the *t* in tube. "You see, Larkie, I'll get along there, when I go. I can say 'tube' like an aristocrat, instead of 'chube' like a pleb."

"I'm going to the beach now," said Lark. "I have to study my French."

"And I have to study my England."

"But I'll really need my French, when I go," said Lark.

"You'll need more than your French. You know nothing. I've forgotten more than you know." Henry Watter leant toward her. "For one thing, did you know they like to drug young girls? For the white slave trade. One of the girls at the office, way back, disappeared. Never heard from. Apparently she accepted a drink from a stranger. The world's a tricky place." He straightened. "Come on, Larkie, test me."

Lark sighed. "Name three of Shakespeare's clowns," she said.

"'Alas, poor Yorick,'" said Henry Watter. "That's one."

The lorikeets were calling out. The *tableau* had broken formation and the birds were falling over one another in anticipation.

Henry Watter looked around to check that Mrs. Watter was still in the kitchen, then whispered, "I'm going on Jack Davey on the radio. Don't tell your mother. I'm going to win my fare to London. I'm going to be a contestant." He placed *Bartlett's Familiar Quotations* in Lark's hands. "Test me, Larkie."

She let the book fall open. "'There is a tide in the affairs of men, which, taken at the flood, leads on to fortune.'"

Henry Watter sat up straight. "'Omitted, all the voyage of their life is bound in shallows and in miseries.' W. Shakespeare, *J. Caesar*. Act four, scene three."

Mrs. Watter was putting out the bread soaked in milk and honey. The beaks of the lorikeets hit the tin pans like gravel falling on a tin roof.

"She thinks this is Jerusalem," cried Henry Watter. "Get the cat. Set it on those birds." He fell back into his chair. He shook his head for a while, then picked up the dictionary and continued to memorize it. "Martello tower," he said, "a circular, masonry fort." He jumped to his feet. "Masonry. I think I'll work a bit on my project." And he fled through the kitchen down the back stairs to the basement.

Mrs. Watter was at the sink. She shook her head. "He takes out two books at a time from the library." She lowered her voice and placed her hand on Lark's arm to detain her as she walked with her books to the back door. "But you'll note that sometimes he holds the book upside down. And I do believe he thinks he is a writer or something. He keeps scribbling things in an exercise book. I find it under the mattress when I turn the bed."

The hammering had started in the basement. Mrs. Watter had let go of Lark's arm and was now talking to herself. "He'd do better to do something about that grass, rather than hammer that wood."

With her books under her arm and the beach umbrella over her shoulder, Lark walked along Park Avenue to the path that led to the beach. She hoped to find Solomon Blank there. They had been doing things together, going out, for some time. Lark had gone with Solomon to see *Cat on a Hot Tin Roof,* and Solomon had asked Lark if she could put on her nylons the way Elizabeth Taylor had in the movie, a kind of peeling-on motion. Solomon had graduated and no longer had final exams, only his research on Renaissance drama, and he was waiting to hear from the dozens of universities abroad, where he had applied to do his doctoral research.

Solomon's younger brother, Marshall, a year or so younger than Lark, was in the schoolyard, mowing the lawn, earning his pocket money. That was a good sign. It meant that the Blanks were around, not off at their country house or at a family luncheon in the eastern suburbs or at some church function.

The four Blank boys were named after islands in the South Pacific—Gilbert, Ellice, Solomon, and Marshall.

"Better than Guam," Solomon said. "Or Nauru."

"I wish I were named after an island," cried Lark, "or that an island were named after me."

"You'd have to own one," said Solomon, who had already traveled a lot. "Then you could name it what you wanted."

The Blanks were the most exotic family in Park Avenue. Mr. and Mrs. Blank had even taken their four sons to England for a year, for the culture, when they were all very young, and they had traveled through France, since Mrs. Blank believed the family name was really Blanc, even le Blanc, and went as far back as Charlemagne or William the Norman. For a while she tried to have people pronounce their name Blong, as if it were French. Solomon's great grandfather, Charles Blank, and his great grandmother were said to have Christianized the entire South Pacific and written books about it. Mrs. Blank sometimes called them the Charleblancs, to which her husband replied that Charlatan might be closer to the truth. It had been ascertained that Charles Blank had frequently drunk and joked with Robert Louis Stevenson.

Lark pushed hard on the rusty metal catch of the old canvas umbrella. Another year and she should have enough money to go away. That was all she wanted, to go away—and to find true love, if possible. She lay on the sand and started with *L'Etranger*, trusting that sentences like "I was almost blinded by the blaze of light," "the sand was hot as fire," and "now and then a longer wave wet our canvas shoes" would be useful during her future adventures, away. Two flies buzzed around her, alighting on her lips and nostrils, and as she read, she had to keep brushing her hand against her face.

Solomon Blank threw his car keys on the pages of Lark's book. She had not sensed his walking toward her across the sand. "'*La campagne bourdonnait du chant des insectes,*'" she said to Solomon.

"'The countryside was throbbing with the hum of insects.' I'll be needing that, when I go away."

Solomon was shaking his head to get rid of the two flies, which had transferred their attention to him. He sat on the sand beside her and rubbed suntan oil on her back.

"'Can you justify the following being regarded as a short story?'" Lark asked, looking out to sea. "'What does the author achieve within the severe limits he has set himself?' That's the kind of question I'm going to have to answer." She continued, quoting, "'"To die like Joan of Arc," said Terbaud, from the top of a pyre built with his furniture. The Saint-Owen fire-brigade hindered him.'"

Solomon laughed. "That's not a story."

"Why not? You have plot, character, a protagonist who wants something urgently, in this case a death like Joan of Arc's, an antagonist, in this case the fire-brigade, and you have a sense of time and place," said Lark. "That's all a story needs. Three lines. Less."

"But there's no development, no dramatization."

And then Mrs. Baker came huffing past, since it was Saturday and not a sign of turpitude to be on the beach, and stopped to shout that it was a hot day, like a furnace. Solomon continued to rub the oil on Lark's back, Lark agreed that it was a hot day, and Mrs. Baker passed on to pitch her umbrella a little farther along the sand next to a friend, and her chattering began again. "Like a parakeet in a cage," Lark said.

Lark's mother remarked that Mrs. Baker had seen Lark on the beach with a young man. Mrs. Watter was sorting through a cardboard carton of old papers.

"I was only with Solomon Blank," said Lark.

Lark's mother asked what he had been doing.

Lark frowned and thought. "Possibly he was helping me put up the umbrella."

"Mrs. Baker said that Solomon Blank was rubbing oil on you."

"That's right," said Lark. "That's what he was doing."

"Then why didn't you say so?"

"Is this a quiz?" Lark asked. "A test?"

"Please, Lark, your attitude." Mrs. Watter sank into a nearby chair. "It's your dignity I'm thinking of."

"I warned you it's tricky," Henry Watter called from his chair. "'Get thee to a nunnery.'"

"I just have to sit down for a minute." Mrs. Watter fanned at her face. "Then I'll make us a cup of tea, Henry."

Lark thought it would not be long now before she left.

"I'm leaving," Solomon Blank had told Lark as he smoothed the oil over her back and arms. "I have the fellowship. Champaign-Urbana."

Lark had hunched over her book. She wished that Solomon would fail at something. "'*Rester ici ou partir, cela revenait au même,*'" she had said, surly. "'To stay here or to leave, it comes to the same thing.' And are you sure you can study Renaissance drama at Champaign-Urbana? It sounds to me like a place to study cocktail parties, with wine and urbane chatter and all that."

"Sour grapes," said Solomon. "In America you can study everything everywhere. You'll be going soon, too. Everyone does."

They went down to the water's edge and walked along the bright sand to the sandstone rock platform at the base of the weathered cliff. They walked around to the blowhole, out of sight of the beach. The sun glinted on the mica and quartzite fragments in the stone. The sea gulls picked at the bits and pieces of oysters and periwinkles. The sea was calm. The waves welled up, rose, like a loaf of bread, and spilled gently across the rock shelf, wetting their feet. The blowhole, a fissure in a section of the rock shelf that descended in a convex curve to the water, gave out a thin spray of water with each new set of waves. Solomon and Lark were able to stand right beside it and hold their arms out over the spray, although every now and then the water shot up unexpectedly high and on rough days had even claimed a life or two. Solomon and Lark moved away and lay down together on the rocks. The water, tepid from its journey across the warm rock shelf, slid under their backs. Lark's head rested on Solomon's shoulder.

"I've never even met an American," Lark said.

"You're giving me a golden shoulder," Solomon said. He rumpled her short, fair hair and kissed her.

"It's probably just my hair coming off on your shirt," Lark said sourly, and sat up.

"Perhaps you'll end up with me in Champaign-Urbana. Who knows?"

"End up?" said Lark. "We would just be beginning." She watched the sea gulls tapping at the shells. "I want to go to Paris. 'You'd like living in Paris, too,'" she quoted. "'And of course we could travel about France for some months in the year.'"

"Paris?" said Solomon, puzzled, sitting up. "I've been there. I have to go to America. Sometimes I have absolutely no idea what you're talking about."

"Camus," said Lark.

Very far out a ship was gliding past, a freighter heading north, for Newcastle or Gladstone, and then possibly farther, across the Pacific to America.

"Could I come with you now?" Lark had asked into Solomon's shoulder.

"I'll write," Solomon had said. "I'll tell you what it's like, away. We'll see what happens. I'll miss you, you know that, don't you?"

"Can you justify the following being regarded as a short story? 'Silot, a valet, established an attractive woman in the home of his absent master at Neuilly, then disappeared carrying away everything but her.'"

A man was now squatting beside the blowhole, and cringing

behind him was a thin boy wearing a bright red beanie over his tousled blond hair. The man sat the boy on his knee and held his legs out over the fissure. When he heard the whistling, windy approach of the sea under the rock shelf, the boy was frightened, too frightened to scramble away, and Lark thought of calling out to the father, telling him not to torture the boy, but she did nothing. When the water surged up through the blowhole, it sprinkled the boy's legs, causing him to shriek and at last wrestle his way off his father's knee. "You are such a scaredy-cat," the father said. The man took the woolen beanie off his son's head and held it out over the blowhole, letting it go when the water spurted up, to see how high the water spout would carry it. He did this several times, until the beanie was sucked down the fissure with the receding sea.

Solomon leant back and squinted at Lark. "You could be a boy, about twelve, whose mother will insist on his getting a haircut because he's beginning to look like a girl."

Lark pulled at her hair, bringing it forward over her ears and forehead.

"I've got to get back," Solomon had said, opening his eyes and looking around. "My mother will be furious if she knows I'm around the rocks." He stood up. "She doesn't want me to get into trouble before I go away." He straightened his shirt. "I think she's glad I'm going." He looked at his watch. "Lunch. She'll be furious."

"You sound like a boy yourself," said Lark, "scared of your mother."

"You didn't go around the rocks, did you?" asked Lark's mother. She had recovered from Lark's attitude and was back at the carton of papers, holding up drawings done by Lark as a child, pictures of perfect families, mothers and fathers with sons and daughters in equal numbers, all with names and ages printed under their shoes, all arranged by height. She was glancing through the letters Lark had written when she had been sent away to the mountains.

"I don't remember," said Lark.

"Mrs. Baker said you went around the rocks with him," said Lark's mother. "You know what happens around the rocks. It's not nice for a girl, for one thing, and for another the waves can be dangerous. They can kill."

"And watch that blowhole," said Henry Watter. "That blowhole is the thing to watch. It can creep up on you. On this continent nature has gone berserk." He looked back at his book. "Did you know that Mousehole is pronounced Moozel, in England? It's a town. Therefore, blowhole should be blew-el."

"Solomon Blank's leaving," Lark said. "You don't have to worry about him and me any more. He's off, lucky devil."

"Please, Lark, no language," said Mrs. Watter. She handed Lark the letters. "You might want to keep these. They're of historical interest, perhaps. They show your fear of atomic bombs at a very early age." She turned the drawings toward Lark. "But you don't want these any more, do you? I always thought you could grow up to be a commercial artist, such a good job, good pay, but I don't think there's any point saving these. I don't think you'll be a commercial artist. I don't think you have the gumption. I think you're too caught up with your university friends. But remember, a woman has to be able to earn a living, to stand on her own two feet. Just look at me." She spread her hands wide and shrugged. "I can't do anything." She walked to the window and contemplated the clothes on the line and the long grass. After a while she said, "We'll rent a sheep." She turned back to Henry in the armchair. "I hear you can rent a sheep for one week a month to keep the grass down."

"More wildlife?" groaned Henry Watter. "You're joking."

"Or a goat," said Mrs. Watter. "But goats eat more than just grass, they say. Sometimes they eat your gravel path and your washing and clothes pegs." She took a deep breath. "I'm going to polish some of my stones."

. . .

Lark walked slowly along the cliff road from the house to the little school with the iron fence. Solomon Blank had flown off to America.

"We'll have to fly," Mrs. Watter had said once, when Lark was very young and they were running late for the bus into town. Mrs. Watter had seized Lark's hand and run down the front path, hauling Lark along, who expected that at any moment they were to rise into the air and fly to the bus.

Lark stopped at the school gates, leaning her forehead against the bars, her eyes closed. The cicadas were shouting, like a male chorus, causing the air to throb, the sound waves almost palpable. She heard again those mouth organs, the recorders, triangles, tambourines, little drums, and the sound of spoons beating against saucepans, and saw those children, some fifty of them, parading in a circle around the school lawn, looking neither happy nor sad. The older ones, Solomon Blank among them, were playing the musical instruments, the younger ones were banging the spoons and saucepans. Lark was crying because she had only two spoons to beat together. The headmistress stood on the school veranda and announced several times, wringing her hands, "We have won the war in Europe, children. God was on our side. Hitler and the Germans have been brought to their knees."

A girl who was a celebrity in the school because she had been in England when the war broke out was allowed to plant a tree in a special ceremony.

"VE Day will be our May Day forevermore," said the headmistress. "And now there remains only the Pacific to be won."

In the cloakroom Lark stole the woolen beret of the girl who had planted the tree. She crammed her own Panama hat on her head, trying to tuck the beret under it, out of sight. When the girl cried that she could not find her beret, the teacher wrenched the Panama from Lark's head, exposing her in front of all the children. Her face leant down into Lark's, and

Lark thought of smashing it, like the face on the eggshell.

"Two hats?" the teacher said, dangling both in Lark's face. "Get your own beret, if you want one."

But with wartime rationing, only the rich had woolen berets.

"What is May Day?" Lark had asked her father.

"Mayda?" He sat up, his book face-down on his knees, delighted with the question. "Mayda is a legendary island southwest of Ireland, and west of Brittany."

"May Day?"

"You mean Mayday! That's an international distress call. Do you want me to teach it to you?"

"No," said Lark. "I'll never need to know that."

Then she remembered leaning against the mulberry tree and watching her mother chop the head off a chicken. The body ran around the yard. The Pacific War was over and they were celebrating with a special chicken dinner. The Bakers took down the flags of the allies, which they had flown every day of the war, and offered the French flag to Lark. Lark was surprised that the blue, white, and red cloth was woolen and extremely rough to the touch. She wrapped the flag around her, like a cloak. She put on her father's gas mask and crept to the fence and peered over at the Bakers' boy. He ran to his mother, screaming that there was a monster on the back fence, and Lark heard Mrs. Baker telling him that the Watters were a strange lot.

"You see," said Mrs. Watter, "all that smashing of Hitler on the eggshells really helped. We won the war. They drew the Kaiser on my eggshells when I was a girl, and we won that war, too."

For several years Lark's school report read: Lark imagines difficulties where there are none; her ability to lead in a helpful manner is developing slowly; her ability to work as an individual could be better; her ability to solve problems could be better; her concentration could be better; participation in group conversations is improving.

It was decided that Lark had been upset about something for years. It was thought that the war had affected many children. She should go away for a while, to the Blue Mountains, said Mrs. Watter, to herself, since Henry Watter wanted no part of sending the child away. And off Lark went for a month to a children's boardinghouse, in the middle of winter, where she was the only guest. It was not the kind of journey she had been planning. She did not want mountains. "Remember about maintaining your toothbrush, when you go," Henry Watter whispered to her. "Trouble with your teeth when you travel is a catastrophe."

The first night Lark turned the tap full on to rinse off her toothbrush. "That's the way my father taught me to rinse my toothbrush," she explained, rather proud of the technique.

"Damages the bristles and wastes water," said the woman in charge of the boardinghouse, perched on the edge of the bathtub.

Lark dried her brush on her towel, aware that the woman was noticing the drying of the brush in particular. "He said the brush goes mildew in the wretched climate of this accursed continent if you don't dry it," she said.

"Spreads filth on the brush," said the woman. "And don't use words of that ilk in this house."

Lark wrote that she was ready to come home after only two weeks: "I am very unhappy in the mountains. One of the things she says about me is that I'm spoilt. I can't eat her rhubarb. And she says 'ilk.' I know I should stand up to it, but I can't. Another thing is that I clean my toothbrush in the wrong way. Will you please get me away from here? When I wrote this I was crying. I can't help it. Your loving daughter."

Mrs. Watter wrote that she had paid for the full four weeks and that the change would be good.

Lark wrote: "I heard over the news on the radio that an atom bomb is going to be dropped in Sydney, and that after the fire come the ashes which fall and cover everything. It is true. Please get me home. Your loving daughter."

Just a few days later Henry Watter appeared on the veranda of the boardinghouse at six in the morning, banging on the wooden door. He had traveled all night on the milk train, and Lark could see that he had his pajamas on under his suit. He had come to take her home.

When they arrived back in the house on the cliff, Mrs. Baker in her front garden, noticing the pajama cuffs, shook her head. And Mrs. Watter, shaking her head, said, "Henry, you really shouldn't have fetched her. The change was supposed to be good. You were supposed to have four full weeks of rest," leaving Lark in some doubt as to who was supposed to be getting the rest and for whom the change was intended.

"Thank you for saving me," she told her father.

"Ask me the stops on the first air route from Sydney to London," Henry Watter said to little Lark. "It won't be long now, before I go." Then he continued, without waiting for her to form the question, "Sydney, Brisbane, Gladstone, Townsville, Karumba, Groot Island, Darwin, Kupang, Bima, Surabaja, Batavia, Klabat Bay, Singapore, Penang, Bangkok, Rangoon, Akyab, Calcutta, Allahabad, Gwalior, Karachi, Gwadar, Dubai, Bahrein, Basra, Tiberias, Athens, Brindisi, Rome, Marseilles, Mâcon, Southampton, London."

Lark lifted her head from the fence rail. The cicadas, accompanied by lawnmowers, were still at it.


For her Qantas interview Lark wore a floral blouse buttoned to the neck and a dark green linen skirt with four buttons at the back, forming the four points of a square, like the buttons on a man's double-breasted jacket. She thought she looked rather like an air hostess already.

"With those buttons, I hope you don't have to sit down," Lark's father said.

He was sitting at the kitchen table, waiting for his lunch. Lark, dressed for the interview and with her coat on already, was grilling him a lamb chop. In her coat pocket she carried Solomon Blank's first letter. "The leg season has arrived here; legs are visible again after the winter, decked in the new season's Bermuda shorts in subtle variations of color, cut, and style. The legs thus exposed show the same variations, not always so subtle, but often of interest to a lonely male doctoral student." Solomon Blank seemed to be in the most exciting place in the Northern Hemisphere, and acculturating very easily.

Lark dumped the chop on a plate next to a mound of lettuce and pushed it in front of her father.

"I'm not a rabbit," he said. Lark grabbed the lettuce in one hand and thrust it back into the crisper. Henry Watter lifted the chop with his fork and peered at the plate. "It's a case of excess blood of the lamb. Please."

Lark flung the chop back onto the griller. She looked at her watch. "But I have to go."

"You'll go, all right. And when you go, you'll be in trouble your first day. You'll see. It's not straightforward, the world." Henry Watter waved her to the chair opposite him, then looked around to check that they were alone. From under his cardigan he pulled out a sheaf of paper, both sides of each sheet covered with his beautiful handwriting. "Read this," he whispered.

"'Ash,' by Sydney London?" Lark took the pages, turning them over.

"My pen name," he said. *"Nomme de ploom."* He leant foward to confide in her. "Sydney to London, understand? I'm entering the *Daily Mirror* short-story contest. One thousand pounds, first prize. It will be my spending money in London, after I win my boat ticket on Jack Davey."

In the story a man was standing shaving, examining his lean, square jaw in the mirror.

"But don't tell your mother," said Henry Watter. "She doesn't read the *Mirror* and will never even see it when it wins."

The lamb chop was burning. Lark leapt up and forked it onto the plate, a hard, black little knob. "I have to go," said Lark, stuffing the manuscript into her handbag. "I'll read this when I'm there."

The secretary told Lark to take off her coat before she went in to the personnel officer. "He has to check your deportment," she said. "In the meantime, I'm sorry but he is running late, so you'll have to wait, I'm afraid, if that's all right."

Lark perched on the edge of an upholstered bench, avoiding sitting on those buttons. She read her father's manuscript. Every morning when the man looked in the mirror he saw that another feature had changed. The eyes were blue, no longer brown. The hair blond, not brown. The mouth had become a thin line that bent in a half smile. He began not to recognize familiar faces—his wife, his daughter. Everyone was a stranger. One morning he looked in the mirror and could not recognize his own face. He seemed to be a child, not himself but some other child. But when he spoke he recognized the voice and knew that the boy—or it could be a girl—in the mirror was indeed he. And then the voice ceased altogether, leaving the child in the mirror mute, and before his own eyes, the blond, blue-eyed child in the mirror crumbled into ashes. The man who shaved leant forward, his forehead resting against the mirror, and saw on the bathroom floor, reflected in the mirror, the ashes of the image.

"You can go in now," said the secretary. "Take off your coat. He needs to see your figure and your deportment." Lark abandoned her coat and entered the huge office, where a man in a brown suit sat behind a desk at the far end and watched her as she walked to him. She was still clutching her father's manuscript.

"Why," he asked, "do you want to be a Qantas air hostess?"

He tapped a pencil against his finger, as if he had asked a riddle about the meaning of life.

Lark hesitated, suddenly conscious of the pages of writing she held on her lap. She thought of saying she had always admired Qantas and had wanted to serve that particular company ever since she was little.

"I want to get away," she said. "I want to travel."

"What's that?" the man asked, indicating the papers in Lark's hands.

"Just," Lark knew the word "fiction" would alert this man to all kinds of shortcomings in her and in her family. "Just nothing." She smiled weakly. It was unusual for anyone to carry about bundles of paper covered with writing.

"I see," said the man. "You do realize that in addition to a deep desire to serve others, our hostesses have to be good-looking girls. The best of the crop. Our passengers demand no less."

Lark had to walk out again, across the vast floor, with that personnel officer watching those four buttons and judging.

In a postscript Solomon Blank had added: "I'm going shopping with a lady friend who will help me choose a pair of Bermuda shorts for myself, in one of those outrageous plaids that used to make us laugh at Americans."

Lark wrote to the student newspaper on the subject of colonialism and imperialism. "We must stand on our own feet," she said. "We must support the newly emerging forces in their struggle against imperialism. If we continue to toe the line drawn by America, we will always lose the race."

Lark met her first American in the cafeteria line at the university. She had hidden an extra pat of butter under her bread roll, which was something they all did, to save the extra penny. Everyone was saving to go away.

"Americans have lost all sense of culture," said this voice behind her. Americans were rare enough in Sydney to make Lark turn around whenever she heard an American voice in the tram or a shop. He was short, with light brown curly hair that touched his collar and covered his ears, which meant that he did not get it cut every two or three weeks like all the young men she knew. It gave him a softness, and he wore horn-rimmed glasses and a baggy tweed jacket with leather elbows, which also added to this gentle demeanor. He held a camera up to his face, as if it were binoculars, and scanned the cafeteria. This was Tom Brown and he seemed to know a great deal.

"Americans have lost all sense of history and beauty in their language." This Tom, without taking the camera away from his face, was addressing the young woman next to him, Donna Bird, editor of the student newspaper.

Lark had watched Donna Bird for several years as she floated around the quadrangle, looking like some kind of court jester, always arguing and waving her arms about, always surrounded by groups of the important students—the libertarian who wore no shoes and tied his khaki trousers with a piece of rope and wrote lewd columns for the newspaper; the architecture student who was caught by a security guard on the floor of the library stacks with the psychology fresher; the leader of the student conservative club who was known only by his initials.

Donna Bird always wore a sun visor, trailed a scarf around her neck, and carried a diary, one of those exercise books that children used in primary school. Donna Bird covered her diaries in brown wrapping paper, on which she lettered a quotation. On the cover of the present volume, clamped under her arm, was written, "'We must take the current when it serves, or lose our ventures.'"

That day Donna Bird was wearing gray slacks, gray socks with silver threads, brown leather sandals, a gray turtleneck sweater, sunglasses, long, gold clip-on earrings, and, of course, her sun visor and one of her scarves, chiffon with a brown and white snakeskin design, wrapped around her neck several times and hanging limply. Today she had braided her long, curly, red hair in an original way and kept fingering it as she spoke, tossing it around, then stroking it as she responded to Tom, looking at herself every now and then in the glass of the food cases.

"Americans think they can do what they like," Donna Bird murmured. "They write n-i-t-e instead of n-i-g-h-t, c-o-l-o-r instead of c-o-l-o-u-r, c-e-n-t-e-r instead of c-e-n-t-r-e. Such laziness, such sloppiness. They obliterate the history of our beautiful language."

Tom had to let the camera go and bend down to hear her. "You're absolutely right," he said.

"You're not like an American," said Donna Bird. "You could be English." Apart from murmuring when she spoke, Donna Bird turned every sentence into a question. "You could be English? You're not like most Americans?" was how she sounded.

Tom smiled, his mouth turned down, his head inclined to one side in self-deprecation. "Oxford straightened me out," he said.

Lark stood still, listening. Tom Brown and Donna Bird, engrossed in their pronouncements, pushed their trays along the metal ledge and bumped into Lark's tray.

"Americans don't know their arse from their elbow," Tom was saying. "I should know. They're too concerned about making money to take the time to write the *u* in colour. Lazy sons of bitches."

Lark nudged her tray along. Such language. Such imagery. So vivid. So free.

"What's this you've got here?" the cashier asked. She had lifted up Lark's roll and was pointing at the pat of butter squashed under it on the plate.

Tom burst out laughing. Lark blushed, exposed as a thief and humiliated before this learned and well-traveled, urbane American.

Tom turned to the cashier. "Please don't touch the food with your hands," he said to her. "It's against health regulations.

You've been handling money. And money's filthy, in every sense of the word."

The cashier dropped the roll back on the plate.

Tom took the roll and placed it beside the cash register. "She can't eat that now." He turned to Lark. "Go and get yourself another bun. And here," to the cashier, "here's a penny for the pat of butter."

The students in the line crowded around. "Here's a bun for the girl," said one. He grabbed a new roll and threw it down to Lark. Tom caught it and placed it on her tray. Lark hurried off to a table in the corner and sat looking out the window at the hockey field, wishing she was in a canoe on some lagoon in the middle of some atoll in the middle of a calm ocean, or perhaps walking on fine yellow sand. She opened her book and read, moving her finger along the line, mouthing the words, *"Et nous avons vu, très loin, un petit chalutier qui avançait, imperceptible-ment, sur la mer éclatante."*

"So? 'We saw in the distance, a little fishing boat impercepti-bly moving on the dazzling ocean.'" It was the American, Tom, reading over her shoulder and placing his tray on the table be-side hers. He took Lark's book. *"'Marie a cueilli quelques iris de roche. De la pente qui descendait vers la mer nous avons vu qu'il y avait déjà quelques baigneurs,'"* he continued for her, in what seemed to Lark to be flawless French. "'Marie picked some rock irises. Descending the steep path to the sea we saw that there were already some bathers there.'" He tossed the book aside and sat down. "Good for you," he said, "fighting the system like that. Butter belongs to the people. Butter and guns and art. They should be free, and if they're not, the people should take them."

Donna Bird had followed Tom and stood for a moment before deciding to place her diary and her tray on the table and share the American. She took out her fountain pen, opened the diary, and started scribbling in bright green ink. Every now and then she placed her hands over the open pages, as if the entire student body might try to read what she was writing.

"Just jotting down a thought or two," she whispered to Tom, who bent close to her to listen. "I have a continuous diary from the time I was four, when I began to write?" Tom nodded at her, approving. "You just have to hold all the volumes in your hands to know that you are indeed alive and have been alive?"

Tom lifted Donna Bird's hands from her diary, which he closed and held for a moment in his own hands, as if he might take the oath.

"Why 'take the current' et cetera?" Tom asked, examining the quotation on the front cover.

"Because," said Donna, "I have already used '*Lasciate ogni speranza, voi ch'entrate,*' and '*Allwissend bin ich nicht, doch viel ist mir bewusst.*'"

"*Touché,*" cried Tom, "sonofagun. *Allwissend* what? German is the weakest of all my languages."

"'I'm not omniscient, but I know a great deal,'" Donna said.

"You're a fine, fine writer," Tom said to Donna. "Truly fine." He handed Donna's diary back. "You're an original."

Lark loathed Donna Bird. But she thought this Tom was wonderful, and had thought so even before she discovered, as he talked to her, that he was the most talented and accomplished person in the world. He addressed political rallies, spoke French and possibly dozens of other languages, and had studied at Harvard and in England and Europe. And he had chosen to sit with her, even though she knew she had made a fool of herself at the cash register.

"Why did you bother to come all the way out here, to Sydney?" Lark asked.

"Let us just say that the world is my oyster," said Tom.

"Mine, too?" said Donna Bird, without looking up. "I guess you'd call me cosmopolitan?"

"Guess," said Tom to Lark, "why I'm here."

Lark shrugged and made a face. "I can't guess."

Tom laughed. "Anyone can guess," he said, and stopped laughing to wait for her to try.

Lark simply could not guess, although she very much wanted to. She could tell that this attractive man liked guessing games, and she would have liked to play it the way he wanted.

"My ancestor was Robert Brown."

"Robert Brown?"

"Scottish. Botanist. Came to Australia in eighteen-o-one. Observed Brownian movement in eighteen twenty-seven."

"Brownian movement?"

"The irregular zigzag motion of minute particles of matter suspended in a fluid. Also, he discovered the cell nucleus in eighteen thirty-one."

"Are you a botanist?"

Tom shook his head. He waited for a few seconds. "You'll never get it. Anthropologist. I used to study Javanese village life."

"And now?" Lark was catching on. She could at least ask the required questions and thus spend time with this man without running out of words to utter. It was similar to testing Henry Watter in one of his categories.

"Now? Urban anthropology. I keep a close watch on contemporary life. I'm a social theorist, and in my spare time, a critic of society."

"You're the first social theorist and critic of society I've ever actually met."

Donna Bird looked up, slapping her hands down on her pages, having ignored Lark's attempts to talk to Tom. "It makes you feel your life is a river, continuous, flowing, with a purpose or destination? Keeping a journal? Gives you a sense of your own history? You ought to try it?" She addressed Lark for the first time.

"The only thing I've done since I was four is keep a suitcase packed, ready to leave." Lark paused, then coasting along in the interrogative, asked Donna, "Did you say you were cosmopolitan?"

"Well, basically English?" Donna replied modestly, going back to her writing.

"She was marooned there during the war," said Tom. "But she's been all over, with her father, of course, and met everyone."

"Her father?"

"You don't know who her father is? Manfred Bird?"

"Manfred Bird?"

"Surely you know of Manfred Bird? Professor Manfred Bird?" He placed the emphasis on "of" and then on "Professor."

Lark sat still, not even shaking her head. She had never heard of Manfred Bird. Donna's page was almost completely covered with her green words. She never looked up, appeared not even to hear.

"Manfred Bird is my mentor. He holds a chair at one of our great Ivy League institutions. And he has refuted several prevalent but false concepts about primitive societies. He knows the Queen of Tonga, the Rockefellers, and Tom Lehrer. And they know him. Donna is his daughter. Didn't you get to know Michael Rockefeller?"

"Our fathers were among the first art collectors to foresee the value of Oceanic art," said Donna. "They knew it would be revered one day."

"You should see Manfred's apartment in New York," said Tom. "Crammed with stuff. A museum."

At least Lark had heard of the Rockefellers and the disappearance of Michael in West New Guinea, West Irian as she carefully called it now, and she already disliked anything Donna Bird and her family might have done. "Didn't they say that he was just a plunderer, stealing art from societies that couldn't protect themselves?"

"It's called preservation," said Donna quickly. "Sometimes

the natives just threw away the stuff, their funerary carvings and so on. The Rockefellers and my father just wanted to preserve art. Art is what matters."

"And he didn't just take stuff," said Tom.

"Certainly not. He brought the natives things they very much craved, begged for—knives, axes, cooking pots, cloth, and so on. And I can tell you that for weeks after the canoes overturned and he was carried out to sea, the natives kept watch for him on the beach? That shows you whether he was a plunderer or a friend."

"Couldn't he be both?" asked Lark.

"She's still young and inexperienced," said Tom to Donna, at the same time patting Lark's hand in a fatherly way. He turned back to Lark. "Donna should know," he said gently, like a doctor at an invalid's bedside. "After all, she's the one who knows them all. Say," and he turned back to Donna Bird, "what say we take her in hand? Our next project?" Donna Bird raised her eyebrows, and with it the visor, then went back to her writing without answering. From his pocket Tom drew forth a pack of photographs, portraits of twenty young men and women, full face and profile. "Look." He flourished them before Lark, beautiful mug shots. "They're from ten different countries—we were all together last year studying in Europe. What a waste of time. Grooming people for the system. Same as Harvard. A waste."

"It must have been wonderful to be in Europe," said Lark.

Tom shrugged and shuffled through his photographs.

"It's all friable, wherever you are," Tom said.

Donna Bird looked up again and laughed for a minute or so. "Friable," she said. "Friable." She placed her hand on Tom's tweed sleeve.

Lark could think of nothing clever to say to this American Tom. He would surely get up and leave her, at any moment, with the clever and original and cosmopolitan Donna Bird.

"Is Champaign-Urbana a wonderful town?" she asked.

She still carried Solomon Blank's letter in her pocket. "I asked a girl out," he wrote. "You have to go out on dates in America, otherwise they think you're odd, it doesn't mean any-thing—and she said she was very sorry, but would I give her a ringcheck. I said, yes of course, but being a careful scholar I enquired what it was exactly that I was to give her, and where could I get one." And while he had not mentioned again that Lark might join him, he had said that he remembered her head on his shoulder, "or was it just a bit of your hair? Just joking." And he had said that he missed her.

Tom was shaking his head, looking at his photographs, smil-ing in recollection. "You've got to be kidding. New York might be a wonderful town, but Champaign-Urbana is the armpit of America. Do you call everything wonderful? That's sweet, but it sounds a bit callow."

Lark contemplated the armpit image. Donna Bird closed her diary. She touched Tom's sleeve again. "It's to be expected, don't you think? I distinctly remember the word 'callow' when I came across it for the first time. They had given us a book in school called *English Short Stories of Today*. In one of the stories, a passenger on a ship in the Middle East seems to know every-thing. In the heat he advises everyone to drink hot tea." She turned to Lark. "You can be sure that everything that happens recurs. Every tragedy, every humiliation, every image that im-prints itself on the mind, every incident, even every word that is spoken or heard in a certain context will recur in a different form and be relevant much later on? That's why there is no such thing as tragedy or error? No such thing as meaning?" She pat-ted her diary. "This tourist tells everyone to keep out of the breeze and turn off the electric fans, fancy gadgets he calls them, in order to keep cool. He boasts that he is an experienced sailor, not a callow tourist. Of course, he is wrong. He nearly gets everyone marooned and killed by Arabs on a desert shore. But that was when I understood the word 'callow.'"

"*Brava!* You are just great," Tom said to Donna Bird. He turned to Lark. "You know that embarrassment with the American warship?"

Lark shook her head.

"You don't know? You don't know what Donna and the others did?" He inclined his head at Donna Bird, who was now chuckling as she wrote. "You know that the ship was in town for ceremonies to commemorate the battle of the Coral Sea? Well, Donna and the others rowed around to its far side and climbed on board and set off all the alarms, as if there were an enemy attack. The captain was demoted for having let it happen. Don't you read the papers? That was Donna here."

"We were proving how easy it is to manipulate the authorities?" said Donna Bird. "I love practical jokes? They can be so pedagogical."

"We're planning another one," said Tom. "A biggie. We want to educate society."

Lark sat silently. What could she say? The ports of call on the sea route to Southampton? The names of the states in alphabetical order?

"We had an air raid today according to the radio," Solomon had written. "But since I didn't see any atomic bombs falling I can only assume that it was a joke, or perhaps a civil defense effort. I was in Washington D.C. with a friend over Easter and viewed the Constitution, the Bill of Rights, and the Declaration of Independence in their bombproof, shockproof, fireproof, helium-filled vault. I had no idea that America was such a complex country, and I never suspected that their traditions were in any way valid or serious. I came away quite overwhelmed and can now think of America as more than a huge imperialist financial machine, the home of the Midwest, the bomb, the hot dog and the musical doorbell."

Lark took a breath. "You're absolutely wrong, you know, about the American language," she said rapidly, to Tom. "The Americans standardized their spelling before the British. They decided to go back to the pure Latin endings, -or and -er, for instance, instead of -our and -re, which come from the French. After that the British standardized and, just to be different from the Americans, chose the more recent French endings. So, in a way, the American language is more pure."

Tom wagged his finger at her. "That's very good," he said. "But are you sure of your source?" He passed his photographs to Lark. "Okay, the education of, what did you say your name was? Okay. The education of Lark. Lark? Okay, lesson number one. See if you can tell me where each person is from."

Lark guessed them all wrong. Tom beamed. "No one ever gets them right. You're so literal-minded." The young woman with long blond hair and a round flat face was French. The dark woman with heavy eyebrows was Swedish. The narrow-faced man with a thin mustache was German. Tom laughed. "It just goes to show that you mustn't trust even your own eyes. That's what Manfred Bird has done for anthropology. Lesson number one completed." He shuffled the photos and retrieved the blond woman. "This French girl was my girlfriend for the year. Agnes. Very attractive."

Lark found that she was jealous.

"A wonderful, beautiful person," said Donna Bird. "Her father acts for Manfred in his European dealings." Donna Bird, with a blissful half-smile on her face, had swiveled around in her chair and was now wielding Tom's camera, focusing first on Tom, then turning away and surveying other tables.

"I heard that Agnes tried to kill herself after I left. I hear she's in so-so shape." Tom was shaking his head. "A terrible waste of a beautiful person. The mothers of all these beautiful European girls wanted them to marry me." He pulled a face

indicating modesty and puzzlement. "I think it was just because
I was from America, land of the giant refrigerator."

Tom stood up. "We have to plot a big prank, shatter some
complacency, change society." He took his camera back from
Donna Bird. "Then I want to do some photography—the *urbs*,
the strand."

"The Strand Arcade?"

"Strand as in beach, the littoral."

Lark was still struggling to say something of interest.

"I feel now that it is time for me to attend to other matters,"
Solomon had ended his letter. "So if you will excuse me I will
just sashay over to the cocktail bar and rustle up another mar-
tini, straight up, and do-si-do into and out of the kitchen, where
I know the olives and twists are kept."

Lark's mouth was dry. "Did you know," she gasped, "that 'on
the beach' was the expression they used in the South Seas last
century for men, Europeans, who had gone off traveling and
run out of money and luck and were marooned, on the beach,
literally?" All she had to offer she had acquired, unwillingly,
from testing her father in his many and various categories of
passion.

Tom laughed, his laughter forming a gentle musical phrase.
"Say, that's pretty good. I like that. You should come with me,
sometime, to the beach, when it's not raining."

"Will you give a ringcheck?" Lark said.

"Ringcheck?" Tom looked down at her. "Good grief. You
mean rain check? Where did you pick up that dated cliché?" He
spread his arms wide. Donna Bird was gathering her things together. "Meanwhile the world is waiting to be saved." Donna
stood up beside him, like a queen next to a king on a coin or a
postage stamp. "Colonized people are struggling for independence, and Australia, which still does not admit anyone with a
less than white skin, is teamed up with America supporting imperialism. At the same time the new Nazis are gaining strength,

as if there had been no war at all." He raised his voice, no longer soft and confiding, to include more of the cafeteria. "And soon anyone will be able to build a nuclear bomb of some sort. They won't need a sophisticated delivery system, just the bomb, which could be driven into Manhattan in a semitrailer or sailed in on board an old ship. You'd have to find someone willing to drive the truck, ready to die for his cause, but that would not be hard to do. Just think of those Japanese pilots and one-man submarines during the war." He stopped and looked around the cafeteria, then smiled down at Lark, before continuing just as loudly. "The desire to penetrate is not sexual. Rather, it's part of our deep need to return to the simplicity of the single cell. Jung didn't take the idea of collective unconscious far enough."

Lark smiled at him, trying to say something, striving to cope with the attention that was now directed from all quarters at her and Tom and Donna. At least Tom seemed to like her, she thought.

"Did someone mention sex?" cried a student.

"Where? Where?" responded others.

"Lesson number two," Tom said to Lark. His voice had lost its stridency and had slid into a gentle vibrato. "To be unafraid to take a stand in public." He put his hand on Donna's shoulder. "We have to go. See you around the block."

The letters had been crammed into the tin letter box that sat on the wooden fence by the front gate. A spider had already spun a web over the top of the box. One was from Champaign-Urbana, one from Qantas.

Lark raced up the front steps and into her room. She sat on her bed, balancing the letters in her hand. Perhaps Solomon was sending for her. So if Qantas did not want her, Solomon surely would. Far off a woman seemed to be crying, or crying out.

"We are afraid that we cannot offer you a position with Qantas. We see our air hostesses as ambassadors for our country, and we feel that you do not meet our stringent criteria."

Lark sat for a moment, not daring to open Solomon's letter. The woman's crying was muffled, but quite distinct. Lark sat on her bed and searched through the *Herald* for jobs abroad, anywhere, fares paid. She looked under governess and then happened to see that the *Herald* wanted reporters. Perhaps she could be a foreign correspondent. But a woman was crying for help. The voice was muted, as if it were coming through sheets and towels. Lark went to her mother's bedroom and opened the wardrobe, in case she had somehow been locked in. Then Lark stood again and listened. Someone was now banging on the floorboards. Lark could hear light tapping footsteps on the cement path at the back. She ran to the back door. Her mother, she now imagined, had been trapped in Henry Watter's project, that strange box he had been constructing for so long in the basement. Lark ran down the back stairs to the entrance to the basement.

The door was closed. On the path was a large, dirty gray sheep, which stood for a moment contemplating the door, then hurled itself against it. Mrs. Watter's frightened face appeared at the basement window. The sheep backed away from the door, did a clattering little dance on the path, as if it were winding itself up, then rushed at the door again, throwing itself against the door several times. Then it stopped for a moment, tore at the remains of the mint and parsley that grew under the tap, before repeating the dance on the path and resuming the attack on the besieged Mrs. Watter.

When Lark seized the mop that rested against the wall by the stairs, the sheep turned and hurtled toward her. Lark poked the mop at its face, the gray cotton of the mop head matching and blending with the sheep's head. The sheep stopped and sniffed at the mop. Lark poked it and the sheep backed away a few steps, sniffed at the mop again, then backed away as Lark pressed forward.

Mrs. Watter opened the basement door and peered out.

"Go upstairs quickly." Lark was trying to shout in a whisper, trying not to distract the sheep from its exploration of the mop head.

But Mrs. Watter's footsteps on the path reminded the creature of its mightier mission, and with a snort it charged at Lark, who dropped the mop and found herself rushing to the basement door, where Mrs. Watter stood transfixed. The two women pressed the door shut as the sheep resumed its battering. The rooster in its coop began to crow.

"I didn't mean to get a wild ram," said Mrs. Watter, close to tears. She looked out the window. "My parsley and my mint." She shook her head. "And I rented it for a week. I didn't tell your father. I was trying to hang out the clothes. They brought it this morning. I've been here for hours."

Lark was examining the long wooden crate that Henry Watter had been building. The corners were beautifully mitered. "The project has grown."

"What do you think it is?" asked Mrs. Watter. "I ask him but he says there's no news as far as the project is concerned." She took the cotton drawstring bag in which she had collected for years old rags and old stockings and began sorting through it. "It'll cut costs when it's time for him to go, he says. I thought it was a glory box for you. To put sheets and things in for when you married."

Lark lifted the lid of the crate. Inside was stored a bolt of quilted green cloth and the World War Two gas mask.

"Then I thought it was for his war collection. He was very, very affected by the war memorial in Canberra as you know. But now I worry that he is building his own coffin," whispered Mrs. Watter. "That would certainly cut costs when he goes." She had separated the stockings from the rags and was rolling them into neat little balls.

Lark closed the lid and sat on the crate. She picked up Mrs. Watter's stone-polishing barrel, which always contained pebbles in the process of being smoothed and polished, and began to turn the handle.

"It's very considerate of him, when you come to think of it. But it's morbid." Mrs. Watter was forced to raise her voice over the noise of the tumbling stones.

"I think I'll be leaving very soon." Lark was remembering the Qantas letter on the floor of her room above them, and next to it the unopened letter from Solomon Blank.

"You must finish your university. A woman has to be able to take care of herself, stand on her own feet." Mrs. Watter spread her hands, palms up, and looked at them. "You only have to look at me." She paused and listened to the sheep. "I didn't tell your father." She was shouting, nodding at the door. "He'll be livid. You'll always get low pay and no benefits without finishing your uni. I've worked so hard."

"I'll get a job with security in a year or two. I really need to go now." Lark turned the handle of the barrel faster.

"There's no money, no security, if you don't finish your uni." Mrs. Watter pursed her lips so tightly that they disappeared. "Don't you value security? Don't you value money? A penniless woman is quickly a victim. People take advantage. She loses her dignity. Look at me. And you have only six months until your final exams."

"Money is important," shouted Lark, trying to please. "I want it more than anything else." But that was not true. What she wanted more than anything else was to get away, away from that basement where a bad-tempered ram held them prisoners, away from that house, and away from the continent altogether. What she also wanted was to find true love, someone to be close to, forever.

Mrs. Watter sniffed. "And you're just the type that would need money."

"The type?" Lark let go of the barrel handle. She should disengage herself. Dialogues such as this one could only bring misunderstanding and trouble. She did not even know what they were discussing. The stones in the barrel slowly came to rest.

"Some people can scrimp, but I don't think you can. Your head is in the clouds."

"Everyone can scrimp if they have to," said Lark. Her tongue was heavy. She thought she might just lie down on the cement at her mother's feet and curl up, or she could crawl into Henry Watter's project and go to sleep for a long, long time. "I've been saving, scrimping."

"Of course everyone can scrimp," said her mother. "But you don't like to, that's the point."

"There's no virtue in scrimping." Lark's voice was slowing down.

"You don't have to tell me that," shrieked Mrs. Watter, and the thumping at the door stopped for a moment, as if the sheep were pausing in order to listen and comprehend. "I've scrimped all my life." She held up the bag of rolled nylon stockings. "There's no virtue at all. I'm just a fool." She paused, contemplating the stockings. "But these are just right for tying up the tomatoes and the vines. It would be silly to have thrown them out. After you've lived through a depression you can't throw anything away."

The thumping at the door resumed.

"It's that Solomon Blank, isn't it? Easy for him. The Blanks have money. But remember that families with money don't like it leaving the family. And he's the one with all the degrees. And he keeps them. They don't rub off on you, even if you are his wife. You're too young, anyway." Mrs. Watter went to the window and stared out. Her agitation had evaporated. "I think ducks would be best. They'll get along with the rooster, and the eggs are so rich, so good for cooking. I'll stretch chicken wire across the whole backyard, from one fence to the other, and they can roam where they like. That'll keep the grass down." She came back and sat down and took the stone-polishing barrel from Lark and turned the handle quite happily, humming to herself.

The door above slammed shut and footsteps walked, or rather danced, into the kitchen. There was one heavy step followed by several light steps and a skip, a little polka, rather like the sheep's dance on the cement outside.

"It's your father," said Mrs. Watter. "In a good mood. He must have been to the library." Her voice was now soft, its usual whisper. Lark might even have imagined the bitter exchange about scrimping and pleasure. "He doesn't tell me anything, he just comes and goes as he pleases, in and out, but I see that he is going to the library almost every day now, two books at a time. That's too many books, for a normal person."

Lark climbed on Henry Watter's box and banged at the ceiling with the hammer handle. The polka above stopped. Lark banged again.

The battering at the basement door continued. Lark banged on the ceiling twice, Henry Watter stamped on the floor twice. Lark banged three times, Henry Watter stamped three times. "In the basement," Lark cried. "Help us," the two women cried. Lark jumped down from the box.

"He doesn't know about the sheep," said Mrs. Watter. "He'll get a shock."

They stood at the window to watch Henry Watter's rescue attempt.

The sheep had heard the new footsteps skipping down the stairs and was standing alert, ready to charge the newcomer or to continue the assault on the door, whichever seemed to offer the most reward. Henry Watter was in his best navy-blue suit. His black shoes were shining. His chin was fresh and smooth from a recent shave. He paused at the bottom of the stairs, while his jaunty step and expression changed to heavy fury. He took off his jacket, seized the mop as if it were a foil, and advanced on the sheep, his legs bent in the stance of a fencer.

"Hah," he cried, lunging at the animal, which had remained stationary, puzzled. "Hah," and he poked it. "Hah." The sheep clattered backwards along the path. "Hah, Wooliam the First, hah, Wooliam the Second, hah." The sheep had retreated beyond the laundry door, into the grass. Henry Watter leapt after it, and for just a second looked down at his shining shoes embedded in the long grass and his freshly pressed pants cuffs that would pick up the pods and burs of this wild lawn. The sheep scraped at the grass, getting ready to charge. "Hah, Woolfred, hah, Woolbur," cried Henry Watter and galloped forward. The sheep turned around and ran down the hill to the gum tree, with Henry Watter behind it, swiping wildly with the mop. And then those shiny shoes skidded in the grass and Henry Watter slipped and slid onto his bottom.

Mrs. Watter and Lark had crept out of the basement, Mrs. Watter pausing for a moment to touch the remains of her parsley and mint under the tap before scurrying up the stairs to the kitchen. Lark was about to follow her when Henry Watter fell. She ran to him and helped him up. There were tears in his eyes. "Mind my shoes and my trousers," he said. He waved his fist at the sheep. "Who brought that wild thing into our compound? Don't tell me, it's a rhetorical question. What's the point of having a compound at all, if the outside world can penetrate at will?"

"Quick," said Lark. The sheep, although standing rooted and trembling a little under the tree, looked as if it could spring into action again at any moment. Henry Watter and Lark scrambled back to the path and the stairs. "Were you going somewhere important?"

"Only to Jack Davey," said Henry Watter bitterly. "That's all. I was on my way to win my fare to England, that's all. But your mother didn't know anything about that. All she knows is to adopt wild fauna and get grass stains all over me."

"You were very brave," said Lark, pushing open the kitchen door. "I hope you win, and I hope your story wins, too."

Mrs. Watter was running water into the kettle.

"Don't tell your mother," said Henry Watter out of the corner of his mouth.

He stood in the kitchen while Lark inspected his clothes.

"I'll just make a cup of tea," said Mrs. Watter, placing the kettle on the stove and shooting the flint gun to light the gas jet. "We've all had a shock."

"There are no grass stains," said Lark, swiveling Henry Watter around like a store dummy. "I'll just brush off the burs, and I can fix your shoes easily."

Henry Watter stood still like a little boy while Lark brushed his trousers and his shoes.

"The grass was so long," said Mrs. Watter. She placed her hand on his arm, but he shook it off. "You were very brave."

"I have to go," said Henry Watter.

"But don't you want to sit for a minute and have a cup of tea?" Mrs. Watter was fussing with the tea caddy and the tea cozy.

Henry Watter ran to the front door. Lark followed him. "Wish me luck," he whispered.

"I'm just going to sit for a minute," wailed Mrs. Watter, fanning her chest with her hand.

"Shall I bring the tea?" Lark asked, closing the front door.

Mrs. Watter nodded. Her lip was trembling. "I've had a shock."

Lark patted her shoulder. "I know. That was a terrible experience."

Lark went into her room and picked Solomon Blank's letter from the floor.

Solomon Blank wrote: "Summer in Champaign-Urbana is a time for socializing in a capitalistic sort of way, and I am drastically short of money. Yesterday, accompanied by a person of the female persuasion, I went out purloining tomatoes from the university orchard. You would have recognized us as accomplices because we both wore our Bermuda shorts and also our legs, quite tan by now, I should add. It doesn't mean what you think. In America it's just a social necessity to have a companion of the female sort. Hope your studies are going well."

Lark wrote to Solomon Blank: "'A certain man is absent from his own country for many years; he is persecuted by Neptune and deprived of all his companions, and left alone. At home his affairs are in disorder—the suitors of his wife dissipating his wealth and plotting the destruction of his son. Tossed by many tempests he at length arrives home, and making himself known to some of his family, attacks his enemies, destroys them, and remains himself in safety.' This is essential, according to Aristotle. The rest is episode. Merely episode. I hope to be leaving very soon myself."

To Mrs. Watter, at dinner, she said, "You don't have to worry about me. I'm not going. Not just yet."

"It's that Solomon Blank, isn't it?" said Mrs. Watter.

"Hey," cried Tom Brown as Lark passed by.

He was sitting on the stone wall on the south side of the quad with a group of students from the newspaper, including the columnist Perce, the one who went barefoot and used a length of rope for a belt. Lark looked around, in case Tom was addressing someone else nearby. He nodded and pointed at Lark and beckoned her to him.

She was wearing her air hostess skirt and a twin set and felt terribly, terribly ordinary as she approached Tom and his bohemian group.

"Not bad ankles," said Tom.

Perce pulled up his trouser leg and turned his foot this way and that. "Thanks," he said. Then he gave Tom a punch. "Listen, we don't compliment our women here. It makes them think you like them. Gets their hopes up."

Lark stopped at the edge of the group. Tom patted the stone wall beside him. "Come, sit." The conservative leader known only by his initials was wearing a monocle, which he turned on Lark as she slid by him and the half dozen others ranged around Tom. Donna Bird was not there. "Don't take any notice of F.X.," said Tom.

"You can call him Fux," cried Perce, "or if that's too hard for you—get it, too hard?—Fix." Lark tried to look as if she was accustomed to this sort of thing, consorting with the student notables.

"So," said Tom, "what's new? *Est-ce-que tu as trouvé 'quelques iris de roche'?*"

Lark shook her head. "Nothing really."

The others were observing this encounter with casual interest.

"Who's the new female, anyway?" said Perce. "Just out of the cradle, by the look of it."

Everyone fell silent and looked at Lark, waiting for Tom to explain her. She knew Tom was considered a catch, with his impeccable credentials—a Harvard degree, which he scorned, and a degree from Oxford, which legitimized him in Australia, and his championing of good political causes. Women of all nations wanted him, and the mothers of these girls, in Oslo, Milan, and Paris, had not minded their daughters sleeping with him because they hoped their girls would marry this clever American Tom. Yet here was this Lark, on whom he was lavishing attention, mute beside him, and now Perce was demanding to know her credentials. Tom frowned. Lark waited for him to speak for her, to tell them that she served some purpose.

"Can she talk?" F.X. called.

"I heard her say two words," said someone else.

Lark looked at her knees. She did not belong with this illustrious group. She had nothing of importance to say and nothing to contribute. Tom had even said so. Henry Watter had always said so. She knew nothing.

"Say something, Larkie," said Tom. He leant back and waved both his arms, like a conductor trying to get more sound from a floundering section of his orchestra. "You can do it. Lesson number two, taking a stand in public."

She could just leap down from the stone wall and rush from the scene, across the quad, down the stairs, and onto Parramatta Road and maybe get hit by a car. She knocked her heels against the stone. Tom put a finger under her chin and lifted her face to look at him. "Larkie, show them," he said to her, and Lark, looking back down at her knees, said, "One must remember that the Constitution of the United States, the Bill of Rights, and the Declaration of Independence in their bomb-proof, shockproof, fireproof, helium-filled vault, make it clear that America is a complex country, with valid and serious traditions, and remind one that America is more than a huge imperialist financial machine and the home of the Midwest, and the bomb, and the hotdog and, and Bermuda shorts."

"Good grief," said Perce.

"That's poetry," said F.X. "Pure poetry."

"Listen, I've got an idea," said Perce, and everyone turned to him. He was addressing Lark. "Why don't you just hang your hymen on the wall and have done with it?"

Lark tried to laugh along with everyone. Tom put his arm around her shoulder. "She's okay. She's my friend. Deep down she's a critic of society, a rebel." He stood up. "Back to the books," he said. "Come to the library with me, keep me company."

"'Attaboy, you can get her in the stacks," cried Perce after them. "Let me know if I can be of help."

"He's alluding to an assault on virtue," said the student who was named End of Tether, after a race horse. "Dearie me."

Gratefully Lark followed Tom up the stairs to the library.

"Don't take any notice of them, they're just boys," said Tom. "You'd know that if you had traveled and met other kinds of men. And Tether just imitates them. That's what women tend to do, imitate men, when they think they're breaking away from old molds. It's the drive to reattain the single-cell state."

"They don't worry me," said Lark, which was not true. But she thought that Tom was very wise.

Tom led Lark along the aisles of the stacks to the table where his work was spread out. The floors, of translucent glass panels, made them sound like tap dancers. "Onward and upward," he said and threw himself sideways into the chair, his legs sticking out across the narrow aisle. "I have to put in a couple of hours, then I'll take you to coffee." He flexed his fingers and arms as if he were about to play the piano.

Lark was standing next to the Bs in the anthropology section and found Manfred Bird's volumes before her eyes. "Where's Donna Bird today?" Lark asked. She needed to know why Tom was asking her and not the illustrious Donna to coffee.

"She's a busy woman," said Tom. "She has deadlines."

Lark wandered along the aisle of Bs. She searched for Blank, Charles, Solomon's ancestor. Among the books written by various Blanks, she found *My Life in the Service of God in the South Pacific* by Charles, and next to it a book by a Frederick Blank, who was the first man to ride a single horse across the North American continent, from Catalina Island in California to Coney Island in New York.

She heard Tom groaning and stretching, and then she heard the murmuring. Lark had not heard any footsteps on the glass, but then Donna Bird moved by creeping, sidling. Lark walked back toward Tom's corner, letting her shoes clatter as much as possible, both confirming her substance and warning the murmurer and the groaner of her approach. Donna Bird was bent over Tom's table, her hand resting on his shoulder. Their heads were close together. She was wearing another of her scarves wrapped around her neck, and the sun visor across her eyebrows. Around her neck she wore Tom's camera, which dangled onto Tom's thigh as she leant over him. Tom let out a long bray of laughter. "That's really brilliant," he said, patting Donna on the hip and leaving his hand there.

Lark's footsteps made them both look around, but Tom's hand did not drop from Donna's hip, and she did not step away from him. "I have to go," said Lark.

"Don't leave me," cried Tom and held out his other arm, which suggested that she should go and stand on his other side so that he could put his free hand on her hip, a pretty *tableau*. Lark hesitated, then walked toward them. He seemed to like her, want her around. Donna tapped his shoulder and pointed back at the paper on his table. "This is how we'll do it."

Lark stood beside Tom, and indeed his arm did go around her waist. "This is a great idea," he said to Donna, and to Lark he said, "Just give me another five minutes or so with Donna to get this thing straightened out. Then we can have coffee."

Lark went back to Frederick Blank's book and copied the information about the horse ride across the North American continent. Then she wrote a letter to Solomon, at that very moment in the middle of that very continent, no doubt eating tomatoes with an American girl in Bermuda shorts. "Why don't we do something inventive like your namesake?" she wrote. "We could go from island to island. Together." Than she moved along the aisle looking for Robert Brown, the Scottish botanist who had discovered the nucleus of the cell, observed the zigzag movement of particles suspended in a fluid, and was responsible for producing, ultimately, Tom Brown.

The student notables were still sitting on the stone wall when Tom led Lark out of the library. Donna Bird followed at her own pace.

Perce let out a howl when he saw them, lifting his chin and drawing out the sound: "Ooooooooo." Then he stopped his noise and asked Lark, "Well, was it as good as it's cracked up to be?" He danced up to Lark, his bare feet making a swishing, shuffling sound, and examined her face. "Personally, I'd rather have a nice cup of tea, wouldn't you, when you come right down to it?"

Lark hoped that Tom would pass right by them, without stopping to resume his sitting and bantering and endless talking. Lark willed him to keep moving, to proceed to the cafeteria so that they could have coffee, together, alone. "So what's happening?" Tom asked and stopped in the middle of the group.

"We're going to Dixon Street for some tucker," said Perce. He patted the knot of his rope belt, then, since Lark was watching him, he pointed at the rope knot and said, "My do-it-yourself tummy button."

Lark looked away.

"Sounds good to me," said Tom.

Donna Bird had slid up beside them.

"Let's go, then?" she said, and taking Tom's arm led the ramshackle little band across the quad.

Lark, while considering extricating herself and just going home, found that Tom had caught her arm and was pulling her along. "It's called educating Lark," he said to her. "You're my current project. Lesson number three is about to begin."

Lark had never been to Dixon Street, had never eaten a Chinese meal. The only rice she had eaten was boiled with milk and sugar for breakfast or baked along with the roast on Sunday. She gladly would have confessed this to Tom, since her ignorance seemed to increase his enthusiasm for educating her, but she would have died before she confessed in the presence of the cosmopolitan Donna Bird. She sat between Tom and Perce. Donna was on the other side of Tom. Lark watched while Tom and Donna reached out with their chopsticks and selected pieces from the many dishes on the table, then she took up her own chopsticks. She hesitated. Donna Bird, expertly conveying her food to her mouth, was watching her. The others had already drunk a lot of beer and were shouting at one another about Freud and Marx.

"It all has to do with the transfer of materials across cell boundaries," Tom said to the table at large. "The urge for all matter to merge through diffusion and osmosis—rather like pressing the 'liquefy' button on the blender."

Perce lifted his beer high into the air and began to pour it in a long stream into his mouth.

"That's disgusting," said Tether languidly.

The Chinese waiters were hovering about, smiling, expecting trouble.

"When molecules collide and become uniformly distributed, that's diffusion," Tom continued. "Water passes without interruption into and out of cells through their plasma membranes—that's osmosis. Then there's active transport, of course."

Perce gulped and paused for a moment in his beer-pouring and swallowing. "You want water passing into and out of, without interruption? I'll give it to you." Perce stood on his chair. "I am the cell. Water passes into," and he poured the beer into his mouth. "Water passes out of," and he went to untie the rope around his waist.

"That's not actually funny," said Donna Bird.

"I thought you liked jokes," said Perce, pouting. "I was being funny." He sat down on his chair, sulking.

"Perce is more like the primitive heterotroph than most of us," said Tom. "And that's why, in the end, we will blow ourselves up, the whole planet. It will give us a deep satisfaction, returning us to our origins. Here," and with his chopsticks he chose several morsels of chicken and pork and placed them on top of Lark's rice. "This is the way they do it in Singapore." He smiled in a fatherly way, then he turned toward Donna and began talking quietly about the implications of the White Australia policy in the context of the independence movements and decolonization going on in the developing world. But his arm rested along the back of Lark's chair and his fingers were tapping on her shoulder as he spoke.

Tether stood on her chair and tried to climb onto the table. Lark tweezered a piece of chicken with her chopsticks. Another young woman spun the Lazy Susan in the middle of the table. Lark got the chicken to her mouth. The Lazy Susan spun faster, sending soy sauce and mustard and hot sauce and chopsticks flying. A glass broke. Lark quickly took a mouthful of rice, using her spoon. The men continued to drink their beer and shout. "For God's sake, Tether," Perce said, "why don't you just hang your hymen on the wall, yet again, and have done with it?" The waiters moved in quietly, deftly, smiling. They removed the Lazy Susan, flicked the broken glass into a dustpan, and mopped up the spilled sauces. They had done this many times before. This was how things were.

Emboldened by Tom's fingers on her shoulder, Lark said, as he paused in order to eat, "I have been assessing the impact of de Gaulle on France and of Sukarno on Indonesia, and I think they are very alike."

"What do you mean, alike?" Tom said slowly, smiling. "Explain."

"Well," Lark said, searching for an explanation and wishing she had said nothing, "I just think de Gaulle and Sukarno are alike, that's all."

"My advice is," said Tom softly, giving Lark's shoulder a squeeze, drawing her a fraction closer to him, inclining his head toward her so that his curly hair touched her cheek, "if you don't know what you are talking about, say nothing."

Lark decided to cut down on speaking and to listen all the time. She had so much to learn. She leant back so that she could feel Tom's arm across her shoulder.

Tom straightened up and took his arm away. He adjusted Lark's fingers on her chopsticks. He rumpled her hair. "But I liked that letter you sent to the editor about American imperialism in the developing world," Tom said. "Good job." Then he flicked at her short hair, to make it stand up in spikes.

Donna Bird, her sun visor pulled down to her eyebrows, took out her diary and her fountain pen and started writing down her thoughts. She was smiling a little, as usual.

Tether, standing on the chair again, yelled, "You must never ask a Chinese person where the lavatory is," and she knocked over several chairs as she jumped down and lurched toward the rest rooms.

Lark knew she was very lucky to be sitting in this restaurant with uninhibited, politically aware students. Seminal, she guessed they were.

Perce suddenly was shouting at her, pointing at her with his glass of beer. "Perhaps she irons shirts," he said, waving his glass. He took a gulp. "Perhaps she irons a good shirt. That must be it. As long as her virtue remains unassailed, she'll iron good shirts."

Lark looked in dismay at Tom, waiting for him to do something to save her from Perce, who was now putting his arm around her and breathing his beery breath all over her.

"I think you've got a fan," said Tom. "He likes you."

Donna leant close to Tom. "Sometimes I think they are no different from every other Tom, Dick, and Harry—sorry, Tom, I don't mean you, of course—nothing to do but talk about sex and get drunk?"

"Have to go to the bog," said Perce, standing up, leaning on Lark's shoulder, then lurching off. "The constant flow of molecules and matter."

"I simply can't wait to get out of this decadent, corrupt, bourgeois, mediocre, boring country," said Donna Bird, holding onto Tom's sleeve and drawing him away from Lark and back to her. "I've been back too long. It's time to go again. Soonissimo. And Manfred wants me to come. I haven't seen Portia for several years, or their new baby. Portia and Daddy now have four boys. And he says one of his friends—they met during the war—will be bringing his ship here soon. A freighter. The passage is cheap."

"You want to leave, too?" Lark asked. She was hoping that Perce would die in the lavatory.

Donna kept her eyes on Tom for a second or two before answering Lark. "Of course," she said. "I've never been able to stand it here for very long? Manfred, that's my father, got away just as soon as he could and wouldn't dream of coming back unless it can be added to his ticket at no extra cost on his way to or from one of his islands, and even then only for a week or two. One of his European friends had a daughter born here, and he called her Barbara, for being born in the land of the Barbarians."

"I've always wanted to go to some island," said Lark.

"Did I tell you, Tom, that Manfred has decided that travel is narrowing, rather than broadening? He now advocates that everyone stay put?"

"It's easy for him," said Lark. "He's traveled already. I've been saving for years, everything I've earned during the holidays and from part-time jobs."

"Hey," said Tom to Donna. "We could give her a job, couldn't we?"

Donna Bird frowned.

"We need someone to photograph the kidnapping."

"Kidnapping?" Lark breathed.

"Shhh," said Donna Bird. "We still have to plan it."

"Plan?"

"Not here," Donna Bird hissed.

"Empirical pedagogy," Tom mouthed at Lark in an exaggerated way. Donna smiled, making clear that she and Tom were partners in this undertaking. "We need someone to photograph it, for the press."

"I don't know how to take photographs," said Lark.

"We'll teach you," said Tom. "I have my camera. And if you're any good, you can work with us on *Strange but True*."

"Strange but true?" Lark asked. Tom always began at the end, and Lark had to ask question after question to get to the beginning. It was what she had hated about "No News." The servant should have told the master straight off about his wife running away with another man.

Donna considered Tom's suggestion about giving Lark a job. She did not look overjoyed at the idea.

"It's a rag, a scandal sheet, American, of course. We could do with help," Tom explained.

"What kind of help?"

"We write stories, fillers for them. With photos. You know, mother eats babies, that kind of thing. The pay is good. They like weird news from down under."

"It's something we do on the side," said Donna. "I am primarily interested in changing the world, educating the masses, empirically? Being involved? I would like to make the world a stage on which I direct a mighty piece of theater, beyond street theater, global theater, watched by everyone in the world. A mighty, pedagogical practical joke, with the impact of a hydrogen bomb."

Perce returned from the men's room, pretending to cry. "My shirt got wet," he said, bending down to Lark. "Would you wash it for me, please? And iron it?"

"Leave me alone," said Lark quietly, angrily, pushing him away.

"Aw, hey, be a sport," said one of the others. "He's only drunk. He can't help it."

Donna Bird was still talking to Tom. "People would be participants without knowing it, a bit like the people who get together to form, say, a living flag, or the members of a band who form numbers on a football field. They can't see the flag or the numbers, although they are part of it, but it couldn't exist without them. I would have people taking actions they never knew they were capable of." She looked around the table. "What's the

thing you are least likely ever to do?" she called to Perce, who
was sitting at a slant on his chair.

"Me?" he replied drunkenly. "Wear a dress and fuck a man."

"Then," said Donna to Tom and Lark, "in my scheme, Perce
would find himself willingly putting on a dress and doing just
that, but he would also be part of some larger drama. If you are
afraid of the sun, like me, you would find yourself immersed in
the sun and loving it."

"You're afraid of the sun?" Lark asked. "I thought you were
allergic."

"It has been suggested that they're the same thing?" said
Donna. "And what do you fear?"

Lark thought for a moment. She sometimes thought she was
afraid of everything.

"She would never break the law or destroy property," said
Tom. "She'd be afraid to do that, right, Lark?"

"Well, I wouldn't destroy anything, people, objects." Lark
was aware she sounded like a goody-goody.

"Wouldn't you kill Hitler?" Tom asked.

"I suppose so. Then I would be doomed, too. But that would
be the price, I suppose, for saving the world. The death of an
individual is nothing really, is it?"

"Then with the world as my stage, my canvas, my text, you
would consciously choose to break the law, and you would destroy property. Afraid to take action, you would be suddenly
bold."

"What would I find myself doing?" Tom asked.

Donna put her chin on her hand and contemplated Tom.
"You're a hard case. You perhaps would settle down and get
married and have children?"

"Me?" Tom laughed.

Lark said, a little lamely, to reassure Tom that it had not
crossed her mind that he should be thinking of settling down,
"I'd rather hope to find myself doing something about changing
the world, contributing in some way."

Donna looked scornful. "Very noble sentiments."

"You can begin to contribute tomorrow. I'm speaking at the rally," Tom announced. "You should come and hear me. I'll teach you to take photos, and you can be the official photographer."

"Rally?" Lark regretted, once again, her ignorance.

"Yes, really," Tom said, and let out a few bars of his laugh.

Donna Bird raised her eyebrows. "You don't know?" She looked at Tom from under her visor, as if to say "callow."

"You should come," said Tom.

"Where is it?" Lark asked.

In answer to the next questions that she was forced to ask, Tom told her, "At seven. You should be there. We need bodies. And at some stage you have to stand up for things you believe in."

Again, after the right questions, Tom told her that there would be a party afterwards at his flat in Glebe.

While Donna and Tom discussed the speech Tom was to make at the rally, giving an American perspective on White Australia, Lark ate her meal, morsel by morsel, slowly. She felt miserable, and yet she also felt she had begun to live, and she had not even run away yet.


Even at the front gate Lark could hear the hammering. Henry Watter was at work. Again, two letters waited in the letter box, one from Champaign-Urbana for Lark, the other from the *Daily Mirror* for her father. From the size and thickness of the envelope Lark knew that his story had been rejected. He had never mentioned the radio contest again, and she felt she could not ask. As for Solomon Blank, she tore open his letter and read it as she walked slowly down the path to the front door.

Solomon Blank was facing a long, hot, lonely summer and could no longer do without the steady companionship of a female. He had succeeded in meeting a fairly attractive, fairly blond American, as tall as he was. They had been to New York together. "It's the most dazzling and energetic place I've been to," he wrote. "The center of the universe. You should see the real Park Avenue." And in the postscript, he said, "Aristotle? Episode? Sometimes I have no idea what you're talking about."

"You're home, then," said Mrs. Watter. She was in the kitchen in her hat and coat, peeling potatoes. "I never know these days. Luckily it's stew, rabbit, so there's enough."

From outside the kitchen came a squawking sound. "I had them delivered today," said Mrs. Watter, inclining her head toward the noise. "Your father wans't happy about it, as you can hear, but he did build them an enclosure." As she finished peeling each potato she threw it into a pot of water boiling on the stove. As the potato plopped into the pot, drops of water leapt out and hissed in the flame. "But he'll love the eggs when they begin to lay. He loves a rich cake. He's been so depressed."

"I didn't know," said Lark, going to the back door.

"He hammers all the time. And he's stopped the books altogether, all of a sudden. I don't like it."

At the bottom of the back steps clustered a dozen ducks, honking and squawking, trying to clamber to where Lark stood. "They've escaped," said Lark.

The chicken wire strung across the back yard had come loose.

"He can't do anything right," said Mrs. Watter. "Go down and tell him to fix it. And then tell him to wash his hands and come to dinner." She threw the final potato in the pot, then sighed and said, "Now I can take off my coat and hat and maybe have a quick cup of tea. I just wanted to get dinner started and over and done with. Here." She handed Lark a basin filled with stale bread soaked in water. "That'll make them follow you."

Lark led the ducks, stumbling behind her, back through the chicken wire and down to the gum tree, near the rooster, which was sitting on its crate looking surprised, making a deep sound in its throat, like a growling cat. Lark tipped the bread onto the grass and the ducks fell upon it, tearing it apart with the vigor of carnivores attacking flesh.

In the basement Henry Watter was fixing hinges on the lid of his box.

"They got out of the wire," Lark said. "It has to be fixed again." One side of the box had now been sanded smooth and she put her hand out to stroke it.

"My ark," whispered Henry Watter. "*Le ark*, as you'd say in fronsay. And that's what it's going to be. A lark. But it's our secret, all right? Don't tell your mother."

Lark nodded, not sure what the secret was, but it did not matter, since she had never conveyed any information from one parent to the other.

Henry Watter took a wooden stake and a mallet and went out to fix the wire. "I don't know what gets into your mother. *Forte dux*," he said to Lark. "That's Latin for forty ducks. *Caesar adsum iam forte, Pompey ad erat.*"

Lark waited for the inevitable translation and the ensuing reproach from her mother.

"Caesar had some jam for tea, Pompey had a rat," Henry Watter shouted as he hammered the stake into the ground.

Mrs. Watter considered reference to the eating of rodents to be in the category of "language." "Please, Henry, no language," she said out the kitchen window.

The ducks, having finished their bread, saw Henry Watter at the wire, and with much honking they flew up the slope at him, skimming two feet above the ground. They landed on top of one another at Henry Watter's feet, on his feet, and milled around his ankles as he worked. "Someone'll have to clip their wings." He kicked them away from him. "Far, far too much fauna." He came back into the basement. "One day it'll be kangaroos, you'll see."

Lark did not know what to do with the rejection from the *Mirror*. She could not bear to let him have it. Instead, she told him about her letter. "Solomon Blank has found a steady girl-friend," she said. "Fairly attractive, fairly blond, tallish, and she's American. They went to New York together."

"You're better off without him, Larkie, if you ask me. People from big families aren't a safe bet. They're too self-centered, wrapped up in their own doings, smug. They'll let you down in the end. Those Blanks, going off all the time, with those four boys. Look." He lifted the lid from his box and opened the paper bag that now rested beside the bolt of cloth. "Cadbury's Caramello, Hoadley's Violet Crumble, and Minties. Lots of sugar, for quick energy."

Mrs. Watter was stamping at them on the kitchen floor overhead.

"Dinner," said Lark, then, "There's news from the *Mirror*."

Henry Watter looked at her, questioning, and she shook her head. "Never mind," he said.

"'The mirror would do well to reflect further,'" said Lark, who had seen Cocteau's *Orphée* with Tom at the university film group. She thought her father might be about to cry and hoped that a pun might cheer him up. She nevertheless went ahead up to the kitchen so that he could cry if he wanted to. But he burst into the kitchen behind her and said to Mrs. Watter, "So when do we have roast duck?"

Lark leant against the railing at the Quay, looking down into the opaque, oil-covered water. Tom was almost an hour late, and she began to worry that she would not have time for her photography lesson before her interview at the *Herald*. She was dressed in her air hostess outfit, with a fountain pen and pencil in the pocket of the floral blouse.

"Got tied up," Tom said, and gave her shoulder a pat.

"It's all right," she said.

He looked around. "There's a good spot for us." He stationed Lark at the bus stop directly in front of one of the wharfs. "There'll be all kinds of people here." He opened up his camera and began explaining aperture, focus, shutter speed. "Take one of that old woman," he said.

"She's not that old," said Lark, putting the camera to her eye and focusing. "In her forties, I'd say. Maybe fifty."

"That's old," said Tom. "For a woman. As far as men are concerned, that is."

The woman, dressed in a straight woolen skirt with a cardigan over her neat white blouse, was carrying a heavy string bag. She was talking to a young man, smiling up at him and twisting a strand of her brown hair in her finger.

Lark took the photo.

"And take the man, too," said Tom. He showed her how to wind the film to the next frame.

Lark focused on the young man. He seemed hardly able to move his mouth to speak, and when he did, he answered the woman in monosyllables, gazing out across the harbor over her head. Lark took the picture.

"Now take one of them both. They'll be good for a May–December scandal," said Tom. "Isn't it silly, a woman her age flirting. She should see how she looks."

"Maybe it's her son," said Lark, and felt a terrible sorrow at the distance between that particular woman and man. "She looks very sad. And he is treating her badly."

"Quick, get that drunk," cried Tom.

A man had lurched out of the pub opposite and was weaving across the road to the bus stop. He had drawn out a crumpled handkerchief and was wiping his face.

Lark snapped him.

"Just take everyone waiting for a bus. Make sure you get one of everything—old, young, fat, thin, happy, sad, male, female, elegant, shabby. Get twins, if you can. Twins always come in handy. And we always need babies, and little children, groups of little children."

Lark snapped away, using up one roll of film, learning how to change the roll, and using up two more.

"Sixty should do us," said Tom. "I'll develop them while

you're at your interview and I'll show you what we're going to do with them tonight, at the party."

"Can I take the camera with me?" Lark asked. "It'll make me look the part. You know, foreign correspondent."

The editor interviewing her wore a visor like Donna Bird's. His bald head poked up behind it, making him look as if he were wearing a shiny helmet with a white and green peak. He wore metal garters around his shirt sleeves. Lark sat down in the chair beside his desk. A young reporter brought him several sheets of copy, which he read while the young man stood rigidly beside Lark, waiting, possibly terrified. The editor finished reading, and without changing his expression he ripped the copy in two and dropped the pieces in his wastebasket. The young reporter stood for a moment longer and seemed about to speak, perhaps to ask what was wrong with the story.

"What makes you think you can be a reporter?" the editor asked. He picked up another batch of copy from his desk and looked as if he would start reading it. Lark was not sure if he was addressing her or the young reporter, but since the reporter retreated without uttering a word, she answered, "I shall have my B.A. in December," she said. "I'm looking for a full-time job, a career."

"Our reporters don't need degrees."

"I have studied French."

"Our reporters don't need French."

Lark touched her camera. "I am a photographer and I have published a couple of things"—she was thinking of her letter in the student newspaper—"and I am interested in the world as a whole and I . . ."

"Our reporters don't need to be interested in the world as a whole or as anything, they just have to report. And we have photographers who take the pictures." He passed his hand over his face, brushing away the sweat without moving his visor. "Listen, girlie, you're too educated, you're too big for your boots.

You might look like a schoolgirl, but actually you're already too old," he held up his hand in case Lark was about to protest, "and you're a girl."

Lark opened her mouth to form some retort, some reply. The man continued to hold up his hand at her.

"Our reporters start with us at sixteen and by the time they're twenty-one, they're old hands. And girls only get into trouble. Or they get married. Same thing. You can't count on them. And none of my men want to work with girls." He went back to his editing. "You're wasting my time."

Lark stumbled onto the street and, after walking for some time, onto the bus that took her out to the university. But when it swung around onto Glebe Point Road, she stayed on, deciding suddenly to go to Tom and cry on his shoulder. Although she had never been to his flat, she had long ago ascertained his address.

Tom was at the greengrocer's stand squeezing tomatoes when Lark got off the bus. "I'm famous for choosing ripe tomatoes," he said to her, apparently unsurprised by her appearance on his doorstep. "I can get them at just the right hour for a salad, and at just the right hour for a sauce. You name it. The Tomato Kid, they call me. What can you do?"

"This horrible man spent two minutes with me and insulted me and . . ." To her own horror and surprise, Lark started crying.

"Hey," said Tom. He put down the tomatoes and opened his arms, and Lark let herself be folded against his shoulder. With one hand he picked out half a dozen tomatoes and motioned for the greengrocer to put them in a paper bag. "This is a stroke of luck that you came by at this moment. I need to photograph the wooden crate these tomatoes came in." He eased Lark away from him, lifting his camera from around her neck. He gave her a pat to tell her he would be with her again in a moment, placed the tomato box on the footpath, and took several pictures of the box from various angles. He put Lark against his shoulder again, fished in his pocket with one hand and paid for the tomatoes, thanking the greengrocer for his cooperation, then led Lark across the road and up the stairs to his flat. "I'll make you a tomato salad to knock your socks off," said Tom.

Lark smiled a bit, then found herself laughing.

They had to step over the mail, which had been pushed under the door of the one-room flat.

Tom sat Lark on the bed. "Okay, so some asshole insulted you." He lay down and patted the space beside him. "You didn't learn lesson number two thoroughly." Lark lay down. He patted her shoulder, saying "There, there," in a soothing way.

Lark gasped out her story against his shirt.

"Jackass," said Tom. He kissed the top of her head. "It's a reactionary paper, anyway, the *Herald*."

"I was so upset. I had to tell someone. Nobody wants me." Lark placed her hand on Tom's chest and turned her face up to his.

He kissed her forehead, then pushed her away. "Listen, I do have to go over my speech for tonight." He sat up. Lark's hand fell back to the bed. "I already developed some of the photos you took—they're drying in the bathroom—and still have the others to do." He sprang from the bed. "Why don't you just wait here for a few hours and then go to the rally with us later."

Lark went to the bathroom to wash her face. The drying prints were pegged to string that laced back and forth across the bathtub. In the tub were beer bottles, which were covered in cold water, ready for the party.

"I feel much better," Lark said, happy to be in Tom's presence, alone with him, in his home.

Tom was in the kitchen alcove slicing tomatoes. "First, food for thought," he said.

Lark picked up the mail from the floor and looked for somewhere to put it. The table was awash with newspaper clippings. There was no free surface.

"Just put the letters on top of the fridge," said Tom. "You think this is bad, you should see Manfred Bird's apartment."

"What are these?" Lark was reading one of the clippings. "'A woman who intended to ride her motorbike from Sydney to Perth put her three-month-old baby in a tomato box and tied it to the pillion seat. The baby was sunburnt and charged with being a neglected child when the mother was apprehended in Canberra.'" She waved the clipping at him.

"Ah, that's 'Three-month-old baby arrested and charged.'" Tom went into the bathroom and returned with a photograph Lark had taken that morning at the bus stop. "This is the baby." He rooted around on the table until he found a picture of a motorcycle. "Motorcycle." He pointed at the camera. "And in there is the tomato box." He held up a brochure on Australian marsupials. "Mother confines baby in leather pouch." And he went through the photos kept in a shoe box until he found a picture of a leather bag carried by a woman in a floral dress. "Mother, leather bag, baby. You got more than one baby this morning, didn't you?"

Lark picked up a clipping about a snake that got out of its cage in a pet shop and ate an Angora rabbit. "Snake eats rabbit?"

Tom shook his head and pulled a face, giving her the thumbs down.

"Man eats rabbit?"

Tom turned his thumbs up. "You got it. Father eats daughter's Easter pet."

Lark ran to the bathroom and brought back a picture of the lurching drunken man she had photographed. The handkerchief made him look as if he was dabbing at his mouth, having eaten a hearty meal. "Father?"

Tom held up a picture of a rabbit. "Rabbit."

"But why?" Lark moved close to him to view the rabbit. She touched his elbow lightly.

Tom shrugged. "*Strange but True* will never know. Donna and I get all the small-town newspapers and odd brochures that we can and just lift suitable stories. I change them of course. It's quite creative really. The pay is good enough for vagabonds like Donna and me." He stepped away from Lark into the kitchen alcove and took the letters that Lark had put on the fridge and held one up. "Our latest check, from *Strange but True*. It's beating the capitalists at their own game. It could also be called new approaches to conceptual art. We can do much more if you join us. You can have the photo credits for the lot you did today. The *Herald* will be sorry they let you slip through their fingers."

"I don't think Donna Bird is too keen on the idea."

The door burst open and Donna Bird walked in. Tom had not locked the door behind them when they came in. Donna merely raised her eyebrows and her visor when she saw Lark, then said to Tom, "Do you want me to go through the speech with you?"

The lecture theater was packed. Lark crept to a seat in the back row. Tom was sitting at a long table on the podium next to an important Australian novelist. Donna Bird, at one end of the table, was taking notes.

"People here are afraid," the novelist said, "that if we let brown people into our country we will find ourselves sitting next to someone who has just eaten his grandmother for breakfast." Tom laughed loudly, the audience followed. Donna Bird smiled and scribbled.

Then it was Tom's turn. "While the people of the developing world continue to struggle for independence from their European masters, neocolonialists are gaining strength; while the neo-Nazi movement grows in Europe, Australia supports uncritically American neocolonialism and commits its own barbarism, its own form of Nazism, by not admitting anyone who is not white, white, white. You've all heard of Italians, those well-known Europeans, excluded from Australia because their eyebrows are too dark and thick, of Chinese who are given dictation in Swedish so that they fail the literacy test and are excluded. Because they are not *bianco*, *bán*, *putih*, *weiss*, *wit*, *blanco*, *blanc*."

*Blanc.* Blank. And for a moment, Lark thought of Solomon.

"If you toe the line drawn by America, you will always lose the race," Tom said.

Lark recognized the line from her letter and was happy. After a while she had the courage to get up and stand at the front, to one side, and she began taking photos of the speakers.

Lark carried in beer from the bathtub and emptied potato chips into a roasting pan. She bore the pan into the room full of gesturing, drinking guests, placing it on top of the mass of papers and clippings on the table. She went into the kitchen alcove and hoisted herself onto the counter in order to observe the party. She felt very useful. It seemed that every prominent student from the university was in that room, students she had previously watched from afar, in addition to the barefoot Perce, the fornicating architecture student, F.X., the young conservative in the navy blue suit, and End of Tether. This was the group that had formed around Donna Bird and Tom, and by default around Lark, whom Tom now seemed to expect to accompany him everywhere. She had never imagined she would find herself in such company, but here she was, swinging her legs against the kitchen cabinets in Tom's flat, in the middle of things.

Suddenly F.X., his cup of beer held aloft, came over to Lark on the counter. He leant into the porcelain sink.

Lark guessed he was going to vomit—it always happened at parties, she should have known better than to sit near the sink—and went to jump off the counter. F.X. placed his hand on her knee. "Just inspecting the faucets and fixtures," he said. "These faucets, as I guessed, were manufactured in nineteen fifteen. Of course, it was an informed guess, since all these terraces were put up long before the First World War, with kitchens at the back, and when they were broken up into these little moozels, new fixtures were installed, naturally." He stood up. "Show me a tap or a toilet and I'll tell you when it was manufactured, to within five years." He swung around and pointed his finger at Lark. "Give me two synonyms for the word 'tap.'"

"Faucet, spigot," said Lark. "The words survive in American English but have almost disappeared from English English."

"Ah-ha," said F.X. He tapped his forehead and wandered off.

Through the archway Lark could see Perce standing next to Donna Bird, his arm around her waist. Tom came out of the bathroom flourishing the new photographs. "Mother kills mate, eats babies," he called, holding up Lark's pictures, and everyone gathered around him while he gave a presentation of stories and pictures destined for *Strange but True*.

"You've got to hand it to Tom, he's innovative," said F.X. "Even though he is deceiving the press, mocking the establishment and private enterprise, and challenging the very base of capitalism. Here's to Tom," and everyone drank some more.

"It's called pressing the press into the service of the powerless people, us," said Tom.

"We'll even forgive him for being a Yank," said Perce, swaying against Donna as he downed his beer. Donna set him upright again, then slipped out of his grasp and went to the bathroom. Perce, slowly looking around the room for his next inspiration, caught sight of Lark sitting on the counter, apart and happy. He lurched toward her. "Can you iron a good shirt? Can you bake a cherry pie?" He put his arms around Lark's waist and rested his head in her lap, mumbling and slurping into her skirt, "Can you . . ." He looked up for a moment. "I say, may I?" And he buried his face in her lap.

Lark looked anxiously at Tom, waiting for him to save her from this assault. She tried to pry Perce loose, but he was pressed against her and holding on with all his might.

"You have a real fan there," said Tom. He picked up his camera and took a picture.

"Take one of me?" Donna Bird was standing in the doorway of the bathroom, one hand above her head pressed against the jamb, one hip pushed out to one side, as if she were a torch singer. But she was now wearing a navy blue serge school tunic, a white blouse with a maroon and silver striped tie in a Windsor knot, navy blue stockings and black lace-up shoes. She had braided her hair into two thick schoolgirl plaits and crammed a school Panama on her head. She wore spectacles and carried a Globite school case.

"Wonderful," cried Tom and snapped her picture. "Just wonderful."

Everyone applauded. Perce, plastered against Lark's lap, merely groaned and grumbled as Lark continued to try to get him off her. Tom went up to Donna and inspected her closely, turning her around and whistling. "Perfect, brilliant, superb," he said, as if he had sculpted her himself. "Tomorrow's the big day," he announced. "Be there, the Wynyard ramp, four o'clock."

Lark seemed to be the only one who had no idea what Tom was talking about. Tom had grabbed Donna Bird around the waist and was jitterbugging with her, knocking people aside, carving out a space in the throng.

Perce lifted his head, saw Donna in her school uniform and Tom whirling around, groaned, said "Statutory rape," and vomited in the sink. Lark leapt down from the counter. She could push Tom and Donna aside, fling open the door and leave the flat, escaping down the stairs onto Glebe Point Road. Another fifty pounds, she needed, perhaps only twenty would do, and then she would really be able to leave. She did not need *Strange but True*. These people did not need her, and she did not need them.

She edged her way toward the door, quietly. Tom threw himself against the door, Donna Bird still in tow. "Don't leave me," he said, pressing his free hand to his heart. And then Donna Bird was whirled off in F.X.'s arms. "I don't want you to go," Tom said quietly, putting his arms around Lark and doing a little shuffling dance on the spot, his cheek against her hair. "You're needed for tomorrow."

"What's happening tomorrow?" she asked.

"The Big Joke," Tom mouthed back. "You'll have to photograph it. You'll stay the night with me here, then we'll mail off the pictures and stuff to *Strange but True,* then you'll photograph Donna Bird getting kidnapped by a carload of perverts."

"What did you say?" Lark asked. She was not sure he had actually invited her to stay the night.

Tom looked up at the ceiling. "Are you deaf? You have to photograph the kidnapping of Donna Bird by perverts, all supplied by us. This," he spun her around so that her skirt went right out, "Is Your Life, Lark Watter."

"But you said something about tonight?"

"Tonight you stay, tomorrow we work." He let go her hand, leaving her spinning, and went back into the crowd, where several of the young men and women had hoisted Perce, who had passed out, into their arms and were bearing him to Tom's bed in the corner.

Lark steadied herself against the door, then slipped back to the kitchen alcove, and turned on the tap to get rid of Perce's mess. She cleaned the sink and the counter and collected the rubbish, then leant against the counter, waiting for the party to be over.

"Be a pet," said F.X. to Donna, "and drive me home. We can take Perce's car, he won't be needing it."

Donna was still in her school uniform. "I'm going to help Tom clean up?" said Donna. "And we have to finish putting together the stories for *Strange but True.*"

Tom, Donna, and F.X. were sitting on the floor. Perce was stretched out on the bed. Lark was sitting on the counter. Everyone else had left.

Tom stood up and started looking through the papers on the table, many of them now wet from beer and greasy from the potato chips. Lark jumped down and started removing the party clutter.

"I can't find the copy for three of the stories," Tom said to Donna.

"They're at my place, or the office, I think?" Donna said.

"They have to go off first thing in the morning," said Tom. "As long as you've got Perce's car, why don't you go and get them now. Then we can get everything licked and stamped."

"I can get them tomorrow morning."

"Come on," said F.X. "I'll escort you, protect you."

Tom rifled through Perce's pockets to get his keys. Perce stirred slightly, mumbled something, then went on breathing deeply. Donna hesitated, then noting Lark in the kitchen busy washing glasses and Perce prominently spread out on the bed, she held out her hand to F.X., who pulled her to her feet.

"I'll be back," Donna said. Then to Lark, "Can't we drop you off?"

"It's all right," said Lark, "I can get home all right. I'll just clean up first."

Tom tossed the keys to Donna Bird. "See you around the block." He looked through the papers on his desk, seized a handful and slid down onto the floor, his back against the bed.

As soon as they had closed the door Lark stopped washing the glasses and sat beside Tom, her knees drawn up under her chin. She rested her cheek on her knees, her face turned toward Tom, watching him read. When he looked up and smiled at her she said, "So this is my life?" She touched his arm. He made a kissing sound at her, and she leant over and kissed him.

"Hey," he said, holding onto his papers, which were in danger of sliding off his knees.

"Can't you take a break?" Lark asked.

"Sure," said Tom "Why not?"

He put his papers neatly on the floor and leant back against the bed, his arm around Lark, gazing at the ceiling. "Some party."

"Do you mind if I lock the door?" Lark was thinking of Donna Bird's surprise entry earlier. She quickly locked the door and returned to Tom, who had begun to pick up his papers again. Lark took his hands in hers and they lay down on the carpet.

"I predict," said Tom, "that one day in the not-too-distant, someone, America probably, will try to put a dome of lasers or something over the whole continent, a shield against attack." Lark closed her eyes and snuggled into Tom's shoulder, caressing his chest. Tom kissed her absently. "It's all part of the drive to reattain the state of the single cell, don't you see? Politicians don't understand that this is what's driving them. They think it's strategy. But it won't work, of course. Just as the sperm can, every now and then, wriggle around the edge of the diaphragm and penetrate and impregnate the uterus, so one person, wheeling a nuclear bomb in a wheelbarrow, will slip under the edge of the shield."

Lark sighed and opened her eyes. Perce's foot was right above her, and she examined for a moment the sole of a foot that had not worn shoes for many months, maybe years. It was tough and hard and cracked, like an old rubber tire. He could probably walk on fire. She closed her eyes and went back to kissing Tom.

"What about *Rigoletto?*" Lark murmured.

"I have no idea what you're talking about."

"The single cell. Rigoletto sets up this protective shield around his daughter in the form of a high wall, to isolate her, and as a result everyone, well, the Duke who stands for everyone, tries to get through the wall. The urge to penetrate. Osmosis, wouldn't you say?"

"What are you talking about?" Tom now lay on his back, Lark beside him, her face over his, smiling down at him. His eyes roamed past her, then he, too, saw the foot. He smiled and tapped Lark on the shoulder.

"Look at that foot," he said.

"I know," said Lark.

"You're not looking."

Lark looked up. "I saw it already."

"You've got to admire Perce's feet." Tom reached up and took a pencil from the table, then drew it across the foot. The foot did not move, Perce had felt nothing. "They're like a pair of dirty old boots. Magritte must have known about Perce's feet. He has a painting of them."

Although Lark did not say "Magritte?" it did not seem to make any difference. Tom said, "You don't know anything, do you? As we lie here, at this very moment, Magritte is in Belgium painting his heart out. There's a whole world out there waiting for you, Larkie."

"And I'm going very, very soon," said Lark. She craned her neck to make sure Perce was still sleeping. "I'm going to be a vagabond, too."

"He won't wake up, don't worry," said Tom. He ran the pencil over the foot again, which this time twitched. "He's alive, at least."

"And Donna Bird? She said she was coming back."

"She's with F.X." Tom sighed and put his hands under his head. "Abstinence, then, is the only way to build strength. Abstinence from weapons, and so on."

A few moments later a croaking voice from the bed said, "Do you need help picking the little flower?" Perce's face was now hanging over the edge of the bed. "Happy to be of service." Lark sat up, turning away from Perce and Tom to straighten her blouse.

At the sound of a key in the door Lark leapt up and rushed to the bathroom.

"Here is the copy?" said Donna Bird, waving a folder in her hand. She stood at the door, taking in Tom flaked out on the floor with his shirt unbuttoned, and Perce on the bed mumbling. Lark opened the bathroom door.

"Jesus," said Tom, sitting up, shaking his head. "This flat is the crossroads of Sydney, it seems."

"The little man has had a busy day, hasn't he?" said Donna.

"I was just going," said Lark. Tom should have told her that Donna had the key to his flat.

"I'll drive you home now. Then," this was to Tom, "we'll do that licking and stamping."

"Licking and stamping," cried Perce from the bed. "I'm good at that. So are they. You should have seen what I saw just now."

And obediently Lark followed Donna Bird out of the flat.

It was daylight when Donna pulled up outside Lark's house. The milkman had already been along Park Avenue. On the footpath, hidden from the Watters' house by the hedge that ran along the front fence but in plain view of the street, were several hundred packets of laundry detergent, stacked to form a knee-high wall. A trail of white powder from a broken packet led from the front gate around the side of the house to the back.

"Colorful," said Donna Bird. Then, noting that the sun was out, she reached into her handbag and pulled out her visor.

Lark was embarrassed by the packets of Persil, which had to mean that her father was engaged in some new project. Henry Watter, in his pajamas and dressing gown, came hurrying to the front, bent over, furtive, and lifted two packets in each arm, then scurried back. Lark was aware that while her father was thus engaged, the illustrious Professor Manfred Bird, father of Donna Bird, in his academic tweeds, was somewhere in North America thinking deeply original thoughts or lecturing to a class of eager students on the habits of primitives.

Donna pulled her visor down on her forehead and wrapped her scarf around her neck and chin. She watched Henry Watter disappear, then shrugged and drove off.

Lark waited by the front gate. Henry Watter, when he came

back for more packets, was too preoccupied to reproach Lark for staying out all night. Perhaps he had not even noticed.

"Quick, help me get these out of sight before your mother gets up."

Lark took a load of Persil around to the basement. Henry had opened the lid of his box and was filling it with the detergent packets. All the walls of the box had now been sanded, and one end had been stained. "Time is of the essence," he said.

They ran back and forth for twenty minutes or so, until all the Persil was hidden. What did not fit in the box they hid in the far corner of the basement and covered with the French flag.

Henry Watter lowered the lid and sat on the box. He wiped his forehead with the sleeve of his dressing gown. "Thank you, thank you. And don't even mention it to her."

"Is it a surprise, a present?" Lark asked.

"You know I didn't get anywhere with Jack Davey?"

Lark shook her head.

"The fiasco won't be on the air for a while, luckily. They had it rigged. They knew I knew everything, so they asked me something I didn't know." He tapped the box, indicating its contents. "This is what I won. Persil. They delivered it just now. Your mother didn't see it. I don't need Persil."

"But she's always washing clothes," said Lark. "She'll appreciate it."

"But I'm ashamed," said Henry Watter, "to have tried so hard and to have failed. I'll never get away." He started to cry.

Mrs. Watter's footsteps sounded in the kitchen above. "I'll go and sweep away the spilled powder," said Lark.

"So," said Mrs. Watter at breakfast, "you were with those friends of yours?" She banged a saucepan of water on the stove.

Lark nodded. "A party. All night."

"That American?"

Lark nodded again.

"You weren't the only girl, were you? You know what people say about one girl with many men."

"There were millions of men, all dancing naked."

"Lark, please, language. I have to care about your dignity, since you don't seem to. I don't want you to find yourself in a situation you'll regret later." She dumped a couple of handfuls of oats into the water. "Of course, the Americans saved us from the Japanese, and we are grateful, but when is this one going back to his own country?"

"Soon," said Lark. "Lucky devil. You won't have to worry about him and me."

"Please, Lark." The hammering suddenly started up in the basement. "Go down and tell him his porridge is ready."

Lark was at the Wynyard ramp with Tom's camera around her neck. She stood at the bus stop, and waited, ready for the kidnapping.

A schoolgirl in a navy blue uniform, carrying a Globite school case and reading a little brown book of Vergil, emerged from the underground ramp and stood at the bus stop, a short distance from Lark. Donna Bird. She put the case on the ground between her legs and flicked her braids over her shoulders, looked at her watch, and continued reading. A dozen or so people were waiting for a bus.

A car—Lark recognized Perce's car—with mud over the number plates cruised along the curb. A young man in a suit and hat leant out of the front window, and whistled at the schoolgirl. "I have some very special lollies here in my coat pocket, girlie, want some?" It was Perce himself.

Donna Bird read on, as if she was not sure that the man was addressing her.

"Do you want a ride? We can take you where you're going."

Donna Bird looked up, peering through her spectacles, as if she had not yet understood. "What?" she said, stepping for-

ward, as if they had asked directions from her and she was going
to help.

A woman waiting near her took her arm. "Just ignore them,
dear."

The car came to a stop. The front door opened and Perce got
out—he looked like a clerk or a bank teller. And he was wearing
shoes and socks for the occasion. The other two young men in
suits got out from the back—Lark recognized them as members
of Donna Bird's entourage—and rather slowly, calmly, they
took a few steps to Donna Bird's side. Perce, awkward in his
shoes, or else still reeling from the night before, tripped on an
irregularity in the cement and fell right against Donna, and the
two of them fell to the ground. Lark took her first photo, waiting
until their faces were turned away so that they could not be
recognized. The other two hauled Donna and Perce to their
feet, pushing the woman aside, then, letting go of Perce, who
swayed a little unsteadily, they pulled Donna, kicking and
shrieking, to the car. Lark took her second photo.

The men pushed Donna into the back seat and jumped in
after her. Perce picked up Donna's school case and the Vergil
and fell into the front seat. The car drove off. The good citizens
at the bus stop had just comprehended what had happened. The
car turned up Margaret Street and disappeared.

"I don't believe it," cried the woman, who had been thrust
aside.

"I couldn't read the number plate," said a man.

"She was reading Vergil," said another. "I saw the cover of
the book. That will help find her."

"I didn't see her school tie," said the woman, "did you?" She
had turned to Lark. "Did you recognize the uniform?"

Lark shood her head.

"The Vergil will help," said the man who had recognized the
book. "There can't be that many students at high schools in the
city reading Vergil."

"She has photos," cried an onlooker.

"We have more perverts in this country per head than any other country," said the woman who had tried to save Donna Bird.

By then a policeman had been found and everyone clamored to tell him the story. Lark wound the film off and gave it to the policeman. Then she disappeared, leaving the upset crowd and the policeman.

The *Herald* and the *Daily Mirror* used Lark's photos on the front page the next day, with the story of the kidnapping. Lark was referred to as the mystery photographer, and there was an appeal for her to step forward. And although every Latin class in the city appeared to be reading Vergil, no student of Vergil was reported missing. No one at all was reported missing.

"But why the kidnapping?" Lark dared to ask later at Tom's. She had thought it was a silly idea, although beautifully executed, like a scene in a movie, even with Perce's clumsiness.

Donna Bird sniffed and shook her head at Tom to indicate her amazement at the question. "I think it's time for the Big J," she said, then to Lark, "Jay, jay, joke. You're really coming along. You realize you have broken the law, don't you? Deceiving the police."

"We just wanted people to be aware that this is a country of weirdos," said Tom. "And we wanted to show how easy it is to manipulate the press. If we can do it, Larkie, manipulate the press, then everyone already does it—and that means our government, all governments, any group that wants to exhibit itself." Tom spoke gently. He even patted Lark's head, with Donna and the others watching.

"Did you say manipulate? Did you say exhibit?" said Perce, making a big show of undoing the rope around his trousers.

"Yes," Tom said, responding to Donna. "The Big J, the Really Big J. The world is our text, as you like to remind us."

"I'm leaving," Tom told Lark. "Back to the U. S. of A."
Lark had finished her final exams. She was finally free.

"So?" she said glumly. "I've been expecting you to leave for months."

It was dusk and they were walking along Lark's beach while Tom took photographs of objects found in the sand. Lark was wearing a pair of Black Watch tartan Bermuda shorts, and was aware that people turned to look at this outlandish item of clothing.

"I'll be leaving one day soon, too," Lark said. "We all do. Sooner or later. One way or another."

Tom looked at her, as if he were deciding something. "I think you'd better come to New York, Larkie. Come on."

"Me?" Lark said, then as if putting him to some kind of test, "Why don't you ask Donna Bird?"

"She's already going to New York. She's going to be a critic of society there. And it's time for her to see Manfred again. She hasn't seen him for a couple of years. She has a new half-brother."

"You'll have her for company," said Lark sulkily. "And I don't know anything. You said so yourself." But Lark was in love with Tom, she thought it must be true love, and she was only waiting for him to tell her he loved her, or something close to it.

"You don't know much," said Tom. "Your mind is unformed. But I could teach you." He squatted down to photograph a sea gull that had followed them along the water's edge.

"I don't think I have enough money for New York. I'll need to be able to last for several months once I'm there. I don't care about having the fare back." Lark lay down on the sand.

"Donna Bird has found the cheapest way. That ship, the freighter. The Captain knows her father. I'll have to fly, of course. But you could go on that ship with her. Save some money. It'll be a form of active transport—you will be the material being transported from here, the outside, through the plasma membrane, to the inside, that is, New York."

"Donna Bird doesn't like me."

"You mean you don't like her. She's an interesting person.

One of a kind. And she wants you to travel with her. She'd be the only passenger, otherwise. It'll give me time to find you a cheap apartment in New York, have it ready for you." Tom pulled a letter out of his pocket. "From *Strange but True,*" he said.

"Money?" Lark patted the sand beside her. She wanted Tom near her.

Tom shook his head. "I don't think you have any choice about leaving."

"No choice?" The question and answer method had become routine for Lark.

"They noticed it was the same bus stop in the background of the photos for all the stories we sent them. They're suing us."

"Us?" Lark propped herself on one elbow.

"You, me, Donna. You had the photo credits, remember? I think it's really time for you to leave."

Lark stared at the horizon.

"A *'petit chalutier,'* perhaps?" Tom asked. "You'd be off the beach, you know. It's what you want. And it will be the beginning of lesson number three, getting your feet wet in the real world."

"But do you love me?" Lark asked.

"Love?" Tom snapped another sea gull. "Of course. Sure. Love is a good thing all around." He turned his camera on Lark and took her picture. "You have an interesting face. When you're old, you'll have interesting wrinkles." Lark turned away. "Don't worry, I'm out of film. I didn't get you." He sat beside Lark and put his arm around her. "You do know, don't you, that you can't possess another human being. That would be murder. Murder by osmosis. Diffusion."

The Watters were eating dinner.

"So you're home tonight," said Mrs. Watter. "At least there's poultry. There's enough."

"I'm going," said Lark.

"This bird is tough," said Henry Watter. He looked up. "She's finally going?"

"To New York," Lark said.

"What do you want to go there for?" Henry Watter asked. "England's the only place." He chewed at his food, looking at each piece on his fork before he put it in his mouth. "Tough old bird. Just like your mother." He chewed for a moment. "You don't even know the fifty states, let alone their capitals. You don't even know the stations on the railway line from Chicago to Detroit."

"I can say the states in alphabetical order," said Lark.

"It's that American boy, isn't it?" said Mrs. Watter.

Lark shook her head. "I always meant to go. And I finished my exams. I did what you wanted."

"Well, at least we finally got rid of that rooster," said Henry Watter, chewing. "Next, those ducks."

"And you'll get married, of course. Here? There, I suppose. But small weddings can be simple and dignified."

Lark shrugged. Tom had said nothing about marriage. But it seemed possible. He liked her, liked having her near him.

"Just like a war bride," said Lark's mother. "I remember them after the war, so excited to be going away. I wanted to go, too. I was already married, of course. I just wanted to go away."

"No more crowing in the middle of the flaming day," said Henry Watter. He looked at Lark. "I chopped its damned head off, you know. We're eating it."

"Please, Henry, language," said Lark's mother.

"Throw me the gravy," said Henry Watter.

"Please, Henry, pass," said Mrs. Watter, handing him the gravy boat. She stared out the window. "I used to go down to Pyrmont to see the boats off and throw streamers to all those soldiers and their war brides, sailing off across the Pacific at the end of the war. We'd hold onto the streamers as if we might be taken along, too."

Henry Watter held the gravy in the air, making it sail along, up and down, like a toy boat on the sea. "'Take the current when it serves,'" he said.

"Henry, please, manners."

"J. Caesar. A self-made man. Like N. Bonaparte. Self-made men," said Henry Watter. He stood up. "'And so to bed.'"

Mrs. Watter stood for a moment at the table. "I think I'll just make a cup of tea, then, and sit for a minute before doing the dishes." She put the kettle on and came back to sit down. "We even thought the men going off to war were lucky to be traveling," she said softly. "When I was a little girl, I was taken down to the Quay to wave them off to Gallipoli, as if they were going on a holiday. It was very jolly. And only much later did we learn what Gallipoli really was, that Churchill and our own government had manipulated us, lied to us, betrayed us."

Lark's earliest memory was a picture in the newspaper: an Australian, a prisoner in the Changi camp in Singapore, was about to be beheaded by a Japanese holding a sword. He was kneeling, his arms tied behind his back, his head bowed. To spare the soldier's family at home, the soldier's face had been blacked out.

"Nevertheless it's lucky we got the bomb first," called Henry Watter from the bathroom.

Lark's mother brought in the teapot. She shook her head. "Sometimes," she whispered, "I have absolutely no idea what he's talking about." She sat for a minute, sipping her tea. "Perhaps he's upset about your going off and getting married, to a foreigner. He doesn't take change easily. At least you have your degree. You have more than I."

Lark helped with the dishes, then went to her room to begin packing for the voyage.

Henry Watter knocked on her door and glanced to the left and right along the hallway before he stepped in. He was turning the pages in a book of puzzles. "Here," he said, sitting on the clothes Lark had laid on her bed. "This'll stretch your brain," he said. "You'll need it, when you go, a stretched brain, especially among those Americans. They're quick. You've got to be able to manage on your own."

Lark pulled the clothes out from under Henry Watter.

He began to read: "'Asher, Barker, and Carson work on a train which makes a daily run either from Detroit to Chicago or Chicago to Detroit, both via South Bend.' This is useful already, Larkie, listen." Lark was opening one drawer after another. "Listen." And Henry Watter stopped reading until Lark stood still and listened to him. "'The three men live in the three cities mentioned. Their jobs are conductor, dining car waiter, and guard.'" He held up his hand, in case Lark was about to protest. "'Three men with the same last names, Mr. Asher, Mr. Barker, and Mr. Carson, who live in the same three cities, are regular passengers on the train. The passengers are an architect, an attorney, and a chemist.' You see, Lark, how already you have learned a great deal about American society just by listening to these few sentences."

"I know, for instance," said Lark, "that South Bend is one of the stops between Chicago and Detroit, and that they say attorney instead of solicitor. Is that what you mean?"

"'For each man, find his occupation and the city in which he lives, remembering that one, no railroad employee lives in the same city as the passenger with the same last name; two, the dining car waiter and the attorney are neighbors; three, Carson lives between the conductor's and Mr. Barker's cities . . .'"

"It's torture, what you do," said Lark.

Henry Watter closed the book, keeping one finger marking the page. "I'm only trying to help. If you did one of these brain stretchers a day, you'd be in excellent shape. Nothing would stump you. And you'd keep your brain in good nick."

"I'd be like you?"

Henry Watter looked down at the book, slumping, hurt. "If I'd been doing these all along, I would have won that trip on Jack Davey. My brain wasn't in shape, not limber, not supple." He spoke quietly. "I was only trying to help you. You're the one who's going, you see."

"I'm sorry," said Lark, "leaving you here alone. But I have to go."

"I'll be going one day, too," said Henry Watter. He sniffed and sat up straight again. "When I'm ready." He reopened his book. "'Remembering that four, the architect and the guard do not live in the same city, and five, the guard has the same name as the passenger who lives in Chicago.'"

Lark sat beside him. "It's too hard for me. I don't have your brains."

"It took me five minutes," said Henry Watter. "Do you want me to tell you the answer? You'll never get it, not with your terrible concentration." He stood up. "I have just had an idea for a new project, and I have to go and work on it, my piece of resistance."

Lark dreamt she was waiting for a New York subway to whisk her off to an unknown destination. When the train hurtled into the station, it bore the sign, "Beware the deadly gases of Atmium and Thomium." It was definitely her train. She had to board it, although she had no gas mask, despite her sense of impending doom.

Lark visited Solomon Blank's mother. Solomon's letters to Lark had stopped altogether some months before.

"So you're going?" Mrs. Blank said. She described Solomon's successes in Champaign-Urbana and the successes of his fiancée. "You didn't know? He is getting married," she said, "to a really beautiful American, statuesque, but blond. Real yellow blond, long, natural of course, not pale and short, like yours." She went on to describe the luminous lives of Marshall, Ellice, and Gilbert, now in London, Copenhagen, and Rome. "They are all devoted to me," she said. She reached into the drawer of the telephone table and extracted letters and photographs. "Solomon is contributing an article to a scholarly journal. His fiancée is a lovely girl. They plan to have four children, one after the other. They are so happy. They write regularly, once every month or two."

Lark read the letters, regular tales of regular doings. Solomon's handwriting had not changed in the slightest. No doubt he was indeed terribly happy, as happy as she intended to be.

"Write down his address. They of course will be moving to a house, four bedrooms they have in mind. The two youngest children will have to share a room, when they come along. Solomon and his fiancée would just love to see an old friend from Solomon's early days. And of course, I may never see them again. It is so expensive. And I am old now. My traveling days are over. But they are devoted to me." She pushed a pencil and a piece of paper at Lark. "Oh, I was forgetting. I didn't offer you anything. Do you want a cup of tea, or will you just not bother?"

When Lark saw Donna Bird creeping up the gangplank of the little freighter, she felt a certain dread and a regret at having agreed to take this ship to New York. Tom had insisted that it would be good for her, and she knew she should save the money. But Tom had flown off to America already, and here was Donna Bird escorted by her followers. F.X. strode a little ahead of her, in his polished black shoes and his blue suit, with a red tartan waistcoat, holding aloft his black umbrella to protect her from the sun. "Cleopatra boards her barge," he announced. Perce danced a little behind in his bare feet. He had undone his rope belt and tied one end of it to Donna's wrist, as if he were her pet monkey. End of Tether carried the Globite school case that Donna Bird had used in the kidnapping.

In her gray slacks, gray turtle-neck sweater, gray socks with silver threads, brown leather sandals, the long gold earrings dangling under the brim of her straw sun visor, and a beige chiffon scarf resting inert on her shoulders, Donna Bird looked like some kind of rodent in a school pantomime. She seemed to have contrived to appear even more outlandish than usual, appearing eccentric rather than original, as Tom liked to term it, but perhaps it was because she was away from her usual habitat. Around her neck hung a camera, a rectangular box in a brown leather case. Donna Bird's long, wiry red hair was partly braided and partly hanging loose, and she kept looking at it in the glass of the portholes of the cabins that gave onto the main deck and in the glass of the bookcase in the dining room, where the Captain greeted her, his second passenger.

"So kind of you to have me? Us?" she murmured to the Captain, extending her hand.

The Captain of the *Avis Maris* clicked his heels and bent over her hand, as if to kiss it. "It is an honor to have the daughter of Professor Manfred Bird with us. You will keep us terrible men civilized."

Donna Bird smiled. "I shall be a mouse and stay in my mousehole."

"Moozel," cried F.X.

"And I shan't cause any bother?"

"You are looking at my unusual head?" the Captain asked.

Lark had tried not to notice the Captain's physical attributes when she had boarded and been greeted earlier. He was a small-bodied man, with a large balding head that looked soft all over, almost as if there were no skull within. "No," Lark had answered to the same question. "Not at all."

"Yes," said Donna. "Your head is unusual."

"War. Bad business. And now the world hates to see my head. It is good, the world thinks, that I spend my days at sea, out of sight. That is why I do not like passengers, especially lady passengers, who hate to see me. And they flit-flut all over the place, disturbing my good shipshapeship. Only outlandish lady passengers take a freighter, and we must talk little instead of big at dinner."

"And they bring frightful bad fortune," said Mr. Fischer, the first mate. "This is busy ship."

"They trit-trot all over the place and poke in things. And they are never German. Always outlandish. A German woman knows not to go on freighter. But you, Miss Bird, are A-O.K. You are the daughter of Manfred Bird."

"I shall be a mouse," said Donna Bird.

"Mooze," cried F.X.

After greeting the Captain and his two officers, Lark had even been glad that Donna Bird would be on board, that there would be someone else during the twenty-one days at sea. And then when Donna Bird had crept on board and accepted the Captain's strange head so easily, even enthusiastically, Lark remembered her dislike. Nevertheless, she had stepped forward and greeted her.

"So, Lark," Donna Bird said as they stood on the deck, "just us two? Off to Joke City and to Tom?" Behind her stood F.X. and Perce and the others in disarray, pushing at one another, hopping around. Behind Lark stood Henry Watter and Mrs. Watter, next to a lifeboat. Henry Watter carried a cotton sack with a drawstring on a stick over his shoulder, looking like Dick Whittington going off to seek his fortune. Lark and Donna were like two adversaries with their seconds and backups, about to choose their weapons. The sailors were securing the cargo of aluminum rods stacked on the deck. The last boxes and crates were swinging in nets and being lowered into the hold.

"Ah, I recognize Mr. Watter," said Donna Bird, "and this must be Mrs. Watter?" She stepped forward to shake their hands.

Henry Watter knocked on the side of the lifeboat and listened. "You want to be sure these are seaworthy," he said.

"Ships can be tricky. Storms and such. Not to mention the people—pirates and smugglers."

"A German ship, going to America," whispered Mrs. Watter doubtfully. "I hope you girls will be all right. I've heard they do dreadful things to women and children. If they had landed in England and placed their hands on those princesses, I dread to think." She was fishing around in the overnight bag she had brought with her. "Henry, did you put in the champagne?" Then she found them, three little bottles of pink champagne, labeled "Baby Bubbly." "Henry, you open them. And would you join us?" she said to Donna Bird, then peering past her to the group behind her, she added uncertainly. "perhaps everyone could have a thimbleful—I'm afraid there isn't much." Henry Watter shook one of the bottles, then aimed the cork into the air. "Henry, please." To Lark, she whispered, "Who are those young men?" She wrenched the bottle from Henry Watter and caught what she could of the overflowing champagne in one of the little glasses she had brought with her.

Perce jumped up in the air to catch the flying cork and then, holding it close to his body with both hands, as if it were a football, hunched over and ran down the deck and placed it at the rail. "Try," he said. Perce hopped back to the group. He tapped Mrs. Watter on the shoulder in passing and inclined his head toward Lark. "You've got a little flower there. A real little flower. Does she iron a good shirt?"

Mrs. Watter nodded politely. Perce hopped away. "Are they friends of yours?"

"They are very intelligent," said Lark.

Henry Watter shook the second bottle and popped the cork. Perce and the others had fanned out to form a row of forwards and a row of defense. F.X. caught the cork with the side of his foot and kicked it over to Perce, who blocked it with his knee, brought it onto the deck, then trod on it, to stop it from rolling around. He picked it up in his toes and hopped with it down the deck toward the rail again.

"Hold it?" cried Donna Bird. Perce stopped his hopping and stood still on one foot, the toes of his other foot curled around the cork, while Donna Bird unsnapped her camera. "Take one, action," she cried, and the camera started whirring. The camera that hung around her neck was a movie camera.

Perce resumed his hop and reached the rail. "Try," he cried again. "Now I'm ready to score." He turned and raised his eyebrows at Lark.

"Would you all perhaps like a little champagne?" Mrs. Watter said brightly. "I'm afraid there is only a little." Then, seeing Henry wrestling with the cork of the third bottle, she threw herself at him and seized the bottle. "Please, Henry."

This would soon be over, Lark thought. Only an hour, perhaps less, and she would be gone.

Mrs. Watter pressed something into Lark's hand, something hard and knobbly wrapped in tissue paper. "Look at it later, when all the fuss is over." She handed around little glasses filled with a finger or so of Baby Bubbly. "We'll have to take sips and share the glasses."

Lark slipped the little gift into her pocket.

Perce raised his hand. "Fear not." He opened the school case and displayed its contents, bottles of Tookey's pilsener. "I can't leave home without my bottle," he said, handing around the bottles, while Mrs. Watter gathered back her glasses of champagne.

Perce was making a toast. "Here's to plucky girls and their voyage into the unknown. Here's to pluck in general." And he drank.

"Pluck," everyone echoed and drank.

"So?" the Captain emerged onto the deck. "The pilot is on board. Now we will not bump into things."

"The pilots of Penzance," said Henry Watter, and Donna Bird giggled crazily. "Don't say I didn't warn you."

Loitering behind the Captain was a young, blond man in a white coat, wearing around his neck a metal ring with several keys on it. The steward. He stood behind the Captain, leaning against the bulwark, his arms folded, observing the passengers and their escorts, a rather scornful look on his face.

"'Take the current when it serves'?" said Henry Watter.

"'Or lose our ventures,'" answered Donna, waving her beer around.

Henry Watter turned to her joyfully and clinked his little glass of champagne against her bottle. "Did you hear what she said?" Henry Watter could not believe it. He began again, softly, hardly daring to hope for a reply. "'There is a tide in the affairs of men.'"

"'Which, taken at the flood, leads on to fortune,'" answered Donna Bird.

"'Omitted, all the voyage of their life,'" breathed Henry Watter.

"'Is bound in shallows and in miseries,'" whispered Donna Bird.

"A girl after my own heart," said Henry Watter, grasping her elbow.

"Look at that," said Donna Bird, pointing at a long box that had been lifted by the crane and was swinging low through the air just above their heads toward the hold. Henry Watter and Donna Bird ducked, although the box was several yards above them.

"Looks like a coffin," said Henry Watter.

Donna laughed. "That's really funny. My father says this is an excellent ship. You might know of him, Manfred Bird, Professor Manfred Bird, the anthropologist? He knows and trusts this Captain. In fact, the ship was named after my father, in honor of his work. He often ships his stuff on it. It's a good ship."

Henry Watter nodded. "I'll remember that, if ever I'm wanting to ship my stuff."

"Manfred says the whole South Pacific is going to rack and

ruin. The natives have no interest in preserving their culture. Some people say Manfred is a latter-day hero because he is dedicated to preserving this quarter of the globe from further corrosion. We're very close, Manfred and I. I help him in his work. But I'm trying to save all four quarters of the world."

Henry Watter looked around for Lark. "She's a very bright girl, this Miss Bird. Good to her father." He took both Lark and Donna by the arm and drew them over to the lifeboat. "I'll give you girls a last word of advice. Don't accept drinks from strangers. They slip drugs in them and you'll end up part of the white slave trade." He inclined his head toward the young blond steward.

"Please," said Lark, embarrassed. "That's another era altogether."

"I'm not kidding. I've been around longer than you two put together," said Henry Watter.

Donna Bird laughed, a girlish, tinkling laugh and gave Henry Watter a kiss on the cheek, then slipped out of his grasp and rejoined her friends.

"There's a very bright girl," said Henry Watter. "Here." He pulled a little leather pouch from his pocket. He cupped Lark's hands for her and placed the bag in them. "Ten dollars, United States dollars, in change." He held up his hand. "Don't ask me how I got it. I've been collecting it for you. It's for an ice cream or two when you get there." He looked over his shoulder. "Don't tell your mother."

Lark put the pouch in her pocket, along with the little tissue paper package. The weight of it all pulled her jacket down lopsidedly, and Lark almost cried out, "I don't want to go."

"The pilot is ready," the Captain announced. "All must leave."

Donna Bird and Lark stood at the rail and waved down to the motley little group on the wharf.

"What good fun your father is?" Donna Bird said. "He's such

an original. So intelligent. And your mother, so genteel and refined? So gracious?"

Lark looked at her for a trace of laughter or ridicule, but
Donna's face was shaded by her visor and hidden by her scarf.

Mrs. Watter drew from her copious bag rolls of paper streamers and handed them around to Perce and F.X. and the others.
They threw them up to Donna and Lark, so that quickly the
delicate strands of colored paper formed an arch between the
dozen or so standing on the wharf and the two on the deck. The
gangplank had been drawn up, the lines pulled in, and the an-
chor weighed. Then Henry Watter produced his *pièce de ré-
sistance*. From the cotton bag he drew forth an enormous ball of
old nylon stockings knotted together.

"He is just darling." said Donna Bird. "He has a sense of
humor. He said one of the boxes being loaded was like a coffin."

"That's not funny," said Lark, "or very original."

"I think it could have a body in it, or a bomb. You know,
plutonium, uranium, the works."

Henry Watter gave one end to Mrs. Watter. "Hold tight," he
said, then walked to the edge of the wharf. Mrs. Watter looked
down at the stockings, her head nodding as she recognized her
basement collection. Holding the immense ball balanced in his
palm at his shoulder, Henry Watter sank back on one leg, as if
he were about to put the shot, and bounced a little, getting
ready to heave the ball up to Lark at her rail.

"He is just darling," said Donna Bird to Lark. "I simply adore
him."

Then changing his mind, Henry Watter shifted his position,
having decided that his well-tried lob used against the Bakers'
dog would serve him better, and he bent his legs and with both
hands heaved the ball up to Lark and Donna.

When the others understood what he was about to do they
began to cheer.

The ball climbed heavily through the air, defying gravity, unraveling as it traversed its arc. Mrs. Watter, somewhat bewildered, held onto her end. Lark, dismayed at this last display of her father's, stood still, and it was Donna Bird who leant out and caught the ball at the top of its trajectory.

The little group below cheered wildly. Perce skipped over and shook Henry Watter's hand. F.X. clapped his back. Donna Bird handed her end to Lark. She unsnapped her camera again and filmed the spectacular nylon streamer.

The ship drew away from the wharf. The ball of nylon stockings unwound completely and began to stretch.

"Don't let go," said Donna Bird to Lark.

On the wharf, Henry Watter, diminishing as the ship drew farther into the harbor, took his end from Mrs. Watter and wrapped it around his wrist several times. As the rope stretched tight Henry Watter was pulled in little resisting steps to the edge of the wharf.

"He's going to be pulled into the water," gasped Lark. She let go of her end and Henry Watter went reeling backwards across the wharf.

The ship swung around, blocking Lark's last glimpse of Henry Watter sprawled on his back on the wharf, with Mrs. Watter and the others gathered around him, bent over him the way members of a football team gather around an injured player.

Lark turned away, her hands in her pockets. She took out the pouch of American coins and opened the little bundle wrapped in tissue. Her mother had made her a bracelet of fragments of river stones, polished to smooth pink, gold, green, and red, and dangling from a gold chain. With them was a note. "These stones I collected near home. I hope they help you remember your heritage, your past, your home."

"The fun is just beginning," said Donna Bird, her eyes bright, her hand over her mouth, as if stifling giggles. "What a lark?"

Lark stayed by the rail until the ship paused and the pilot climbed down the side onto his boat and headed back toward the harbor.

# II

The Captain was infatuated with Donna Bird from the moment she stepped on board and showed an interest in, even admired, his strange head. Donna Bird made the Captain forget that they all believed that women on board brought bad luck.

"Where is the other one?" he cried when Lark came in for lunch on that first day. The Captain, at the head of the table, pointed to the seat at his left, on the padded bench that ran along one wall in the tiny dining room. Mr. Blut, the second mate, sat on the bench on Lark's left. The seat opposite Lark, on the Captain's right, was for Donna Bird, who was late, and next to her place, opposite Mr. Blut, sat Mr. Fischer, the first mate. The dining room was like the inside of a trailer or an airplane. Everything had its place, everything fitted neatly. No bric-a-brac.

"*Guten Tag, guten Tag, guten Tag,*" the three men muttered at Lark when she entered.

"Our new lady passenger," the Captain stated rather dully, distracted, waiting for the other passenger.

They all stood up, Mr. Blut making a token rise of a few inches from the padded bench, the table over his knees keeping him anchored in a semisitting position, fixed, like the objects on the ship. They all shook hands. Lark sat down. The chair opposite her remained awkwardly empty.

"It is a fine day," said Mr. Fischer, unsmiling.

The steward in his white coat and the keys dangling around

his neck loitered at the door. He had lunch on the trolley, ready to trundle it over to the table.

"*Bier,* Herr Crouch," the Captain called, and remaining in that slightly slouched, loitering position for a second or two, to show his disapproval at the delay in serving lunch, the steward, Mr. Crouch, went off to get the beer, then returned to his position at the door, leaning against it. He seemed to hold within him the potential for action of some sort, deeply buried.

"*Prosit,*" said the Captain. Lark drank her beer. She had escaped, her adventures had begun, she was drinking beer on the high seas, and at the end of it all Tom was waiting for her. While they waited for the missing passenger, the men tried to engage Lark in polite English conversation. The Captain started telling jokes, beginning with, "Why does the Statue of Liberty stand on Liberty Island?" and answering it himself, "Because she cannot down sit, I mean sit down."

The Captain told Mr. Crouch to ring the bells again, and finally Donna Bird appeared, creeping past Mr. Crouch, yet managing with her conspicuously deferential manner to make him move out of the way. The Captain leapt to his feet.

Donna Bird wore her visor and was now carrying a fan decorated with a woman's face, with the wings of a beautiful insect forming the hair. She looked up to check that the overhead light was off, then slung her visor over the back of the empty chair on the Captain's right. As she sat down, the other two men having more or less jumped up, mumbled their good days, and sat down again, she said, "I'm so very, very sorry? I was exploring, and I forgot everything." She waved the insect fan in front of her face, cooling off.

"Ha, ha," yelled the Captain. "Not much to explore on a little ship like this. And it is not safe below. Stay up. Up stay. Do not flit-flut around my ship. Do not trit-trot everywhere. That is a rule. Even for the daughter of Manfred Bird. And I am the Captain." He laughed as if he had just told another joke, then nodded his pudgy head at his glass and his plate. Mr. Crouch brought them more beer and began serving the herring.

"Is there some secret you don't want me to find, Captain?"

The Captain kept up his laughing.

"So, Lark," said Donna Bird, leaning across and tapping the table in front of Lark's plate, as if they were the closest of friends, "ready to learn about the world? Our Tom will be so pleased?"

"You are friends?" the Captain exclaimed. "Is this a yoke?"

"Jay, joke," said Donna Bird gently.

Lark felt she was watching a play still in rehearsal, the characters still trying to understand their parts, and she felt a terrible terror. The Big J, Tom had said. But by then it was impossible to get off the ship.

"Our lady passengers will now give English lessons, ha," cried the Captain.

Donna laughed, a little giggle. *"Asid raja Nalo nama,"* she said and looked around, pleased with herself, waiting to be asked what it meant.

"What means that?" Mr. Blut, the youngest of the three men, asked slowly and carefully.

"'There was a king, his name was Nala.' Sanskrit. I have been reading some of the tales of power of yore." Donna Bird waved her fan in front of her. "History teaches us lessons about our world, does it not?"

"I agree very much," said the Captain, "but we need magic to change history. Man-made magic. To unmake the bad that is already made."

*"Zauber,"* said Donna, and then, *"Zauberei."*

The Captain guffawed. "Good, good. You know German. *Die Zauberflöte.* One of our best operas." He turned to Lark sitting there stonily and said, "Magic. *Magic Flute.* W. A. Mozart."

"Sanskrit *and* German?" Lark said to Donna, sarcastic.

"It's funny what one picks up?" said Donna. She seemed

pleased to see Lark angry. "One is absorbing, picking things up all the time—information, facts, names—and these things, meaningless in themselves, surface much, much later, in a different form, I assure you?"

"And she will teach us English on this voyage?" said Mr. Blut.

Fine for Donna Bird, Lark decided. Let her teach them English. She would get on with her reading, having planned to get through at least a dozen books in the coming weeks, in preparation for meeting Tom in New York. She had brought *To the Finland Station*, *The Technological Society*, and *The Religion of Java*.

Mr. Crouch withdrew to his position by the door. Donna Bird started going through all the words she knew for herring. *"Maatjes,"* she said. *"Rollmops."* This kept her and the three men busy throughout the meal, recollecting where and when they had tasted excellent herring prepared in a certain way.

"In New York, I shall buy you herring, you and the veneered Manfred Bird," said the Captain. "When we end."

But suddenly, to Lark, the end with Tom waiting there seemed in doubt.

"Revered," said Donna. She looked around the table at the men, one by one, as if she were picking little flowers, and concluded the meal with a final murmur. *"'Allwissend bin ich nicht, doch viel ist mir bewusst'?"*

There was a hum of surprise from the men. "She do know German," said Mr. Blut. "She do not know all, but she know much."

Donna nodded once, to approve his effort, before correcting him. "Does," she said. "She does not know everything, but she knows a lot. Goethe. *Faust*. Another tale of power that is most instructive."

"Goethe is our genius," said the Captain.

"What Goethe and the other greats knew," said Donna Bird,

"is that fear and trembling, *das Schaudern,* is the best part of man, and not, as Aristotle proposed, fear and pity."

"You are a clever lady," and the Captain lifted his hand and seemed about to pat Donna's cheek. But the hand waved instead at the steward. "Herr Crouch will take away these plates," he announced. "And lunch is finished. We all go to work." He leapt from his chair and the two officers half stood up to acknowledge the departure of their lady passengers. For Donna Bird, the Captain clicked his heels together and bowed. "Good lady," he said. "I mean ladies." Then the three men sat back down at the table, suddenly relaxed and happily speaking German again.

Donna Bird stopped at the door. "Oh, Captain, good Captain, I need your help. I wonder if you could do something to cover that light? I'm allergic? All light, artificial and natural."

Lark walked onto the deck outside the dining room to catch a last glimpse of the coast. Donna followed her. Mr. Crouch, who had taken off his white coat, was on the deck before them, leaning against the rail and smoking. Thrown over the rail near him was a blue coat, his cabin boy's uniform. It soon became apparent to Lark that he had an hour off after each meal, between coats, which he generally spent smoking and leaning somewhere.

That first afternoon Lark leant against the rail some distance from Mr. Crouch, looking toward the stern, the afternoon sun and the wind on her face.

Donna Bird stayed pressed back against the bulwark, under the overhang from the bridge above. She had pulled her visor down onto her eyebrows against the western sun and held the fan in front of her chin and mouth. "You heard him talk about secrets. It's very suspicious, I think."

"You're the one who mentioned secrets," said Lark.

"But he's the one saying don't go snooping. And we don't know what the cargo is, remember, apart from those rods, and stacked on the deck like that they could just be a front, a façade, to foil airplanes and surveillance. There's the coffin, of course."

Lark turned to face Donna Bird for a moment, and not being able to stand the sight of her cringing there in her sliver of shade, she turned back to the sea. Donna Bird looked more like some kind of court jester than ever.

Lark held onto the rail, squinting into the horizon. Mr. Crouch had not moved a muscle. He stared out at the water, flicking his cigarette butt, still alight, over the edge of the deck and lighting another.

"Surely that's against ship rules?" Donna Bird said in what was for her a shout, trying to overcome the wind. "Fire hazard?" She seemed more intent on provoking a reaction from the good-looking young steward than on the possibility of fire.

Mr. Crouch, whose name Lark imagined was Krautsch or something like that, was lucky to be German, she thought, and to be spared Donna's stories. Donna laughed her whispery chuckle, and then stepped forward and plucked at Mr. Crouch's sleeve before ducking back into the shade.

The steward moved a step or so away and mumbled something, shaking his head. There was something about him that did not seem quite right to Lark. He looked like a cowboy, a non-American's imitation of a cowboy. Or he looked as if he were acting the role of a pirate in an operetta or a children's movie, with the wind blowing his hair back, one foot up on the lower rail, squinting at the horizon. While he did not look like a real sailor, he certainly looked quite lovely standing there, so tense.

Donna Bird was studying him, too, in this pose. Then she began to speak as if she were continuing an entirely different conversation. "There's the word 'callow,' for instance, which, as you know, Lark, I came across in a story about a pompous young man on board a ship in the tropics who seems to know everything. In the heat he advises everyone to drink hot tea and to keep out of the breeze and turn off the electric fans in order to keep cool? He boasts that he is an experienced sailor, not a callow tourist. Of course, he is shown to be wrong. His stupidity nearly gets everyone killed. Callow."

The steward was gazing out to sea with such a look of distaste that Lark guessed that he had understood what Donna had said.

"That's what I mean about recurring," Donna mused. "Each time the context will be different. And apart from that there is no meaning. The meaning or truth lies on the surface, each time."

That first afternoon Lark went to the bridge and watched the Captain and the two officers doing their navigating. The Captain was charting the rest of the voyage, to Tacoma, then through the Panama Canal to New York. They were to sail due east from Australia, clearing the reefs and other coastal formations, then they were to head northeast. The Captain was checking the readings. He took a ruler, Lark saw him do this, and ruled a line straight up through the Pacific, past hundreds of little islands, across the equator, passing south of Hawaii, to Puget Sound. They had no scheduled stop until Tacoma.

"Once we owned most of this," the Captain said. He scratched his bald head a little, the soft skin moving about as he did so. And Lark shivered. "Now all is ruined. This independence all everywhere is to blame. Before, the Europeans, who know what art is, preserved the art, the culture, the innocence."

"Garibaldi was wrecked in the Bass Strait." It was Donna Bird who had crept up behind them and was watching the charting procedure. She put her finger on the patch of water between the Australian mainland and Tasmania.

The Captain had taken out a length of rope and was tying the wheel into a fixed position. For the next three weeks they were to sail along that ruled line, the wheel tied into position, with no helmsman holding it steady, just an officer checking the bearings now and then, or a sailor standing nearby. It made Lark uneasy. Could navigating an ocean be so simple?

At various spots on the chart coral reefs showed light brown in the light blue of the water. The reefs brought forth from Donna anecdotes about coral.

"There is a poisonous coral, pinkish, that has a fatal sting?" she contributed. "If you step on it, there's no hope?"

The Captain said that later on, out in the Pacific, he was going to stop the ship, if they made good time, so that Lark and Donna could walk on one of the reefs and observe the coral and reef life closely.

Donna clapped her hands. "Standing in the middle of the ocean? Like walking on water?" She then frowned and placed two fingers delicately over her mouth. "Oh, but the sun." She brightened. "I'll cover up very, very well?"

"Are you allowed to do that?" asked Lark. It seemed highly out of order for a freighter to come to a halt in the middle of an ocean for such a frivolous undertaking, and she was scornful of the Captain's allowing himself to be captivated by Donna Bird. "I'm not walking on any coral," she said.

The Captain gave a tolerant smile and put one arm around Donna's shoulder, the other around Lark's. "It is an opportunity to test equipment and for passengers to enjoy. Like on those Queens."

Lark shook herself free from the Captain.

"*Queen Elizabeth, Queen Mary,*" Donna explained.

"I know that," said Lark, irritated.

But Donna was already addressing the Captain again. "Please don't bother about stopping the ship on my account? It's too much trouble?"

"Of course we bother," said the Captain. "Is it not boring on this ship for beautiful ladies? You will walk on coral."

"We'll need sneakers?" Donna stated.

"I'm not walking on coral," said Lark.

"Mine are pink," Donna went on. "In fact, I bought them especially for reef walking. On the Great Barrier Reef. Once I was there," she put her hand to her lips and lowered her voice, "on holiday?" And she told the intricate story of paying a pound for a pair of sneakers and of choosing pink, rather than turquoise or yellow. Donna laughed, and as she continued her tedious story, Lark watched the Captain, bent over his charts, searching for a reef for the coral walk.

"Ha, ha," he said, and marked a spot.

"That's in the middle of nothing," said Lark. "There's no land. I'm not walking on any coral."

"I'll show them to you," said Donna, and she ran or rather sidled out to get her pink sneakers and bring them back, holding up their soles and pointing to the cuts and lacerations made by the coral. "As you can see, the damage wasn't too great. I still wear them. But you can see what coral could do to your feet. Like glass?"

Lark came in to dinner the first night to find the Captain on a chair tying some kind of paper shade over the ceiling light. He was trying to dim the bright overhead light to accommodate Donna Bird, who was sitting in her chair, clasping her hands and looking up at the Captain with a wide, encouraging smile. Mr. Blut, who was sinking into his place on the bench, having jumped up when Donna Bird came in, jumped up again when Lark appeared.

"We all want to see your pretty faces as much as possible," the Captain said, looking down at them, but clearly addressing Donna.

Donna was wearing her formal gray and beige, a long skirt and a blouse, unbuttoned for evening, plus earrings and a brooch of little grapes pinned to the side of her visor. And there was the fan, which she waved back and forth, queen of the *Avis Maris*.

"Oh, you shouldn't, you're so kind?" Donna whispered, to

Mr. Blut for having jumped up and to the Captain for standing on his chair to struggle with the light for her. "I'm so sorry?" Donna whispered. "I'm so sorry to be so allergic? Please don't bother on my account?" In order to hear her the Captain had to stop fiddling with the paper and Mr. Blut had to turn his head so that his ear was toward Donna Bird. "It comes upon you suddenly, this allergy. It came upon me after a visit to the tropics. It can go away, too, I hear."

Lark believed she was exaggerating, lying, and put it down to affectation, some kind of ploy for attention.

The Captain resumed folding the paper shade around the light fixture.

Donna Bird spoke beseechingly, submissively, commanding a response. "Please don't bother on my account?"

"Of course we bother, yes, yes, *nicht?*" said the Captain.

"*Ja, ja,* naturally," said Mr. Blut.

The Captain jumped down from his chair, pleased with his handiwork.

Lark now understood that people always bothered about things on Donna's account.

Then Mr. Fischer, the first mate and engineer, who had not forgotten that women on board tended to bring bad luck, appeared and told the Captain that the paper shade was a fire hazard. The Captain, happily entranced, was losing his nautical judgment. And Donna Bird had to continue wearing her sun visor.

At dinner the Captain resumed his jokes, beginning with, "Where are the queens of England crowned?" pronouncing it crown-ed, two syllables, as if he were reciting a sonnet, and he looked at Donna, a big smile on his face, pleased with his offering. "In the head," said the Captain, answering his own riddle. "The queens of England are crown-ed in the head."

Donna smiled sweetly.

"*Kopf, Kopf,*" the Captain explained to the unsmiling Mr.

Fischer, tapping his own head, the finger making an indentation that remained for a second or so after each tap. *"Kopf,* ha."

"On the head? On, on the head?" Donna suggested.

"On on on the head," sang Mr. Blut.

"Now our ladies will give English lessons," cried the Captain. Donna's scarcely audible voice made everyone else shout.

The fan paused in its scan across Donna Bird's face. "Yes? Certainly, yes."

Lark looked at Donna, trying to make out whether she was being serious or droll. The young pirate, whatever he was, was putting before them his stuffed green peppers, a dish that Lark particularly hated, and which were so khaki and sodden that they could have waited until midnight to be eaten, if necessary, without changing in appearance or taste. The Captain would certainly make no effort to have the schedule of stuffed green peppers changed to accommodate Lark. She would not even consider mentioning it.

"So," said the Captain, turning to Donna, "here is a story, in English, about the opera. We Germans love the opera, but alas, hiding like this at sea, I no longer go to opera. Before the war, then it was the palmy days of culture. Manfred Bird knows culture. It is the reason we are friends. So, the story goes, Brünnehilde sings to Wotan. She must sing, *'Weiche, Wotan, weiche,'* which in English means—" and he searched for the word.

"Surrender," Donna said, nodding encouragement. "'Surrender, Wotan, surrender.'"

"This clever lady knows so much," said the Captain, shaking his head. "Surrender. And also it means 'soft' in German. So, before Brünnehilde takes her big breath to sing, *'Weiche, Wotan, weiche,'* whispers Wotan to her, *sotto voce,* so that only Brünnehilde hears, 'How do you like your boiled eggs in the morning?' and she must sing loud, for all to hear, 'Soft, Wotan, soft,' without laughing. You understand?"

The Captain looked like a soft-boiled egg himself, with his

smooth round head, wider and pudgier at the cheekbones than at the forehead and chin, and a smile that was a perfect arc, painted on by a child. Often, looking at him, Lark saw the eggshells on which she had drawn Hitler and which she had smashed with her fist on the breakfast plate.

Donna laughed a little. She had got the Captain's joke. Then she started with her own story. "I love practical jokes."

"Yes, yes, yes." The men were leaning forward and staring at her lips, following her.

Lark was unwilling to watch those lips letting loose their stories. If she lowered her eyes to the table, all she saw were the green peppers on the plates, half-eaten, sagging. If she raised her eyes, she saw Mr. Crouch at the door, who winked at her, which made her want to giggle. She kept her eyes rotating from one undesirable object to the next, thinking of the worst things in the world—drowning, a nuclear war, chocolate-covered softboiled eggs—to stop herself from collapsing in hysterical laughter when she caught Mr. Crouch's eye.

"I love jokes. But, did you know, you can get killed with a joke, just laughing, against your will?"

The Captain looked hurt and Donna placed her hand on his arm.

"Practical, dangerous, killed, joke," said Mr. Blut, making little haiku fragments, enjoying the words.

"What? No green peppers?" Mr. Crouch whispered to Lark.

"I loathe green peppers," Lark whispered back. "It's possible they can kill you."

Mr. Crouch smiled down at her. "Killer peppers." He took her peppers away and brought bread and fruit.

"You can get killed laughing," said Donna.

Finally Mr. Crouch was able to get rid of all the dinner plates and place before them dessert, a coconut thing.

"Killed, laughing?" asked Mr. Blut.

Donna took a deep breath. "For instance," and she nodded at

the coconut-covered cake before her, "man killed by lamington."

Lark's head was bowed. She was suppressing gales of laughter, which seemed to increase in strength inside her. She was
frightened, imagining that she might never be able to stop
laughing, that she might very well die.

"A lamington is an Australian cake, sponge cake, cut into
little cubes, and each cube is rolled in chocolate icing and then
coconut. Lam-ing-ton."

The men repeated the word. Donna's scarf, a tiresome silk
she had gathered in some place during some other story, dangled
over her plate. Lark waited for her to spill custard on it.

"Such lamington killed?" prompted Mr. Blut.

"It was meant to be a wonderful joke," said Donna.

A scraping fork, a cleared throat, the Captain's chewing,
could blot out her voice. Everything had to stop when she spoke,
Mr. Blut with his fork on its way to his mouth, Mr. Fischer
with an unfinished mouthful resting inside his cheek, the Captain with his knife and fork in the air. A scene from *Sleeping
Beauty,* with Mr. Crouch, the kitchen boy, immobile at the
doorpost.

"The jokers at this party had covered a piece of sponge rubber
with chocolate and coconut and given it to the guest of honor.
He ate it, tried to, and it stuck in his throat. He was dead in a
matter of minutes." When Donna paused, Mr. Fischer was able
to swallow his mouthful and belch into his table napkin. Mr.
Blut, who had been mouthing the words along with Donna,
said, "Stuck, dead minutes." Mr. Crouch yawned from his
doorpost, making his keys rattle.

"I thought you loved practical jokes," said Lark. Her laughter
had suddenly dissipated, leaving her angry at the spell she
seemed to have been under. "I recall you dressed up as a schoolgirl and got yourself kidnapped?"

"I love jokes," said Donna, unperturbed. "By affirming the

spectacle, they educate and teach political realities." Then for the table in general she terminated her tale. "The lamington plugged his throat?"

"Plug throat?" said Mr. Blut.

"I think you're making it all up," said Lark quickly, so that the men would not completely understand. "All these stories, all these people you say are friends of yours." Lark decided that Donna Bird was a chronic liar, had fabricated her way through life, probably to the editorship of the newspaper and definitely to the good graces of Tom.

Donna rose, her face straight and cold. The Captain leapt to his feet to wrench her chair back. Lark got up from her bench and slid out. Mr. Blut half stood.

"Good night," whispered Donna and crept to the door, brushing against Mr. Crouch.

"*Guten Abend,*" thrice.

At the door Donna paused and looked back at the men. Her face was smiling now. She had recovered from her fit of pique. "Say, anyone for a game of poker?"

The men looked at one another. The Captain nodded at them. "Oh, *ja, ja, ja.*"

"And you, Lark? Larkie?" She was imitating Tom.

"Five's a crowd," said Lark. "I hate crowds. And actually I also hate cards."

Finally, Lark and Donna Bird had given up their pretense of friendship. The war between them was now in the open.

The three men followed Donna to her cabin.

Lark returned to her little cabin, a wood-paneled box, rather like a burrow, that was a sitting room, stateroom it was called, with an alcove at one end, which was the bedroom, and a closet off the alcove, which contained the bathroom. Donna's cabin, on the opposite side of the ship, was identical. Lark sat on her couch for a while, dreading the coming weeks, then went out on deck.

There was not much space on the ship for promenading. The main deck was stacked with the aluminum rods, which left little room for the two passengers; only the deck at the level of the dining room and cabins, the little catwalks at the level of the bridge, and a little square deck at the very top of the ship, which formed the roof of the bridge. Lark climbed up the ladder to that topmost square deck. They had left the coast behind and were heading into the dark. Behind them a vague glow marked the residue of the sunset.

Mr. Crouch was there, leaning and smoking.

"Pain in the neck."

"Pardon?" Lark was startled.

"That woman. Pain in the neck, isn't she?"

"You're not German at all." Lark could now hear that Mr. Crouch—Paul, as she came to call him—was a native English speaker.

"Who said I was German?"

Lark had taken it for granted—a German ship, a blond, blue-eyed man called Herr "Krautsch," speaking and spoken to in German—in spite of the lesson in stereotypes that Tom had tried to teach her in the cafeteria with his portraits.

"They like it that I don't know too much German. Just 'More beer' or 'Bring the peppers' is all I need to understand. They're an odd lot."

Lark looked at Paul Crouch, really pleased, both because of the sentiment he had expressed about Donna and the officers and because his speaking English gave her someone on board to feel allied with.

"She'll make dinner take twice as long, and she'll make my days even longer." Paul grumbled, mumbled, not a clear diction. "She's a busybody, a know-all."

Lark could now hear that he was Australian.

"But don't say anything to her," Paul said. "I don't want her after me with her reminiscences and stories and interrogations. She wants to get at me. You saw her this afternoon."

"She thinks we're carrying bodies, or bombs."

Lark did not think to ask him why he had left home, or when. It was logical enough for him to be cabin steward on a German freighter. Australians were circling the globe by the thousands for years at a time. It was one of the things they did. And here on this little ship were three of them, engaged in what was shaping up as some ritual of endurance.

The twenty or so sailors who slept and worked below were rarely evident. Occasionally they could be seen checking the ropes around the aluminum rods on the deck and swabbing the parts of the deck that were not covered by the rods. Occasionally Lark saw large mice of various shades of gray and brown, which she had to admit were probably rats, nipping in and out of the rods.

To escape from Donna Bird, Lark went up to what she came to consider her deck, on top of the bridge. And she went around the ship barefooted. She intended the soles of her feet to become rough and hard, her skin brown and tough, her hair blonder and coarser, as if all of that, too, would free her from Donna Bird's artful pallor and restraint.

Donna spent the days inside, away from the sunlight, usually in her cabin or in the dining room, which became a library and lounge room between meals, where she sat, pale and soft, and wrote. Sometimes she prowled around the ship, "flit-flutted" as the Captain put it, in the early morning or late afternoon, when the sun was not too hot.

It was a brilliant day. The sea was calm. Lark lay on her deck. She looked up and saw Paul Crouch's head, as if on a plate, just a foot or two from hers. Thick blond hair, blue eyes, brown skin, several fine scars under the right eye, and two or three large light brown freckles on his right cheekbone, the mark of Australians who had spent their youth in cars with the southern sun beating down obliquely through the driver's window. She noticed later that on his right arm and shoulder were similar freckles. On the palm of one hand, held at chin level, he bore a tray with a teapot and two cups. He knew that Lark would invite him to keep her company.

He slid the tray onto the deck and hoisted his body up. "You don't want to get sunstroke," he said. "You should wear a hat.'"

"A visor, perhaps?" And Paul Crouch smiled. Lark looked at the two cups. "Hot tea is the best way to keep cool in hot weather," she said, "and stay out of the breeze, it'll only make you hotter," and they both laughed.

Paul Crouch sat down, cross-legged, beside her. They drank their tea, not talking, neither wanting to begin the story of a past life that travelers were always expected to tell. Then Paul pulled off his T-shirt and his sneakers, took a book from his trouser pocket, rolled up his trouser legs, and lay down on the deck beside Lark.

Lark dozed off and dreamt about Solomon Blank. He lived in a glass house, with an indoor pond whose surface was practically obliterated by water lilies. In the dream his wife was short, and hairy, resembling a wombat.

Lark came into the dining room before lunch and found Donna hunched on the bench, on the spot where Lark sat for meals, scribbling in her book in that bright green ink. Donna looked up and placed her two hands over the open pages. "Just jotting down thoughts."

Lark shrugged. Who cared? She turned to the bookcase and then saw that the Captain was standing there quietly, apparently looking for a book, gazing at the titles, his finger moving along the spines.

"You really should try keeping a diary, Larkie," said Donna. "Tom would definitely approve. Of course, in my diaries there's nothing of importance. They have no meaning. I try to stay on the surface, that is true freedom, and to eschew the psychological."

"And to affirm the spectacle, of course. But your diary makes you feel you are a drop in the ocean of life, isn't that right?" said Lark.

"Exactly. I celebrate the ludic and the joke. Playing is itself subversive, and therefore liberating," said Donna, ignoring Lark's sarcasm. "And so, you see, the world itself is my text, the spectacle." Although she still placed her hands over the pages containing her thoughts, she nevertheless flaunted her diary and her writing, as if daring someone to pry. Lark was surprised that she felt no impulse to take a look. She felt rather that the diary would contaminate her, stain her fingers green.

"But since your vision of me is as liar, I am writing something now especially for you, something to make you adjust your view of me. Later you will have it, when I've finished."

The Captain walked over to the table and turned the pages of Donna's diary. "Very good handwriting," he said. "An artist. Very cultured. We value that in Germany." He bowed slightly. "Good morning, ladies." And he left the room.

"I think he is going to make us do it," said Donna. "Walk on the coral."

"I'm not going to," said Lark. "I believe you're egging him on."

Donna looked down at Lark's feet. "Of course you, Lark, will be less vulnerable than I, with those feet and that skin."

"Walking on coral must surely be against the law of the sea," said Lark.

Donna got up and tucked her arm into Lark's. "If you don't go, I won't go. Just think what adventures you'll be able to entertain Tom with in New York. You'll be so worldly. So grown up. That's what you want, right?"

Paul Crouch took to coming up the ladder to Lark's deck after breakfast every morning, bringing tea for two.

"She won't follow us up here into this sun," he said.

Paul had read the entire library on the ship long ago, novels like *Exodus* and popular works on subjects like out-of-body travel, and wanted to start on Lark's books. When she finished one she passed it on to him. Sometimes they read together. She got to know the line of his cheek, the pale freckles, his hair and his hands as they sat reading, and she learned his gestures, his postures, his characteristic noncommittal smile.

Sometimes they talked a bit. Sometimes they lay on the deck silent. Sometimes they stood up and leant against the rail and watched the water and the sky.

"I like this clear sky," said Lark. "Nothing can fall from it. There can be no surprises."

Paul smiled. "Like a piano on the head?"

"Don't laugh. A plane fell into the Empire State Building in New York, you know. Imagine, sitting at your desk and being hit by an airplane."

"You'd have to wear a hard hat indoors. You'd be like Donna Bird."

Lark did not laugh with him. "Then I would be a crank. It's a fine distinction, between being sensible and being a crank."

Now and then they saw birds circling in the distance, and they would know that an island must be off there somewhere. Now and then they saw what looked like a bird but turned out to be an airplane, generally not a high-flying commercial jet but a speedy, low-flying type, military, French or American, patrolling the Pacific Ocean. "Maybe one day it'll be Superman," said Paul, "ready to catch the piano as it falls." The distant birds and the planes were the only signs of life they encountered, if a plane could be called a sign of life. They never saw another ship, and they never saw land.

After a while Lark said, "I always wanted to live on an island, under a sky like this."

And they lay back down on the deck and read their books.

"'*Galeotto fu il libro,*'" croaked a soft voice.

Donna Bird's head had appeared at the top of the ladder. She had a view of their heads close together as they read.

"*The Inferno,*" she said. "Dante. Without that book, which told the story of Galahad and Lancelot and Guinevere, Francesca and Paolo would not have become lovers. At least, that is what Francesca would have us believe. You'd think there would have been something for them to think about beyond each other and sex."

Paul groaned, mumbling something like, "Bloody woman." The more he disliked Donna Bird, the more attractive he seemed to Lark.

Lark looked at Donna's face, the closest she had ever been to it—usually she found herself averting her eyes from Donna's intensity—not that much was visible, swathed as she always was in her scarf and visor and flapping her fan. Her eyes were as blue as Paul's, and Lark could see the pale freckles on her right cheekbone. But Donna looked like a gray, out-of-focus photograph beside Paul's Technicolor moving picture.

"Won't you burn up out here?" Lark asked. She could not imagine what had brought Donna out into the sun.

"The Captain says it's getting close to the time for our coral walk," she said.

"I'm not going coral walking," said Lark.

Paul had become the stage pirate. He stood up and was leaning again, his back to them, still with his trousers rolled up and his T-shirt off, his back and his calves smooth and brown. Paul never looked at Donna, never spoke to her, in fact hardly spoke at all, even to Lark. It seemed powerful to Lark, that he stayed so silent, and so safe. After Donna's little anecdote about the callow traveler that first day, she appeared to ignore Paul Crouch, although Lark was aware of her keeping track of him, of both of them, tracking their movements. And Donna had risked her skin to climb up to Lark's deck in broad daylight, more, Lark now guessed, to check on her and Paul than to announce the coral walk, which Lark still believed was just the Captain's teasing.

"It'll be such an adventure," said the head at the top of the ladder. "But you don't think he's trying to get rid of us, do you? You don't think it's connected with his secret cargo?"

"What secret cargo?"

Donna smiled. "You know. You've heard him. You saw that box."

"You're absurd."

"Of course," Donna went on, "he does know my father, so we'll probably be safe. On the other hand, an accident at sea is always possible, if he thinks we're onto something. But then you think I lie, so you shouldn't believe what I say, and you might as well walk on coral, too."

"I'm not going coral walking," said Lark.

"Tom would be so proud of you?" said Donna, goading. "You could dine out on the tale for months in New York."

With a grunt Paul left his rail, picked up his T-shirt and pulled it on, then lowered himself down the ladder, practically vaulting over Donna Bird, taking care to look at neither of the women. Lark watched his head disappear, angry at Donna's interference.

Donna was absent from dinner. She sent word that she had had too much sun and needed to rest her skin in her cabin. The meal was very quiet. The men exchanged subdued brief sentences in German, which all seemed to concern the condition of the engine, fuel, the weather, and sometimes life in the good old days. There were no jokes, no poker game. The Captain, having told Paul Crouch to take Donna Bird's dinner in to her, hurried through his own meal and paid a courtesy call on Donna Bird in her cabin, as if he wanted to be sure she had not flown off.

It was later, after dinner, on Lark's deck, that Paul told Lark that Donna had been sitting in her cabin with just one little light on over her desk and had just reached her hand around the door to take the tray, so that even the light from the gangway would not reach her.

"She was wearing gray socks," said Paul "but they were over her hands."

"Did she have whiskers stuck on, too? Did she squeak?"

But the next day Donna's head appeared again at the top of the ladder, a pale jack-o'-lantern. Paul and Lark were lying rather close together. Paul had taken off his shirt as usual and lay on his back, his hands under his head. Lark was reading. She could hear the airplanes in the distance. It took her several seconds to understand that the whirring sound she heard was coming from Donna's movie camera.

"I've lost my pen," Donna said. "Have you seen it?" She had dropped her camera so that it was out of sight, below the level of the deck. Only the strap around her neck showed.

Paul took up his book and rolled away from Lark.

"Borrow mine," said Lark.

Donna screwed up her nose. "I could never write a word using a Biro." She burrowed in the bag she had slung over her shoulder and held out a sheaf of papers. "Here, Lark. For you."

Lark took the papers. In columns in bright green ink, filling up each side of each sheet in tiny script, were the names of everyone Donna Bird had ever met. Lark looked at the head just a few inches from hers. "Is this why you missed dinner? You must have been doing this for days."

"You think I make everything up? You think I lie about what I've done, whom I've met?" Donna smiled happily. "You see, there are thousands of names, including the Queen, which was during the war when I was a little girl in England and she was a Girl Guide. You'll see there's the Prime Minister, and of course Margaret Mead. One actually does meet thousands of people in a lifetime?"

Toward the end of the list Lark saw Lark Watter, Tom Brown, and farther down, Paul Crouch. As she held the names she felt trapped, caught in some kind of game whose rules she did not know. "You should try it yourself. You, too, Herr Crouch. Please do it. I'll be happy to analyze your list for you. It's one way of understanding your personal history, Manfred says." She smiled. "You know, river of life, et cetera. And by the way, I went snooping during dinner last night. Everything is locked. But I can tell you, we're not carrying much cargo. We're riding pretty high in the water."

Paul cleared his throat. Donna hesitated a moment, then said, "My skin," and she backed down the ladder, supposedly retiring to her cabin for the rest of that day, too, leaving Lark with the names of thousands in her hands.

Paul rolled back to Lark. "She's batty," he said.

Lark stuffed the sheets of paper away, resisting the impulse to let them fly off over the ocean. She imagined them fluttering off, getting caught in the rigging, littering the ocean. Paul lay beside her, his eyes closed, and he seemed to be smiling at the heavens. The airplanes were flying closer to the ship than usual. Lark saw that Paul was not smiling at the heavens but merely bending his mouth in order to crease his eyes against the sun. He turned onto one side to look at her. His face was almost directly over her and shaded her face. She could open her eyes and look at him, at the blue eyes and brown skin.

Then the airplanes were suddenly upon them. They roared down at the ship, the noise so loud that Lark could compare it to nothing she had ever heard. There were four planes swooping down at them, coming so close to the top deck that Lark felt she had only to reach up to touch them, if she had not been holding her hands over her ears and screaming. She could see the faces of the pilots and crew pressed against the glass of the cockpits, fair young men, looking like Paul himself—blond, brash, and weak. Weak. That she thought Paul Crouch was weak surprised her.

One after the other the planes swept by. Lark thought at first they were intent on bombing the ship. Her view was that of an artistically placed camera in a war movie. And who knew what had been happening in the rest of the world these past few days? Who knew whether these planes had been ordered to begin a new war by strafing and sinking merchant ships in the Pacific?

The planes flew off. Paul, who had got as much of a fright as Lark, put his arms around her. As the planes receded he turned her head to him and kissed her.

And then the planes were back. The four of them again. Paul and Lark kept holding onto each other. Lark had never been so frightened. Paul half turned over to watch them. Again it seemed clear that they would damage the ship, so close did they fly. And so loud.

"Bloody Americans!" Paul yelled. "Crass, crude Americans, wrecking civilization." He had discerned the markings on the planes. He shook his fist at them, while Lark trembled against him. "And you're actually choosing to go and live among them." Paul was now shouting not at the planes but at Lark. She saw that those young faces in the planes buzzing her deck were roaring with laughter. They were pointing at Paul and her lying on the deck and laughing at them. She could imagine their raucous voices. Paul picked up one of his sneakers and threw it at the last plane, which made that pilot laugh in an even more exaggerated way. The sneaker fell back, hitting Lark on the shoulder. Paul threw the other sneaker, which sailed over the rail of the little deck and disappeared.

Lark sat up. Paul pulled on his T-shirt and, muttering about work, climbed down the ladder. And then came Donna Bird's voice, at the foot of the ladder. "Perhaps you saw my pen, Mr. Crouch?"

Lark stopped by the bridge. The Captain was examining the chart. "So, coral," he was saying. Donna stood next to him.

"We're not going to walk on coral," said Lark.

"Of course you walk," said the Captain. "Life is short. I give you adventure, nonbourgeois adventure."

"*Bravo!*" cried Donna softly. Then, while looking at Lark, she addressed the Captain. "Those planes were certainly taking a close look at something."

The Captain slapped his thigh and laughed, as if Donna had

just told a joke. "Those Americans, they think they can do that to Germans, to everyone in the world."

Donna left the bridge. The Captain, without looking up, said to Lark, "So, we see that you and Mr. Crouch are good friends."

Lark blushed.

"Too good, perhaps," said the Captain. "He is the cabin boy."

Lark could say nothing. The Captain, who had begun to alter a few points around the spot he had marked for the coral walk, now looked up at her, his hands at the same time continuing to rule a line. Lark found herself looking back into the bright blue eyes in the soft head, fixed by them, and seeing peripherally his hands continuing to work. She wondered if he had some kind of periscope that had enabled him to watch her on the deck with Paul Crouch.

"Mr. Crouch is the cabin boy, only. Only that." The Captain went back to his charting. "We have him on board only since Perth." He swept his hand over the Pacific Ocean on the chart. "We used to own all this. And now," he snapped his fingers, "nothing. They ruin their islands."

Sometimes it seemed that the Captain, encased in his ship sailing round and round the world, had not heard that the war was over. Lark frowned and backed away, noticing on the way out that Paul's sneaker had been tied to the fire axe that was fastened on the wall of the bridge and was dangling there, bobbing at her.

"Beware of liaisons," said the Captain.

The *Avis Maris* came to a stop. The shuddering of the engines, then the absolute silence, frightened Lark. This was so stupid.

"I can't see any coral reef," she said.

"It is good to test equipment, and we make very good time so far." The Captain was rubbing his hands together as he ordered one of the boats to be uncovered and the winches started up. "Go now," he said to Donna. "Get in the boot."

He put his arm around Donna's shoulder and started to lead her to the boat. His grip was firm. Donna, her visor crammed low on her forehead, her scarf muffling the lower half of her face and her khaki trousers rolled up with the lolly-pink sneakers at the ends of her white legs, held onto Lark's arm. And the three of them stumbled across the deck, as if they were chained together.

"You'll get burnt?" said Donna, looking at Lark who was wearing shorts and suntop and espadrilles, with no hat or shirt, and she wriggled out of one of her several layers, a T-shirt she was wearing under her long-sleeved sweat shirt, and made Lark put it on.

"You're all mad," said Lark. She still believed the Captain was joking.

Half a dozen crew members were standing beside the uncovered lifeboat and helped the two women in.

"Don't push me," Lark yelled, refusing to climb up. She saw Paul Crouch on the top deck above the bridge, leaning on the rail, smoking and watching the sailors prod them into the lifeboat. She felt he could hurdle the rail of the deck, if only he wished to or dared to, and soar through the air and land lithely at the lifeboat. He could stand with his legs apart, his hands on his hips, blocking the Captain's way, and order him to halt, desist, and when the Captain refused, strike him a solid blow. He would then scoop the two women in his arms and fly off with them. He somehow should save these two helpless women from something terrible.

The men lifted Lark off the deck and placed her in the boat. Donna got in on her own. The men climbed in after them. Then Mr. Fischer got in, carrying two large glass salad bowls. The boat was lowered down the side of the ship, something Lark had seen only in the movies, in an emergency, as when the *Titanic* hit the iceberg. As they disappeared over the edge of the ship, Lark looked up at Paul. He moved his hand slightly, just lifting one or two fingers to acknowledge her. One foot remained on the lowest rail, both elbows on the top rail. Having lifted his fingers, he took a drag on his cigarette.

When the boat hit the water, the sailors started pulling away from the ship, with Mr. Fischer sitting in the bow giving orders. The sailors were silent, no joking among themselves. But as they rowed they studied these two women sitting in the stern facing them, the two passengers they knew were on board yet rarely saw, just the glimpse of a scarf here and there, or a bare brown leg disappearing up a ladder.

"But why did he make us do this?" Lark asked Donna. "Just to impress you?"

Donna laughed. "We shall learn something new, perhaps?"

"That foolish man is in love with you. The whole thing is the centerpiece of this voyage."

"And there is no foolish man in love with you?" Donna said.

Mr. Fischer ordered the men to stop rowing. They were now a mile or so from the ship.

"Get out now," he said.

"There's nothing here," shrieked Lark. "We're in the middle of the ocean!"

"Now you get out," said Mr. Fischer, pointing over the side. "Out get. Legs up, over, so," and he demonstrated how they were to swing their legs over the edge of the boat.

"Don't do it," said Lark.

But Donna, having peered over the side of the boat, slipped off her trousers, under which she wore a bathing suit, and swung her legs over, twisting her body and lowering herself into the water.

The ship seemed far off. The ocean surrounded them—there was no land, no break in the ocean surface—and there Donna stood, up to her armpits in water, next to the boat, still holding on with one hand.

"This is wonderful, Lark. You'll never get a chance like this again."

Donna let go of the boat and started to wade away from it, her body slowly emerging, until the water was at her waist, then, about fifty feet away, at her knees. "It's wonderful."

Lark was holding onto her seat in the stern of the lifeboat. Then, knowing she should not panic and scream and lose control, she squinted at the sea, taking it all in, turning her head a hundred and eighty degrees from the ship behind them, scanning the water until her eyes found Donna, standing knee-deep in water, and continuing to scan the full circle, a further hundred and eighty degrees, back to the ship floating in the deep. Where Donna stood the sea was slightly choppy, with little points of miniature waves, little disturbances, different from the broader swells behind them. This subtle change in the texture of the sea marked the reef. As she peered at the water at Donna's knees and tried to see through it, she discerned the brownish surface of the coral and the white of Donna's legs.

"Now you go," said Mr. Fischer. He signaled one of the sailors to help Lark over the side.

Donna was frolicking now, jumping up and down.

"I'm not going." Lark was shrieking again. She pushed at the sailor who was trying to get her legs over the side of the boat.

"*Komm, komm,*" he said, encouraging her.

"This is an adventure," Donna called. "Once in a lifetime." She was standing on one leg like a flamingo, one hand on her hip, one at her eyebrows, peering over the water. "You must take whatever chance you can get to do something you would never do under normal circumstances. 'Take the current when it serves.'"

"Get away from me," said Lark, pushing the sailor so hard that he fell back onto the floor of the boat.

The tide was moving fast. Parts of the coral reef were beginning to be exposed, and the water was almost down to Donna's ankles. She started to walk about, now and then bending down to examine more closely the coral shapes and colors, and at one point she squatted right down and put her face into the water, then lifted it out again, laughing and brushing the water from her face.

Mr. Fischer suddenly remembered the glass bowls. "You take these," he said to Lark. He nodded at a second sailor, the first one having picked himself up, and the two, together, picked Lark up and lowered her over the side. She was yelling at them, kicking her legs. They almost threw her over. Then, when she saw she would not prevail, she stopped screaming and again concentrated on not panicking. She found her footing and clung to the edge of the boat.

"Take," said Mr. Fischer, holding out the two glass bowls.

"Take them, Lark. We can view the coral better." Donna had wrapped her scarf around her face again.

Lark found herself clasping two glass salad bowls to her chest with one arm, clutching at the bobbing lifeboat with the other, trying to find her footing in waist-deep water on the uneven coral. She would not let go of the boat. One of the sailors pried her fingers loose, causing her to lose her balance and stagger in the water.

"Don't drop the bowls. They'll float off or sink," called Donna. "Don't fall. You'll cut your legs on the coral. And I happen to know that coral cuts take weeks and weeks to heal. When I was little we were told that coral cuts and oyster cuts never healed, never, never?"

And again, Lark concentrated on not panicking and not losing balance. She did not want to cut herself on the coral, and she also remembered the treacherous pink poisonous type that Donna had mentioned.

The boat had now drifted off a little. Donna was beside her, taking the bowls and offering her hand, which Lark gladly took, allowing Donna to lead her to the exposed part of the reef.

"They're thugs," said Lark. "Why are they doing this to us? You don't really believe there is a bomb, that they are terrorists, do you?"

Donna laughed. "What I know is they think they are the *Queen Elizabeth.*" She had taken one of the bowls and walked off a little so that the water was up to her thighs. Lark followed her. Donna pressed the bowl into the water, just far enough for the water to come halfway up the outside of the bowl. She bent over and peered into the bowl. "Oh, Lark, you must do this. Now you can see the brilliant colors. And there are fish." She was using the bowl as if it were a glass-bottomed boat. "How thoughtful of the Captain to give us each one."

Lark was standing transfixed. She had let her bowl go, and it was floating off, bobbing away with the current. She was watching the lifeboat drifting and the ship in the distance. Then, as she watched, the men in the lifeboat lowered their oars and began rowing back toward the ship. And Lark stood in the middle of the Pacific Ocean and sobbed. Donna looked up from her bowl and saw that the boat had left them. She rested her hand on Lark's arm.

"They can't leave us here? They'll be back?" Lark cried.

Donna bent down to fossick at Lark's feet, picking up little bits of coral that had broken off. "Here, Lark," she said, holding up a little pale blue, branched piece. "Take this back? A souvenir?"

Lark was looking at the lifeboat growing smaller. Donna slipped the coral into the pocket of Lark's shorts. "You've let your dish go. That's a pity. But come, you can look through mine. We'll share."

She placed the bowl in Lark's hands and then made her hands place it in the water. "Look into it, silly. You'll never see anything like this again." She placed both her hands on either side of Lark's head and pushed it down, so that Lark was looking through the glass at the coral, which, underwater, was as colorful as a garden of flowers.

"That pink coral is there," gasped Lark. "That poisonous one." She looked up, imploring, at Donna. "What'll we do now?"

Donna took the bowl. "Where is it?"

Lark pointed, and Donna guided the bowl close to herself and peered down. Then she burst out laughing. "Oh, Lark, that's my sneaker. Look," and she wiggled her foot around under the bowl. Lark started to cry again, silently, the tears running down her cheeks and dropping into the ocean.

The lifeboat was back at the ship. The tide was nearly as low as it would go and would soon turn. Several hundred yards of the reef were exposed.

"We might as well sit and rest our legs while we can," said Donna, perching gingerly on the coral, her knees drawn up to her chin, sitting very still so that the coral would not cut through her bathing suit. She bent her body over her knees and lowered her swathed head, so that the sun struck no part of her.

"I wish I had a camera?" said Donna, her voice muffled by her scarf.

Lark stopped crying and sat beside her. The tears were still wet on her cheeks, her eyes were fixed on the ship. "They're going to leave us behind."

"I'd reckon we have about two hours until the reef is covered and we can't stand any more?" said Donna. As she spoke, the water was lapping again at their toes and soon was covering their feet.

"Like those galloping tides in England?" said Donna chattily. "The shore is so flat that the sea just rushes in at high tide, like a train. People are always drowning, trying to run away from it. You have to somehow not fight it, but go with it, go with whatever is pushing at you, in order to master it."

They stood up and picked their way to what appeared to be the highest part of the reef. Donna had now let her glass bowl go and was leading Lark. Even at the highest point the water was at their ankles, rising steadily.

"It's hard to believe, isn't it, that this solid wall of coral is alive. It's not that the coral is built by living creatures. It is the living creature itself." Donna stamped her foot in the water. "We are actually standing on living creatures? In fact, if you cut yourself, and a piece of coral lodges in your flesh, it continues to grow."

The water was at their calves. It would get more difficult to stand as the currents of the deepening water began to push at them.

The two women were standing thigh-deep in water. One was upright, in shorts and a T-shirt, no hat, her short hair, close to her head, like a bathing cap. The sun struck her face, rendering it round, flat, almost the color of her hair, without definition. The other was crouched over, her bathing suit just visible below her long-sleeved sweat shirt. Her sunhat and a long scarf, which anchored the hat and wrapped around her chin and neck, obscured her face. They stood braced, their arms outstretched for balance, their legs apart and vaguely outlined beneath the water. The horizon, dividing blue water from blue sky, encircled them. They looked into the distance, expectantly, urgently. As the water swelled and pressed against them they were forced to take little steps, first this way, then that, in unison, two women dancing on coral.

"Look!" cried Lark. "They're lowering the lifeboat again."

The boat hit the water, and the oars began to dip in and out. When the boat reached them the water was at their waists. It was Mr. Blut who now sat in the bow. He brought the boat around so that its broadside was next to Lark and Donna, who both grabbed at it. Mr. Blut lifted their fingers off.

"One first, the other then," he reprimanded.

The sailors hauled Lark in, then Donna. Both sat in the stern, shivering in the wind.

"Ha, ha," said the Captain with his Humpty Dumpty smile as they clambered onto the deck. "You see coral, we check the boot. All is in good order."

Lark stood for a moment, then walked up to him and kicked his shins and punched his chest. He took her wrists in one hand and held her at arm's length.

"You tried to kill us," she yelled.

His eyebrows went up, as he kept on smiling. "It was a yoke, a practical yoke," he said, "for crossing the equator."

"Practical jokes can kill people," Lark yelled.

"But you must go in the water at the equator," the Captain laughed. "It's tradition, and it is the time for yokes. Bad luck if no yoke." He looked at each of them in turn. "Very clever ladies who know so much should know about the equator."

Donna stood adjusting her scarf, pulling on her trousers against the sun. "I love practical jokes," she murmured.

The Captain put his arm around Donna. "Did I fright you?" he asked.

Lark flounced off.

She stayed in her cabin for dinner, and for breakfast and lunch. She placed the piece of coral from her pocket on the ledge beside her bed and next to it her espadrilles with the rope soles that were now torn and ragged.

When she went in to dinner the next night, she wore high-heeled sandals and a long skirt. The others were already sitting at the table, laughing. It was the night for stuffed peppers again and the night that Donna Bird said "mouse."

"So sexy tonight? No more the little child?" the Captain said to Lark. "Such fine shoes? I shall buy some for my lady friend when I am next in New York." He nudged Donna.

Lark sat down without speaking.

Donna Bird was in her most splendid form, chattering about meeting a famous painter, a friend of her father's interested in primitive art, in Paris when she was twelve.

"Ah, that's one thing we Europeans know about, the value of art. And Manfred Bird, too, of course. Even during wartime, we took care of our art," said the Captain.

Donna went on to describe watching an avalanche in the Swiss Alps when she was seven, progressing through interminable interim tales, finally arriving at the Tower of London by river in a special boat.

"Can't you ever stop?" Lark shouted, slamming down her knife and fork.

"Larkie, darling," whispered Donna, "you think I'm still lying?" She smiled, almost happily. "But you never say anything at all. You just sit there, doing nothing. Like a child. You could help out at times."

The three men had given up on Donna's stories, so profuse were they this night. When Lark shouted at Donna, they looked up for a moment, then back to their plates. Paul Crouch, clearing away the remains of the green peppers in his customary state of detachment, looked as if he had not heard anything at all. He brought in the dumplings.

"Our handsome Paul," said Donna. The men were hacking at their dumplings. Donna called them to attention. "We were talking about Mr. Crouch, how handsome and strong he is."

The Captain gave a grunt.

"He could probably leap buildings in a single bound." Donna looked around. "If he wanted to, that is. A lot of little boys imagine themselves to be Superman." The men looked at one another and continued eating. "You can imagine how it happens, the little boy's view of the superhero, looking up at the towering body." Donna's face was radiant, as she recreated the scene. She was like the boy herself, looking up at the ceiling, lifting her head and opening her mouth in wonder, sinking back a little into her chair, as if retreating from that overpowering figure. "That ballooning chest, those muscles, those strong legs in blue tights. You can imagine how impressive, overwhelming, it would be, a little child looking up at that overpowering mouse."

And here she stopped. She seemed surprised at what she had

said, and she looked around the table. "I mean man," she said, and giggled, then remained silent while she finished her dumplings. During coffee and the after-dinner biscuit that accompanied the coffee she said, "Larkie, he is right about the equator and the tradition of playing practical jokes. That had completely slipped my mind as a possibility." She smiled at the Captain. "I conquered a fear. Such fun. So pedagogical. Not bad at all, for a joke."

The men laughed, glad that Donna Bird was herself again. "Equator such fun," said Mr. Blut. "King Neptune is a kind one."

"It was a good yoke," said the Captain.

"Joke?" said Donna. She paused. "We've done something no one else in the world has done. Thank you, Captain, so much?"

"And tomorrow," said the Captain, lifting his glass to Lark, "we have no tomorrow, ha."

Donna chuckled.

"Tomorrow we have no tomorrow," the Captain repeated.

And finally, when Lark refused to play the game of questions and ask why, he said, "Tomorrow it will be today again. We cross the dateline, and when we go east, we have the same day twice. We live a day longer. When we go west we lose a day in our life. Sad."

"Better than losing your life in a day?" said Lark.

"A yoke, a yoke!" said the Captain. "The afraid lady is yoking. She is better again."

"Joke?" said Donna kindly, putting her hand on the Captain's sleeve. "Please, jay, jay, joke?"

"Jay, jay, joke?" said the Captain. "And this is no joke. I have interested news for the lady passengers. We shall stop at an island. We must change course. We must pick up some thing from some island. We have new orders."

"Some island?" asked Donna.

"Some little island owned by some man."

"Why didn't you do something?" Lark asked Paul Crouch when they stood together on the deck later. She felt awkward with him knowing that he had watched their ordeal and done nothing, merely waggled his fingers at them as they descended in the lifeboat.

"There was nothing I could do. It would have been mutiny or something."

"But that Captain is a madman, you know that."

"Anyway, nothing happened. You're safe."

He was right, she supposed. They were safe. But she stayed standing apart from him, leaning on the rail some feet away.

The sudden port of call meant that a new route had to be charted. Lark stopped by the bridge and stood near the Captain as he pinpointed the island and fiddled around with his calculations. He still seemed to know what to do—Lark remembered that first charting, that ruling of the straight line across half the world—despite that foolish coral walk.

"This Pacific, we know it so well," said the Captain.

Lark climbed the ladder to the deck, where she found Paul Crouch, leaning on the rail.

"There's your island," he said.

They stood uneasily together, making a self-conscious, stilted effort to resurrect their conspiratorial closeness, pretending that all was as it had been.

The island was so small that it showed only on large-scale and local navigational charts. The sandy shelf around the island and the river leading into the only port were constantly dredged to make a channel deep enough for a small freighter to come right into the wharf, which ran alongside the main street of the settlement. Offshore, still visible above the water, was the hulk of a ship that had veered into the shallows and become embedded in the sand, perhaps a century before.

The Captain himself sailed the *Avis Maris* up the dredged

channel and docked right in the middle of the village. There were no formalities. A gangplank and ladder construction were let down directly onto the wharf; and a man wearing khaki trousers, a floral shirt, a pith helmet, and sandals came on board; he nodded at the two passengers and gave them permission to wander around. "But don't venture far. Don't go beyond the village. It is too easy to be lost." It was Mr. Weiss himself, introduced as owner of the island. He then turned away and conferred with the Captain and with Mr. Fischer.

During the time the *Avis Maris* was docked, Mr. Weiss spent the days on board, playing poker with the three officers in the Captain's private sitting room, drinking beer, not talking much. At dinner the first night, after Mr. Weiss's departure, the Captain did not speak at all.

"Poker," said Mr. Blut, explaining his Captain's behavior. "Herr Weiss always wins and here we are always poor."

"Always?" said Lark. "You always stop here?"

The Captain looked up. "We stop here sometimes, only."

Early next morning, Lark ventured out. Within half an hour she had walked up and down the main street of the village, a dirt road, and had ascertained that there were a dozen or so side lanes and a railway line, which ran beside the road. A shuttle of open cars sat on the rusted tracks, looking as if they had not moved for decades. A few peddlars of odd bits and pieces displayed their wares—a spoon made from the shell of a coconut, a plain basket, a tin plate. They seemed to have hurried to spread out their few goods as Lark came down the gangplank.

"You have may day in?" asked an old man who was wearing shorts and an old cotton shirt and sitting beside a tin plate containing large seeds on which were painted faces, just a mouth and eyes and a squiggle or two for hair. He held up a seed on which the mouth was drawn as a rectangle, with straight lines up and down forming squares representing teeth.

"You have may day in?" he repeated.

Lark paused. She wanted to keep walking, to run, and to ignore this incomprehensible demand. "I beg your pardon?"

"May day in?" He stood up and approached her.

Lark backed away. He held up his hand, as if to tell her not to worry.

"Okay, okay," he said. "May day in." He pulled up the back of his collar and pointed at the tattered label. "May day in France. May day in Hong Kong." He beckoned to a child in a doorway. The child stepped forward. The man pointed to the scarf he wore around his head. "May day in America." It was one of Donna Bird's scarves.

Lark nodded. "Made in," she said.

The man nodded. "Good," he said. He held out the seed to her again. "Art," he said, then pointed at her sandals.

Lark understood he wanted to exchange his seeds for imported goods. "I'm sorry," she said. "I'm terribly sorry." She hurried on.

"May day in." The peddlars took up the cry, waving the objects they wanted to trade.

Lark had wanted to eat on shore, to get away from Donna Bird and the Captain, but hesitated now to do so; and Paul Crouch, who might have kept her company, had to be on board to serve lunch. In any case, there was nothing that could be called a restaurant, only one or two coffeehouses, little huts, where she could have sat on a stool, half in and half out of the structure, drinking something, trying to ignore the peddlars. She made her way back to the ship.

"They see Europeans collecting real art—clubs and war sticks and death masks and the like—and they think they can trick us into buying anything," said the Captain at lunch. Mr. Weiss was there, sitting in Mr. Fischer's seat, while Mr. Fischer had moved over to the bench, so that Lark, Mr. Blut, and he sat tightly wedged in a row opposite Mr. Weiss and Donna Bird's empty chair. They had waited five or ten minutes for Donna Bird, who still had not appeared. The Captain waved to Paul Crouch to serve the food. "They think we're stupid." He tapped his head. "But they are the ones who are stupid enough not to see we have superior brains."

"That's what the fascists used to say, still say," said Lark.

"You are a child still," said the Captain. "You know nothing of the world, nothing of fascism, nothing of Europe and of history. You know nothing."

"One could ask how these people even know about Europeans and their art collecting. Who taught them about it?"

The Captain did not bother to answer. When Donna Bird was absent, he was always surlier, more belligerent, more himself, as if he could relax. Mr. Weiss looked up for a moment, then went back to eating. He did not speak at all during the meal.

After lunch Lark set off with Paul Crouch to walk the length of the village along the main street lined with houses made of tin, past the villagers offering sad little household items, and up the hill, at the top of which was a church overlooking the village and the river.

"The Captain's crazy, of course," said Lark. "Like Donna Bird. And where is she? Sulking in her cabin? Out trading her bizarre wardrobe with the villagers?"

"Let us hope she's in her cabin. It would be a good sign, the mouse not leaving the ship."

The church, Stella Maris, was of stone, in contrast to the village houses and all the other structures they had seen. A nun in full black habit came out to meet them, speaking first in German, then switching to English.

"I have been forty years here," she said. "I have a degree in English from the university, and I enjoy it when, every sometimes, the *Avis Maris* comes and discharges a person who climbs to this hilltop and speaks with me. In German, in English, it does not matter, but if it is English, then I practice. Perhaps

one day I shall be required to serve people who speak English.
Perhaps one day I will go to America."

"Did you say the *Avis Maris* often comes here?" asked Lark.

An old man, a native of the island, approached them, squatting and waddling forward, a bowl in his outstretched hands.
He said something to the nun, who excused herself and went
inside for a moment, returning with a plate of gray rice, which
she tipped into his bowl.

"This week he is Catholic," the nun said. "We're giving out
rice to attract converts—rice is not native to the island and it is
a luxe compared with the local root. Herr Weiss could do a little
more than he does to help these people, and we have to keep our
numbers up. In return for the rice, they are obliged to come to
church."

The man half stood and backed away, delicately shoveling the
rice into his mouth with one hand.

The nun looked away, thinking. "There is a problem," she
said, leaning toward them. "You may not walk like this, together. We cannot have a man and a woman walking the way
you are. It is not the way of this island."

"We're only friends, walking," said Lark. "You know, walking. Germans walk all the time, I hear."

The nun shook her head. "Do not generalize. These islanders
do not walk. It is not the way here." She looked at them more
closely. "I see you are not Catholic, are you?" They shook their
heads. "Then you will have to go to the Protestants at the foot of
the hill."

"We're not signing up, we don't want rice," said Lark. "We
only came to look at the church and the view, to get off the
ship."

The old nun pointed back down the hill. "It is the agreement
the two churches make for visitors." She turned and hurried
away.

Lark was furious. "Do you suppose the Captain telegraphed ahead to warn them about what he likes to call liaisons?"

She walked to the edge of the churchyard, beyond which the hill fell away to form a cliff, a steeply sloping, sometimes sheer rock face, loose with rubble, which descended to a beach and the river below. A few bathers were splashing in the water. She climbed down the cliff a little, knocking loose a few small rocks and pieces of broken stone and sending them tumbling over the edge, out of sight, to the beach. She found a ledge, somewhat horizontal and broad enough for her to sit. She drew her knees up and rested her arms and head on them. Paul leapt down and sat beside her.

"What a terrible island," Lark said. "They seem to do nothing here. Nothing moves."

She leant back against what appeared to be the firm cliff face, but her leaning dislodged a slab of rock. She lost her balance and was thrown to one side, her body drawn in the wake of the boulder crashing down the cliff. Indeed, she would have fallen if Paul had not quickly put his arm around her shoulder and held her against him.

"You must leave. You must go to the Protestants."

They looked up and saw the nun's head poking out from the rim of the cliff, outlined against the sky, a white moon with a black halo, peering down at Lark pressed close against Paul. Then beside the nun's head appeared Donna Bird's, partly hidden by her camera, which was whirring as she panned past Lark and Paul to the river and beyond. "Fantastic view," she said.

"I told you what is our way here," the nun said, and the two heads disappeared.

Paul and Lark climbed back up to the top of the cliff. Neither the nun nor Donna Bird was in sight. Without saying a word to each other, Lark and Paul followed the dirt road back down the hill, then inland around the base of the hill, away from the river and the village. It brought them to a rectangular tin building.

Two lengths of two-by-four timber nailed together to form a cross were tied to the apex of the tin roof. A man and a woman, husband and wife, Lark assumed, came to meet them. Seeing Paul and hearing his name, they started speaking German, then like the nun, when they realized their mistake, immediately switched to English.

"It is our pleasure to speak to others, every now and then," they said, "when now and then the *Avis Maris* brings someone to us."

"You could speak with the sisters on the hill," said Lark. "Or with Mr. Weiss."

The man hurried inside, saying he had to prepare for the service.

"Our two missions have been here for a hundred years," his wife whispered as he disappeared inside the smaller tin house beside the church building. "It still upsets him to think of it. We Protestants were here first and settled here first, and because we were doing so well the Catholics came. We said they could go to the other end of the island, but they would not leave. They simply took that hill and built that arrogant church. At least we are simple down here, and among the people. It was not fair. Herr Weiss does nothing to stop it. The owners are concerned only with themselves, although they used to be missionaries themselves." She pursed her lips. "And Protestant, too." The lips disappeared. "Commerce controls all," she hissed.

Then, from inside the house, Donna Bird emerged. She looked as if she lived there, although she could have been only five minutes ahead of them. "I have had such an interesting talk with your husband and his assistant," she said. Behind her came a young man in a white cassock, almost skipping from the happiness of talking to Donna Bird.

"Ah, your friend is so interesting to talk to, is she not?" The minister's wife smiled at Donna and held out her hand to her.

"And you will all join us in the service? We love to have visitors, and my husband loves a new audience."

Thirty or so islanders, on their way to the service, had gathered around the three visitors, peering at their faces, fingering Lark's skirt, trying to touch Donna Bird's spectacular earrings and the grape brooch on her visor. Paul and Lark looked at each other and Lark opened her mouth to tell the minister's wife that they would not join the service. But Donna Bird said, "Oh, we would love to," and the three of them were carried along by the cluster of worshipers and swept into the church.

"Why didn't you say something?" said Lark to Paul.

"Why didn't you?" he answered.

The men and women sat separately. Donna Bird took Lark's arm and sat her on a bench among the women on the right. Paul was escorted to the left. The villagers kept their heads turned to look at these newcomers, unusual as they were, and even when the minister and his assistant came in and began the service, the heads did not turn to the front.

The young assistant preceded the minister, giving the signal to the congregation to settle down. But he, too, was searching through the congregation looking for his new acquaintance, and when he spied Donna Bird in the middle of the women's section, he bowed toward her. Throughout the service his eyes scarcely left her.

"This is so interesting?" said Donna Bird into Lark's ear, just as Lark realized that a collection plate was being passed and that she had no money with her. The plate was made of tin, deep enough to serve as a soup bowl as well as a dinner plate. It had a little metal ring attached so that it could be hung from a belt or a nail and must once have been part of a military kit. With all eyes on her Lark received the plate, trying not to rattle the few coins that had been cast in it, and she passed it quickly to Donna Bird, who took it and rested it on her lap. She took off her earrings and dropped them into the plate, allowing them to clatter. There was a murmur throughout the church. What a fine gesture.

In the men's section, Paul, who had change in his pocket, let drop as many coins as he could into the plate, which, in Lark's mind, seemed cowardly, showing that he preferred to emulate Donna Bird rather than align himself with Lark in her embarrassment. She felt betrayed.

The man who had received the rice from the nun at Stella Maris on the hill walked into the church, stooped, although he seemed to be trying to walk as upright as he could manage. Rather then taking a place on the men's benches, he squatted right at Paul's feet and gazed up at him the whole time.

After the service, as Lark and Paul shook hands with the minister and his wife, who thanked them for coming, as if they were parishioners in the suburbs of Sydney, the minister's assistant drew Donna Bird aside. The two of them talked quietly and animatedly in German, with much waving of their arms and smiling and expressing of thanks.

The man who had sat at Paul's feet in the church came and sat at the minister's feet, his bowl once more in his hands, and he asked for food.

"Get up, my man. You need not kiss feet at this church."

His wife took the bowl and ran off, then returned with the bowl filled with what Lark took to be the local root vegetable. The man bowed and went off, again delicately shoveling the food into his mouth with his fingers and thumb, the first two fingers of the right hand scooping up the mash and the thumb pushing it into his mouth like a little bulldozer.

The minister looked for his assistant and beckoned him into the house.

"*Bis später*," said the assistant to Donna and followed the minister, catching the cassock as the minister let it drop from his shoulders.

"That was wonderful?" said Donna Bird. The service had lasted an hour and a half.

"It was terrible, perhaps the worst thing I have ever had to do," said Lark. Donna Bird was smiling, as if she were pleased at Lark's reaction. They were walking back along the main street toward the ship.

"We really wanted to walk a little in the jungle and explore," said Lark.

"We did?" said Donna Bird.

"And you forced us into the church."

Paul was slightly apart from the two women, behind them. Lark was aware that he was watching them walk, watching her waving her arms around at Donna. The islanders watched, too, from the doorways of their homes, from the little benches placed at the edge of the street.

"May day in," cried the children. A little boy, holding a large heart-shaped leaf, offered it to them, fanned his face to show that the leaf was a fan, then offered it again. "May day in."

Donna stopped and tried the fan, then handed it back to the boy. "I already have a fan," she said. She patted him on the cheek. "I'm sorry."

Toward them came running the man who had had his bowl filled twice. He had slipped ahead and was now coming to meet them, followed by several children skipping and leaping. He had in his hands a lamp, like the prize of Aladdin. "*Alt,*" he said. "Very old. Buy."

Donna Bird looked at it for only a moment, nodded, then beckoned to the man to follow her, and she hurried ahead to the ship. Donna disappeared up the gangplank, leaving the man with the lamp standing on the dock.

"Let's walk again," said Lark, reluctant to follow Donna Bird and reluctant to exchange the firmness of the earth for the uncertainty of the ship. "It's strange," she said, as they walked back along the main street. The island children walked behind them, their numbers increasing as they went along. "So strange that those separate groups of German missionaries live on this island owned by a German, without talking, competing for converts, when they could easily meet and talk about *The Magic Flute* and joke about Wotan and Brünnehilde and recall the triumphs of the past." Paul nodded, saying nothing. The soft sound of bare feet in the dust of the road made Lark glance back. "Oh, my God." By now a throng of children was following them. They were jumping about, nudging one another, skidding in the dirt of the street. As Lark cried out one child picked up a pebble and threw it at this strange couple, hitting Paul on the back.

He wheeled around and yelled at them. "What the blazes do you think you're doing?" He picked up a stone and made as if to throw it back at them, a gesture that reminded Lark of Henry Watter dealing with the Bakers' excitable dog. To Lark he said, "Remember what that nun said. It's not what they do here, walk along the street, just a man and a woman."

"They can't stop us from walking, can they? We'll just go to that little beach under the cliff. You're not scared, are you?"

Smatterings of children pursued them all the way through the village and along the path leading away from the Protestant church to the riverbank and the beach. Every now and then, when Paul stopped and looked back at the children, they also stopped, and if he took a step toward them, they took a step backward, like shadows, and then as soon as he started walking again, the children walked, too.

When they got to the beach and started walking on the sand, so yellow and perfect, the children stopped. They stood in the grass, where the path ended and the sand began. They stood, suddenly quiet, watching these two strangers.

"Why do you think they have done that? Why have they stopped?" Lark asked. "Is this a forbidden place?" She wanted Paul to be able to answer her questions. She wanted Paul to be strong. But he had deserted her again, depositing those coins, leaving her to fend for herself.

They walked on, leaving the children behind. The hill and the cliff were above them, the Catholic church out of sight over its rim. They rounded the base of the hill. The village and the children were now obscured.

"What's wrong? What has happened?" Lark asked. She held onto Paul's arm. "But what is that smell?" A stench like an open sewer or rotting rubbish assailed them.

"Oh, God," said Paul. He stopped and drew Lark to a halt beside him.

The stretch of sand before them was covered with refuse in which sea gulls were ferreting for morsels. And then, farther on, they saw several villagers squatting on the sand, their backs to the river. This golden beach was the village rubbish dump and the village latrine. Paul and Lark fled back to the village. The children, who had waited at the edge of the sand, knowing, howled with laughter.

In the main street they met the man from whom Donna had bought the lamp. He was wearing Donna's red plastic raincoat, snapped right up to the neck, and using her black umbrella as a walking stick. As they passed he nodded, smiled an appropriately refined smile. The children still followed them, all the way back to the ship, pushing each other and hooting and yelling, "May day in, may day in."

After the feel of the land, the ship seemed tiny and stuffy. Lark went up to her deck, where she found Donna Bird and the Captain leaning against the rail, her rail. They were close together, Donna Bird's head inclined toward the Captain's shoulder. They must have watched Lark and Paul retreating to the ship, pursued by the mocking children. Donna, holding a bunch of brightly colored flowers and even wearing her visor, looked almost lovely.

"What do you expect?" said Donna Bird, when Lark told the

story of the beach fiasco. "Do you think the whole world has your values? Why should these villagers not see a strip of sand and a tidal water as a utility, something to be used? You expect everyone in the world to think a strip of yellow sand is for romance?"

"We only wanted a place to sit in peace. And you?" said Lark, recalling Donna's spectacular, misguided trading activities. "You persuaded that man he needed your plastic raincoat and your umbrella in this heat, on this island. You're no better than a nineteenth-century European trader, getting rid of your surplus on the natives."

"In addition to the lamp he gave me a woven fly whisk." Donna simply ignored the point Lark was trying to make.

"So you got a bargain—a lamp and a fly whisk for a five-dollar plastic raincoat and umbrella. Don't you understand the meaning of what you're doing?" Lark was enraged.

"I told you, there's no such thing as meaning. The truth is apparent. The man wants my umbrella and raincoat. I want his fly whisk and lamp." She looked at the Captain. "Perhaps we can put kerosene in the lamp at dinner tomorrow." Then, nodding at Lark, "Now that's what I'd call romantic."

Lark closed her eyes and leant against the rail for a moment. "There must be somewhere to walk to, somewhere we can go," she said wearily.

"These people are just wonderful, aren't they?" Donna said, raising her eyes toward Lark, out of breath with the pleasure of it all. She held up her flowers. "Aren't these beautiful? I found them growing by the jungle paths." She held them out to Lark, who backed away, refusing to take them. "And their customs? A group of children already took me along some back paths a little way and I visited their homes? There's so much more to them than meets the eye of the jaded Westerner, don't you think?" She touched her hair, flung it back over her shoulders and hooked it behind her ears. "They will show me their dancing. I have started to learn the language. I can say, 'Did you catch the wild pig?'"

"And did you?" said Lark sourly.

Donna Bird laughed. She seemed delighted when Lark showed her irritation. "Very good, Lark. The mission school is rehearsing a production of *Our Town,* in the native language. Manfred, by the way, would love that, since he thinks people should stay at home. Thornton Wilder writing from New Hampshire has a timely message for these islanders. I'm going back to help them in the morning. They have trouble saying the words."

"You're the right person," said Lark. "You have no trouble saying yours."

Donna Bird laughed again. "'Take the current when it serves,'" she said. "Oh, Captain, the minister's assistant wants to give me a hat, woven by his grandparents. It's decorated with hair and feathers and spiderwebs. It's beautiful. But do you think I'll have trouble with customs in the United States?"

"There are ways," said the Captain.

"And what does the minister's assistant want in return? A tissue?" asked Lark.

Then the noise of something that sounded like a tank or a tractor made them shield their eyes and look along the road to where it turned into a jungle path and was swallowed up in the trees. From the trees, hurtling along the path, burst forth a large cube of a vehicle, on Caterpillar tracks, painted in camouflage, a kind of open-topped tank that could ford rivers and practically scale cliffs. Tied onto it was a long, narrow box.

"Ah-ha," said the Captain. He nodded and went down the ladder. The vehicle rumbled rapidly along the village road, the villagers finding it an unusual enough sight to run alongside it, trying to keep up. A young European man, blond and tan, was sitting on top in the driver's seat, yelling and yelping as if he were at a rodeo. He kept up his swift approach to the ship, until

it looked as if he would drive straight off the wharf into the
water. He applied the brakes and halted the vehicle almost on
the spot. The Captain was at the foot of the gangplank. He
called half a dozen sailors, who brought a dolly and climbed up
to unload the box. The men strained to wheel the load on board.

"Do you realize," said Donna, leaning over the rail until she
had lost sight of the dolly and its load, "that that box is absolutely identical to the long box we saw loaded on board in
Sydney?"

"So?"

"Well, it contains either another coffin and corpse or,"
Donna was now turned away from the dock, her elbows propped
on the rail behind her as she gazed into the sky, "or else it's the
second half of the bomb. They'll assemble it on board, you see.
Uranium and stuff from Australia, the mechanisms smuggled
here from . . ."

"From where, then?"

"Well, from the French bases in the Pacific." Donna looked
sideways at Lark. "You don't believe me, do you? You still think
I'm lying?"

Lark was uneasy. "You have no way of knowing that. You
can't possibly be sure that they're coffins. Or bombs." Lark
mumbled the last words. She had not wanted to utter them, to
go along with what Donna Bird said.

The *Avis Maris* was to leave after lunch the next afternoon,
when the tide was high. Paul and Lark had their morning tea as
usual on the top deck. Donna Bird remained out of sight, in her
cabin, Lark guessed, having suffered from too much light the
day before, or else she had slipped ashore before breakfast to
coach the children with their play.

"I wonder why we stopped, then? What is in that box, rather
those boxes, since there was one like it taken on board in
Sydney?"

"Come on," said Paul. "She's crazy, you know that. You know not to believe her. She only likes to disconcert and trick."

"Then let's walk once more," said Lark, again wanting to distance herself from the ship and feel the earth before casting off into the Pacific. They climbed down the ladder to the bridge and then down to the main deck.

The Captain emerged, calling to Mr. Crouch that he had some chores for him to do before they set sail. He set him to polishing the brass fixtures in the dining room and the brass hinges on the doors and portholes, hardly the most urgent task. But it certainly prevented Paul from going ashore again with Lark.

He got out the rags and the polish. "You go. I'm not my own master, remember, just a follower of orders." He picked up Donna's visor, which she had left hooked over a brass handle of the bookcase, placed it on the table, and began polishing.

Lark stood for a moment, frowning. She had dreamt that she was wearing that visor and was out in the sun for several hours. When she took the visor off, her face was burnt dark pink, with a brilliant white line above the eyebrows where the visor had rested.

Lark went for her last walk alone, taking with her some salami and cheese from the galley. She had decided to skip lunch on board. She walked along the main street and up the hill to the Catholic church.

The good sister, having expected to see Paul Crouch beside her, nodded with some relief, gave a kind of curtsy and hurried past this Protestant intruder, resisting the urge to exhibit a few English sentences. Lark walked to the edge of the churchyard and peered down at the beach, where beyond the broken stone of the cliff she could now discern the villagers at their ablutions, seriously bobbing in the water, rinsing off. Then she walked down the hill, along the path past the Protestant church.

"Your friend was here, too, very early," called the minister from his veranda. "Good morning, how are you? Very well, it is to be hoped? My assistant took her to spend time with some of our children, to learn to speak with them and ask questions about our island, the culture, the life, and to make film. We are not very interesting for outlandish cosmopolitans, I'm afraid, but she is charming, charming."

How did Donna Bird do it? People were drawn in without fail, happily allowing her, a scavenger, to pick at them.

Lark nodded, waved, and passed on. At the other end of the village she found another path and an inlet with a patch of sand that seemed never to have been used for anything. The sand was golden, unmarked. Lark found a rock to perch on and took out her little picnic. She was at last on an island in the Pacific, in that different place she had always longed for. It was peaceful enough on the surface. But she did not belong. And she was glad that she did not. She could see that she was not wanted here. She closed her eyes and tried to understand why she was so frightened.

A few sea gulls flew down, curious. Several more landed. They stood in a semicircle around Lark's rock. The sea gulls took a few steps forward. Lark drew her legs up, close to her body, unaware of the birds. She rested her head and her arms on her knees. At the movement the sea gulls moved back a little, then pressed forward again.

Solomon Blank was now probably settled in a house with empty bedrooms waiting to be filled with babies in an unlikely place called Champaign-Urbana. And beyond him there was Tom Brown in New York, whom she intended to love forever, if she ever escaped from this island, which at the moment seemed like the whole world, her oyster.

There were perhaps fifty sea gulls within ten feet of Lark, stepping forward and surrounding her. One of them, like a company commander, walked right up to Lark's sandals and trod on her toe, one of its spiked claws digging into her skin. She looked up. Then dozens and dozens of sea gulls seemed to be upon her. She clapped her hand to her mouth, to stop the scream, and while some of the birds flew off, the others stayed there; and when she jumped to her feet, the salami and cheese dropping from her lap, several sea gulls flew at it. Lark shrank back, believing that they intended to tear her to shreds. The sea gulls carried off the food, and the paper and plastic it was wrapped in, pursued now by the dozens of others, screeching and wrangling with one another for a share in the prize. A single shred of plastic fluttered at Lark's feet.

She ran back through the village to the dock, pushing her way through several dozen villagers who were gathering to watch the departure of the *Avis Maris*. The gangplank was being raised, but when the crewmen saw Lark, they lowered it again.

"We waited," said Mr. Fischer sternly, standing at the top of the gangplank. "And Miss Bird? Is she not with you?"

"She is already back on board," said Lark, out of breath, re-membering the visor on the handle of the bookcase. "You didn't sound the horn. I could have been left behind. Is it another of your jokes?"

"We sounded," Mr. Fischer said. "But in reality, passengers do not belong on a freighter. They disturb things, make waves, where before was smooth."

Lark stood on her deck. She would wait to see if Paul came to her, and then she would tell him about the sea gulls. She watched the ship distance itself from the dock, packed with the villagers, who were watching the ship grow smaller as they themselves grew smaller in Lark's eyes. They looked like so many gray and brown creatures, crowded along the wharf, jumping, waving, seething almost, like rats confined on a ledge in a lab experiment. Then Lark saw a little figure in brown and gray, looking like a leaf or a stick, scampering along the main street and onto the dock. It was unmistakably Donna Bird, wav-ing something—the new rush hat. And she was probably shouting, if indeed she was capable of raising her voice enough to shout. The ship was some way down the river, and Donna Bird was already a tiny little thing, standing at the edge of the wharf.

At first Lark was annoyed. Here was Donna Bird, once again, making a spectacle of herself. Just like her. And why had she left her visor behind? To trick everyone? What joke was she engineering this time? Lark watched Donna Bird's waving thread of an arm holding the round balloon of the hat. Then the arm stopped waving, the hat seemed to be on the head. Both arms seemed to be close to the body, the hands at the face. Was she crying? The ship sailed on. Lark stayed on her deck, watching Donna shrink from sight. Finally she forced herself to climb down to the bridge, where she found the Captain at the wheel and Mr. Fischer staring back at the land. Lark said nothing. She withdrew. Surely Mr. Fischer, too, had seen Donna Bird running along the dock.

Lark climbed back to her deck, confused, staying there until the land had completely disappeared and they were at sea again. She had deliberately left Donna Bird stranded on a remote Pacific island. It was likely that Mr. Fischer, at least, had done the same thing. And if that was so, what would he do to her, the remaining, unwelcome woman on board?

Paul vaulted up the ladder and came to Lark's side.

"She's not in her cabin," he said. "I've looked everywhere." He was distraught.

"Her visor was in the dining room," said Lark, not able to look at him.

"She is nowhere," said Paul. "I think she has been left behind."

Lark joined him in the search, going to Donna Bird's cabin, walking through her sitting room into the sleeping alcove and bathroom, as if Paul might have overlooked her and Donna would be found crouched in a corner. Donna Bird's bright green fountain pen was on her table. Her visor and fan were next to it, presumably placed there by Paul, and next to them the flowers in a jar and the lamp filled with fuel and ready to light the evening meal.

They combed the deck, looking in the lifeboats and behind coils of rope.

"Damn," said Paul.

They went to see the Captain.

"She went to look for you," said the Captain to Lark. "We would soon leave. It was late, half twelve, and we were ready. She was good and went to find you."

"But her sun visor was here?" whispered Lark, imagining that Donna Bird was still capable of turning up. The whole crew was now searching for her.

"She left the ship," said the Captain. "She said not to worry, she knew where to find you. You say she is back, so we sail."

They were now several hours away from the island. The Captain radioed Mr. Weiss on the island and eventually received the reply that Donna Bird had been found and was staying in one of the villages. After conferring with Mr. Fischer, the Captain decided, reluctantly it appeared, that he could not go back for her. She was to wait for another ship or for some little boat going to one of the bigger islands for supplies. "Native boats are always going there. And she is her father's daughter. She will have ideas of her own. But what will I tell him?"

"She could be there for months," Paul said to Lark. He was distressed. "I should have seen that she was not here. I can't stand her, but I wouldn't have wished her left behind, would you?"

And Lark felt guiltier than ever.

At dinner, after the ritual scraping of chairs and leaping up by the men when Lark entered, silence prevailed until Lark asked the Captain, "What is in the box you took on board?"

Paul Crouch lounged morosely in the doorway.

The Captain, who was eating, looking at his plate, lifted his head briefly.

"What do you guess is in it?"

"A—a body? It looked heavy enough." Lark attempted to smile, to indicate levity, trying to keep the fear and trembling out of her voice. "Like the one taken on board in Sydney."

"Ah, yes, a coffin, of course. Why not a sarcophagus? A man in a sarcophagus, a heavy sarcophagus." The Captain winked at Mr. Fischer, but without smiling. "The lady makes good jokes."

"A German man in a heavy sarcophagus," said Mr. Fischer.

"A heavy German man in a heavy sarcophagus," said Mr. Blut, joining in the game.

Lark looked at Paul Crouch, and while she understood that the men were ridiculing her, she was thinking about the days it would take to transport a corpse across the ocean, and she smelled the stench of bodies, in advance, seeping up through the layers of the ship to her deck. "Why not a burial on the island, or at sea?"

"They will with their own people rest," said the Captain. "No man wants to rot among primitives." He returned to his eating.

"They always bury them at sea. I've seen it, in war movies."

"That war," growled the Captain. "But we like to be buried at home."

"That is the way we like to do it," said Mr. Blut, feigning good cheer.

They were teasing her, so seriously, with such determination, that Lark now believed that something was wrong, that something terrible was being planned.

Mealtimes became funereal, with Mr. Blut and Mr. Fischer lapsing back into German, speaking only sporadically, the Captain hardly at all. The Captain was morose, slamming his knife and fork and glass down on the table, striding noisily along the gangways, turning corners abruptly. The men made no attempt

to converse with Lark. While she was blamed for causing
Donna Bird to miss the ship, Lark began to believe that it had
been arranged, the ultimate practical joke. But she was not sure
who the joke was on.

Paul had packed Donna Bird's things, leaving her suitcase on
the bed, the visor, fan, fly whisk, and lamp on top, as if they
were to receive the burial at sea. Lark, standing before them,
took the whisk and the lamp, and tucked them into her own
luggage. Then she went back and took the visor, too. Lark wrote
to Tom, protesting her innocence in the abandoning of Donna
Bird, then tore it up. She wrote to Solomon Blank: "Here is a
voice from the past," and tore it up.

Lark still went to her deck during the day, wearing Donna
Bird's sun visor all the time. She had begun to feel dizzy, the
sun seemed hotter and fiercer. She wrapped a long cloth around
her like a skirt, over her shorts, to protect her legs. As soon as
they reached Tacoma, she would get off immediately and go by
land to New York. She would not stay on this ship a moment
longer. In the meantime, the remaining weeks on board seemed
interminable.

Two days out from the island the ship gave an enormous
lurch, then a series of jolts, as if it were descending a staircase.
Lark was lying on her deck in the sun, alone. Her book flew out
of her hands, across the deck, and slid under the railing, going
over the edge down past the bridge. Lark slid across the deck
behind it. The jolts continued. There was a creaking of the
whole ship, a crashing of the aluminum rods on the deck, a
general breaking and shifting, falling and clanging. When the
ship subsided, the deck was at a slope, and Lark was lying
against the rail. The cloth wrapped around her had come loose;
the visor had fallen off. She got to her knees and crawled out of
the cloth, up the slope of the deck to the ladder, peering out over
the edge.

The crew was scurrying around beneath her, shouting. This

was the first time she had seen the whole crew at once. She could not tell what the trouble was, or if the ship was going to sink. Then she saw that the sea was a light blue, and therefore shallow, and she understood that the ship had run aground. Holding onto the rail, she slid her body around, her legs toward the ladder, which, as she swung her legs over and started down, swayed with her. It had been jarred loose by the impact and was swinging free, held only by two screws anchoring it at the top. Her weight on the ladder made the whole thing break away and fall to the bridge deck with a tremendous clatter, which nevertheless went unnoticed in the general uproar. She was left with the top half of her body bent over the deck, her hands holding onto the bottom rail, her legs waving in the air, searching for a foothold. She eased herself down a bit, with a toe hooked onto one of the brackets that had secured the ladder. Her other foot edged down toward the next bracket. She look down and saw Paul Crouch standing at a slant, as if he were leaning into the wind, holding onto a bracket to stop himself from sliding. He was smiling up at her, not a smile, just a bent mouth.

"Help me," she said.

It was simple enough to get off the ship. They had been able to lower the lifeboats. The crew stayed on board to work the winches and dump the aluminum rods to make the ship lighter. Lark was placed in a lifeboat with four oarsmen, and they sat some way off, watching the jettisoning of the rods, keeping their distance in case the ship should subside or list further. Military airplanes flew low over the ship, then disappeared. Lark sat all day in the lifeboat, at first bent over, trying to protect her face and neck and legs from the sun, until one of the sailors hauled out a flag tucked under one of the seats, which Lark was able to wrap around her, like a cloak.

Before nightfall the rods had gone, the tide had risen and the ship sat higher in the water, floating, at first listing a little, then straightening up.

When it was dark and the tide had risen, the ship was as ready as it could be, and they climbed back on board. The Captain's face sagged. "This was not foreseen," was all he said, before lapsing into silence for a few minutes. Then, "We will end in Tacoma. No New York now. We need to put the ship in the hospital for a diagnosis."

The Captain and Mr. Fischer spent much of their time below, leaving bridge duty to Mr. Blut. The wheel had been tied in place again.

"They fix something," said Mr. Blut, when Lark asked about their absence. "Busy, busy."

Bombs, thought Lark. The boxes surely were the two parts of a bomb, waiting to be assembled, as Donna had insisted. She was worldly and knew about these things. The Captain would unite the boxes, link them.

Lark took to eating her dinner in her cabin. She said she was sick, which she truly felt she was. Paul Crouch, now remote and cool, brought her dinner on a tray at night. Whenever the Captain caught sight of her, he tapped his head and nodded at her. "Hat," he said, pulling down the corners of his mouth. "Too much sun. Far too much sun. It harms the head." As soon as her ladder was fixed and secured once again, Lark climbed to her deck, to lie there, doing nothing, thinking nothing. Paul Crouch no longer climbed the ladder in the mornings bearing tea.

Lark packed her bags. She wanted to put her things in order, as if to be ready for whatever happened next. Among her clothes she found the list of names which Donna Bird had left in her hands early in the voyage. At the top of the list, Donna Bird had written, "The Book of Names." Lark sat and read the list, page after page. She came to Tom's name and her own. Right at the end, after the names of the Captain and Mr. Blut and Mr. Fischer and Paul Crouch, were the words, "At Tention, Dan Gereux, Bom Beenbas, Des Troyship, Avan Tarriverusa," as if they, too, were just more names. *Attention, dangereux, bombe en bas,* destroy ship, *avant arriver U.S.A.* Warning, dangerous, bomb below, destroy ship, before arriving U.S.A.

"Can't you find out what is really in those boxes?" Lark asked Paul Crouch when he brought her next meal, breaking days of silence. "I have to know."

"I'm not Superman," Paul said tersely. He pointed at the tray. "Here. Food. I can't just break open the lids of coffins, boxes, whatever they are, with my bare hands."

"Can't you steal the key or something?" Lark sat hunched on her bed, miserable, frightened, the recipient of Donna Bird's legacy. "What is in them, then?"

Paul shrugged. "Drugs? Weapons? Explosives? Corpses? I neither know nor care."

Lark took out the list of names and pointed to the words at the end. Paul frowned at them.

"Don't you see? She says it's dangerous, there's a bomb," Lark said.

Paul was silent for a while, then he looked up at Lark's wild face. "Say, you'd better stay indoors. You look terrible. And you know she likes jokes. She is always saying so."

Lark tried to descend into the hold but found everything bolted. She climbed to her deck and on the way paused on the bridge, contemplating the fire ax, then the radio. She wanted to summon help, but she had no idea how to work the radio. She had never learnt the Mayday call. So Lark decided to destroy the ship. She would have to set it on fire.

She wrote to Solomon Blank and to Tom Brown, beginning, "By the time you read this, I shall be . . ." and getting no further.

Everything on board seemed to be metal, with the exception of some of the decks and the paneling in the cabins. And she had no gasoline, nothing in enough quantity, to start a conflagration that could not be controlled. All she had to do was disable the ship, attract attention somehow, get help.

She simply took Donna Bird's lamp, emptied the fuel onto her sheets, and set her bed on fire. She could not believe she was doing this, trying to destroy a freighter, and prepared to die in the process. The bedspread and sheets smoldered, resisting the sluggish little flames. All Lark had to do to put out the fire was roll up the bedding and smother it. Then she remade the bed, with the burnt sheet and bedspread at the foot, tucked out of sight.

Lark sat up. Someone was climbing the ladder. If it was Paul Crouch, she would confess that she had allowed Donna Bird to be left behind. It was the worst thing she had done in her life.

The Captain's head appeared. He stopped climbing and rested his arms on the deck, and then his head on his arms, Humpty Dumpty balanced on his wall. Lark drew away from him. She had not seen him for several days. Perhaps he had found the burnt bedding. She thought of lashing out, of kicking the Captain's face, a football just a short distance from her, sending him off the ladder. But it would not kill him, and then he would really come after her.

The Captain hoisted himself right up onto the deck. Lark jumped up and backed away, against the rail. "This is an unlucky ship," said the Captain. "Two bad things happen to this innocent ship." He walked toward her, his arms out.

"It was an accident," Lark cried. "I didn't mean it." She pressed back against the rail. "Stay away from me." And then she started to scream.

"Poor Miss," said the Captain, advancing, taking her by the shoulders. "I know you are unhappy, to lose Miss Bird, and also sick."

"Don't throw me overboard," Lark cried. It seemed that was what he had in mind.

The Captain folded his arms around her and held her against his chest. With one hand he felt her forehead. "A terrible thing," he said. "A tragedy. You will go to bed, and we shall bring soothing food—soup, brandy—until you feel much better. We do not want a third bad thing to happen."

Mr. Blut and Mr. Fischer appeared. *"Hilfen Sie mir,"* said the Captain. "Help me."

"Leave me alone." Lark could not move, imprisoned in the Captain's arms.

"Such to-do," said the Captain. With the help of the two officers, he dragged her across the deck, handed her down the ladder. "She shall remain in her cabin." As she was being maneuvered along the gangway to her cabin, Lark glimpsed Paul, ducking into the galley.

"Is this drugged?" she asked, when he bought her crackers and soup. She was sitting on her bed, looking away from him. "Why didn't you do anything?" she asked. "Why didn't you help me? Why do you let them keep me a prisoner in my cabin?"

"I was in the galley getting lunch," said Paul. "And the Captain says you're sick, from all that sun."

Lark beckoned him to her. "It was an accident."

Paul frowned, not comprehending. Lark pulled out the sheet and bedspread and showed him the rather insignificant burns. "I didn't mean to."

"Take it easy," was all that Paul Crouch said.

"They said once that I had a sense of impending doom," said Lark.

"It would be hard not to have a sense of impending doom on this ship," said Paul Crouch. "It was just one of Donna Bird's jokes, that list of names."

Many days passed, and while Lark remained in her cabin, out of the sun, away from the company of the officers and Paul Crouch, the *Avis Maris* had sailed into winter. Lark had lost her feverishness but still thought of the two boxes in the hold and of

Donna's list of names with their hidden warnings. She went on deck in the dawn as they passed through the Strait of Juan de Fuca into Puget Sound. Dozens of little fishing boats were already out, tossing in the winter waters. It was still possible, she thought as she hugged her inadequate sweater and Windbreaker around her, that the *Avis Maris* was the delivery system for a bomb that was contained in those boxes and intended for New York.

"And this is warm, mild." The Captain was standing beside her. "Wait until you spend Christmas in Chicago, and New Year in New York." He blew through his lips, making a sound to indicate the degree of cold and rubbing his hands together. "I am like a passenger now. Like you. We have the pilot on board. He is in charge. I can have some entertainment, like on the Queens. Ha." He pointed all around. "You see, America. In New York you see the same, only it is a big bridge and the Statue of Liberty standing on her island. That is the joke I told you in the beginning. She cannot sit down. Perhaps she could lie down, if she got tired." He laughed a few short bursts, and stopped. "It is good this bad journey is finishing. The end is soon. I must go below." And he left Lark at the rail.

The end is soon. Lark looked after him. The end. And below were those two boxes, lying side by side, surely transformed by now. Lark watched the little fishing boats toiling, taking on dimension and detail and color in the new light. She could now distinguish one boat from another and sometimes, if the craft was close enough, its skipper and crew. Then she remembered that the Captain had mentioned the pilot.

On the bridge the pilot was standing at the wheel. Mr. Blut, dressed in blue serge with gold trim ready for shore, was off to one side sorting through charts.

"Good morning," said the pilot to Lark. This was her second American. "A good voyage?"

Lark stood close beside him. "In the hold," she whispered,

"there is something strange, something not right." She swiveled her eyes toward Mr. Blut, whose legs were planted on the periphery of her vision. The toe of one shiny black shoe was tapping. "Two boxes, like coffins, possibly bombs."

"Hmm?" said the pilot, half listening, smiling, not really trying to comprehend. "Boxes, you say? Coffins?"

"Coffins?" came a booming, blustering voice. The Captain had entered. "Ha, ha. There are no coffins, just cargo."

"But he said there were coffins in the hold," said Lark. She had nothing to lose now.

"Exactly," cried the Captain. "No bodies, and no coffins. It was a joke." He shook his head at the pilot. "That one," indicating Lark, "does not understand a joke. She has no humor."

"Ah-ha," responded the pilot. He nodded at the Captain.

Lark stepped away from them.

"She has been very ill. Too much sun. Far too much sun. All the time she lies in the sun." The Captain tapped the side of his head, and again Lark watched the little indentations left behind by his finger.

"I've been sick?" Lark asked, at the same time deciding that she should disembark just as rapidly as possible. "Yes, that's it." She backed away from the pilot and the Captain, toward the door.

"She is a land lover," the Captain joked after her.

"Not a sailor at all." Mr. Fischer had appeared at the door, causing Lark to jump and turn around. He stepped aside to let her pass. "Women on board, bad news."

"We hope you will be very happy in our country," said the pilot.

"She will be happy," said the Captain. "She is a land lover, not a sailor at all."

Lark stood on the main deck, with her luggage at the spot where the gangplank would be lowered. She now reasoned that if she left the ship her premonition about the bomb would be false. The ship would not blow up, as long as she was not on it thinking her thoughts. The gangplank was lowered, but she was not allowed to disembark. A port official had to board first.

"You are wanted in the dining room," said Paul Crouch, who had slipped up beside her and slipped away again, quietly and quickly, after delivering the message.

An immigration official in white shirt and navy pants had set up a card table at which he sat awaiting her, the only passenger. The Captain appeared to be explaining the absence of the second passenger.

The immigration official stood up when Lark entered. He leant over the table, his arm outstretched. At first Lark thought he wanted her to hand something over, her passport perhaps, but he seized Lark's hand and shook it. "Welcome to the United States of America," he said. He shook her hand vigorously again. "We are a friendly nation. Be open, frank. Don't hold back."

The third American. He, too, sounded like all the men in all the Hollywood movies she had ever seen. "Thank you," she said.

He motioned to her to sit at the chair in front of the card table while he examined her documents. Lark looked around. The Captain stayed close by, standing over them.

The formalities over, Lark dashed down the gangplank onto the wharf, then quickly turned and, looking up, saw Paul Crouch leaning on the rail of her deck. He gave her a slight nod.

While the taxi driver loaded her luggage into the trunk and onto the seat next to him, Lark looked back at the ship. Paul Crouch was still there, leaning and smoking. He threw his cigarette away and acknowledged her departure by moving his wrist and lifting his fingers slightly.

As they drove away she looked anxiously back in the direction of the wharf. "Just take me to a train station," she said to the driver.

"We don't use trains much, anymore. Buses are what we use. Greyhound."

Lark said the train station would be fine.

"Greyhound would be cheaper," said the driver. "Ninety-nine days for ninety-nine dollars. Dollar a day. And faster than a train."

"The train station will be fine."

"Are you sure you're old enough to be traveling alone? You look like a runaway to me."

The train station was deserted. The ticket window was closed. Lark placed her bags on a bench near a telephone. With Henry Watter's leather coin pouch looped over her wrist, she prepared to telephone Tom in New York.

"Operator?" she said, again mimicking the movies, "I want to call long distance." She opened her address book and gave Tom's telephone number.

"I got off in Tacoma," she told Tom, suddenly aware that she had traversed the largest ocean, changed hemispheres, passed from summer to winter, and endured a great deal in three weeks. "The ship changed its route. It needs repair. It ran aground."

Tom did not seem terribly surprised to be hearing this news. "No wonder the Germans lost the war," he joked, not at all curious. It was as if she lived around the corner and he had seen her just the other day. And Tom never asked questions. Lark could not recall Tom's ever having asked a question, about anything. And she was glad, otherwise he would ask about Donna Bird and want to know her whereabouts. "It'll cost you money," he said, "leaving the ship on the west coast, traveling across the country."

"It's a good opportunity to see America. I don't have much luggage."

"So, Larkie, now you have gotten your feet wet in the big, bad world, thanks to active transport."

Lark paused. She wanted to tell him about the mad Captain, and about the coffins and her attempt to destroy the ship. "Active transport?"

"The cell uses energy to transport materials through the plasma membrane. It's all part of our drive to return to the unicellular condition—remember?"

"I've been at sea for weeks. Out of touch."

"Most theorists, Darwin, et cetera, would have us believe that we are driven to develop and become more and more complex. But the reverse is, in fact, true. We are just following a very roundabout route toward simplicity. Einstein recognized it."

The operator interrupted, asking Lark to deposit more coins. As they clinked into their slots, Tom continued. "And so, you are here. The membrane, the U.S.A. in this case, has folded in, forming a pocket, which fills with fluid and particles from the surroundings, in this case you and that ship."

"I don't know what you mean. I've been at sea."

But Tom went straight on. "The membrane then closes over the pocket and releases the particles, poof, into the cell. And so, you are here, in the cell. *Fin, fine, Ende.*"

Lark let a few seconds pass, to make sure Tom had stopped talking. "This sounds very silly, I know, but how hard is it to make a bomb, a big bomb that would destroy buildings?"

"Ah-ha, exactly, you're catching on. That's why we're on our way to blowing up the planet. It's a deep, unacknowledged need—the satisfaction of returning to the single cell state."

Lark leant against the wall of the phone booth, more confused than ever about the *Avis Maris* and the bomb that Donna Bird had insisted was in the hold. At least she had begun to try to tell Tom, and if he had deflected her confession, well, it must mean that what she had to say was not really important.

"So I'll be seeing you," said Tom. "Take care. Have fun."

But Lark was not ready to relinquish her connection to Tom and be left standing in a phone booth alone in a deserted train station. To keep him talking to her, she asked a question. "Don't you want to know about Donna Bird?" She would have to tell him sooner or later, and if she did it now, on the telephone, he would not be able to see her face and detect her dissembling. He waited for her to explain. "She stayed behind. On an island. To educate the people there." That sounded entirely plausible. In fact, Lark liked the sound of it very much. She went on. "Like Sylvia Ashton-Warner and the Maoris. They needed her more than Manhattan does. She was helping them put on plays and appreciate their own culture."

"She's an original," said Tom. "But damn. I rented an apartment for the two of you. Now you'll have to manage the rent on your own."

"I shall be there in two weeks or so," Lark said, although he had not asked. "I'll let you know exactly when."

"It's a great apartment," Tom said.

She hung up. From her address book fluttered the piece of paper on which she had copied the address and phone number of Solomon Blank when she had visited his mother in Sydney before she left. Then the phone rang, which was surprising to Lark, since it was a public telephone. When she answered it, it was the operator telling her the final cost of her New York call and directing her to drop the coins into the box.

Lark, who still held a fistful of coins and the slip of paper, telephoned the Blank household in Champaign-Urbana. "I hope you are sitting down," she said, when Solomon picked up the phone. "This is a voice from the past."

# III

Solomon was at the train station in Chicago to meet Lark. She saw him pacing up and down the platform, peering in through the smoked glass of the cars, trying to locate her. He was wearing a sheepskin hat, rather like the hats that Russians wore in Hollywood movies, and a sheepskin overcoat that almost reached the ground. There was a sad look about him, weighed down, almost obliterated by his clothing. As she stood in the aisle waiting to alight, Lark was able to watch Solomon swiveling his head, looking anxiously at each emerging passenger. Then, as Lark climbed down the metal stairs to the platform, he was there beaming up at her, holding his arms out to give her a hug. He held her close for several seconds, pressed against his coat, much longer than she would have expected from a newlywed husband. He held his cheek against her hair and breathed in. Then he held her from him and looked at her, shaking his head in disbelief, before embracing her again.

"Amanda insisted that I come," he said. "She said that it would be terrible not to see an old friend who has come so far and that she could manage quite well on her own for an afternoon and an evening. And if she had an old college friend passing through, she would certainly expect me to allow her to go and see her, or him, as the case may be. She told me to come." He held Lark from him again to look at her. "I drove for hours to get here, over icy roads and through sleet and snow flurries, and then I was here early and your train was late." He was extremely pleased to see her, and he stood looking into her face, rubbing his hands on her arms, along her jacket. "I think you'll be needing warmer clothing."

"I'll buy something in New York suitable for the Northern Hemisphere."

"But I wanted to walk you along the Lakefront, to show you how handsome Chicago is. I love the lake, although it doesn't much resemble our ocean, or our beach, or our rocks."

"I'm glad to be away from them," said Lark.

"You'll see, after a while, that you'll need to be near the water, too. I often drive in to Chicago just to walk along the shore of the lake, although right now it's all white, covered with ice. And since we had a blizzard last week, everything is also covered with snow. You can hardly tell there's a lake there. It looks like a field." He looked at Lark, then down at his coat. "Perhaps we can wrap this around us both. It's pretty large." He pulled the front of the coat away from him, to show how large it was and how little space he took up inside it. "You can't get by without the proper clothing in this part of the country. We were lucky—at home there was no need for a complete new wardrobe in winter, no heating bills; you should see what Amanda and I pay to heat our house." He let go of his coat and it fell back against his body, drooping to the ground. "This belonged to Amanda's father. He was enormous." He patted his coat again. "Amanda takes after him." He picked up Lark's bags and carried them to his dark green station wagon. "I've rented you a room in this motel. It's cheap. I could stay over, too, if you wanted me to. I'm sure Amanda would understand."

They drove through the snowy streets, Solomon turning to Lark often and grinning. He patted her arm, then pulled her closer to him. "It's been a long time. Put your head on my shoulder. Come on." And he placed one arm along the back of the seat and around Lark's shoulders, drawing her closer.

The motel was a few miles from the center of the city, a two-story blond-brick building among car lots and supermarkets.

"It's cheap. I checked you in already," said Solomon. "And it won't matter, once we're inside, where we are. We can just talk and talk."

Solomon took Lark's bag and a small duffel bag of his own, and led her past the desk clerk and a cardboard placard propped on an easel in the lobby announcing that the motel was the venue for the reunion of the Children of the American Revolution. Stuck up at various points were arrows and little cards announcing CAR This Way. Solomon flung open the door to the room. Two full-size beds separated by a narrow table took up most of the space. On the bed closest to the window was spread a towel, and on the towel sat, a little unsteadily, a bottle of champagne, two glasses from the bathroom, and a packet of Cheddar cheese and crackers.

"To celebrate," announced Solomon.

Beyond the window came the sound of water splashing and children shrieking. Solomon walked over and pulled back the curtains. "Your view, *madame*."

The glass of the windows was steamed over, dripping with condensation. Instead of looking out over whatever terrain the outskirts of Chicago might offer, the window looked in over the motel swimming pool. Dozens of Children of the American Revolution, all of them remarkably chubby, were shouting and climbing up the ladder to the diving board from which they plummeted in quick succession, sending water over the edge of the pool across the tiles where the parents of the revolutionary children sat talking, apparently contentedly, on the green carpeting. The shouts and splashes of the children echoed and reverberated under the fiberglass dome that enclosed the pool and the courtyard. Sleet was falling outside, rattling on the dome like gravel. On the window Solomon wrote with his finger, "Welcome to the U.S.A.," then opened the champagne.

Solomon gave Lark to understand as they talked, sitting together on the second bed, that he was extremely happy with his research on Renaissance drama and with his lovely wife. Perhaps it had only been his overwhelming outer clothing that had given him that dejected, powerless look at the train station.

"Amanda is very creative," Solomon told Lark. "She makes paper. At the moment she sells stationery for a local printer, but she is really a gifted artist. When I get my tenure and my textbook makes me a millionaire," he smiled weakly and looked up at the ceiling—"just joking—I'll set her up in her own studio and she can just make her paper." He put his arm around Lark and kissed the top of her head.

Lark leaned neither away from him nor toward him. "Your mother said you were planning to have four children. She said you have their bedrooms all ready, and their names, too."

Solomon reached out and touched the bracelet on her wrist, fiddling absently with the polished little pebbles. "Ah, yes. That, too. Amanda wants lots of children. She can paint while she has babies." Solomon brought Lark's hand closer to him so that he could turn the bracelet and examine each stone. "These are from home, aren't they?"

Lark nodded.

"It is beautiful." Solomon kept holding Lark's hand.

"I'm glad you're so happy," said Lark. "So happily married." With the sound of the children smashing into the water behind them they could have been beside an ocean. The sleet on the fiberglass dome could have been the sea gulls picking at bits and pieces of oysters and periwinkles on the rock shelf. For a moment Lark let herself lean against Solomon. "It almost sounds like home, doesn't it?"

"Let's go and walk beside the lake for just a little while. I want to tell you something." Solomon pulled Lark to her feet. "It'll be like going around the rocks. Then we'll have a wonderful dinner. I've made a reservation, overlooking the lake. You'll love it."

They drove to the waterfront, then trudged across the park, stumbling in the snow. The wind came in brief gusts, striking the snow in different spots and sending it swirling into the air, the way bombs falling from an airplane into an ocean send up spray as they hit. Solomon held Lark close to him, and they hunched over as they walked. When they reached the waterfront, Solomon unbuttoned his coat. He slipped his left arm out of its sleeve and held the coat open. "Come in beside me," he said. Without hesitation Lark nestled against him. "Put your right arm around my waist," Solomon instructed, "and your left arm into the sleeve of the coat. Now, come in close, kind of sideways." He placed his left arm around her, under the coat. "There." And using Lark's left hand and Solomon's right hand, they managed to button the coat up again. "I don't think we belong in this climate, actually."

Lark was pressed against Solomon's side, her head against his shoulder. She felt like his Siamese twin, and she was certainly warmer, although to move forward with him she had to walk in a kind of sidestep. They careened forward, the wind blowing them along, like runners in a three-legged race at a Sunday school picnic, each trying to get used to the other's rhythm and step.

"Let's just pretend it's a beach," said Solomon, "in summer. And we're taking a romantic walk around the rocks."

"With no Mrs. Baker passing by to declare how hot it is and checking up on us. Oops." Lark slipped in the snow that had hardened to ice at the edge of the shore. Because she was so firmly attached to Solomon, buttoned into his coat, she was saved from falling.

"Mrs. Baker?" Solomon asked.

And Lark explained. He remembered nothing about rubbing suntan oil on Lark's back and Mrs. Baker's walking by, saying that it was as hot as a furnace that day on the beach before finals several years before, and he remembered nothing about throwing his keys on the pages of *L'Etranger*.

"At home the other night, after you telephoned, we sat in the breakfast nook and took out my old slides."

"You don't actually have a breakfast nook, do you?" Lark did not like hearing Solomon mention "breakfast nook" and "home" or use the pronoun "we," which so clearly excluded her. It was very lucky that she had fallen in love with Tom Brown. "I wanted to show Amanda who you were. There's one of you and me on a picnic in the Blue Mountains. You're trying out my crutches."

"Crutches?" Lark remembered nothing about Solomon's breaking his leg and nothing of going on a picnic and trying out his crutches. "Are you sure?" She shivered. "Perhaps it was someone else who was with you?"

"And there's one of me playing your pianola and you singing."

"But I don't sing," said Lark.

Solomon Blank drew them to a stop. "Behold, my Pacific," he announced, sweeping his right arm across in front of them, taking in the entire lake, which stretched white before them, merging with the white of the sky. "I don't think we fit in here," he said into Lark's hair. "I don't think we love each other," he whispered.

Lark at first thought he was referring to her and him, but then, on contemplation, realized that Solomon was still talking about Amanda. Then she realized that the ground they stood on was moving, floating. Lark looked around as best she could, over the collar of the sheepskin coat.

"We've wandered onto the ice," she said.

"Oh, my God," said Solomon, trying to look around and take some action, hampered though they were by encasement in the same overcoat. "When I say three, we'll jump. One, two, three."

They threw themselves off the ice onto the snowy shore a couple of feet away. Lark struggled out of the coat, hoisted herself to her feet and began to run back to the road, toward the city, where the lights in the tall office buildings along the lake glittered in the dull winter daylight.

"Wait for me," Solomon cried and loped after her.

"Just take me back to the motel," gasped Lark. "I don't want any more nature, ever, ever again."

"Here, get in my coat again. It's too cold for you like that."

Lark stepped away from Solomon as he approached, opening his coat toward her. "I'm okay on my own," she said. "I'm okay, okay?"

"You're so cute like that," Solomon said, stumbling after her. "So angry. Like a cross little boy."

"Mr. and Mrs. Blank?" the manager of the restaurant greeted them that evening and sat them at a corner table, next to a large family group of several adults and many teen-aged children.

"She doesn't love me, anymore, I'm sure of it," Solomon said.

"You said you were happy. You have a breakfast nook and empty bedrooms waiting to be filled with children."

"She would be glad for me to go, I'm sure of it."

The lights in the restaurant suddenly dimmed, and a train of waiters and waitresses emerged from the kitchen bearing a birthday cake with flaming candles. The group at the next table burst into song. "Happy birthday . . ." they sang, and the whole restaurant joined in.

"But you've only been married a little while." Lark had to shout to be heard.

Solomon nodded gloomily.

The lights came back on. A young woman in a black dress and white apron was standing beside them, as if a lamp had been rubbed to produce her. "I'm Amanda," she said. "Mandy. I'm your waitress this evening and I recommend the flounder."

Solomon looked quickly at Lark before picking up his menu. Lark saw that he was blushing, as if a waitress called Amanda was capable of detecting his identity. But the name had made them awkward. They ordered and ate quickly without saying much.

Back in the motel room, with the Children of the American Revolution still diving and swimming and shouting, Solomon asked Lark if she wanted to see a picture of Amanda. Lark took the photo. She was a fairly blond, fairly attractive young woman, as tall as Solomon, and as sad as Solomon had looked through the train window. At least no one would ever call her cute or mistake her for a schoolboy.

"She doesn't need me, anymore," said Solomon. He turned toward Lark and held his arms wide. "Let's go to bed."

"Together?" Lark replied, in something of a squeak, and almost flew into his arms.

"I don't mean to play on your sympathies, of course," said Solomon.

"I'm going to New York," Lark said. "And you are going to Champaign-Urbana."

Solomon nodded glumly, then looked at his watch. "I suppose I should be getting back." But he sat down beside Lark on the bed. "I needed to get away for a few hours. I suppose I ought to be getting back home, then. Still, this has been the happiest day of my life."

"We could both be dead," Lark said, "if we'd been carried into the lake on the ice floe."

Solomon sighed. "But I don't mean to play on your sympathies. It's just that sometimes I feel that we, you and I, should have stayed at home. Together."

"But you Blanks were always off. You can afford to recommend staying put. Anyway, it's too late now."

Solomon stayed sitting and talking, taking Lark's hand. Lark thought of changing her mind and asking him to stay with her.

"Amanda will be worried," Solomon said, not moving. "What I mean is, sometimes I think even if I didn't marry you, I should have married an Englishwoman. England and the English are more compatible with us."

Lark stood up.

"I could stay," Solomon said. "Amanda wouldn't mind. She's very broad-minded."

"I'll walk you to the lobby." She did not want to hear any more about his domestic situation and his unhappiness. She wanted to be free of it, free to be in love with Tom Brown now.

"Wait," said Solomon. "I have to take home something. Some kind of present, to prevent unnecessary strife." He took Lark with him into the souvenir shop in the hotel lobby. He fingered the scarves and the necklaces. "She's tall," he said to the saleswoman.

"Like me?" the saleswoman asked, coming out from behind the counter and exhibiting her height.

"Taller," said Solomon.

"Then she can take a bold design," said the saleswoman and pointed to a scarf with ugly red and blue marks on it.

"Would you like one, too?" he asked Lark.

She shook her head, and waited while the scarf was paid for and wrapped.

"I'm sorry," said Solomon as they walked back into the lobby. "But she'd be furious if I didn't bring something back."

Lark shrugged. "She's your wife."

Solomon put his arms around her. "I have become a pathetic provincial, a nobody," he said, "while you, Lark, are about to begin a magical life in the greatest city in the world. At least, I deserve a kiss, don't I?" And he kissed her in the lobby of the hotel, a real kiss, and Lark responded, remembering how much she had loved him, how much she had wanted to follow him to America, to be with him forever. Then she watched him drive off into the white city.

Lark awoke to find the round face of a little boy in a swimsuit pressed against her window, staring at her. The splashing and shouting in the pool had started up again. It was as if those children had never gone to bed at all. The boy ducked away and ran across the tiles and into the water.

The light under the fiberglass dome was gray and dull. Six inches of snow had fallen during the night, coating the dome and blocking the morning light. Lark poured out the unfinished champagne, then packed her bag and checked out.

"Plane would be faster, and bus would be cheaper than train," the desk clerk told Lark.

"But I'm not in a hurry."

The clerk made a face. "Nothing to see between Chicago and New York, believe me." But he telephoned to get the times of the trains to Detroit and on to New York. "You know you can go direct to New York. You don't have to go through Detroit."

"I'm not in a hurry," said Lark.

The clerk looked Lark up and down. "Shouldn't you be in school?"

At Union Station a man and a woman, each hauling suitcases with wheels and tethers like little dogs, bumped into Lark as she sat on her suitcase, hunched over against the cold.

"Is this the train for Detroit?" the woman asked.

"I asked a woman at the front of the line," Lark replied. "She said it was the train to Detroit."

"Oh, you AHsked, did you?" The man was imitating Lark. "Are you English or just affected?"

"Henry!" said his wife, admonishing, then cajoling, "So where are you from?" Lark hesitated. "Mmmm?" the woman persisted.

Lark looked around, as if the information might precipitate some kind of trouble. She mumbled her answer.

"That's the same as English," said Henry.

"No, it's not," said his wife.

"We had an exchange student from South Africa staying with us when our son was in high school," said Henry.

"South Africa is nowhere near Australia," said the woman. "New Zealand is."

"We're going to Ann Arbor, we're from Chicago," said Henry. "Our son is picking us up. He goes to school there. Architecture."

"It's a very good school," said the wife. "One of the ten best. Henry, my husband," she nodded at him, "Mr. Parker, is an architect. Our son takes after him."

The line started to move, and Henry and his wife pushed ahead of Lark and were swept away.

The guard helped Lark up the steps into the car. On his lapel was a badge bearing his name: P. R. Przylucki.

A mother with three girls pushed past Lark. "Where is she?" the mother shouted. She was tall, authoritative, self-absorbed. She had long, blond hair and wore a pink coat, and was frowning as if she were in charge of the whole world.

Through the loudspeaker came a voice. "This is equipment number three fifty, about to depart for Detroit, Michigan, stopping at," and Lark sat quickly on the arm of a seat with her pen poised over the first page of a little notebook, "Hammond-Whiting, Michigan City, Niles, Kalamazoo, Battle Creek, Jackson, Ann Arbor, Dearborn, and Detroit."

"Excuse me," the mother said, bumping Lark aside. "We're trying to get to our seats. I have three children here, and I have to get them to their seats."

Large families, thought Lark. She feared she would have to hear this voice all the way to Detroit. Then miraculously the mother called out good-bye to the three girls. "Good-bye, darlings, sweeties. Have a wonderful time with Daddy." She blew kisses all over the car. "I'll call you tonight. Love you." She went to stand on the platform, where she blew kisses continuously at her girls, who sat looking down at her through the tinted glass and blowing kisses in return.

"Please have your tickets ready, and I hope you have a pleasant trip," concluded the voice over the loudspeaker. "All aboard." And the train slid away from the kissing woman in the pink coat.

Lark wrote in her notebook: Parker, architect; Przylucki, guard.

A young woman, older than Lark, threw herself into the seat beside Lark. "Oh, my God," she gasped. "I almost didn't make it. If it hadn't been for my R.A. I would have missed the train. I have a bad back and I can't lift my own suitcases. But my R.A. did it all for me."

"R.A.?" Lark asked.

"Research assistant," said the young woman. "I couldn't live without one."

Mr. P. R. Przylucki was moving through the car. "Three for Detroit, one for Dearborn here on the aisle, two for Ann Arbor on the window, Kalamazoo here on the aisle. Have your tickets ready." And behind him came the conductor writing numbers on the back of the passengers' seat tickets and sticking them in the luggage racks. When the conductor bent over her, Lark saw that his name was Dash, P. Dash. And when he had moved on, she wrote down his name: Dash, conductor.

The young woman next to her was still collapsed in her seat, fanning her face with her hand and gasping.

"Ladies and gentlemen," came a new voice over the loud-speaker. Lark picked up her pen. "May I have your attention. My name is William Washington, and I am your bar café car attendant for the duration of your journey. The bar car is open and has cocktails, food, coffee. I hope we can satisfy you, or come near to it." Lark was listening in wonder. "I would name everything we have, but it would take up too much of your day. The food car is located toward the front of the train—that's the direction in which you are traveling."

"I think a beer will be in order for me," said Lark's neighbor.

Lark wrote down: Washington, dining car waiter.

"We would like to take this opportunity to inform you that we will be stopping in Hammond-Whiting in approximately four and a half minutes to pick up passengers."

"I'm Pinky Boucher," said the young woman next to Lark.

"I'm a chemist at Northwestern, and I'm going to visit my sister and her husband, who is a tenured professor at Wayne State." She leant back and closed her eyes.

Lark wrote down: Boucher, chemist.

"Why don't we stop at South Bend?" Lark asked.

Pinky Boucher shrugged. "It's not on the route, I suppose."

A lanky man sitting in the seat in front yawned loudly and stretched, his left arm reaching so far back that it nearly hit Lark in the face. He struck up a conversation with a young woman student sitting across the aisle from him.

"I was supposed to go deer hunting this morning," he said, "but it is too wet and windy, and I already shot a deer, anyway. I'm an attorney."

"My brother's an attorney," said the student. "In Detroit too. Maybe you know him? Marlon Larson."

"Marlon? Sure I know Marlon. We went to college. I used to give him my statistics to do. I never analyzed my own statistics, I just got Marlon to run them through."

"He's my brother. I go to Notre Dame. I was supposed to be on a plane to Miami yesterday, but here I am going back north, heading into the cold instead. The Miami trip fell through. I'll tell him I saw you."

"Tell him you saw Bernie Herbert."

Lark wrote: Herbert, attorney.

"Come with me and have a beer." Pinky Boucher was addressing Lark. Lark, with her notebook in hand, followed her.

P. R. Przylucki was sitting in the bar car, drinking coffee from a Mickey Mouse mug. A jelly donut rested on a paper plate in front of him. "When I get home to Detroit . . ." he was saying to P. Dash, who sat in the booth opposite him.

"You have tomorrow off," said P. Dash.

"I'm going to rest up," said P. R. Przylucki. "You have the day after tomorrow off."

"I've got to get down to South Bend to see my mother," said P. Dash. "I won't have time to rest up."

"Two beers," Pinky Boucher said to the café attendant, who wore his W. Washington name tag on his pocket.

"You from Chicago?" he asked her.

She nodded.

"Great city," he said. "Great place to live. You, too?" he said to Lark. She shook her head. "Great place to visit, too."

Pinky Boucher threw herself onto a bar stool—she always moved in a sudden impulsive way—and folded her legs under her, so that sitting cross-legged on the bar stool, she looked like some kind of flower on a stem, sprouting from the floor of the café car.

"I'm twenty-eight and I've been married two times," Pinky said to Lark. "I've lived in fifteen different cities, went to seven different schools, I was born in South Bend, Indiana, and we moved to Washington, D.C., then California, then Los Alamos when I was seven. My father was a physicist working on the bomb." She raised her beer as if toasting either her father or the bomb. "What a scene. We should have stayed in South Bend. My baby brother was born in Los Alamos and died when he was two months old. They took away his body, and to this day we don't know where he is buried. They won't tell us. They didn't want anyone to examine the body or talk to the people on the project. Then we moved outside of Princeton." She drank her beer. "Where we met everybody who was anybody. When your father brings Einstein, Delmore Schwartz, and von Neumann home to supper, you are in awe of no one, ever. Look at my marriages. The first time it was a Princeton undergraduate, the second time I ran off to the Midwest with someone I just met, and now I'm thinking of marrying my R.A." She sighed. "But I can't bear children. What about you?"

"Children? I don't know." Lark had been thinking that Americans gave the essentials, did not indulge in the episode. Which was Solomon Blank's specialty.

"I mean everything."

Lark thought for a moment of parceling up her life for this

stranger, telling it the way Aristotle summarized Ulysses' story. But "I'm going to New York," she said to Pinky Boucher. "Probably to get married."

"Ladies and gentlemen, we would like to take this opportunity to inform you that we will be stopping in Niles, Michigan, in approximately four minutes. For those of you traveling farther east we will be changing to Eastern Standard Time at Niles. It is now eleven thirteen, exactly. Please take this opportunity to check the area under your seats and on the racks above you. Make sure to take all your personal property with you. Good day."

"Well, good luck," said Pinky Boucher. "Marriage is a tough business. If anyone knows that, I do."

When Lark got back to her seat she wrote to Henry Watter: "These are the stops on the railway line from Chicago to Detroit: Hammond-Whiting, Michigan City, Niles, Kalamazoo, Battle Creek, Jackson, Ann Arbor. Dearborn, but we do not pass through South Bend. Your brain stretcher was wrong. The architect is Parker, from Chicago; the chemist is Boucher, from South Bend; the attorney is Herbert, from Detroit; the guard is Przylucki, also from Detroit; the conductor is Dash, from South Bend; the waiter is Washington, from Chicago. This is what some call empirical education."

Lark dozed all night on the train from Detroit to New York. She opened her eyes at dawn to see a fleet of black ships on the Hudson, outlined against the pale sky. There appeared to be hundreds of them, massed ready to attack her, the sisters of the *Avis Maris* come to avenge her.

"The mothball fleet," said the conductor, whose name was now Flagg. "Old commercial vessels waiting on the Hudson in case there is a war and we need ships to be outfitted in a hurry. You never know these days, with the Russians and crazy things happening all the time. And the · bomb. Remember the Germans."

Lark remained awake as the train sped down the east bank, with the water only a few feet away, past the Palisades, then along the Harlem River, and into Manhattan and the tunnel that brought the train to Grand Central. Lark was aware that this was the most significant day of her life, that she was about to ascend to the surface of Manhattan and begin a new life, although Manhattan was not exactly the island she had had in mind when she packed her bag and planned her escape as a child in that house on the cliff in Park Avenue in that beach suburb of Sydney.

Tom was actually waiting at the exit from the platform. Lark recognized his shape, his waving arm as soon as she stepped off the train. She had telephoned him from Detroit, but she had not expected to see him, imagining him to be too busy to take a morning off to meet her.

"You look great," he said. "So tan. Like a Californian kid." He put his arm around her and gave her a squeeze.

"Don't call me a kid, please."

"Kid, kid, kid," said Tom.

While the taxi driver loaded her luggage into the trunk of his cab and onto the seat next to him, Lark looked away from Tom. As they drove she looked anxiously out the window.

"You look as if you're sick or something," said Tom.

"That Captain was mad," said Lark. "He made us walk on the coral in the middle of the ocean. He stopped at this tiny little island just to take on board this box, which he said was a coffin, but it matched exactly a box that had been loaded in . . ."

"Riverside Drive," said Tom, sweeping his hand across the window of the taxi, displaying the park and the Hudson as if he were a real-estate salesman. "Walking on coral. You lucky devil."

Lark paused, looking at the scene. Two thoughts came to her. She was away from home and words like "lucky devil" could be uttered without her mother saying, "No language." And Donna

Bird had indeed pointed out that the coral walk would make a good anecdote for Tom. "It was great," Lark said. "We just stood in the middle of the ocean. It was like walking on water. It was wonderful. A once-in-a-lifetime chance. Such an adventure. I'll show you my espadrilles, all cut up, and the piece of coral I kept as a souvenir."

Tom was looking out the window. "That's called really getting your feet wet."

"The island was wonderful, too."

"Get it?" said Tom. "Feet wet."

Lark gave a smile. "I get it. On the island the people were so interesting—the children were putting on a production of *Our Town*, and we went to a church service that lasted an hour and a half." She gave him a quick look to gauge her effect. "There was so much more to them than meets the eye of us jaded Westerners."

"Stop here," Tom cried to the driver through the partition. Then, "You should write it down." He handed the money to the driver, who held it in his hand for a moment, staring at it, then he looked back at Tom.

"Two bits?"

"Two bits," said Tom, and got out.

"Two bits?" said Lark, scrambling out behind Tom.

"Two bits," said Tom.

Lark waited for him to explain what it meant. Finally she asked, "What are two bits?"

"A quarter. Twenty-five cents."

The driver was leaning across the front seat, holding the coin out to Tom. "Here, take it. I don't need to take two bits from anyone."

"Okay," said Tom, and walked over to the window and took the money back.

Lark stood on the sidewalk, again waiting for Tom to explain. He pocketed the money and said nothing. "What was that all about?"

"That? Oh, he thought I should give him a bigger tip." He picked up the bags. "But I work hard for my money."

Tom threw open the door to the apartment and led Lark down the hallway to the living room. "Your quarters, *mademoiselle*." He threw open the French doors that led onto a little balcony overlooking the street and the university where he taught. He beckoned Lark to him and put his arm around her. "Welcome to Manhattan."

Lark nestled against Tom, shivering in the cold, and looked at the layers of buildings—red brick against stone and glass, gray cement against a gray sky, where airplanes seemed to duck in and out, now visible, now hidden by the tall buildings. Next door, where a new building was going up, a crane was poised like a giant bird on its giant leg.

Tom waved his free arm. "To the left New Jersey, to the right Harlem. And inside those buildings directly in front of you are three different libraries."

Through the bare branches of the trees growing out of the sidewalk, she could see the students bent over their books in one of the libraries. Lark vowed to spend as many hours as she could in those libraries, emulating those clever students, studying to become a worthy companion for Tom.

Opposite was a dormitory, where students lay on their beds or sat at their typewriters. She could actually hear their typing. In the faculty house, next to the dorm, a gathering of academics toasted their guest speaker. And from the terrace of the restaurant on the roof of a building above and beyond the applauding academics the diners looked down at the city, past Lark's apartment, at all this stone and brick and asphalt.

On her doorstep, Tom told her, among the children playing hopscotch and roller-skating and the drivers searching for parking spaces, could be a South American Communist who had been tortured for years in his homeland, or a lawyer who had prosecuted at Nuremberg, or a future National Security Adviser. "And if you watch long enough," Tom said, "you'll see a bag snatcher making a dash for the park. I give you the world, at your doorstep."

"Where is your apartment?"

"What's the matter, don't you like this place?"

"It's lovely," and indeed it was. So much light and space. "I just wanted to know where you would be."

"My place is small and filled with my junk, over by the river. Not roomy like this. I have needed to be alone." Lark nodded, disappointed. "I'll help you furnish this place." Lark was about to say she had very little money. "We'll do it for under a hundred dollars, you'll see. And I'm quite a handyman. I like working with wood."

"Is there anything you can't do?" Tom Brown seemed perfect. And this was now her life, near him. Perhaps this was her island, after all. Yet she felt gloomy. If only Donna Bird did not show up, evidence of her bad deed.

"Of course, there's my furniture you can use."

"You have extra furniture?"

"I thought I'd move in here with you."

Lark thought she must have misunderstood. "What?"

"If you don't mind me for a roommate, of course."

"No, no, that's wonderful."

"There are two bedrooms—I need to be alone, of course."

So, they were going to live together, after all. He had planned that all along. "But we'll share things? We'll talk?"

Tom laughed. "If you're good, maybe more than that. Look." Tom pointed at a white-haired man scurrying by. "That might be a Nobel Prize winner. That woman with the dog might be a famous novelist. And that," he pointed at a blond woman in lace-up boots, "might be a terrorist making bombs in her basement."

The mention of bombs made Lark ask again about the *Avis Maris*, reluctant as she was to change the subject from the idea of Tom's moving in with her. "Do you think there could have been a bomb in those boxes?"

Tom laughed his wonderful, hearty laugh, forcing Lark to smile, then laugh along with him. "Show me those shoes you said were cut up by the coral. Let's talk walking on coral first." Tom held her tighter. "You must be cold." He drew her inside and closed the glass doors.

Lark rummaged through her suitcase and held the espadrilles aloft. She turned the soles up. "You see, those loose ends of rope, cut by the coral?"

"You could have done that with a knife." Tom was still laughing, enjoying teasing her.

"Wait," she said, scrambling away from him. She searched for the piece of coral in the pockets of her various shorts and shirts. "There." She handed it to him.

"You could have bought this in some souvenir shop in Sydney, or Tacoma, for that matter." He tossed the coral in the air, butted it with his forehead like a soccer player, then kicked it with his heel and caught it.

Lark sat on the floor. "Now about bombs. Seriously."

"Seriously," said Tom, "anything is possible. If you can even think of it, then it can be done." And he laughed again, falling down on the bare floor. Lark lay down beside him. "And if you're good," he said, sitting up, "I'll give you your mail now." He pulled a light-blue airmail letter out of his pocket. Lark grabbed it and sat up.

"I do believe," Mrs. Watter wrote, "that this is the first time I have ever used an aerogramme in my entire life." The folded letter had been addressed to Lark, care of Tom. "I thought I had lost your father the other day. He went around the rocks. I had gone into town early to shop, since we had had about a fortnight of constant rain, but it stayed fine for that day. I like to go into town, especially to some of those current affairs talks they have in the evenings. I generally do not stay in that late. I have to make sure I am on the bus and on the way home, because your father frets if I'm not there, and he needs his dinner on time. When I got home he wasn't there. I could tell he hadn't been in all day—no telltale sand on the floor from the beach. I ran around the rocks, thinking he had been taken by the blowhole. And there he was, at the edge of the blowhole, just staring. So I brought him home. He says to tell you that Sydney time is ten hours ahead of Greenwich mean time. He is still building in the basement, so that is a good sign. He fixed a lock on the box the other day, but he did it wrong. He fixed it so that the thing locks only from the inside. But I didn't say anything to him. He's so sensitive to criticism and interference, and so alone. Too, I think he misses you. As we all do, of course."

"What are these?" Tom was examining the metal lamp and the fly whisk that Lark had taken from Donna Bird's cabin. He held the whisk and whirled it around his head, making a figure eight. "A Polynesian pompom?"

"Those," Lark said, "are, I suppose, artifacts. From the island." She paused. "Actually, they're Donna Bird's. I didn't want them to get lost." Another pause. "She seemed to value them."

"That's very thoughtful of you." Tom got up from the floor and pulled Lark to her feet. "Let's take a turn around the block. We can take these things to Manfred."

"Now? Couldn't it wait?"

"It's only around the block. I want to show you my turf. He'll want to hear about Donna. Come on."

Tom was so energetic, dazzling. And they were going to live together in this dazzling, energetic city, center of the universe. "I'm glad you're going to be my roommate, and not Donna Bird."

"You need someone to show you the ropes," Tom said. "Otherwise you might get into trouble."

Lark and Tom forced their way down the windy hill to the river. Tom was carrying the fly whisk and the lamp in a plastic shopping bag that ballooned in the wind.

Lark held onto Tom's arm and leant her head against him.

"It's ten degrees colder down here by the river than where we are," said Tom cheerfully, swinging the shopping bag.

We. Lark loved the word, now that it was uttered by Tom and embraced her. We. Tom and Lark. And the prospect of facing Donna Bird's father, the legendary Manfred Bird, did not seem such a terrible ordeal, after all.

They heard no sound after they rang the doorbell.

"They must be out," said Lark, hoping for a reprieve. "We can come another time."

"Don't be silly. They buzzed us in downstairs. They're definitely home. It always takes them a long time to get to the door."

Then, with no preliminary sound or footsteps, the door opened a little way and a woman's round, placid face appeared in the opening. Her gray hair was braided and tied in blue ribbons, on which her name, Portia, was stenciled in red. Her face was smooth, young, but her manner and expression seemed much older, so that Lark could not tell if she was twenty or fifty. Portia pulled the door open a little more.

"Can you get in? Menfred has piled stuff in the hallway and I can't get the door open any further." Portia's mouth hardly moved when she spoke. She seemed reluctant to let the words escape and fly away. At rest, the lips came together into a little rose, giving the impression that talking, uttering words and sounds, was vulgar and altogether to be done as discreetly as possible. "He's awaiting a new shipment of really good stuff, so he's pecked up some old stuff and he's going to donate a lot of it to museums. Then we'll be able to move around a bit."

Lark squeezed through the opening and into a dark hallway, which, she saw after her eyes adjusted to the gloom, was completely filled with boxes and crates. It looked like a warehouse, an ill-kept stockroom.

"Just walk straight through to the living room," said Portia.

Walking was hardly possible. Among the boxes was a narrow path, like a track through the jungle, barely wide enough for a body to pass, and every now and then, where a box protruded beyond the others, Lark had to turn sideways.

Tom was crashing along behind her. "How's the old man?" he asked Portia over his shoulder.

"He's livid today," said Portia. "Fit to be tied. I'm gled you're here. You can distrect him. He just got beck some proofs and they're botched." At times the vowels were like prisoners, crowding forward in her mouth, awaiting their chance, even if it meant twisting forth in a distorted form.

Lark stood at the entrance of the room to which the jungle path had led her. Tom bumped into her. "Hey," he said.

On the wall directly opposite Lark was a long wooden rack, elaborately carved, with masks that looked like decorated human skulls in every opening.

From behind Tom, Portia called, "Go on in. Find somewhere to sit."

Lark shuffled her way into the room. The floor was completely covered with stacks of newspapers and journals. Every horizontal surface was similarly obscured—the radiator, the table, the file cabinet. A path led through the papers to the kitchen and to several of the chairs, which like the floor were all stacked with papers. Lark had seen disorder and disarray before, but not to this degree. But above the debris, which formed a knee-high layer on the floor, was an extraordinary order. Fixed to the walls were shelves and glass cases and hooks, as in a museum, where objects that Lark guessed Manfred Bird had collected on his travels were displayed. His "stuff."

Running the length of the wall, beneath the rack of masks, which dominated the room, were several brackets on which rested a long pole carved in the shape of a crocodile, with carved turtles and cicadalike insects, possibly praying mantises, infesting its back. In the corner, the height of a tall man, was a hollow log, with a carved head at the top and a hole like the slit of a money box along its length. In a glass case completely covering the adjoining wall were fans, bowls, clubs, paddles, masks.

"Sit anywhere," said Portia. "Menfred doesn't mind if you sit on his papers. Just don't disturb the order, that's all."

Lark picked her way along one of the paths to what she guessed was a chair, on the seat of which was a stack of manila folders. Tom remained standing, having picked up one of the journals and begun leafing through it. Portia stood at the door, her hands clasped, smiling. Then she flicked on the light and the track lighting along the ceiling lit up the wall displays, the outlines of the carvings forming shadows on the wall behind. Portia flicked on another switch, and the lights within the glass cases came on.

"That'll give you a better view. Everyone who comes wants to see Menfred's things. They're temperature-controlled in those cases. That basketry deteriorates so quickly in the humidity."

What had looked like a pile of rushes, with illumination became a basket with legs and arms, mimicking a decapitated body.

"Impressive, isn't it," said Portia when she saw Lark looking at the bowl. "It's made from sago spathe and was used in ceremonies that preceded headhunting raids. Menfred, my husband, who as you know is a famous anthropologist and is tenured at the university, has spent a lifetime collecting. He recognized the value of primitive art before almost anyone with the exception of Picasso and some of those Frenchmen. And he has single-handedly saved Oceanic art from destruction by time and by the natives themselves who don't see anything in it. Menfred has some of the rarest and best specimens extant. Sit down. Please."

Lark sat gingerly on the pile of folders.

"Where's everyone?" Tom asked.

"I've sent the boys out to play. They're under the thrit of dith not to come beck until dark." She paused, pursing her lips. "The boys bother Menfred when he's trying to work, and they make such a mess in the house. Little sevidges. We should donate them to a museum." Portia giggled, placing a few fingers in front of her mouth to hide the display. "They could keep them in glass cases all clean and out of mischief and tex deductible.

The baby's asleep, of course. He won't be any trouble until he starts meddling with Menfred's stuff."

Tom tossed the journal back on its pile. "So, Portia, what are you working on these days?" Tom was driven to ask a question. Lark attributed his apparent discomfort and preoccupation with the journal to his awkwardness at her own presence on what he called his turf.

"You won't believe it. I'm scrambling Menfred's files." She nodded at the file cabinet in the corner, draped in papers and books. "There are dozens of others in his study. I'm changing the labels. Menfred thinks there's going to be some kind of Communist revolution soon, and they'll seize all his stuff. So we're subverting our own system, overturning the right classifications, before they do. I'm keeping a code, of course, so that we'll know what's what."

"Do you think it's really necessary?" Tom asked.

"Menfred thinks it is. He's got a lot of sensitive material in the apartment and in the files." She smiled at Lark. "And what will you work on, now that you're here? You have no job, Tom said? It's possible Menfred could find you a few hours' work. He needs a girl Friday."

A rumble and a growling reached them from several rooms away.

"That's Menfred. I told you he's like a wounded tiger right now."

Along the hallway came what seemed to Lark like giant footsteps, and she was overcome with a fear and trembling, *das Schaudern*, the best of man, as Donna Bird would have pointed out. "He's a pit, really," said Portia in an aside to Lark. "I was one of his students. His bark is worse then his bite."

"Who is it? I wasn't expecting visitors," growled the professor, as he made his way with delicacy past his boxes and crates.

"It's only Tom," called Portia. "And a friend."

"Whenever these illiterate typesetters come across a three-letter word, they think any three-letter word will do, any word at all." At the doorway stood a lanky white-haired man who seemed to stretch to the ceiling. He was all angles, his jaw, shoulders, elbows, knees, prominent. His hair stood on end in thick spikes. In the doorway, knees slightly bent, eyes darting about, ready to spring, he looked like a piece of his own art collection. "I just got my proofs on slash-and-burn, and of course they're atrocious," he bellowed.

"He's upset today," said Portia.

"They send them to the Philippines to save money and then primitive ignorami do the typesetting. Before that it was Hong Kong, same thing."

"The publisher says it saves an awful lot of money, but of course in the ind we pay because Menfred has to spend all his precious time correcting them and then correcting them again."

So this was Manfred Bird, father of Donna Bird, who was stranded at this moment on a minuscule island because of Lark. And standing next to him, giving a simultaneous interpretation of his words, was Portia Bird, Donna's stepmother.

"Sit, Tom, sit," said Portia.

Because of the clutter in the room, no one moved. Lark sat upright on the folders opposite Manfred and Portia at the door, and on the path between them stood Tom, characters waiting to be told their next lines.

Tom looked around, chose a path, and maneuvered along it to an upright chair in front of one of the cases. He turned around and before sitting said, "This is Lark. Tell him about Donna."

"Well, where is she?"

"On an island," said Lark, the first words she had uttered since arriving at the Birds'. She cleared her throat. "She knew that the islanders n-needed her. She is helping them."

"Helping? How?"

"Helping them to understand their own culture."

"I've been wanting to see her," said Manfred.

Portia patted his arm. "There, there," she soothed. "She'll turn up one day, when you least expect it. She's so independent. She's helping people. Doing worthwhile work."

"A one-woman Peace Corps. She should have been quadruplets," said Manfred Bird. "She's very, very intelligent, you know. An IQ off the charts. Wins all the prizes. Since she was in kindergarten." Lark could not tell if he was mocking or serious. "And that rascal, the Captain? He said he had changed his plans, trouble with the ship. He didn't come to New York."

"We ran aground," said Lark.

"Good grief. He didn't tell me that. No wonder he wrote and didn't telephone me. He knew I'd murder him if I spoke to him." Portia patted his arm again. "He could have lost all my stuff. It could have gone to the bottom. The ocean is filled with lost treasures."

"And now that governments of these countries are making it harder for experts like Menfred to get the art out and save it, every shipment is doubly precious," said Portia. "Luckily Menfred has ways to carry on his mission to preserve it all."

"I didn't know you had stuff on the *Avis Maris*," said Lark.

"Of course. I've known the Captain since the war. He had to surrender to me. His ship was filled with tapestries he had managed to rescue from the peasants. German peasants were no different from other peasants. They were cutting up these priceless treasures for blankets. We hit it off immediately. Portia, where's my stool?"

Manfred Bird had decided to sit, since the conversation with these visitors showed signs of going on a little longer than most conversations that took place in that apartment. Portia squeezed past him, then returned with a carved wooden stool. Manfred held it up for Lark to see. "A debating stool, from the Sepiks, New Guinea." He placed it in the doorway and sat down, peering over the low wall of newspapers.

"Was it in boxes? Your stuff?" Lark asked. She looked at the carved pole and the log figure with the slit along the torso. "Man-sized boxes?"

"What happened to the cargo? That Captain is a coward. He's a good fellow, but a coward."

"Only the aluminum rods were ditched," said Lark slowly. "How do you get your stuff, then?"

"I have my ways," said Manfred.

"He has chennels," said Portia. "Contects."

"Portia is his New Zealand connection," said Tom, who had been uncharacteristically silent.

"I'm from New Zealand," said Portia. "My family has always been in government, public service."

"And the island and Mr. Weiss? Is he a connection, too? And the *Avis Maris?*"

"Don't interrogate him," Tom said quietly to her. "Here, Manfred." He reached into the shopping bag on the pile of magazines beside him and held up the lamp and whisk. "Lark brought Donna's stuff for you."

Portia shuttled over to get the objects and take them back to Manfred, winking at Tom and smiling in gratitude.

"Ah-ha," said Manfred. "That lamp, metal, must be from the East Indies somewhere, not Polynesia or Melanesia. Maybe Sumatra. Maybe Nias."

"She got them from a man in the street on the island, who now wears her raincoat and carries her umbrella."

"A chip off the old block. She's devoted to me. The perfect daughter. She helps me with my work, my investigations. Now, luckily, I have Portia, while Donna goes off all the time." Portia winked at Tom again, while Manfred, who looked as if he might cheer up a bit, examined the little lamp. "My network is getting wider and wider," he said. "Like the old routes they used to follow in their canoes. Stuff is finding its way along the trail to me, and my trail is finding its way farther and farther to more stuff. Of course, this lamp is not strictly in my area of expertise, but I can tell it's of interest historically and artistically. I'll get the museum to evaluate it. It could pay for Donna's trip."

Portia left his side and sat on a stack of journals near Lark. "He's such an original," she confided. "A first-rate mind. Everyone adores him. He's a pit. He's courageous, too. You know what he did on his first field trip?—that was before I married him, of course, when field work was still relatively new—he destroyed all the statues in the village he was studying."

"What on earth for?" Lark asked.

"Well, they were all male figures with erect penises, really large, much larger than life, really quite out of proportion. So he cut them off, the penises. He told the villagers they were obscene."

"I thought that's what anthropology was all about, statues, rituals, perceptions of the world. I thought anthropologists were supposed to be neutral, blend in."

"Menfred knew that it was the Westerners bringing with them their obsession with sex and power that had influenced the art of the people. The statues weren't truly indigenous."

"Ah-ha, you see," said Tom. "Another example of the yearning to return to the state of unicellularity. The obsession with sex and penetration has nothing whatsoever to do with sex and penetration."

"Now this fly whisk," said Manfred, flicking it around. "This is the real thing. Donna certainly has an eye."

"He believes," said Portia, "that those who make art and by extension those who revere art and preserve it, are very far along on the road to divinity. They have a lot of mana. That's why this shipment is so important. It contains an ancestor pole—he's already collected one for each of the boys, like that one." She pointed to the long carved pole resting on brackets on the wall. "This new one was to be for Donna."

"If anything happens to it," growled Manfred. He stood up

and reached across what seemed to be the whole room and seized one of his skull masks and wiggled it at Tom and Lark.

*Das Schaudern, das Schaudern,* Lark chanted to herself, like a little *Lied.*

"He's just joking," interpreted Portia. "Ancestor poles are used in ceremonies to incite the living to avenge wrongs done to them." She stood up. "Shell I make coffee? Wouldn't you like a glass of water?"

Manfred looked alarmed.

Lark stood up. "Let's just not bother. We should really be going."

Manfred eased himself off his stool, picked it up and placed it on top of a pile of journals so that Lark and Tom could pass into the hallway and leave.

At the door Portia said, "We are very gled to meet you. Tom told us you were coming. We were rather hoping that Donna would settle down with Tom, who is like a son to Menfred already. But never mind. Donna has whims of her own, and if she chose to stay on the island, then so be it."

Portia opened the door, and three boys, ranging in age from six to twelve or so, darted past Lark and Tom as they stepped into the corridor; they scrambled over the boxes and past Portia and disappeared into the gloom of the hall.

"Little sevidges," said Portia. "They were in the corridor all the time, waiting."

"It is cold outside," said Lark.

"Boys, you promised," Portia called after them. She turned back to Tom and Lark, smiling. "He'll simply murder them one day."

Tom hugged Lark to him as they staggered back up the hill in the icy wind that came off the river. "So. How's that for your first afternoon in New York?" He smiled a little but seemed subdued. "Manfred doesn't give just anyone an audience."

"Do you really like him?" Lark welcomed the cold after Manfred Bird's suffocating living room.

"He's my mentor. I owe my career to him."

"I think he really is mad. And he talks like a Nazi."

"Everyone admires him," said Tom. "No one says anything bad about him, ever."

"How can you go along with it, that performance? That conceit?" Lark was exhilarated because Tom seemed depressed, vulnerable, and he even seemed to be about to agree with her on the subject of Manfred.

"I am like a son. He has been grooming me ever since I was his graduate student to replace him, take over the department when he retires."

They walked for a while in silence. Lark felt she might burst from the excitement of having Tom so close.

"Say," Tom cried suddenly, shaking Lark from his arm. "Look at that!" He went to the curb, where a padded armchair had been placed under a tree, near a trash can on the corner. It was a comfortable-looking old chair with a floral slipcover. Tom sat himself in it, crossing and recrossing his legs, then sinking down with his legs stretched out in front, like Goldilocks seeking the right position. "What people throw away in this capitalist society!"

"It must belong to someone," said Lark.

Tom sprang up and circled the chair, giving it a little kick now and then and a slap on the arms. "Not bad for free." He motioned to Lark to help him pick it up.

"Isn't this stealing?"

"Trust me," Tom said. "This is the way it's done here. People don't leave things on the sidewalk if they don't intend someone to take them. The only crime is that we have constructed a society in which it's easier for people to discard perfectly good items than to keep them."

Lark and Tom lugged the armchair back to the apartment.

Tom placed it in a corner and sat in it, his arms and hands placed squarely on the arms. He was looking into the distance, his head on one side, as if he were listening for something, getting acquainted with the chair.

Lark ran water into the kettle to make tea. "You should stand up to him," she said, trying to get Tom's attention back to Manfred Bird and have him side with her against him. "You and he have nothing in common. You and he hold opposite views. You're one of the people he would call a Communist. It's because of people like you that he's scrambling those files of his." She stood at the door of the living room, measuring her effect on Tom. "And I thought you said art belonged to the people. Remember? Butter, guns, and art. Manfred doesn't think so, stealing and hoarding all that stuff."

"Manfred is people." Tom shook his head and frowned. "And Manfred is the most brilliant anthropologist in the world."

"I don't believe it."

"You don't know anything about anthropology." Tom's voice was sharp, warning her not to press any further. Then suddenly he held his arms wide open. "Larkie, come here and sit on my knee." And when she had done that, he said, "Let's go to bed."

"Together? Now? You really mean it?"

"Strange but true. Take me to bed," Tom said, "and then you can stop talking about Manfred."

And finally Lark and Tom made love in the apartment they now shared in Manhattan. The whole voyage and miseries of the past weeks now seemed worthwhile. She had reached Tom, after the vicissitudes of her journey, and he had accepted her, even needed her.

"I've decided to give a party in your honor, to introduce you to all my friends."

Lark was half asleep. Tom poked her awake. He sat up and began pulling on his clothes. "A peanut party. It's BYO." He pronounced it to rhyme with Ohio, then leapt up. "Got to get to work. All play and no work makes Jack a dull boy."

"Beewhyo?"

"B-Y-O. Bring your own, booze, that is. You just bring your charming self. I'll supply the nuts." He bent over and poked her again. "Get it? Nuts."

"I get it."

"We'll invite everyone I know."

Lark stood among Italians, Germans, Dutchmen, and Jamaicans, among Carnegie Fellows and Woodrow Wilson Fellows and Rhodes Scholars, the so-called cream of the world's young people, who would one day be prime ministers and diplomats and publishers of influential newspapers.

Elizabeth, an old college classmate of Tom's, was there, with her husband, Jean-Claude, a French nuclear physicist. And there was one Russian, whom everyone fussed over. It was hard to get real Russians, Russians who were not refugees or émigrés, to come to a party.

"I have fever," said the Russian Yuri apologetically, and stayed in the old armchair in the corner all night, looking ill. "But I want to come to this American party, so I come." He spoke English with difficulty. "Excuse, please. I do not say well. My English is very basic." He said that he was a writer, an analyst of society, that he was interested in contemporary Western culture, and that he hoped to write a monograph. He took out a little note pad and wrote everyone's name down. "I do not remember names well," he said.

"Alas, poor Yuri," Tom kept saying, prolonging laughing at his pun as he wielded his camera, snapping more portraits for his collection.

"Not me," said Yuri, holding his hands up every time Tom turned to him with his camera. "I am ugly."

Elizabeth questioned him about the role of women in the Soviet Union, Tom commented on industrial development, Jean-Claude asked about the Soviet stance toward nuclear disarmament.

Lark handed around peanuts, then stood by the double doors at the balcony, fiddling with her glass, nodding now and then at someone, anyone, in order to demonstrate that this was not a mute, not a dummy, that Tom had brought with him to New York.

Tom turned one of the coffee tables upside down to show the guests at the peanut party how easy and cheap it had been to make them. He had devised them himself—planks of wood, beautifully oiled by Tom, with painted coffee cans for legs.

"You can count on Tom to come up with something different," Elizabeth called, and Lark was pleased this was the man she had chosen to follow and love truly.

She and Tom had pasted khaki burlap on the walls and pinned to it Beardsley prints and a Javanese batik. In the corner was a New England cheese mold. They had gone through the streets at night picking up old furniture, discarded and intended for collection by the sanitation department.

Tom, having finished the demonstration with the coffee tables, was now waving his arms at the apartment.

"We didn't choose any of this just because it made a good conversation piece or fitted in with the décor," he was saying. "There's an interesting story to tell about every object in here." He slapped the arm of Yuri's chair. "We found this on the corner the other day. Those Beardsleys I came across in San Francisco on the way from Sydney. The cheese mold is a friend's, maybe we'll make some cheese one day." He looked around for Lark. "Larkie, show them the bookshelves." And he threw himself onto a pile of cushions on the floor.

As if she were displaying a coveted prize in a game show, Lark walked to the shelves, which covered one whole wall, and touched them with one hand, smiling at the guests. "He just got the cheapest lumber and hammered it all together himself," she squeaked. "Isn't it comical the way the sloping floor of this apartment makes them look as if they might keel right over?"

"Give them a push, Larkie," Tom said from the floor.

Lark touched the shelves, and the whole structure swayed. Tom laughed uproariously. "And the marble," he called.

Lark took a marble from the top shelf and placed it on the floor. "It doesn't stop rolling until it has reached the other side of the room," she announced.

The guests watched the marble roll across the room, some of them skipping out of the way, Tom calling out, "Come on, faster," as if it were a horse.

After the marble disappeared under Yuri's chair, Tom looked at his watch.

Lark went back to stand by the balcony doors. Elizabeth came up to her and put her arm around her. "It's great you're here. Jean-Claude and I are going to France." She patted her abdomen. "We're going to have a little Frenchman in May. We hated to leave Tom without someone. Most men can't get along very well alone. Say, Tom's quite something, isn't he? Quite a catch. You should get married. You're a cute couple."

"I'm not clever enough for him," said Lark.

"Don't kid yourself," said Elizabeth. "I'll tell you something. Just subscribe to *The New Republic, The New York Review of Books,* and read I. F. Stone's *Weekly.* That's all it takes. Don't tell him I told you that." She looked around guiltily, then giggled. "If you were mixing with the Ford Foundation lot, all you'd have to read is *The New Yorker,* and that would do it. It takes a bit more work to be on the left, to be a critic. But personally I can't wait to get away from all this." Then realizing she might be misunderstood, she said, "Not this party, of course, great party, but this," and she indicated the university, New York City, the whole country.

"I like it here," said Lark.

"But I grew up here. That's the difference," said Elizabeth, and wandered off.

A young Irishman came and stood next to Lark. He glowered at the guests ranged again around the feverish Yuri in Lark's living room.

"He's no writer," said the Irishman, nodding at the Russian. "He's a spy. K.G.B., of course. What I object to is his sullying the name of real writers."

"It's possible," said Lark, "that everyone in this room is a spy. You could be I.R.A., that German could be N.A.T.O."

Tom was standing on a chair with his camera, photographing Yuri over the heads of his admirers. Yuri was writing down yet another name. "How you spell that?"

"Tom could be C.I.A.," said Lark. She was glad to be talking to someone, glad that someone had come to stand beside her and replace Elizabeth.

"That's daft," said the Irishman. "The West is free. We don't spy on people. Our governments don't lie. They, the Communists, lie. And the British, of course."

Lark turned to take a good look at him, to see if he was being sarcastic. He was drinking his beer, staring at the crowd at the other side of the room.

"Perhaps he is writing a polygraph," she said, then, when he did not respond, she asked, "And what do you do? What are you working on at the moment?" At least she had learned the right questions.

"I'm a writer," said the Irishman.

"It's possible, in that case, that all the people in this room are writers, if they're not spies," said Lark, sighing.

The Irishman looked down at her. "I'm a real writer," he said. "Poetry." He pulled from his pocket a copy of his book and let Lark hold it.

This was the first poet Lark had ever met. She said the title aloud." "*Alone in the Garden*. The Garden of Eden?" She toyed with the idea of being alone in Eden. Had Adam been alone in the garden, the species would not even exist. If that were the case, Tom's theory of a unicellular unconscious would not be necessary.

"Of course not," he said. "Gethsemane."

"Gethsemane? Oh, Gethsemane," said Lark quickly. She had always thought Gethsemane rhymed with Charlemagne, and she was glad to discover her mistake, since she had already blundered by making Yosemite rhyme with Vegemite.

"Allow me to present my book to you. I always carry a copy with me so that I can give it away," said the Irishman. He took a pen from his pocket. "But first I must inscribe it. What did you say your name was?"

"I'm the guest of honor, actually," said Lark. "This party is supposed to be for me. I even live here."

The Irishman did not look up from his poised pen. "What is the name?" And he wrote, "For Lark, may she at Heaven's Gate sing."

"I don't sing," said Lark. "I don't do anything."

The Irishman pocketed his pen. "When I was eighteen, I decided there were three things I had to do before I was twenty-five. First, to write a book and get it published. Second, to represent Ireland in the Olympic Games. Third, to get a master's degree in America. As you can see, I have achieved the first. I can assure you that I have achieved the second. I have run for Ireland. And I am on my way to achieving the third, with eighteen months left."

"I only wanted one thing," said Lark, "and that was to run away. I have done that. Well, two things. I wanted to find true love, too."

"I have applied to the Harvard Business School," the Irishman went on. "I wrote and asked Ted Kennedy for a reference. The Kennedys come from the same town as my grandfather. I told him we were more or less cousins. Ted has invited me to Hyannis to visit."

Three boys in gray serge trousers and yachting jackets, look-ing like miniature men engaged in a guerrilla action, suddenly appeared before Lark and the Irishman, surging around them, burrowing past them, easing them to the side of the balcony doors. They opened the doors, flung the wide, and lined up on the balcony. These were the Bird boys. The tallest boy dug in his pockets to find objects to drop over the edge. Within a sec-ond or two he was releasing paper clips and pieces of paper onto the street below. Cold air gushed into the apartment.

"Boys, boys, cut that out," bellowed Manfred Bird's voice from the other side of the room. At the same time Portia ap-peared quietly at Lark's side and was pulling at the collars of the boys' blazers. "Remember, boys," she said softly, "you're under the thrit of dith to behave like gentlemen for the rest of your lives." She turned to Lark. "They have promised to behave themselves until they are at least seventeen years old or go to college and leave the nest, whichever comes first. That was after we discovered them throwing water bombs and once a co-conut from our windows onto the Drive. As you know, we live in a spacious apartment on the river. Menfred's a tenured, full professor. He will murder them if they throw anything else. Boys, you promised." She yanked one boy at a time inside and closed the doors. "Such bed boys. Sevidges," she said happily, hardly moving her lips. "No bitter than sevidges in the jungle."

The boys went off prowling around the living room, stubbing their shoes against the chairs and the little coffee tables.

"Thrit of dith," Portia called after them.

Lark smiled slightly at Portia, whose gray hair tonight was pulled back into a pony tail. She had not asked Tom if the Birds were coming, feeling that if she did not mention their name, they might not appear.

"I have just heard that my stuff has been impounded in Taco-ma. It's not on its way here at all. An investigation, can you believe it, and me the best anthropologist this country has." Manfred Bird was yelling loudly enough for the whole room to hear, although he was addressing Tom, who rocked back and forth on his heels, his hands in his pockets, adhering to his informality. "That's tough, Manfred," he said.

"Imagine, investigating my stuff. That's petty bureaucrats for you. I'll have to call in the big guns from D.C. if this doesn't cease. I had valuable stuff in that shipment."

The guests drifted away from the feverish Yuri, sunk deep in his chair yet conversing bravely, and gathered around the impressive Professor Bird.

Portia, next to Lark, was shaking her head. "He gets so upset," she said. "That's my husband for you. The students just adore him."

"Professor Bird," said Elizabeth, "would you share with us your current thinking on north-south relations?"

"I'll tell you one thing," Professor Bird barked at the room in general, "I'm going to have to spend all my time on leave just changing 'the' to 'are' and 'was' to 'its.'" He looked at his watch, as if his leave was about to begin any minute. "The proofs of my latest book have been botched, once again, inevitably."

"We've got a sabbetical," Portia said. "We're leaving at the end of the semester for the Pacific again. He has so much groundbreaking work still to complete."

"And I'll tell you another thing," yelled Professor Bird, "travel doesn't broaden, it narrows. People should stay at home. Whole societies have been destroyed overnight because of tourists and bureaucrats. Soon there won't be any work for me to do, no society to observe or investigate. It will be too late."

"But you travel, sir," said Jean-Claude deferentially, laughing at the same time to show he was joking.

"I'm an anthropologist. I am obliged to travel. It's absolutely a condition of the profession. I and my family blend in. We don't spoil things. But I'd rather stay peacefully at home."

"He has to check a few things for his book," said Portia to those near her. "He's trying to whittle a few anthropological myths down to size. And he's always looking to expand his collection. For posterity. If we ever divorce, I'll hev to hev hef—that'll be enough to live on for some time," and she let out a long giggle to show that she was joking.

"You should all stay at home." Professor Bird leant against the table, still addressing the guests in the room as if he were giving a lecture.

"Go home, all of you," Professor Bird was shouting and pointing at the guests. "You're from Trinidad? Go home. And you? France? Go home."

"Oh, dear, I hope the boys aren't being bed," said Portia. "I don't see or hear them. I'd better go and look."

"What are you working on now, Professor?" Elizabeth asked.

"Hm? Working on? Names. I collect names now."

"How very, very interesting," said Elizabeth. "Names, collecting names. How original. Ah, for what purpose, then, sir, are these names being collected?"

"They're for my Book of Names. I'm collecting every name on earth. My daughter helps me. We're like geologists collecting rocks."

"Ah-ha," said Elizabeth, as if everything were now clear. She nodded thoughtfully.

"The Russian collects names, too," the Irishman called out, still standing next to Lark.

"Ha, ha," croaked Yuri, placing his notebook of names in an inside pocket and holding his jacket closed. "I have bad memory."

The Irishman snorted. "And so does the K.G.B., I suppose."

"The C.I.A. collects names, too, remember," someone responded. "They'd love Manfred's list. Maybe he's their supplier of names."

And everyone burst into laughter at the notion. Lark frowned, remembering Donna's list of names in green ink and the hidden message about the bomb. Perhaps it really was just a list of names, after all, collected for her father.

Portia led the three boys back into the room. The oldest stumbled over one of the low-slung coffee tables, kicking it partway across the room. One of the coffee-can legs came loose and fell off, and the plank of wood that formed the tabletop tilted, sending all the ashtrays and glasses spilling onto the floor.

"I can fix it or make another one," said Tom. "No sweat."

"Thrit of dith" said Portia to her boys, wagging her finger at them. Clearly they had been up to something.

"I'm afraid I found them going through your clothes," she said to Lark. "They said they were looking for a piece of string."

"I'll show you what I mean," cried Professor Bird. "Everyone," he called out, bringing the room to attention. "Take a sheet of paper. Write down what I tell you. I'll show you what I mean. Empirical education, it's called. Much better than my explaining." He clapped his hands. "Paper? Paper?"

Portia ran to Tom, who was picking up the debris from the collapsed coffee table. "Do you have paper?"

Tom called to Lark. "Paper? Do you have paper?"

Lark gave him a yellow note pad. Tom handed it to Portia. Portia took it to Professor Bird, who, with a wave of his hand, directed her to distribute sheets to everyone in the room. "Pencils?" he called, and the same procedure was followed, until everyone held a pen or a pencil, ready to play his game. "Boys, boys, come along, you join in, too." The boys shuffled toward him. "We're about to play the Game of Names."

"Boring," muttered the oldest boy. "Do we have to?" asked another.

"Of course, we'll all play." Professor Bird looked around the group, beyond Portia and the boys. "The Game of Names is enlightening, and it passes the time. And each time you discover new names."

The boys groaned.

"Sit, boys, sit," said Portia, and the boys fell to the floor sullenly.

"You begin at the beginning. The aim, eventually, is to write down the name of everyone you have ever met. Everyone. It's an undertaking of years. You write down the name of your father, your mother, brothers and sisters, then aunts and uncles, the first people you remember, such as your doctor, neighbors, cousins. Then take, say, your first-grade class and write down the name of the teacher and the other pupils. But tonight we'll just do last week. Write down the name of everyone you met last week."

Yuri stood up, buttoning up his jacket. "I must go now," he said. He looked at his watch. "I am expected in Rotterdam."

"Rotterdam?" everyone protested. "That means we won't be able to continue the dialogue begun here tonight," one said.

"Maybe he means Rotterdam, New York," said another.

"Sorry, sorry," said Yuri. "I must write my monograph in Rotterdam. My plane leaves soon from Kennedy." He turned to Jean-Claude. "I enjoy our conversation. I am interesting to know that we shall soon all put a nuclear bomb in a bathtub. Ha, ha."

"Maybe even in the trunk of a car, one day soon," said Jean-Claude.

The Russian patted Jean-Claude on the back in a feebly jovial way. "Ha, ha, very interested."

Professor Bird nodded curtly at Yuri. "He should be going back to Moscow, where he belongs." He strode over to where Lark was standing, to watch from the sidelines, as everyone said good-bye to Yuri and wished that he would return soon. Again, the scene before her seemed to Lark to resemble a work-in-progress, a play in its early stages.

"Write, everyone, write," directed Manfred Bird, after Yuri had left.

"Oh, this is fun," said Elizabeth, and started scribbling lists of names.

"I'll tell you the story of your life, just from the list," said Professor Bird. "I can tell by the names. I'm an anthropologist. I'm sensitive to names. Come on"—he saw that Lark was not writing—"write."

Because Lark was unwilling to attract his attention any further, she began to write. But she went back to the beginning. Henry Watter, Alice Water. Mr. and Mrs. Baker. Solomon Blank. Gilbert Blank. Ellice Blank. Marshall Blank. Mr. and Mrs. Blank. And so on. If she was lucky, she would not have to speak with Manfred Bird at all the whole evening. She wondered why Donna had tried to goad her into writing down her own list of names on board the *Avis Maris*. Was she just an extension of Manfred Bird, the ideal daughter, like Anna Freud, assisting him eternally, ceaselessly, no matter where in the world she was?

Professor Bird paced up and down, like a proctor in an exam.

"Solomon, Gilbert, Ellice, Marshall?" Elizabeth was peering over Lark's shoulder.

"They were named after islands in the Pacific," Lark whispered to her.

"No talking," said Professor Bird.

"Sorry," said Elizabeth, going back to her own list.

Professor Bird cried out, "Time's up. Let me have your names." He seized Elizabeth's list, and Jean-Claude's. As he held his hand out for Lark's, she found herself holding onto it.

"I'll keep mine. I haven't finished."

"But I will interpret your life. It's a game, for you. For me, it's my work. I need your list." He tilted his head and read Lark's list sideways. "You started at the beginning. I said to do last week. Well, let's see, Watter, Baker, Blank. Anglo-Saxon names, and distorted French, possibly Huguenot. Could be in Britain, or any of the British colonies or excolonies. No other children's names for a while—this must be an only child. No aunts, no uncles. This family is isolated. Solomon, Gilbert, Marshall. Hmmm. Names of islands in the Pacific. This family is probably involved in some way. Their ancestors should have stayed at home. The world would be better off."

"You heard me talking to Elizabeth," said Lark. "And you already knew my background."

Professor Bird stood back, offended.

"Here," said Portia to her husband, "interpret my list."

"I know your list already," said Professor Bird. "I know who you are and everything about you. You are my wife."

Portia drew back her list, unperturbed.

Professor Bird seized the list of his oldest son, and opened his mouth to read it aloud, then stopped. He folded the list. "You go to the bathroom and wash out your mouth, young man." He pointed at the boy, then at the door. The boy scrambled to his feet, and his brothers jumped up beside him. They raced out of the room, exploding in giggles.

"He's going to murder them one day," said Portia. "We had to bring them with us, or the babysitter wouldn't stay with the baby. She says all four are too much." Portia pursed her lips happily at the combined effect of her boys.

"Interpret mine," said Elizabeth.

Professor Bird took her list. "I'll just take them with me. They're for an article I'm writing. Portia, we can deduct the bottle of wine we brought from our taxes because I'm doing my work." He gave a laugh. "Help me collect them, will you?"

Portia scurried around the room taking the sheets of paper, now covered with names, from the bewildered guests. "He's really a pit—all bark and no bite, really," she said, as she went around.

"I'll just keep mine," said Lark, who would have swallowed her list rather than let it fall into the hands of Manfred Bird, who stood before Lark again, waiting for her to hand over her list.

"Say," cried Tom, "here's something you ought to see, Manfred." He disappeared and came back holding aloft Lark's espadrilles. "How would you interpret these? Their history?"

Professor Bird frowned at the shoes, turning them over gingerly. "Cut up," he said. "Glass? Walking around New York streets would do that to a rope-soled shoe."

"Coral," said Tom triumphantly. They could been his shoes. It could have been he who had made the coral walk. Yet Lark had felt that he had not believed her at all when she told him. "These shoes have been walking on coral, in the middle of the Pacific." He twirled them around on his fingers. "Tell him, Larkie. She was with Donna, you remember, Manfred. They coral-walked together."

Now Lark felt suddenly important, valuable. Tom was pleased with her after all. She could contribute, even if it was only a pair of rope-soled espadrilles.

"She's an original," said Professor Bird.

Lark smiled modestly.

"That Donna of mine always was. If anyone would go walking on coral she would be the one."

"We both walked," Lark insisted, even though she knew she had had to be forced into it. "It was such fun. It's not every day you get a chance to walk in the middle of the ocean. We were crossing the equator and had to be dunked in water for good luck."

"What an adventure," said Elizabeth. "I'm only going to France."

"France is not 'only,'" protested Jean-Claude.

Elizabeth patted his cheek and kissed her lips at him to placate him.

"You should all stay home," said Professor Bird. "You're all spoiling the world. It's getting harder and harder for us anthro-

pologists to do our work." He frowned. "And then when igno-
rant, left-winged governments interfere with your work—they
impounded my valuable stuff. Customs was told there was
something suspicious about the cargo."

*Das Schaudern, das Schaudern,* Lark hummed. She was the
one responsible. She had told the pilot on the *Avis Maris.* He
must have been listening to her, after all.

"They say it could be a federal case—international theft of
art work. They're out to get me because I am not afraid to speak
out with unpopular ideas."

But it was finally Donna Bird's fault that the father was in a
fix. She had gone to great lengths to persuade Lark that the
cargo was suspicious and dangerous.

The doorbell rang. It was the downstairs neighbor. "What is
this? A brothel?" He was holding out items of Lark's underwear.
"Some kind of joke? These were being draped across my window
sill."

"The boys," Portia gasped and dashed into the bedroom. "You
bed boys. You promised."

"I'm terribly sorry," said Lark to the neighbor, taking back
her clothes.

"It was just the boys," said Portia, from the doorway of the
bedroom. "They were just lowering things, on a string. An experiment, I'm afraid. They're always experimenting. So curious. Typical boys."

The neighbor stormed off.

"It's all right," said Lark to the Bird family, although no one
was actually offering her an apology. But it was just, in a way,
that the Bird boys, Donna's half-brothers, should embarrass
her. It was a kind of repayment, for what she had done to
Donna.

Portia hustled the boys out. "We should go, Menfred. The
baby-sitter, remember?"

"Wait," said Tom. "Just a moment." He drew Lark with him

to the center of the room. "You know the reason for this gathering?"

Lark smiled brightly around the room.

"To meet Lark, of course," said Elizabeth, smiling at Lark, giving her a wink to remind her that they had shared intimate information about Tom and the key to cleverness.

"That was the pretext," cried Tom. "I wanted to announce some wonderful news, that I—" and for a moment Lark thought he was going to announce that they were getting married, although as far as she could remember he had never suggested it to her. She hoped that one day she would be qualified to marry Tom, after she had improved her mind. She was thinking of enrolling in a Ph.D. program, in history or sociology, so that he would want to listen when she spoke about the outcome of elections or economic policy.

"I wanted to announce that I have been given a grant to travel this summer. A generous grant, I should add."

Everyone cheered. "Great, wonderful, good old Tom."

Tom put his arm around Lark and looked down at her.

"You didn't tell me," Lark whispered, about to cry, but still smiling since everyone was looking at them, the happy couple.

"What about me?" was what she wanted to cry out to him.

"Lark's coming, of course. We're going to turn her into a social critic."

"When are you going, exactly?" someone asked.

"A-ha," said Tom. "It's a surprise."

"You'd do better to stay put and publish some solid articles," said Manfred. "Work on something substantial, mainstream. Look to your mentors."

Later, after everyone had left and Lark and Tom were picking up peanut shells and glasses and ashtrays, Lark asked where they were going, but Tom wagged his finger at her and shook his head. Then she asked, somewhat timidly, "Do you think we might get married? One day?"

"Married?" Tom hesitated. He gave Lark a bear hug and kissed her. "Let's just put that on the back burner."

Lark saw a stove with pots boiling away on front burners and a little bridal couple, up to their necks in hot water, simmering on the back burner.

Tom returned from teaching his first class of the new semester. It was the day after the peanut party.

"In class I sat at the back," he told Lark. "The students didn't even realize I was the teacher. That shows you the kind of authority that a desk at the front of a room bestows on a person."

Lark went to him and touched his shoulders. He dropped his head to show that he would accept a massage of his tense neck and shoulder muscles.

"What kind of practical joke was that?" Lark asked. "The poor students must have been confused."

"It's a political tactic, Lark. Don't you see? I sat there at the back of the class for ten minutes. The students were getting restless, shifting around, looking at their watches. Finally, I said, very quietly, 'When are you going to get your act together? Are you waiting for some authority figure to come along and tell you what to do? When they tell you to go to Vietnam, are you just going to go?' They froze in their chairs and sat very still, saying nothing. 'I thought you guys might want to have a say in your own curriculum, define your own syllabus, teach one another.' And do you know what one of them said? 'We're here to learn, sir.' 'Sir,' he said. Sir!" Tom was shaking his head. He shrugged Lark's hands from his shoulders. "It seems you have to force freedom on some people, lead them to water and make them drink."

Lark stood on the balcony again. The crane, on its long leg, had added to its own height and raised itself one story, keeping pace with the rising height of the building under construction.

"That Irishman thought the Russian was K.G.B.," Lark called back into the room.

"Maybe he's gone to Rotterdam to count N.A.T.O. ships," said Tom. "Just joking. It's the West that is busy counting these days."

"Then do you think Manfred is C.I.A.?" She went to the bookshelf and took down *Alone in the Garden,* riffling its pages as if it were a book of moving pictures.

Tom shook his head, shrugged, and waggled his toes in time to "The Trout" on the radio. Tom was sitting in the comfortable armchair in the corner next to the swaying bookshelves, his papers and books spread in concentric circles on the floor surrounding him. "Thank God they're giving us a break from Telemann," he said to his papers.

"He's a poet," said Lark. "The Irishman." She dangled the book at Tom. "My first poet."

"Here, show me that book." Tom looked at the first few pages, then threw the book down. "This is a vanity press. That asshole paid to have his own book published."

Lark took in a breath, not so much at the revelation as at Tom's metaphor, which never failed to produce for her the literal image.

"He ran for Ireland in the Olympics."

"All he probably ran for was coffee," said Tom. "He's a reactionary crock of shit. And a liar."

Lark paused to consider this new image. "Then why did you invite him to my party?"

"The Irish quota. Just joking. He is one of the Carnegie Fellows and some of my best friends are Carnegie Fellows, and sometimes even Carnegie Fellows can be lemons. That guy's a fake." The phone rang. "He seems to have impressed you. But then, you aren't used to meeting the cross-section of types we get here, just as a matter of course." Tom went back to jotting in his note pad.

"I thought he was dreadful," said Lark, crossing to the phone. "Hello?"

It was Elizabeth. At the same time, someone else came on the line. A man. Elizabeth said, "Hello," and the man said, "Hello?" and Lark said, "Hello?"

"This is my phone number," Lark said to the strange, third voice.

"I know," he said.

"Who are you?" Lark asked. "Why is my phone connected to yours? Where are you?" She heard another voice in the background calling out to the man on the line. "Shit," the man muttered, and hung up.

Elizabeth laughed. "It's some kind of surveillance. They're probably watching Tom. It's well known that universities spy on their teachers these days."

"Couldn't it just be crossed lines?"

"It's more likely to be a tap," said Elizabeth, "and that's not even being paranoid. Say, I wanted to thank you and Tom for last night. Great peanuts."

"Tell her to come over," said Tom. "Immediately." He waved some papers in the air. "I've got this questionnaire and I need subjects."

"Don't you think it was just crossed lines?" Lark asked Tom when she was off the phone.

He gave a little snorting laugh. "If you have any sense at all, Larkie, you'll just take it for granted that the phone is always tapped. Always. Period."

Lark went to the balcony to watch for Elizabeth. "This is a test of the emergency broadcast system," the radio announced, and there followed a long shriek from a siren. How could Manhattan ever be evacuated? Just the cars parked on this street would have trouble lining up and turning north to get away.

"We could get out your car and go to the beach," Lark said. "We could walk along the sand. I'd like to see some ocean."

Tom kept his car in a garage and never used it. It was too much trouble to walk to get it and too much trouble to park once you got where you were going, Tom explained. He pulled a face, shook his head, and indicated the papers on the floor.

Lark saw that farther down the block, a man was walking back and forth on one section of the sidewalk, passing and re-passing a green station wagon. When he got past the station wagon, each time he stopped and looked around to see if anyone was watching.

"I think that man is about to steal a car," Lark said.

Tom got up and looked, then drew back. "Get out of sight," he said. Lark was leaning out over the balcony, about to start shouting. He put his arm around Lark's shoulder and drew her to him, his hand pressing her head to his shoulder in an un-expectedly warm gesture. Lark stayed still in the circle of his arm, feeling the cotton of his shirt against her cheek, his chin against her head.

The man was standing beside the station wagon. He had a short blade in his hand, which he inserted between the door and the body of the car, and ran it quickly up, then down. Then he unlatched the door of the car, got in, and drove off.

"We should have shouted out at him, stopped him doing that," said Lark, ashamed of what she had allowed in exchange for an embrace.

"Maybe it was his car." Tom went back to his chair. "In any case, the people have a right to take the material possessions of the rich, which are created through the labor of the poor." But he looked uncomfortable, and Lark knew he had been afraid. "Remember, this is New York. You can get hurt. People carry guns. You're not in Sydney now." He looked up at her and tried to make her smile at him, then shrugged when she turned away. "It was just one small event in a day of small events."

"We should have stopped him. Why did we hide? Like mid-dle-class cowards?"

Tom cleared his throat. "Come here and sit on my knee, Larkie."

Lark stayed standing, looking at him. Tom patted his knee. "Come on. I want to propose. I've been thinking. Let's get married."

The doorbell rang, and Elizabeth walked in, beaming.

"Congratulations," she cried. "You're under some kind of surveillance. That's called really making it in these parts, Lark. Your Tom is a better guy than we thought."

"Tea?" Lark asked.

"She can't let anyone in the door without offering tea," said Tom. "Come here, Larkie, and let me give you a hug. It's cultural, you know. Someone walks in, Lark's right hand reaches for the kettle and her left hand turns on the faucet." Lark, smiling like a good sport, went to stand beside Tom in the chair, and he put his arm around her legs and gave her a squeeze. "In Australia I drank so much tea that my back teeth sang 'Anchors Aweigh.' Ladies would ask me if I wanted a drink, and of course I always did, but what they gave me was tea."

Lark saw a chorus line of teeth—molars, bicuspids, incisors, the lot—dancing on their roots, kicking high and singing on the deck of a ship that floated on an ocean of tea.

"Well, actually, I do feel like tea," said Elizabeth, winking at Lark.

"You don't look like tea," said Tom.

"What kind do you have?"

"Pardon? Oh, just tea."

"Then just tea will be great," said Elizabeth.

Lark went to the kitchen. She suddenly felt tired. It seemed that every day she had to be alert in order to comprehend the forces around her. It was the feeling she had had all the time on board the *Avis Maris*. The world was indeed a tricky place, as Henry Watter had warned. But she had to remember that everything was going to be all right. Tom wanted to marry her.

"Did you ever feel any anxiety about the possibility of a nuclear war or a nuclear attack?" Tom asked Elizabeth.

"What?"

"Significant, moderate, slight, none?"

"Significant, why?"

"Did you ever have any nightmares dealing with a nuclear war or nuclear attack? Often, occasionally, once or twice, never?"

"Say, what is all this?"

"He'll never tell you," said Lark, poking her head around the kitchen door. "He likes you to guess."

"Dreams? As opposed to nightmares?"

Lark bore in the tray with cups and the teapot covered with a tea cozy knitted by her mother. "It's a survey, Elizabeth, for a seminar in political ideas."

"You've gone and told her and spoiled it," said Tom.

"I have dreams," said Lark, "all the time, about deadly games, war, explosions. Often it's an atom bomb dropping on Sydney, but the other night I dreamt the two towers we can see from here exploded and we had to breathe air filled with radioactive particles the consistency of gravel."

"We'd better call in Dr. Freud," Tom said, then asked Elizabeth, "Did you ever makes plans to move to another part of the world to escape a nuclear war? Often, occasionally, once or twice, never?"

Elizabeth laughed. "We're going to France fairly soon," she patted her abdomen, "and taking little Henri here. That'll be right in the middle of things, when the big bang goes off." She turned to Lark, hunched over the teapot, pouring the tea. "Gorgeous tea cozy," she said.

"If the U.S. does become involved in a nuclear war, how much chance do you think there is of your community or city being attacked? Very real danger, slight, no danger, no opinion?"

"Very real," said Lark.

"Elizabeth?"

"Very real danger, I'd say."

Lark handed the cups around, waiting for Tom to tell Elizabeth about his proposal.

"How would you describe yourself politically? Moderate, radical, conservative, liberal, other?"

Elizabeth shrugged. "Radical? Moderate? Moderate radical? It depends. What about you, Lark?"

Tom seized the tea cozy and put it on his head. "Lark has no opinion," he said, mimicking a woman's voice. "But we're trying to get her to say 'radical' when asked that question."

"Cute hat," said Elizabeth. She looked from Tom to Lark. "Why don't you two get married? You get along so well."

"You must have E.S.P.," said Tom, looking disappointed. "That's exactly what we're going to do. In the not-too-distant. I was just about to tell you."

Elizabeth kissed them and clapped her hands, crying out at the wonder of it all.

"It's not going to be your conventional kind of marriage. We think of it as partly satisfying the unicellular urge to merge," said Tom. "Right, Lark?" Then, seeing her dismay, he added, "Just joking."

After Elizabeth had gone, Tom picked up his books.

"You're leaving?" said Lark.

"See you around the block," Tom said. "I'm going to the library. And please, don't humiliate me in front of my friends."

"Humiliate?" Lark searched back. Could it have been the tea cozy, or her dreams?

"You said I like to keep people guessing, that I don't tell things straight." He went to the door.

"I'm sorry," said Lark. "I didn't realize."

He came back from the door and kissed her lightly, then tickled her. She writhed away, squealing. "Get out," she cried. "Away with you."

Tom stopped. "If that's how you want it." He picked up his books again and walked down the hall.

"I didn't mean get out," Lark said.

"Then why did you say it?"

"That's what I say," she said. "Get out. It means stop that. It's cultural, like tea." She took his arm. "I don't want you to go."

Tom looked at his watch. "I have to go, anyway. Lots to do."

Lark wrote to Solomon Blank. "I hope you are well and happy. I really enjoyed seeing you in Chicago. Sometimes I feel the need to talk to someone who knew me as I was, who knew the streets I used to walk, and the beach. Also, my good news is that I am getting married. To an American. To a social theorist. Greetings to your wife."

"An early wedding present. Household effects," said Elizabeth. She was standing at the door of Lark's apartment with several shopping bags filled with household items—a breadboard, an espresso coffee pot, an egg whisk. "We can't take everything to France with us, so we're bequeathing them to you and hope they bring you good luck." She handed the bags to Lark and sighed, rubbing her back with one hand. "I am certainly very, very pregnant," she said.

"I'll make you some tea," said Lark very quietly. She did not want Tom to tease her. "Come and sit down."

Tom came up behind Lark and peered into the shopping bags. "Loot," he said. "I was thinking about what we should do for our wedding, since we don't want an ordinary, bourgeois affair like everybody else."

"Uh-oh, you can trust Tom to come up with something different," said Elizabeth.

Lark and Elizabeth followed Tom into the living room.

"I can only stay a minute. Jean-Claude said he'd pick me up here," said Elizabeth.

"In Java, when someone wants to celebrate something, the whole village joins in," Tom said. "For instance, you'd rent a film and a screen and a projector and run the film in the middle of the village for everyone. People would just walk by and sit down on the ground and watch, on either side of the screen." He was lifting the items out of the shopping bag, one by one, nodding in approval. "We'll have our wedding outdoors," Tom said. "When it gets a bit warmer."

"Do you know someone with a garden you can use?" Elizabeth asked. "Someone with a brownstone or in the suburbs?"

"We don't have any rich friends. We'll have it on the street right outside," said Tom, triumphant. "Anyone and everyone can come. We won't send out invitations. We'll rent a film, et cetera, and then stick up notices all around the neighborhood telling people to come and watch a film for free. Manfred will love it." He grabbed Lark and waltzed her around the room. "It'll be a riot. Different. Not one of these routine, hypocritical affairs. I don't mean you and Jean-Claude, Elizabeth. He's French. He's got a tradition to perpetuate."

"What do you think, Lark?" Elizabeth asked.

"Where will you show the film?" Lark was confused, dizzy. "Will they allow you to do that?"

"Allow, allow. You're still so worried by authority." Tom waved his arm, then seized Lark's hand and swung her wide. "It'll be a like a street fair. It's easy to get a permit. Maybe the *Times* will cover it. There's plenty of time to organize it. It'll be like organizing a political action."

"What film shall we have?" Lark gasped, breathless from whirling about.

"*The Sky Above and the Mud Below.*" Tom was doing a kind of solo jitterbug, holding onto Lark and pirouetting, snapping his fingers. "Manfred recommends it. Anthropological. About New Guinea. Made by some Frenchmen, or Swiss. They really understand human nature."

The doorbell rang, and at the same time the telephone. Lark let Jean-Claude in, then picked up the phone. "Who is this?" It was a woman's voice. Then there was the sound of another receiver being picked up. "Hello?" Lark said. There was silence. Then one receiver was hung up, followed by the other.

Tom had been telling Jean-Claude about his wedding plans. *"Très original,"* said Jean-Claude.

"Make sure you do it before we leave," said Elizabeth. "We wouldn't want to miss it."

"We'll do it in May, when it's warm. On May Day? No, that's too hokey."

"Mayday is a distress call." Lark paused. "There seemed to be two people on the line just now. But neither spoke to me. Just a woman asking 'Who is this?' Then two people hung up."

"You've got to hand it to them," said Tom. "The university, the C.I.A., F.B.I., whoever, is hard at work, keeping us under surveillance."

"Why us, you?"

Tom shrugged. "We seem like troublemakers, that's all. We don't go along with the party line, we question authority. Once the technical ability to gather and store information is acquired, then information must be gathered and stored. It seems to be a law of postindustrial society. Just as, when we had an atom bomb, we used it. And that's why we'll have a nuclear war sometime. The weapons exist, they demand to be used."

"Soon you'll be able to make a bomb and drive it across France in a little Citroën, a little *deux chevaux.*" Jean-Claude pretended to be driving in a little car, putt-putting along as if he were in a horse-drawn cart.

Solomon Blank wrote, in his first communication since the meeting in Chicago: "What a pleasant surprise to hear from you. Amanda is pregnant, just as we had planned, and I have revised my article for the scholarly journal. Amanda, after some considerable effort, has at last found a job, part-time, which unfortunately she will have to leave when the baby is born, of course. Of course, we are very, very happy. Everything is turning out just as we had planned and hoped. We don't get to New York at all in the ordinary course of events, so we both offer you our best wishes for your impending marriage. You will find that being married to an American is quite charming. If you ever happen to be in the great Midwest, we would both be very glad to see you both. It's really quite civilized here in Illinois."

And then there was a postscript: "I have often worried about the letter I sent you once defining a baseball term which I misheard. I thought the word was 'ringcheck,' and it was, of course, 'rain check.' I don't suppose it matters much, and now you won't have any occasion to use it. It just shows how unreliable I am."

"Tea?" Lark asked.

Manfred Bird turned on her, frowning. "I just stopped by to give a word of advice to young Tom. Since he's getting married tomorrow, I thought he would have nothing more important to do than to consider my comments on government and secrecy." He pushed a flat brown-paper parcel into Lark's arms. "Our present. As I recall it, the week before a marriage, the groom isn't needed at all and is largely in the way."

Inside the parcel was a cane tray in a design of squares. "Don't worry," said Manfred, "it's not from my collection, so you can use it."

"I'm glad you didn't give us one of yours," said Lark. At first she had thought it was the basket with the arms and legs and no head that she had seen in Manfred's cabinet.

"Portia bought it. It's Japanese, I suppose."

"I got the permit to show the film in the street, my students are taping up the notices all over the place, and Elizabeth and Jean-Claude have delivered the press releases," said Tom. "It has taken months to organize, but now it's all done and I've got nothing to do. Lark is going out." Tom had told Lark she made him feel guilty for liking Manfred and was uncomfortable with Lark and Manfred together. "She's going to The Strand. She's been looking for a wedding present for me, and I told her I wanted a book. I told her to surprise me. The Strand's the best place, don't you think, for surprises?"

Manfred looked at his watch.

"I'll just put the kettle on," said Lark. "You can make the tea, or coffee, as you wish."

Manfred Bird had already begun his analysis. "I do not agree with the author of the article that, because of the surveys and opinion polls that are now prevalent in this country, Americans are the most nakedly exposed, and in this sense the most unfree, people in history. That's balderdash, the idea that the government's security system is destroying this society because it permits the Executive to deceive and manipulate the people."

"You could argue, I must insist, that if the security system were removed, lying by the government would be more difficult," Tom offered. "The people have lost their privacy. Only the government retains privacy."

"The government knows best—at least the right government knows best, not our current one. And Tom, be careful when you talk about mendacity. Our government doesn't lie. We are free. Except when petty bureaucrats use their power and impound, for instance, my stuff. There's rare Aboriginal and New Guinea art there. They'll probably wreck it."

"If the security system were removed, it would be more difficult for the government to lie," said Tom.

They did not hear the doorbell ring. Lark answered the door. A smiling young Chinese man stood at the door.

"I'm the telephone repairman," he said. "I'm new to the job. But they told me you have a problem?"

He had come to check the line, as Lark had requested. He went to the basement for a while, then came back and said he had found an extra line leading from their telephone line to the basement of the new building next door. Then he said, "But don't worry, miss, I cut it." Off he went, smiling, pleased.

"But we could try," Tom was saying, with no idea that the repairman had come and gone, "having a time limit on government privacy, say a couple of months, after which all activities would be made known to the public."

"What on earth for?" cried Professor Bird. "The public doesn't want to know."

"Perhaps the public doesn't know that it needs to know."

Lark listened happily from the kitchen. Tom was right. He had his own ideas, and he was at last trying to stand up to Manfred Bird. A good sign. "I shall go now," she said to the two men.

"I thought you'd gone," said Tom.

"You're still here?" said Manfred Bird.

"Peace," said Tom.

In the dark aisles of The Strand Lark was uneasy. The lights were dim, and she was finding it hard to read the titles. She ran her hand along the spines of the books. She was in the section on war and had fingered Masefield's *Gallipoli*, wondering if Tom would like that, then she contemplated a book on the great escape from Dunkirk. She really had no idea how to amuse him, surprise him. He seemed unsurprisable. He knew everything. Even if she wore a panda suit to the wedding, he would not notice, or at least would not comment on it.

Then she found it, Charles Blank's autobiography, *My Life in the Service of God in the South Pacific*. It was the book she had touched while she waited for Tom in the stacks at the university in Sydney. Lark took the old volume from the shelf and found, as the frontispiece, a photograph of the man himself, with the same perplexed expression that Solomon Blank often wore, an expression that could slide into one of sadness or hurt. "It is an offense," she read at random, "for a native to sit with his legs outstretched, and unpardonable to be stingy, especially with food." Perhaps this book would surprise and amuse Tom. She went to the cash register and paid for it, then, reluctant to return to the apartment while Manfred Bird and Tom were conversing, she went back among the books, and leaning against one of the shelves she continued reading the book. "They are kind, lovable, polite in intercourse, but extremely sensitive to insult. Wars are carried on for generations. When they are about to enter battle, the two sides have ceremonial drinks together, then say 'Shall we trample grass?' and the battle begins."

Lark felt a hand on her arm and heard a whisper close to her ear. "So, the battle begins?"

It was Donna Bird, smiling broadly, as if they had seen each other only the day before, rather than months ago on the island. She was holding a book with a worn gray cover. *"My Life in the Service of God in the South Pacific?"* Donna said, turning over the book Lark was holding and peering at the title.

"What are you doing here?" Lark snatched the book back, holding it close to her.

Donna Bird proffered the book she was holding. "This is the book I was telling you about? *English Short Stories of Today?"* Again, she spoke as if they had had the discussion about that particular book just yesterday. "I just found it—this is a wonderful bookshop, I'm so glad you have discovered it, it's one of New York's truly great assets—my copy in school had a red cover. And here," she was turning the first few pages, "you see, callow, this tourist I told you about." She pointed at the page and read aloud. "'I'm not going to sit and catch pneumonia under those fancy gadgets like a callow tourist.' That's what this young man, Leonard, is saying. He has ordered them to scrap the electric fans on the ship. In the tropics? You see, I don't lie."

"What are you doing here?"

"What everybody does here, running into people, buying books. We all go round and round the world, remember? It's just one of the things we do. We just circle the globe. Adventurers, you might say. Or vagabonds?"

Lark backed away. Donna Bird was no longer wearing her visor. Her hair was now shorter, flying free, curly, bushy, forming a nest for her head, but she was still tossing it around as she spoke, as if it were still long. She looked Lark up and down, leaning back and peering at her in the gloom of the shelves. "And how is our Tom?"

"Tom?" said Lark, as if she had no idea whom Donna was referring to.

"And the rest of your voyage on the *Avis Maris?* How was that? Pretty peaceful?"

Lark wanted to rush from the shop, but Donna Bird stood in front of her, blocking her escape. Donna Bird stepped close to Lark. Lark drew in her breath. She was hardly able to breathe. That face was so close that Lark had to turn away, weak, resting her head against the books on the shelf. She ran her fingers along the books, along the bindings, as if each might let out a separate note, a cry, when touched.

"So afraid?" Donna's whisper was almost inaudible. "Because you left me stranded on the island? Because you saw me on the dock waving, running to get the ship?"

"Leave me alone." Lark pushed Donna Bird aside and ran to the front of the shop, turning to see if she was being followed. She saw a shadow at the end of one of the aisles. She ran past the cashier onto the street, still clutching *My Life in the Service of God in the South Pacific,* open, to her chest. Outside she leant against the wall, catching her breath. The cashier had followed her. "Where's the fire?" he asked, and took her book, checking to see that she had not stolen it.

Lark ran to the corner and looking back, saw a dim figure standing in the doorway of The Strand. She ran around the corner, along the block, and around the next corner, so that she would be out of sight if Donna Bird came in pursuit. As she slowed to a walk, several blocks from The Strand, she wondered, looking over her shoulder every now and then, if she had imagined the encounter with Donna Bird. After all, she had been holding the book, reading about customs of the people of the South Pacific and about their long feuds and their behavior toward enemies. The aisles of The Strand were dark and the shadows could be easily misconstrued. How could Donna Bird *not* appear before her, given such conditions?

Lark threw herself down on a bench in the square, dropped her book beside her, hitched her skirt above her knees. She stretched out her legs, reached her arms along the back of the bench, dropped her head back, closed her eyes, holding herself out to be warmed by the sun. Then, conscious that she must be drawing great attention to herself, she sat up, stood up, straightened her skirt, picked up her book, and after a brief look around her, ducked into the subway.

When Lark arrived home, Manfred Bird had left and Tom was involved in a long phone conversation with the secretary of a hated colleague in his department. His feet were on Lark's desk, the television was on. The secretary needed to discuss with Tom the affair she was having with a certain prominent member of the department, for it appeared that the wife might be on the point of discovering it all.

"Far out," said Tom. "People aren't possessive any more, jealousy is a thing of the past. Nobody owns anybody. He's free, you're free, she's free. Just hang loose." He began to offer sympathetic and lengthy advice, then said, "Hey, hold it, I've got to take a leak."

The secretary held on at her end of the line while Tom went to the bathroom.

"Hi," said Lark, as Tom passed her in the hall on the way.

"Hi," said Tom. "Don't hang up the phone, I'm still talking to Mimi."

This gave Lark time to reconsider the encounter in the bookstore. By the time she got off the subway and had seen the notices for *The Sky Above and the Mud Below* tacked on trees and railings and posts, confirming the present and her marriage to Tom the following day, she was sure that the Donna Bird she had seen in the bookshop did not exist.

Lark prepared a cheese soufflé, using stone-ground wholewheat flour and a salad with walnut oil imported from France, which Tom ate while he talked on the phone. "I'm having a gourmet omelette here," he said to Mimi, between mouthfuls. "You should see it." Then he called out to Lark. "She says to tell you you're terrific."

As she ate, perched on a stool in the kitchen, Lark decided not to mention the Donna Bird episode. She washed the dishes, then went to the bedroom and laid out the long white cotton dress she had bought for the wedding. Then, since she could hear that Tom was nowhere near finished talking to Mimi, she started putting away her winter sweaters and socks, slamming cupboards and drawers.

"Hey," said Tom, coming into the room after a while. He had finished his telephone conversation. "The phone tappers would have enjoyed that phone marathon I just had with Mimi. All that info about who is sleeping with whom."

Lark was standing on a stool poking a sweater into the top of the closet.

"Anything wrong?" Tom asked.

"Just a bit tired. Long day."

"Mimi really needed my help tonight," said Tom. "She's in a real mess. I can't tell you about it. She wouldn't let me go. I don't know, but women just seem to confide in me. I've always been a crying towel, since way back." He sighed and rubbed his cheek against Lark's leg. "One of my students even sent me a note the other day—would you believe it?—that ended, 'Of course I'm in love with you.' It was a female student, of course."

Lark hopped down from the stool, gathered up her mittens and long johns, and hopped back up.

"Hey, don't put all those sweaters away. You'll be needing one or two," Tom said, suddenly remembering he had exciting news for Lark.

"What do you mean?"

"You'll be needing a sweater."

"Oh?"

"Yup. It's going to be colder, at night, you can be sure of that."

"Where?"

"Where we're going this summer." Tom sat on the bed, fingering Lark's white dress.

"Where? The North Pole?" Lark stood still on the stool, holding the mittens and underwear.

Tom shook his head happily.

"Alaska? Chile? Bhutan?"

Tom shook his head. "Come on, be serious. Not that cold. You'll just need a sweater, that's all, in case it's cold."

"Are you going to tell me for once, without putting me through these wretched hoops of yours?"

"Ha, it suits you, a little burst of temper. Good. Shows spunk."

Lark burst into tears.

"Jesus," said Tom. "What's gotten into you? You really are on edge. It's the wedding, isn't it?"

Lark dried her tears and got down from the stool. "I'm sorry. Where are we going this summer, Tom?"

"Guess," said Tom. He was putting on his beige pajama cutoffs.

Lark sighed. "The Falkland Islands."

"Be serious," said Tom. He climbed into the bed, which he had made from two slabs of foam glued together, which rested on two doors, which in turn rested on several cinder blocks. "You'll never guess."

The phone rang. It was Solomon Blank. "I've been trying all night to get you. I can't talk long. Amanda will be back any minute. I just wanted to wish you well, and I wanted you to know, if I weren't married already, I would want to marry you myself." And without giving her time to say anything, he hung up. Lark stayed holding the phone, wondering what she would tell Tom, then she replaced the receiver and quickly picked up her white dress and hung it on the closet door so that she could see it as she lay in bed.

"You'll never guess," said Tom from the bed.

"In that case," said Lark, "why don't you just tell me." She put on one of Tom's old shirts.

Tom picked up a copy of *Dissent* and began turning the pages.

"I'll be back in a minute, then you can tell me." And Lark left the room.

When she came back, Tom said, "You were a long time."

"I just had to see something."

"Guess."

"France."

"How did you guess? You knew all the time, you heard me on the phone."

"I must have E.S.P.," said Lark, getting into bed. "And anyway, tell that Mimi, or Peepee, or whatever her name is, to cry on another towel."

"Shame on you, Larkie," said Tom. "You're jealous." Lark said nothing. She turned away from him. He rolled toward her and put his arms around her, fitting himself against her back, his cheek against the back of her head. "We'll leave in a couple of weeks. It can be our honeymoon. We can stay with Agnes and her mother in Paris, and with Elizabeth and Jean-Claude for free. Mmmm, Larkie, what do you think?"

Asking her opinion and giving out so much information all at once was Tom's way of apologizing to Lark, making amends. She wanted to say something about Manfred Bird, his stupidity, since that seemed to be one way of aligning Tom with her, but it would spoil this moment. She turned around and nestled into Tom's chest, then thought about Solomon Blank and his phone call. Fortunately she loved Tom now.

That night Lark awoke suddenly. Her dress on the door looked like someone standing watching them. Then she saw a shadow. "There's someone on the fire escape," Lark whispered to Tom, sound asleep beside her.

He leapt to his feet, his fists up, his legs apart, bent. "What? What?"

"That shadow," Lark said. A man seemed to crouch on the fire escape, his round back casting a blurred shape on the window shade.

Tom jumped toward the window, landing in the same position, fists up, legs apart, bent. "Move it!" he screamed. "Move it!" The shadow seemed to move only slightly. He jumped at the shade and wrenched it down, then let it fly up and spin around and around, the tassel on the cord hitting the pane and frame with every revolution.

There was no one, nothing, on the fire escape. Tom was now fully awake and seemed surprised to find himself stationed pugilistically at the window in the middle of the night.

"What?" he asked.

"There was someone on the fire escape."

Tom grunted. He threw up the window and leant out and scanned the air shaft. "No one here."

"There was someone there," said Lark. "I think." Tom turned slowly to look at her. "Your shouting must have scared whoever it was away."

Tom leant out the window again. "Get out!" he yelled. "Get out!"

A couple of lights went on in windows opposite. Tom returned to Lark. "Now that was cultural. I really meant it when I yelled 'get out' to that guy you say you think was there." He sat on the edge of the bed, shaking his head.

"I'm awfully sorry," said Lark.

Tom stood up. "I think I'll get something to drink." He stumbled out of the bedroom in the dark, and as he passed the front door there was a tremendous clatter, as if a set of pots and pans had been turned over, followed by a thump, as Tom fell to the floor. Lark rushed into the hall and turned on the light. Tom lay on the floor, cursing. Next to him lay a large saucepan, a saucepan lid, and a tin wastepaper basket, with its contents, crumpled sheets of paper, scattered around him.

"I'm sorry," said Lark. She knelt and righted the basket, popping the balls of paper back in.

Tom sat up. "What the fuck is this collection of percussion?" He picked up the saucepan and its lid and banged them together, like cymbals.

"Sh." Lark grabbed at his hands. "Everyone'll hear."

"Everyone has heard already, when I ran into this scrap heap," said Tom. "They are waiting for the show to begin." The cymbals clashed.

Lark sat back on her heels. "Sometimes I hear someone trying the door. I think I hear someone. Often when you're not here." It was Donna Bird she always imagined tracking her down, coming to take her revenge.

The cymbals clashed once, twice.

"Please don't;" Lark begged. "This is New York. You said so yourself. There are break-ins."

Tom sat on the floor, his back against the wall, his bare legs out in front of him. "You set up this booby trap every night?"

Lark shook her head. "This is the first time. I would have taken it down before you woke up."

Tom heaved himself off the floor and threw himself into the armchair in the living room. Under the chair Lark had hidden *My Life in the Service of God in the South Pacific*.

"I got you a present." She looked at the clock. "It's past midnight, so I can give it to you. It's our wedding day." She knelt down to pull out the book, and still kneeling, Lark held out the book on both hands to Tom. While she held it, his page boy, he started turning the pages. "I'm thirsty," he said.

"Ah, a ceremonial drink," said Lark, and went to the kitchen. "That's what the two sides used to have before they went into battle, in parts of Polynesia." She knew she was taking a risk talking about a Pacific island, because it raised again the issue of Donna Bird and her whereabouts, but she desperately wanted to keep Tom placid and happy throughout this day. Everything seemed so precarious. She stood for a moment. "There's a bit about worms, did you come across it?"

Tom stretched out his legs and yawned.

"There are two mornings a year when they stop everything and hunt sea worms. The sea worms only come two days a year. The coral reefs are crowded. And the canoes get so full of worms that there is no room for the people. They have to swim back to shore beside the canoes. Now that I know what a coral reef is like, having walked on one, I'd hate to catch worms on one." Lark was attempting levity. "Isn't' it a great book? Don't you just love it? I always wanted to live on an island," she babbled, running the water until it was cold, then got out ice cubes, placed them in a plastic bag, and smashed them into little bits so that they would melt more quickly, the way Tom liked it. "But I don't want to any more. The worms come to the surface of the lagoon and when you put your hands in the water, they just hang onto your fingers and you fling them in the canoe. That's how you catch them." She brought the glass of ice water into the living room, where Tom lay slouched in the chair. "And then the worms break up into small pieces, all by themselves. They seem to prepare themselves to be eaten. They cooperate, so willingly." She dipped her finger into the water, about to flick some of it onto him. But she saw that he was asleep.

She took the water onto the balcony and stood there, leaning. In the street below, in response to Tom's application for a permit for the outdoor wedding and film show, tied to the trunks of the gingko trees, were the notices from the Police Department telling motorists not to park on this particular street on this particular Saturday. At the corner were the barriers the police would use to close the street to traffic.

In her last letter Mrs. Watter had written: "We have had several nasty decapitations. At Wiseman's Ferry, where they water-ski, skiers have fallen into the water and been chopped up by other speedboats while waiting to be picked up. And all in that beautiful countryside, with the fruit trees coming right down to the river. Dreadful. So much for life and progress in the Southern Hemisphere. I'm sure you have more interesting tales to tell. Your father says to tell you *bon jour*. He has been studying French in secret. I found the books under the mattress. Don't mention it to him. He doesn't know I know. They changed your old school into a nursing home, and old Mrs. Blank is in it. She says her boys are devoted to her, but I don't see them visiting her, in their far-flung corners. We are all without our children. We are glad you are so happy and will be thinking of you on the day."

Lark dressed carefully in her long white dress and sandals. She held a bunch of daisies and daffodils, although the florist, when he learned that it was to be a wedding bouquet, had said they were not appropriate. The sun was shining, and in a few weeks it would be summer.

"You ought to wear something on your head," said Elizabeth, who had come to help Lark get ready. She was wearing a white shirt belonging to Jean-Claude as a maternity smock, over trousers that might have been Jean-Claude's pajamas. She held up a white kerchief, then a white cap, rather like a painter's cap, then a piece of netting into which she had threaded flowers, all of which Lark brushed aside. Head coverings, particularly the netting and flowers, reminded her of Donna Bird. "You can't go bareheaded."

"Beheaded? Oh, bareheaded." Lark seized the kerchief and tried twisting it into a band to tie around her head.

"That's nice," said Elizabeth.

But Lark threw it aside. The twisted cloth, resting on her forehead above her eyebrows, reminded her of the dream she had had on the *Avis Maris*, when she wore Donna's visor in the sun and was left with a white mark across her forehead.

The police barriers had been set up at either end of the block. The street was clear of cars. On the sidewalk outside Lark's building was a collapsible table on which rested plastic glasses, flagons of California wine, and paper plates piled high with crackers and cubes of cheese. Milling about on the sidewalk and the road were dozens of people, those who were friends of Tom and Lark and those from the neighborhood who had read the notices for the film and had come to have a free drink and snack and to watch a free film. The screen had been set up in the middle of the road, the projector on a card table a short distance from it. The wedding and reception would take place in the last light, the film would begin as soon as it was dark.

Tom himself was down there. Lark leant against the balcony rail and watched him. She had often seen him in his OshKosh overalls standing on the corner with young women in identical overalls, looking up at him as he gestured and talked, taking in the world.

Today Tom wore pale-blue cotton trousers and a white Nehru jacket. He stood below Lark, talking wildly and laughing with a man wearing sandals, jeans, and a plaid shirt. This was a college friend of Tom's, recently ordained, who had traveled from Boston to perform the ceremony. Lark had not met him before. Their laughter reached Lark on the fifth floor. On a canvas director's chair sat Professor Manfred Bird, with a glass of wine in his hand. Around him gathered half a dozen of his

students, eagerly listening as he talked apparently continuously.
One of the students pulled out a little note pad and took a few
notes. Portia, having wandered around the periphery of the
crowd, finally sat herself down on the curb, her baby toddling
beside her. Her three older boys, their socks collapsed around
their ankles, raced up and down the street, dodging among the
wedding guests and at one point knocking down the screen.

"Boys," cried Portia, leaping to her feet and seizing the oldest
by the sleeve. "He'll kill you one day."

The baby began to cry, and with Portia distracted, the boys
went off to surround the projectionist, who was fiddling with
the placement and focus of his projector.

Elizabeth came to Lark and said, "It's time."

Lark locked the apartment, descended in the elevator to the
ground floor, and walked out onto the street. There was no al-
tar, no apparent focus for the ceremony. Lark poured herself
some wine. She looked around. Tom, catching her eye, lifted
his glass to her.

The minister turned to look, and seeing the bride in her long
cotton dress, said, "Okay, then," quietly, so that only the few
people who stood near him realized that the ceremony was under way. The minister beckoned to Lark. "I imagine that you,
Tom, agree to take," he hesitated, unsure of her name, "Lark—
is it?—for your wife, and Lark, I imagine that you don't mind
taking Tom for your husband, right?"

Both Lark and Tom nodded and said, "Right."

"If anyone has any objections, now's the time to say so," said
the minister.

There was a yell from the projectionist, followed by the clatter of running feet as the Bird boys fled to another part of the
street, with Portia's reasonable voice crying after them, "You
promised!"

"Goddamned kids!" the projectionist said.

The clergyman, who had halted the ceremony to observe this

incident, continued. "Then, I guess you are man and wife." He looked around. "Hey," he added. "That's neat-o, keen-o, far out, and groovy."

And that was that. Manfred Bird had not even stopped talking.

Then came a voice, soft, strong. "Wait."

It was Donna Bird.

Manfred Bird let out a cry, leapt out of his canvas chair, which fell over and folded up on the ground, and strode to Donna. He gripped her shoulder with one hand, surveying her, nodding his head. "My girl," he said. "She's back," he called to the assembled crowd, "from working in the field." He started applauding. "The more credit to her." The people around joined in the applause, which swelled across the street, through the crowd of friends who had come for the wedding and the passers-by who had come for the film, most of them believing they were applauding the happy couple.

Portia made her way to Donna Bird's side. "Every day he asks for you," she said. The boys knocked aside the spectators and ranged themselves around their half-sister, examining her, looking for things about her that they could touch or purloin. "This is Rodney." Portia held up the baby, lifting it off its feet, straight up, like a rocket taking off, level with Donna Bird's face, then, as the baby's legs flailed and its mouth opened to begin screaming, Portia lowered it back to the ground.

"Donna Bird!" That was Tom, pressing through the crowd that had left him and Lark standing alone. "Sonofagun. What luck. You've come at just the right moment."

"I thought I would be too late?" said Donna sweetly.

"We're just about to roll the film. It's dark enough. *Sky Above Mud Below*—you'll love it."

A van pulled up at the corner, and from it issued a cameraman from a local news station and a reporter, who walked toward the crowd around Donna Bird. The cameraman, catching sight of the projector and the projectionist sitting on a stool beside it, stopped to chat with him.

The clergyman stood on the periphery with Lark.

"Where's the wedding?" the reporter asked.

"We've just joined these two young people in matrimony," said the clergyman.

Another round of applause went up from the crowd around Donna, Tom, Manfred, Portia, and the boys. Manfred Bird had just recited some of Donna's accomplishments.

Lark, in a state of terror and remembering Henry Watter's warning about big families sticking together, like a team or an army, waited, outnumbered and hopeless, for Donna Bird's next move. She looked up to the sky and prayed for something to fall and hit her on the head.

The cameraman joined the reporter, and they pushed their way through the crowd. "Let's get the happy couple," the reporter said.

"No, not that one," cried the clergyman. "This is the bride, here."

But the camera light was on Donna and Tom, and the tape was running.

Lark turned away and began walking to the corner. She thought she would get a bus, the first bus that came along, and sit on it until the end of its route. She hesitated. She had no money with her, and she had to decide quickly whether to go back past the crowd and into the apartment building in order to get her purse or whether to keep walking.

The clergyman followed in the wake of the reporter and the cameraman.

Seeing that all attention was on the television crew and Donna Bird, Lark turned around and, holding up the skirt of her dress, tiptoed quickly back toward the apartment.

"You've missed the ceremony," said the clergyman. "They're already married. I just did it."

"Could you go through it again for us? We need something light for the late news. They'll kill us if we go back empty-handed."

"Well, I'm agreeable," said the clergyman.

"Wait," said Donna Bird. "I had hoped to be here before the ceremony, but it was only now, as I made my way toward my father's apartment, that I saw the wedding notices tacked to the lampposts and realized the wedding was taking place."

"I didn't know you were back," said Tom. "I would've delivered you a notice personally."

The clergyman caught sight of Lark disappearing into the lobby of her building. "Hey," he cried, "we're going to re-enact it, for television. This is really something. Go get her."

Elizabeth and Jean-Claude detached themselves from the crowd and ran up to Lark. "This is really something. What a very good idea of Tom, to do a press release and have us take it around," said Jean-Claude.

"It's not every day you can get on the news," said Elizabeth. "All the stations are trying to build up their local news coverage. They think there's an audience for it, in addition to the national network news. Light news. Fluff."

"Lark could have told me yesterday," Donna Bird said to Tom.

"Yesterday? You saw Lark yesterday?"

Lark, led into the ring by Elizabeth and Jean-Claude, a criminal caught in the act of escaping, heard Tom's question, his first question.

"We met in The Strand," said Donna Bird.

"And didn't she tell you about the wedding? Didn't she invite you to come?" Tom turned to Lark. "Is this true?" Three questions.

"And what is also true is that she deliberately saw to it that I was left behind on that island, so that she could get to New York first and marry you."

"Is this true?"

Lark shook her head. "She brought it upon herself."

"What island?" the reporter asked, waving to his cameraman to shift from Tom and Donna to Tom and Lark. "Can someone tell me who exactly got married?"

"I performed the ceremony," said the clergyman. "Just five minutes ago." The cameraman swung his camera to the clergyman.

"Are you sure?" said Professor Bird. "I didn't hear anything."

"It's a new-style wedding," said the clergyman. "We just said the words in a relaxed way, as if we were chatting at a party."

"Who's he?" asked the reporter.

"I'm the clergyman."

"No, him," nodding at Professor Bird. "Father of the bride?" The camera swung to Manfred Bird.

"That's Manfred Bird, the anthropologist, father of this young woman, Donna Bird, his daughter by his first marriage, and this is Mrs. Portia Bird, the present Mrs. Bird, and their four sons."

"And who are you?"

"I am Tom Brown, urban commentator, social theorist, disciple of Professor Manfred Bird, and tonight the groom." The camera swung back to Tom. "This wedding is my way of showing how community can exist in the *urbs*."

"And her?" indicating Lark. The camera shifted to Lark.

"She is my wife, who stands accused at the moment by Miss Bird of certain wrongdoings."

"Are you sure?" Professor Bird asked the clergyman again.

"I'm sure," said the clergyman. "I did say if anyone objected to come forward."

"I didn't hear," said Donna Bird. "I had scarcely arrived."

The camera turned back to Donna. The crowd of onlookers followed the camera. Someone in the crowd said, "It's called street theater, it's new. They plan it in advance, then make it seem spontaneous, and the spectators are supposed to join in, feel involved."

"Goes back to the tradition of the Passion plays," said a man neatly dressed in gray trousers, an open-necked shirt, and a cashmere cardigan. "That's my field. I'm a medievalist. This is probably a modern Passion play."

"What does the bride herself have to say?" someone shouted. "Let her speak. It's her wedding."

Lark opened her mouth to speak.

"Wait," said Manfred Bird, holding up his hand. "We'd better do this properly."

"What about the movie?" someone from the crowd asked. "We came to see a movie."

"All in good time, my good man," said Manfred Bird.

"They're doing a live show first," someone contributed.

"We're going to show *The Sky Above and the Mud Below*, about society and customs in the jungles of New Guinea. It's new," Tom explained in an aside to the reporter. "I wanted to show these *urbs* dwellers that we can be as close as those New Guineans, as the people of any traditional society."

"Now," Manfred Bird looked around, then, picking up the canvas chair that he had knocked over and placing it on the curb, he said, "we need someone to hear the case that Donna wants to make. It seems that this marriage may well be fraudulent."

"You do it," said Tom.

Professor Bird pondered the suggestion, then shook his head slowly. "I must declare myself ineligible, because I am the father of the plaintiff."

"I'll do it," said the clergyman.

"We need someone who is disinterested," said the television reporter, beginning to catch on. "You're a witness, clearly. You need someone from the crowd. Why not him?" He pointed at the man in the cashmere cardigan. "He knows about passion, he said."

The man shrugged, looking around, and since there seemed to be no objection from any quarter, he stepped forward. He shook Manfred Bird's hand, saying "I think we've met? At faculty meetings or at the faculty house?"

"Please, allow me to contribute this debating stool." Manfred indicated the director's chair.

"What about a jury?" The reporter was about to count out twelve people, when Professor Bird said, "The whole village will be the jury."

Lark, who had stood in a kind of daze, again feeling that she was in the middle of a play in progress, still afraid of Donna Bird and of being exposed for having left her on the island, finally was able to ask, "What am I accused of?"

"She's right," said her supporter in the crowd. "She hasn't done anything wrong. This is a democracy. She's just gotten married, that's all, and since when is that a crime? Leave her alone."

All this time the television camera was taping.

"I accuse Lark Watter of deliberately stranding me, Donna Bird, on a remote island in the middle of the Pacific Ocean six months ago, so that she could get to New York before me and trick Tom Brown into marrying her."

"Whoa," said the medievalist in the canvas chair. "Hold it. Start at the beginning."

Donna Bird told how she and Lark left Sydney in order to come to New York, in her case to earn a living as a writer and reunite with her father, in Lark's case to learn about the world and broaden her views and also, Donna now realized, to capture Tom. Her voice was clear and carried through the crowd. No one had any trouble hearing her.

Tom testified that he had expected them both and had rented an apartment for them to share. He said he was surprised that only Lark had eventually shown up, but he had believed her story about Donna Bird's choosing to remain on the Pacific island to help out the islanders.

"She is public-spirited," Manfred Bird contributed. "She always served others. It's in keeping with her character that she would wish to help those less fortunate than she. We all swallowed Miss Watter's account."

The judge held up his hand. "Wait until you're called on to take the stand," he said, and turning to Tom continued. "Had you asked either of the young ladies concerned to marry you, or given either one to understand that you would marry her?"

"If I was in such a hurry to get to New York," Lark objected, "why didn't I just fly from Tacoma? Why did I take three weeks to cross the country, taking even longer than the ship would have taken to get to New York?"

"That is a good point," said Lark's supporter.

"Please don't interrupt the proceedings," said the judge. "Wait until you are called on."

"Now that I come to think of it," Tom said, "Lark never seemed to really like Donna Bird, right from the beginning."

"Can you cite instances of the form in which this dislike manifested itself?"

Tom thought for a moment. "Well, I don't ever recall her addressing Miss Bird directly. I don't think she said more than a sentence or two to her the whole time I saw them both together."

The crowd murmured a little, some saying that was a good indication of the tension that must have existed between the two women, others saying that there's no law that two people have to talk to each other and that as evidence Tom's assertion was not admissible.

"When did the idea of marriage come into it?"

"Although I had never mentioned marriage until I proposed a few months ago, Miss Watter herself had suggested it soon after she arrived."

"Mrs. Brown, don't you mean?" cried Lark's supporter.

"And how did you respond to her suggestion?" The judge pressed on.

"I said, let's just put it on the back burner."

"Why, then, did you propose marriage at a later date?"

"We had watched a man steal a car. Then he proposed. Perhaps he wanted to buy my silence." Lark surprised herself with her statement.

"No speculation about motives," cried several people in the crowd.

"Order, order," said the judge. "The defendant will have her chance to speak."

But Lark's supporter in the crowd was too fired up to stop. "What about love?" he cried at Tom. "You mean you asked the poor girl to marry you and you didn't even love her? That's deception, cold-blooded deception, if you ask me. What was she supposed to think? She thought you loved her." The crowd was swayed and murmured its approval. Love was a good cause.

"Order, order." The judge nodded to Donna Bird to speak.

"I can prove that she was jealous of me and wished me ill," began Donna Bird. "All the time on board ship she was rude and insulting to me. When she came across me writing in my diary—I have kept a diary since I was four—she mimicked me and said, It 'makes you feel you are a drop in the ocean of life.' She mocked me when I got involved in helping the natives with a production of *Our Town*. When I quoted something in Sanskrit and then something in German, she said 'Sanskrit *and* German?' placing the emphasis on 'and' in a sarcastic tone of voice."

"You know Sanskrit?" asked the judge, interested.

"A little," said Donna Bird. "I can quote from the *Upanishad* and the *Mahabharata*."

"How interesting," said the judge. "I have a friend, a Sanskrit scholar, who when he went to India for the first time, tried to speak to the porters at the airport in Sanskrit." He burst into laughter, joined by Donna Bird and Manfred Bird. "He was astonished that no one understood him and thought it demonstrated the decline of that great civilization."

"Get on with it," said the television reporter, looking at his watch. "We've got to make the late news."

"And after I single-handedly tried to keep the conversation alive at the dinner table, she asked me if I ever stopped, in a mean way—she was criticizing my conversation—and after I had recounted several anecdotes, she called me a liar. She said I could not have done what I said I had done or met the people I said I had met. And so I went to my cabin and wrote down the names of all the people I have ever met—it took days—and gave it to her, just to show that we meet thousands of people in our lifetimes and that I do not lie."

"Where is it? Your list?" said Manfred Bird. "I need it for my work." He nodded at everyone around him. "She is a chip off the old block, like minds, so intelligent."

"She has it, or at least she had it. I don't know what she did with it." Donna Bird pointed at Lark. "A lot of work went into it. Then, after the church service we attended on the island, when I said it was wonderful and uplifting—and it was, for we were afforded a glimpse of the customs of these islanders—she said it was the worst thing she had ever had to do."

"She told me she loved the church service," said Tom to the clergyman. "I believed her. She spoke as if she was involved with *Our Town*. I believed her."

"She called attending a church service the worst thing she has ever had to do? Did I hear you correctly?" the judge asked.

Donna Bird nodded. "Moreover, she said I forced her, that was the word she used, forced her, and the steward into the church."

The crowd hummed again, some saying that freedom of religion was one of the basic rights of this democracy and included the right to have no religion, others insisting that anyone who could scorn a religious service would be capable of anything, including stranding a friend on an island, and still others protesting that Lark was right, church services could be pretty tedious and pointless.

Donna continued. "She wanted to spend all her time with the steward, with whom she had struck up a liaison, and whom she had turned against me. I was so lonely on that ship, for there were only we two passengers, and she and that steward, cabin boy really, kept avoiding me, eluding me."

"She chose to stay in her cabin," interjected Lark. "She's allergic to all light, natural and artificial. She has to wear a hat indoors and out, night and day. I was the one who was lonely."

Donna Bird smiled at the crowd and shrugged, and, by touching her hatless head, indicated that Lark was lying. "Exactly. She struck up a liaison with the cabin boy."

"Is that true?" Tom asked Lark.

"You had your own liaison," shrieked Lark at Donna, "with that soft-headed Captain."

"Donna and the Captain?" questioned Manfred, nodding slowly, taking it in. "She is an original. Well, what can I do? At her age she's her own person. I just don't want to know about it."

"Order!" cried the medievalist, and motioned to Donna to continue.

"And she made me go coral walking. She knew I could not take too much sun at the time."

"But she said she went on the coral, too," Tom chipped in. He looked at Lark. "You told me you went coral walking. I believed you."

"The Captain forced us both to walk on coral. He was mad. I can prove it." Lark turned to Elizabeth. "Go upstairs and get my espadrilles from the closet, and the piece of coral on my chest of drawers." She gave Elizabeth the key. "Quick."

"And worse, worse for me," Donna continued, "when I went to look for her on the island—she was missing and the ship was going to leave; I could have left her behind if I had chosen—she contrived to get back on board without my knowledge and allowed the ship to depart, leaving me stranded on an island where ships rarely stopped, where there was no airstrip, nothing."

Lark stood with her head bowed, her hand to her eyes, covering her face. Her other hand, holding the daisies and the daffodils, hung by her side.

"Give her a break," said the kind man in the crowd.

"But she did something wrong," said someone near him. "You can't go leaving people on islands and expect to get away with it."

"I can prove it," said Donna Bird.

"We'll hear from the defendant," said the judge.

Lark managed to pull herself together, suddenly trying to marshal a defense. She threw the daisies and daffodils to the ground, dabbed her eyes with the corner of her dress, and began. "She didn't like me, right from the first day that Tom noticed me and talked to me. She wanted Tom for herself. She even talked to him of settling down and having children. She was always trying to keep us apart, she didn't want me to work with them on *Strange but True* stories. On board the ship she constantly goaded me about Tom, telling me, for instance, that if I went coral walking it would make a good story for Tom, it would entertain and impress him. In fact, I think she planned the whole journey by ship rather than by air in order to keep me from Tom. When she saw Tom liked me better, she set me up. It was a joke that she had planned. She intended to remain on the island all along. She's always staging practical jokes." Lark was guessing, but as she developed this idea, she became convinced that it was the truth.

"She's just falling back on psychology, plumbing the depths, interpreting," objected Donna Bird. "The truth is on the surface. Look only at what happened. Look at the facts."

The judge held up his hand for Donna to cease her interjection and nodded to Lark to continue.

"She thinks jokes are educational, subversive. The ludic,

she calls it. The world as text, she calls it. Ludicrous, I call it." Then Lark recounted the kidnapping, which had been designed to show how easy it was to manipulate the press.

"She's right about manipulation," cried her supporter. "Look at that television camera now, at this very moment."

The judge held up his hand.

Lark told of the ringing of the alarm on the American warship and was about to tell of the *Strange but True* hoax, but thought better of it, since it reflected badly not only on Donna Bird but also on Tom and her. "And then she tried to get me to blow up the ship."

"Blow up the ship? Destroy property? Commit a terrorist act?" The crowd reacted to this allegation very strongly.

"Quick," said Lark to Jean-Claude, sensing that she was ahead, "go up to my desk. There's a folder with pages and pages of names there, in green ink. Bring it."

Elizabeth had just emerged from the building with the espadrilles and the coral. She gave the key to Jean-Claude and brought the espadrilles and coral to Lark.

"You see," cried Lark, exhibiting the soles of the shoes. "They're all cut up from walking on coral. I had to do it, too. She tells lies, you see. She thinks anything is justified, if she is making a point."

"What point is she making by setting it up so that it would appear that you left her behind on the island?" asked the judge.

Lark thought for a moment. "So that she could turn up like this and win Tom."

A murmur swept through the crowd.

"I was forced to walk on the coral. The Captain forced me, and she walked on coral, too. The only difference is that she wanted to and I didn't. We both could have been killed. And this is the coral I got while we were on the reef. She even slipped it into my pocket and said that I should keep it as a souvenir."

The judge inspected the shoes and passed them into the crowd. They were handed around and examined.

"You could do this with a razor blade," someone suggested.

"That's exactly what I said when I saw them," said Manfred Bird. "Just walking around New York streets would do that."

"Why would I cut up a pair of espadrilles?"

"Why, just to be prepared for Miss Bird's accusations and to support your claim that you actually went walking on coral." This was Tom, looking perplexed, angry. "And did you actually have an affair with that cabin boy?"

"You have always said that no one possesses anyone else."

"Then I guess I have to rule that the shoes are circumstantial evidence," said the medievalist judge.

"And the coral?"

"I guess you could also pick up a piece of coral anywhere. I've seen bits like this for sale in tourist shops in the Caribbean," said the medievalist. "And we're losing our focus. The issue is, did she or did she not deliberately leave this young lady behind on a remote island?"

"She tried to get me to destroy that ship," Lark shouted, sensing that the opinion of the crowd was now swinging away from her to Donna Bird. "Anyway, she herself says that there's no such thing as tragedy or error, that things just recur in different forms.

Jean-Claude returned and gave Lark the list of names. Lark turned to the last page. "See? Listen to this." She read the words first as names, then joined together as warnings.

"They could be names," said Donna Bird defensively. "If you'd traveled as much as I have, you'd know that people have all kinds of names, that are strange to you who grew up in a homogeneous society. I collect people with funny and strange names, which is why they are on that list."

"And she helps me," Manfred Bird added.

"What if I had actually destroyed the ship? Or if I had been caught trying to? You must have wanted me to be arrested for terrorism or mutiny." Lark addressed the crowd. "She wanted me permanently out of the way, so that she could get to New York and have Tom for herself."

"Where's your sense of humor? Your sense of the ludic?" asked Donna.

"I can see how it could be considered a joke," said Tom slowly, pondering. "After all, Miss Bird is an aesthete, and the spectacle is the ultimate victory for the aesthete."

"Everything so far is just the word of one against the word of the other. Speculation. Their evidence isn't hard. We have no proof," said the medievalist judge. He stood up, as if his task was finished, and the crowd applauded him.

"But I have proof," said Donna Bird, "proof that she was in conspiracy with that cabin boy and that she left me on the island deliberately. It was a premeditated act." Donna Bird reached into her bag and pulled out a box of film. "I filmed it all."

The crowd gasped. Followed by the television camera, Donna Bird walked over to the projectionist, who had fallen asleep sitting in his little chair, waiting to be called on to run *The Sky Above and the Mud Below*. "Run this," said Donna Bird, shaking him. The man jerked awake, shook his head to clear it, recollected where he was, then threaded Donna Bird's film into his projector. "They're going to have to pay me overtime," he said.

Before the streetful of people—friends and strangers—Donna's movie of life on the island unfolded: the nun, the Protestant church service, the village, and the children's production of *Our Town*. On film it all looked pacific and romantic.

"She's remarkable, isn't she?" said Manfred Bird to Portia. "The boys will be the same when they're older."

Then suddenly, there appeared a sequence of shots of Lark and Paul Crouch, first lying close together on the top deck of the ship, him leaning over her as if he was about to kiss her, followed by the scene on the cliff below the Catholic Church, when Paul Crouch had held Lark to him to prevent her falling, after she had dislodged the stones. Finally, there was a shot of the *Avis Maris* pulling away from the island, taken from the dock, and on the top deck above the bridge was a tiny, ill-defined figure.

"You can't prove that's me or that that person, whoever it is, is even looking your way!" Lark shouted.

The long shot zoomed in to a close-up, and although the figure was still small, clearly it was Lark standing there, her short blond hair and tan skin clearly discernible, staring straight into the camera's eye.

The photograph was on the front page of *Strange but True*. Lark had left the wedding party, after Donna Bird's incriminating film, and was walking in her white dress along Broadway, determined to walk and walk and not return until the late news containing her humiliation was over. Then she could go back to the apartment, pack her suitcase, and run away. She had not made a plan beyond escaping, beyond just leaving with a few things.

She picked up her skirt as she stepped off the curb and crossed the road. She was hungry and thirsty, having had nothing at all during all the evening's proceedings—she did not know whether it should be called a wedding or a trial—and the luncheonette on the other side of the street was still open.

The man behind the counter was pleased to see a customer. Most people at this time of night wanted only to get the first edition of the Sunday papers. They merely came in, paid, and left again.

"You look as if you just got married," he said and slapped a glass of water in front of Lark as she sat on the tall metal stool at the counter. That was when she saw the photograph. She looked around the store partly to make sure there was no television set going in any corner and partly to insure that she was alone, since the last store she had entered, the day before, had

produced from its inner recesses Donna Bird. On a rack opposite the cash register and along a low counter beneath the store
window were the magazines and newspapers, and among those
magazines and newspapers was the latest issue of *Strange but
True,* and on the cover of *Strange but True* was Lark's picture.
The picture was credited to Tom Brown. It was the picture
Tom had taken at the party in his flat after the rally in Sydney.
Lark was sitting on the kitchen counter, and the barefoot Perce,
drunk at the time, clung to Lark with his head in her lap. Taken
by surprise by the camera flash, Lark's mouth was open, giving
her an almost joyful expression, rather than exposing the revul-
sion and disdain she had felt at the time. The caption read: Too
Shy to Propose, Man Begs Ex-Wife to Be His Proxy and Pop the
Question to Wife No. 2.

The story accompanying the photo, with Tom's byline, recounted how after his divorce this Englishman, who was so shy
that he could not even face a camera without panicking, had
asked Wife No. 1 to propose on his behalf to Wife No. 2. "'We
divorced because of his extreme shyness,' said Wife No. 1.
'Sometimes he couldn't even talk to me. But he's improving all
the time, and he's a really sweet person.' Wife No. 1 helped him
out when he started dating after the divorce, telephoning young
women he was attracted to and arranging dates. Sometimes she
would take him right to his date's house and ring the doorbell,
just to get him started. 'I hope she'll be very happy with him,'
said Wife No. 1 of Wife No. 2."

"What'll it be?" asked the counter man. "I'm afraid we're all
out of wedding cake tonight." He was pleased to be expanding
his joke.

Lark ordered a donut and a cup of coffee, and considered
things. Along with the donut and coffee the counter man
slapped down the check.

"I haven't got any money," she said. "I forgot. I just ran
away, you see."

"You won't get far," said the counter man, removing the plate and cup. He made a performance of tipping out the coffee and replacing the donut on its stand. "I should have known," he said into the air. "Nuts come in all ages, shapes, and sizes."

"I should have eaten it before I told you," she said. "It was an honest mistake."

"That would have made it simple for me. I just call the cops when someone doesn't pay. You could have spent the night in jail."

"So give me back the donut and coffee," said Lark. "Jail sounds good to me."

"Crazy," the man said. "Go on, leave, don't bother me."

While he was wiping down the counter, Lark got down from the stool, still holding *Strange but True,* still thinking, and walked back to her apartment. It was after midnight when she rang the bell, for she had also walked off without her keys and had no idea if Tom or anyone else would be there. The street door buzzed open, and when she rang the bell of her apartment, Tom, wearing a sarong, flung the door open.

"You ran off, we need to talk," he said, stern.

Lark pushed past him into the living room. "We do need to talk." She spread the newspaper on the coffee table. "How could you do this? You must have sent in this story and the photo weeks ago. And yet you said nothing to me."

Tom looked at the newspaper, then seized Lark and started dancing around the room. "That's great, wonderful, far out, that's the best news I've had all day."

"Stop, stop," cried Lark. "You've made a fool of me in every way, at our wedding and now this."

"At the wedding I'm not sure who made a fool of whom. I felt pretty deceived myself, and I had to watch you making love with another man, a cabin boy no less, on my wedding day." But he had picked up the paper again and was reading the article.

"I'm going to leave, you needn't worry."

Tom was not listening to her. "You know what this means, don't you?" He looked up. "We're exonerated. They've forgiven us. That's what it means. Even if they tracked us down with their lawsuit, they wouldn't have a leg to stand on because they've continued to use our work. Don't you see? It's like adultery. If you sleep with your wife after you've discovered she has a lover, it's tantamount to forgiving her. Legally there's no case." He twirled around the room. "How do you like my honeymoon sarong? I wanted to surprise and amuse you."

Lark sat on a cushion on the floor. "I think it's despicable of you even to consider using my picture like that."

Tom stopped twirling and sat beside her. "You didn't think it was despicable when you took photos at the bus stop and got the credit. It could be argued that it was despicable to abandon Donna Bird on that island."

"It's despicable to make my wedding a fiasco."

"It's despicable to trick me into marrying you."

"And it's despicable to ask me to marry you without loving me. I really loved you."

Tom put his arm around her. "So, it comes down to this. You left Donna Bird behind and I used your photo." He kissed her. When she did not respond, he gave her a little tickle. "You wanted to marry me, and I asked you to marry me. We're even," and he kissed her again, "Mrs. Brown." He lay on the floor with his head on the cushion and patted the floor beside him. "So we'll just have to make the best of it."

"Then you do love me?"

"Mmmm," said Tom. "That, Mrs. Brown, is a question without meaning. You're quite a spunky young woman. I like it. Arguing suits you. You have mastered lesson number two, making a show in public, and also lesson number three, getting your feet wet in the real world. You were a match for Donna Bird, more than a match—if she had not had that film, you would have won the case. You're coming along nicely." After a while he mumbled, "You missed the news. What a gas. We were on it, the last item. It was very funny. It's not so hard to influence the press."

Lark shook her head. "You're impossible." She could either laugh or cry. "Do you realize that I even shoplifted that newspaper? And I'm not sorry. The guy in the luncheonette deserved it."

"Then, Mrs. Brown, I'd say you are coming along very nicely indeed, learning your lessons well."

"How many lessons are there?" Lark asked, staring at the ceiling.

"Only one more," Tom mumbled, then turned over and fell asleep. They were awakened by the telephone at eight the next morning.

"I just wanted to say good-bye? Did I awaken you? Awfully sorry, of course, but I'm leaving for Europe."

It was Donna Bird. Lark handed the phone to Tom.

"So, you're going today," Tom said. They talked for several minutes about Donna's itinerary and the friends she would be staying with, including, in Paris, the family of Agnes Comet, Tom's old girlfriend.

Lark tickled his feet while he talked, and when Tom hung up he said, "I'm not ticklish. I trained myself out of it when I was in grade school, and after that no one could get at me, tease me or affect me. I have been safe ever since. "So," he put his hands behind his head and contemplated the ceiling. "Our Donna's off to conquer new worlds."

Lark was delignted. "Who is she going to persecute now?"

"Now, now," said Tom. "You yourself know firsthand that the world is her stage, that she has to keep moving, engaging in new enterprises. To her, that is freedom."

"She's dreadful, and you know it."

"Let's not get nasty about Donna Bird."

"All the Birds are dreadful. And all views Manfred Bird holds are opposite to yours. He probably gives those names of his to the authorities. Manfred Bird tyrannizes. So does Donna Bird. They all do. They are like an invading army."

"He is a father to me. I can't just dismiss him."

"He's dangerous. He's also a crook. Nevertheless, you, who aren't afraid of authority, succumb to him, to them all. You are a hypocrite."

"He is grooming me to succeed him."

"Then you are an opportunist."

"I told you, he is a father. You can't harm the father. Perhaps someone else will, but the son himself can't. Or the daughter." Tom put his head in his hands.

"He probably informs on you. What do you think those lists of names are for? His files?" Tom was right, Lark thought. Perhaps there was hope for them together. "He's bogus and devious." She was enjoying herself enormously.

"He is exactly as he appears on the surface," said Tom through his hands. "The man has no depth. I know that."

Lark felt like crying tears of sheer joy. Tom actually was agreeing with her. Tom was criticizing the great Manfred Bird. This was the most intimate conversation she had ever had with Tom. And for the first time, Tom was quiet, not performing.

The telephone rang again. "You take it," said Lark. She believed it was Donna Bird again and wanted now to see how Tom would deal with her.

Tom shook his head. He reached out a hand, picked up the receiver, and handed it to Lark. "I can't," he whispered, and she had to answer.

"This is your telephone courtesy representative," said a woman's voice, smiling, unctuous. "I am calling to report that there is nothing wrong with your telephone."

"What about the extra line leading to the building next door?" Lark asked.

"Who told you about that?" the courtesy representative asked sharply.

"The repairman," said Lark. "He was very courteous."

"He should not have told you about that," the courtesy representative snapped. "He had no authorization to say that. That was confidential. Disregard entirely what he told you. I am calling to inform you that there is nothing wrong with your telephone."

"She said it was confidential," Lark said, which made Tom sit up.

Tom smiled and ran his hands through his hair. She could see that he was still with her, that he was still himself. "You know what confidential means, don't you?" he said quietly. "It means that hundreds of people in hundreds of offices have access to detailed information about you, but since it's confidential it means that you're the one who's not allowed to see it. And we acquiesce, because the government reassures us it's in the interests of national security. Governments lie."

Lark knew that Tom was right—for her life and indeed all their lives had been filed away, somewhere—and that he was right about most things that had to do with public policy. She regretted her doubts about him and what, this morning, had seemed like her petty-mindedness. He had already taught her a great deal. To her surprise and pleasure, she found that this first morning of her marriage she was glad to be beginning her life with this man, Tom Brown, whereas the night before she had been about to escape from him, to flee. She felt fortunate, at last. It was as Tom had promised, her horizons had been broadened. Donna Bird was out of the way, seemed finally to have been put to rest. Tom could now pay full attention to Lark, and Lark could at last relax and enjoy her life with him.

Lark and Tom spent one quiet, happy day together, then the next day Agnes Comet, who had tried to commit suicide when Tom had left her, telephoned from Paris. She had terrible news for Tom and desperately needed his help. Donna Bird, passing through, had given her his number. Her father, a lawyer, was in jail. He had been investing clients' money for his own purposes, buying up art works, and was unable to produce the money when clients had called for it. He was being held in debtor's prison, and Tom simply had to fly over immediately to help Agnes and her mother raise the money to pay back his clients and get him out of jail.

"Of course I'm coming, immediately," said Tom, looking at his watch. "I'll fly this afternoon. I'll be with you tomorrow."

"You're going now, today, this very moment?" Lark was dismayed.

Tom was shaking his head. "That Agnes. You know, she's one of the most intelligent women I have ever met, a first-rate mind." Tom dialed the travel agent. "Change of plans, Mavis," he said, "I'll have to leave this afternoon." And he secured his ticket.

"We've only been married two days."

"Lark, please don't be so possessive and so deeply conventional. You can't appropriate me. That's the same thing as murder. This is an emergency. I have to go. Agnes's mother is a very old friend. I have to help her. And this whole thing is likely to make Agnes flip." He went to his desk. "Luckily everything I'll be needing in Europe is already organized." He placed two boxes of note cards of blue, yellow, green, and white and several folders of clippings and notes in a duffel bag, then he stuffed underwear and shirts and socks and sweaters on top of the note cards and folders. "You can come over as we originally planned, in two weeks, and I'll meet you in Paris."

Lark stood on her balcony, watching the street. She had lost him. She had had him for just one day. There was no point in even trying to be a first-rate mind and to discuss the outcome of elections and economic policy and the arms race. And then another thought crossed her mind. "This isn't another joke, is it?

You didn't plan that phone call, did you?" A dark green station wagon was maneuvering into a tiny parking space, inching back and forth. Lark had grown accustomed to noticing green station wagons, like little remnants of Solomon Blank. A man got out and stood stretching on the sidewalk. It appeared to be Solomon Blank himself.

"Don't be absurd," said Tom. "In this world, emergencies occur, you know."

A woman, the same height as the man, fairly attractive, fairly blond, carrying a baby, emerged from the green station wagon. Lark watched them for a second or two, unable to shout. She ran down to the street, down the five flights of stairs, but the man and his family had disappeared. She ran to the corner, and down the block to the next corner. Then she walked home.

"I thought you had run away," said Tom.

"I thought I saw someone I knew," said Lark. "But I must have been mistaken."

"Don't do that," he said, "don't make me panic like that. And Larkie," he hugged her extravagantly to him, a stage hug, "don't be selfish. I have to help Agnes and her mother. We'll be together again in no time."

When Lark looked down at the street again, the station wagon had gone. She shrugged. Perhaps it had never been there in the first place. Lesson number one, as Tom had taught her— don't necessarily believe what you think you see. Later she watched from the balcony as the yellow taxi whisked Tom off to Kennedy.

Mrs. Watter wrote: "He is interested in genealogy now, ever since he finished his project. And he has written to a lord in England suggesting that they are related. He would like to have ancestors. What next? I wonder. I hear there are many people on this continent who believe they are related to English aristocrats. It's quite an antipodean delusion, I hear. I dread to think what the lord will answer. Don't tell him I called it a delusion, though. I think he misses you. He mutters a lot, about arcs and larks. We are glad you are happy now. It is not such a terrible thing to be settled, you'll find. And you'll be interested to know that I have started a native garden, with bacon-and-egg, black-eyed Susans, sarsaparilla, flannel flowers, and, I hope, touch-wood, a waratah. It's just a small contribution to preserving this natural heritage of ours."

## IV

Off Lark flew on a chartered jet that left Kennedy seven hours late. It was the best deal in trans-Atlantic flights the travel agent had been able to find, and it was just as well she was flying cheaply, since Tom had had to pay the full regular fare.

The night before she left, Lark dreamt that President de Gaulle was asking for volunteers. Lark kept trying to raise her hand and cry out, *"Je, je,"* but the only sound that came from her mouth was a kind of hum. The good part of the dream, Lark felt upon awakening, was that she had understood de Gaulle when he spoke French, although she was aware that the answer she was struggling to emit was ungrammatical.

Lark took Dramamine at the airport, just in case she got airsick, since it was a small, older plane, but because of the delays, she kept taking a dose every four hours until the departure. She fell asleep in the middle of the chicken cacciatore. When she awoke she found there was a piece of unchewed chicken resting in her mouth, which confused her. They had cleared away the dinner tray while she slept, and the chicken in her mouth at first seemed to have no relation to anything around her. She swallowed.

"Oh, Tom," she whispered to the passenger next to her. "There's something I never told you," and slept again, vaguely aware that she had addressed a complete stranger by her husband's name, and had wanted to confess to him her role in the investigation of Manfred Bird's shipment of artifacts.

Lark telephoned Tom at Agnes's flat before she cleared customs.

"*Oui, allô?*"

"*Est-ce-que je pourrais parler à Tom Brown?*" Lark had written the sentence down on a piece of paper. She spoke each word clearly, excited at last to be speaking this language.

The woman did not answer, but Lark heard her call Tom. "*C'est ta femme, comment s'appelle-t-elle?*"

Lark was too pleased to have understood to be concerned with the tone, the content.

"He comes," said the woman.

"*Merci beaucoup,*" said Lark.

"You're welcome," said the woman, who Lark guessed to be Agnes's mother and who, Lark also guessed, must be extremely upset about her husband's detention, which would account for her brusqueness.

"Your plane is so late," said Tom. "I finally gave up calling."

"I'm sorry," said Lark.

After she passed through customs, she realized she had left her collapsible luggage trolley at the phone booth, and as she waited for Tom, turning her stone bracelet around on her wrist, the catch broke and the bracelet fell through a grating. Lark knelt down on the pavement, her forehead resting on the grating, trying in vain to see the bracelet.

"Good grief, Lark." Tom was there trying to haul her to her feet, the passers-by pretending that this woman hunched over on her knees with her head on the ground was nothing out of the ordinary. "For God's sake, get up. Are you ill?"

"I lost my bracelet, that's all." Lark wiped her forehead with her palm.

When Tom saw that she seemed to be all right, he softened, smiled, and held open his arms for her. "You had me worried. I thought at first you were some mad woman praying. Then I recognized the jeans and jacket and the behind in the air." He gave her a playful pat. "Just joking."

"I've even missed you," said Lark, with a little laugh to show that she, too, was joking, although the heaviness from the loss of the bracelet was still with her.

"We really did a good job with raising the money. Mission accomplished. We have almost the full amount pledged. Monsieur Comet will be out in a few days, I hope. I can't carry this." Tom picked up Lark's bag and put it down again. "I'll throw my back out. These soft French beds have been murder."

Lark saw that Tom was still lost to her. He was off and running, and she wondered how she would ever catch up, retrieve that moment of understanding that they had experienced, that perfect day of peace, after Donna Bird had left, before Agnes Comet had called.

"I can carry my own bag," said Lark. "Only travel with what you can carry yourself, has always been my motto. Ever since I was four years old."

They walked to the car, Tom with the palm of his hand at his waist, the fingers rubbing his back, to show that he was indeed incapacitated from sleeping on a soft mattress. "Madame Comet wants us to stay with them for as long as we can."

"Can't we get a hotel room?"

"They'd be terribly offended if we moved out. And besides, it'll save us money, which would be better spent on wonderful food, and you'll be able to see Paris while I finish off my fundraising chores. Madame Comet cooks a mean meal. You've got to hand it to Frenchwomen." He kissed a thumb and a finger to show how good her cooking was. "And they're so grateful for my help that Madame Comet is letting us use her little Citroën— you'll love it, a tin can held together with rubber bands—while we're in France. She's dying to meet you. Agnes, too."

"A little Citroën, a *deux chevaux*, is big enough for a bomb," said Lark brightly. "That's what Jean-Claude said."

Tom opened the door of the car for Lark to throw her bag in. "We called and wrote to everyone who has known the Comets and appealed for help. It was pretty simple. We said it was a misunderstanding, of course, that Monsieur Comet was in prison, but in the meantime they should send in contributions to get him out. It was like fund-raising."

Lark was taking in the road signs, the place-names, saying them to herself as they passed the exit signs on the expressway into the city, striving to appear normal. Every now and then she looked at Tom's profile as he talked, and then she remembered that she was married to the most handsome, most talented man in the world. My husband, she thought, without pleasure, for he had gone from her; my clever husband. Then she remembered Portia Bird saying, "My husband, the tenured professor," as often as she could, and looked out the window again. She wanted things to be straight between them.

Lark moved close to Tom and put her hand on his thigh. He placed his hand over hers. "There's something I never told you, several things, about Manfred Bird and me," Lark said. She rested her head on his shoulder, this moment of confession helping her to feel closer to him, to feel like a wife.

"And there's something I want to tell you." Tom swung off the expressway. "There's something I ought to tell you before we get there. *Salot,*" he called out the window at a driver who had cut in front of him. "*Espèce de . . .*" he could not find a word bad enough but gave the driver the finger instead, a gesture different from its American equivalent. Tom could gesture in French and English. "If Cécile, Madame Comet, says anything about Agnes and me sleeping in the same bed, don't be upset. They were short of space and Agnes has been too upset over her father to be alone. She needs a lot of comfort, you know, a friendly shoulder to cry on. She's a bit shaky emotionally at the best of times."

"You slept with Agnes? We've been married less than three weeks and you slept with Agnes to comfort her?" Lark was screaming, yelling, punching first Tom's arm, then the door of the car. "Let me out, stop this tin can and let me out." She tried to unlatch the door.

"*Mon Dieu,*" muttered Tom. "Take it easy. I told you, it was nothing." He reached over, pushed Lark's hand out of the way, then held the door with his right hand, pinning Lark with his arm back against her seat. The car swerved. Other cars around honked their horns. "*Cochon, salot, espèce de cochon,*" rang out from the other drivers.

"You'll get us killed," and Tom edged over to the curb and stopped.

Lark made another effort to get free and leave the car. Tom grabbed her by the shoulders, shook her violently until she relaxed and let herself be shaken. Then he let her go, and she subsided into her seat.

"Nothing happened," said Tom. "I didn't know you were going to react so crazily. I only told you in case *Madame* makes some kind of joke about it. She has a great sense of humor and likes to joke. I didn't want you to get the wrong idea." He paused. "You're a big girl now, remember. I thought you'd grown more than that."

Lark was whimpering now. "Take me back to the airport."

"Don't be ridiculous. Jesus, I didn't expect the shit to hit the fan. I didn't even expect there to be any shit. I was just helping out old friends, who I've known years longer than I've known you, the same as Manfred Bird. I know how much you hate him and resent my friendship with him."

"But I am your wife," said Lark.

Tom groaned and beat his fists against the steering wheel. "There's one other thing you ought to know. Donna Bird had to fly back to New York. Manfred has been arrested. There's going to be a trial. He's accused of larceny, smuggling, and fraud.

Everything." He looked at her coldly. "That ought to please you."

Lark could see nothing. A gray veil had been drawn over her eyes, as if someone had put drops in to dilate her pupils, blur her vision. She turned to Tom but could not see him. She reached out her hand to see if he was there. He took it as a gesture of reconciliation and grasped her groping hand and kissed it. "There, there Larkie, I didn't mean to shock you. But this is the real world, remember." He shook his head. "Jesus, you frightened me with that outburst. It's not like you."

Lark still could not see. She believed she had gone blind. She reached for the door with her free hand. "Ah, ah, naughty, naughty," said Tom, reaching over and taking that hand, too, holding both her hands in his right hand, the way a rider holds both reins. "Come on, kiss and make up," he said and kissed her cheek and ear. Lark did not move away, which he took as a good sign. "When we get to the Comets, you can go straight to sleep. You're overtired, I can see that."

Lark blinked, trying to dismiss the gray veil.

While Madame Comet had insisted on speaking English on the telephone, as if Lark's French were too painful, in person she spoke rapidly in French.

"*Elle est douce, très docile, une bonne femme, je crois, et malléable?*" She addressed this to Tom, indicating Lark with a nod. "She looks like a child. She should do something about that short hair."

Tom explained that Lark was fatigued from the journey.

"Ah, *fatiguée*, but are you sure? *Vous vous êtes marriés combien de semaines?*" She was raising her eyebrows and nodding in a knowing way.

"No, it couldn't be that," said Tom.

Madame Comet and Agnes had not been home when Tom parked the car outside Madame Comet's flat near the Champs Elysées and led Lark inside. He was carrying her bag now, since she seemed incapable, and he also held onto her as she stumbled and tripped over the doorstep, then bumped into a skinny little table just inside the door. "Steady," said Tom. Then he thought for a moment and asked, "Did you drink a lot on the plane?"

"Dramamine," Lark said. She was concentrating on getting her vision back. The gray had lifted and the pupils seemed to be contracting. She could see the shapes of the pieces of furniture and the brightness at the windows. Tom led her into a bedroom and placed her on the bed. "Is this the bed?" she asked, and sank into sleep.

At dinner, Lark had trouble following the conversation. It was all so much faster than she had expected. She was still working out *"malléable,"* whether it was *"mal et"* something, and they were discussing her illness, or something else altogether, when the conversation moved on. She heard Donna Bird's name and the word or words *"panneroppe,"* or perhaps *"pas neroppe,"* or *"pain eroppe."* After considering that there was perhaps a type of bread called Eroppe bread, or Roppe bread, she finally seized upon Pan-Europe, and gathered that they had been talking about some sort of new political activism designed to unite all the countries of Europe, which Donna Bird had had to give up because of Manfred's troubles. But by then the conversation had progressed even further from Lark's grasp.

Lark was glad that she could not follow everything, that she could plead language difficulties for not joining in, not that anyone seemed to care. She had turned leaden, getting heavier and heavier in the limbs, so that it was hard to pick up a fork, hard to chew, hard to stop the eyelids from descending. Agnes, who had appeared just before dinner for the first time, was also eating in silence, leaving all the talking to Tom and Madame Comet.

Agnes was a plump young woman wearing, that evening, a voluminous paisley shift. Her face was certainly the face of the photograph Tom had shown Lark what seemed like years ago in the cafeteria in Sydney, heart-faced, with blond hair now falling straight and severe to her shoulders. It was a little face that did not belong to the large body. At least Lark was able to discern this. And she could also discern that Agnes was listening attentively to Tom, that her silence was caused not so much by bad temper or shyness, but by admiration of Tom, who was now gesturing exaggeratedly, fluently, pushing his lips forward to form his words well and to show that he was completely at home with this language and in these surroundings. Frequently he laughed, and even his laughter seemed to be in French, and incomprehensible. He reminded Lark of Donna Bird at dinner on the *Avis Maris*.

"He talks like one of us," said Madame Comet to Agnes. "He could be French."

Lark was working hard at remaining upright, moving her fork to her mouth, in order to stop herself from just lying down on the floor and never getting up.

Tom was telling jokes, anecdotes from his childhood. Since Lark knew most of his stories by now, having heard them dozens of times, intimate stories that he told to new acquaintances, using the same words, the same phrases, the same pauses each time, she even recognized some of them in their French versions and punctuated with *mon vieux* this and *mon vieux* that.

For some reason Madame Comet was turned toward Lark and was holding up her little finger, waggling it at her, a gesture Lark did not comprehend. Then in English, she said, "We French have a culture and a sense of history that no one else in Europe possesses, or even in the world. In the little finger of even the lowliest French grocer or laborer," and here she grasped her little finger to emphasize her point, "there is more culture and more history than any American possesses in his entire body—or any *colon,* for that matter."

"*Brava!*" cried Tom, clapping.

Lark had no idea what they had been talking about. Madame

Comet turned back to Tom. "She will learn a lot this summer in France."

"There are exceptions, of course," said Madame Comet, softening a little, and she lapsed back into French and seemed to be saying that Tom, for instance, was *très cosmopolitain, un citoyen du monde.* Manfred Bird, too.

The gray began to descend again. Lark's eyelids kept moving to a close, like a curtain, a portcullis.

"*L'enfant est fatiguée,*" said Madame Comet. "*Vite, vite, allez au lit.*" Lark got up. "And you don't have to worry about leaving Tom with Agnes," added Madame Comet in English, "I'll see that they behave."

The three of them laughed at the joke, and Lark fled from the room, escaped, and again fell onto the bed. But she had trouble sleeping. She lay heavily in bed, and when she did sleep she had dreams that woke her up. She dreamt of a field of cattle, all standing in rows, humming, a male chorus, and then the sound of her own voice, humming, awakened her. She could hear Agnes and Tom in the living room talking loudly and rapidly, Tom's guffaws accompanied by Agnes's prolonged giggling. Lark did not sleep again until the birds started to sing, just before dawn. When she awakened she could see clearly again. The gray had gone. Tom was there, beside her, his mouth straight and stern in sleep.

Lark slipped into the kitchen to sit and think. She turned the faucet on only a little way and let the water hit the side of the pot, as if she were pouring beer, so that the noise would not bring Agnes or Madame Comet bounding into the kitchen.

She sat quietly holding her eyes. She still had no plan, still did not know what to do.

"This is not the way we make coffee in France." It was Madame Comet, taking the pot off the stove, substituting the espresso pot. "And we use the small electric coil, otherwise it wastes electricity." Lark got up. "Stay there, I'll do it."

Some time later, when Tom wandered in scratching his chest with one hand and rubbing his hair with the other, he said, "It has all fallen into place. I must have been puzzling this out while I slept." In the hand that was scratching his chest was also a sheet of paper, which he flung on the table.

"You mean you actually slept?" said Madame Comet, with a wink and a smile at Lark. "Agnes hasn't even stirred yet. They talked all night, you know."

"I wrote it down when I woke up, look," said Tom, pushing the paper at Lark and at Madame Comet. Then he picked it up himself and read out loud, "What is neocolonialism?" He held up his hand in case they might try to answer. "It is the control of export industries. That's it."

"*C'est vrai*," said Madame Comet. "He knows, that one, he could be French. I must rush. I must visit Fernand this morning and tell him the good news, how much money we have."

For the next few days, while Tom and Agnes finished their fund-raising, Lark went for walks through Paris, deliberately not noticing which way she turned, seeing if she would find the way back to the flat or get lost.

Tom laughed when she told him this. "You should take pebbles, or breadcrumbs. I'm really sorry I can't show you the Paris I know so well. Next time. Maybe on the way back, when we return the car."

"Don't leave," Madame Comet begged them. "We won't be able to manage. You are part of the family. Agnes really needs you."

"We'll be back," said Tom.

"How can she say that, about Agnes, in front of me?" Lark said as she packed the last of their things. She thought she sounded like a nagging wife and regretted her question.

"I told you," said Tom irritably, "I keep Agnes stable. She relies on me. I told you what happened once before when I left." He passed his finger across his throat.

"Why didn't you marry Agnes?"

"She has a first-rate mind," said Tom.

"I've hardly even seen her since we've been here. She only seems to come out at night, when I'm in bed already." And again Lark regretted her tone of voice, the whining quality.

After Tom had pulled the car up in front of the building, Lark still sat in the passenger seat while he went in to get their luggage. She did not want to see Madame Comet or plump Agnes. She wanted to watch the two women and Tom haul the luggage out, without her help. She wanted to stay in the car as if she were at a drive-in movie. But when Tom said, "Lark?" and motioned to her to get out, she did so, and she shook hands and said, *"Au revoir, madame, au revoir, Agnes."*

While Tom ran inside to check that they had left nothing behind, Madame Comet put her arm around Agnes and shook her head. "It's not right, you should have had him, you are the one for Tom. It's a joke. That young *colon* only pretends innocence. She has tricked him." She spoke in French, but Lark suddenly knew she had understood every word.

Lark read the road signs as they drove south and then east, *chemin de fer, chute de pierres,* and so on. She kept a list of the towns they passed through: Corbeil, Fontainebleau, Montereau, Sens, Villeneuve-sur-Yonne, Joigny, Auxerre, Courson, Coulenge, Clamecy, Varzy, Premens, Nevers, Moulins, Riom, Clermont-Ferrand, le Mont-Dore, Besse en Chandess, Murat, Aurillac, Entraygues, Estaing, Espalion, Mende, Gorge des Tarnes, Gorges de l'Ardèche.

Tom kept a list of the photographs he took: Clermont-Ferrand from Puy-de-Dôme, Puy-de-Dôme from Clermont-Ferrand; cathedral tower; Basilique de Notre Dame du Port; Romanesque tower; gargoyles; Romanesque doorway; statue over Murat; Entraygues, center; Entraygues, thirteenth-century bridge; Gorges des Tarnes; Gorges de l'Ardèche.

That summer the wasps were particularly bad. Every morning when Lark slipped and clattered down the cobbled lane to the bakery, several wasps followed her, attracted to her yellow dress and drawn along in her wake. If she ran from them, they teemed after her and bumped into her when she stopped. They terrified her.

Lark was hating this summer in France. She now thought she might be pregnant. It was one more thing she had to tell Tom. Tom was always reading or talking animatedly to Elizabeth or Jean-Claude, taking turns with them holding the baby. And while he no longer seemed to talk to Lark or look at her, he often sat with his arm around her or his hand resting on her knee, and she had the feeling she was somehow essential to him, like the paper that is wrapped around a bowl and tucked into the crevices when the bowl is packed in a box.

If Lark listened, beyond Giscard d'Estaing this and Pompidou that and Mitterrand something else, she sometimes learned new things about Tom. She learned that he loved the fireside scene between the two naked men in *Women in Love* and the novels of Hermann Hesse.

Elizabeth passed the newspapers on to Lark every day, but the stories Lark remembered were the fillers, the items about the Indiana woman who crawled and rolled through the snow with two broken legs after her car had run off the road, and the lady from Toledo, Ohio, who took a taxi to San Francisco. And now she was reading insect stories. That morning she had read of a man from Vienne who inhaled a wasp. The wasp stung his throat, the throat swelled, blocked off his windpipe, and the man died.

To get to the bakery she had to steel herself. She walked deliberately, with her hand over her mouth and nose, breathing slowly and quietly. Clustered about the bakery door were more wasps, and inside the display windows, crawling over the fruit tarts and the sugared bread, more. The girls behind the counter did not seem to care. They chatted and laughed, with their mouths wide open, moving the breads and cakes and flicking at the wasps. The first time she had gone in, one of the girls had cried, *"Bon jour, madame,"* and the other had said, *"Il fait beau aujourd'hui, n'est-ce pas?"*

*"Oui, mais les insectes . . ."* Lark had answered, wanting to say that the wasps bothered her but not able to find the words. *"Mais 'la campagne bourdonnait du chant des insectes,'"* she said instead.

The girls had screamed, laughing. "Ooh, she speaks French so well," one said, and the other agreed, *"Oui, oui,"* taking in her breath as she spoke, and to emphasize it she shook one hand in the air, as if she were drying nail polish. *"Formidable."*

It was torture now to go there, but it would have been worse to have stayed in the house and confessed the reason. Lark remained outside in the square until the crowd of customers in the bakery had thinned. She watched the slate-green Rhône. In the middle was a flat rock, a miniature island, which once caught the fancy of a king, who had ordered a table and banquet to be set. He sat on the rock and feasted, with the water swirling by. And he watched while one of the servants bringing him food drowned.

"Good morning," the girls behind the counter sang when she walked in. "What can we give you today?"

As if they did not know. Every morning she asked for eight rolls, two for each of them, and a long loaf for lunch.

Lark escorted the wasps back up the lane to the house. She could slam the door on them, but by the time breakfast had been set on the terrace at the back under the grapevine, the wasps had found their way up the front of the house and over the top and were swarming about them as they sat down.

If a wasp alighted on the butter or fell into the milk jug, Lark ate her roll without butter and took her coffee without milk. She had read that a startled wasp deposited its sting in fright, and that once deposited in food, the sting retained its poison for some time.

She spent most meals walking about the little terrace, turning away from the wasps and smuggling every piece of bread to her mouth. Tom and Jean-Claude laughed at her. Her behavior irritated them both.

"If you move they'll follow you even more," Jean-Claude said. He sat impervious, the brown and yellow striped bodies coasting about his head.

"You'll get an ulcer if you spend every meal on your feet," Tom informed her. "Relax. Enjoy yourself."

"Women rarely get ulcers," Elizabeth said.

There was nowhere for Lark to go to get away from the wasps. The fig trees and vegetable garden made the next terrace, set into the hillside above the house, impossible. Indoors was just as bad. With the shutters open, the wasps flew freely in and out, hovering over the fruit bowl, the sink, and even the bathroom fixtures.

Sometimes, when the others were busy outside, she could close the shutters and doors and stay in the house.

One morning, before the others awakened, Lark took ten empty beer bottles and placed an inch of sugar and water in the bottom of each. She stowed the bottles at intervals around the terrace, behind rocks and plants and other objects to keep them out of sight. Then, as she stood and watched, wasps flew to the bottles and crawled inside, then fell into the sweet water. She planned to empty out the dead wasps every morning and refill the bottles with sugar and water.

Lark was washing her hair over the stone sink in the kitchen. Tom and Jean-Claude sat outside and watched Elizabeth bathe the baby. She had cleared the breakfast things and placed a blue plastic bathtub on the table on the terrace.

From the kitchen Lark could overhear everything they said. She could see them if she raised her head. Tom watched Elizabeth wash the child in the tub. Then he stood up and wet his hands in the bath water and lathered them with soap and tickled the baby all over. Elizabeth ran inside to get her camera. Jean-Claude laughed.

When Elizabeth had taken the photo and finished bathing the child, she wrapped him in a towel and handed him to Tom. Then Jean-Claude asked Tom why he and Lark did not settle down and have a family.

"Plenty of time," said Tom and shrugged and laughed. "Things are fine as they are. Why change it?"

"You'd enjoy being a father," Elizabeth said. She went and stood by Jean-Claude, her hand on his shoulder. Together they watched their child on Tom's knee.

"Time enough for all that," Tom said. He held the child above his head and made him laugh.

Lark watched Elizabeth take another photo.

They sat outdoors, in a small café by the river, and ate fried fish and fresh melon. In the dusk the wasps had thinned out, and those that still flew about had become more attracted to the street lamp behind them. The baby slept, covered with mosquito netting.

"If life could always be like this," Elizabeth said. Jean-Claude rubbed the back of her neck.

Tom told a story. "This reminds me of the night I liberated myself."

Jean-Claude leant back in his chair, Elizabeth leant forward toward Tom. Lark sat quietly and ate the little fish. She had heard this story several times.

"You've no idea what a simple gesture can do to free you from the pressures and hypocrisies of a lifetime," Tom said. "There were eight of us. Two were young priests. We had cooked that steak over the open fire and eaten it with bread and salad and wine. We sat around the fire. Everyone was in a good mood. We sat or lay in the grass. A bit like now. Then suddenly I knew what I had to do. I stood up and took off my clothes, and I jumped over the fire. Then everyone stood up and threw off their clothes, and we held hands and danced around the fire. Those of us who dared jumped over it. Everyone except the priests. They just sat there, in their clothes, looking a bit uncomfortable. But they still sat there, watching, taking everything in. They could have walked away if they had wanted to. They didn't have to watch. We had a ball. We jumped and ran and horsed around. It's the most natural thing in the world, to go about naked. Here we all were, just jumping about and laughing. There's nothing to it, just taking each other's bodies for granted. The guys tried to jump on some blonde and make it with her. She led everyone on, but she wasn't having any."

Elizabeth turned to Lark. "Where were you? Were you liberating yourself?"

Lark shook her head. Tom laughed. "She was busy making tea in a teapot and putting on the tea cozy. Just joking. I didn't know Lark yet. God, you'll never know. It's the most natural thing in the world. Everyone's so hung up about nudity."

"You'd better be careful back in New York, when you're talking to Manfred Bird." Elizabeth giggled. "Remember what he did to those statues."

"Poor Manfred," said Tom. "He must be off his gourd, with this arrest and trial coming up."

Lark counted the number of little fish heads left on her plate. She had eaten thirty-two while Tom told his story. Jean-Claude paid for the meal while Tom was still fumbling in his pocket for the money. Lark felt ill.

They decided to go swimming. There was a stream, a tributary of the river, some ten miles south of the house. Just before the stream joined the river it made a sharp turn. On one side of the turn the water ran deep and swift, swirling against a bank of sheer rock. On the other side the current was slow and edged its way around a deposit of sand, forming a small beach.

Lark put on her bathing suit and joined the others outside the house.

"Your swimsuit's gotten too small for you," Tom said. "It must be all these rolls and croissants and nothing to do."

Elizabeth and Jean-Claude turned to look.

"Stop it, Tom. It's fine," Elizabeth said. "There won't be many people at the beach, anyway."

"It won't hold," said Tom. "The hook at the back will snap as soon as she starts to swim."

He was right. And the suit was old. It had seen her through many Sydney summers at the beach.

"I could wear nothing if it snaps," Lark said. "I'm not hung-up about nudity."

"Don't be silly," said Tom.

"I have a second suit I could lend you," said Elizabeth, in a kind voice."

"It wouldn't fit her," said Tom.

Lark shrugged. "It doesn't matter. I probably won't go swimming, anyway. I have a book I want to read."

Tom put his arm around her shoulders. "That's solved, then. Let's go."

"You can read out loud to the baby," said Elizabeth. "He loves women's voices."

When they got there the sun was high overhead and slightly to the south. There were about twenty people on the beach, in the water, and diving from the rock face on the opposite bank.

Jean-Claude and Tom ran straight to the water. When he was halfway down the beach Tom came running back and kissed Lark. "Sure you're okay?" he asked, and then ran back to Jean-Claude in the water.

Elizabeth fussed about setting things right for the baby. She spread a padded plastic sheet on the sand and on the sheet a white towel. She placed the child on his stomach on the towel, and then she fiddled with a parasol so that its shade fell over the baby's body. Over the parasol she draped mosquito netting, which she anchored with shoes and bags and some stones at the edge of the plastic.

She stood back and admired the construction. "That should keep him safe," she said.

Jean-Claude and Tom called her from the water. They splashed and ducked each other to show her how wonderful it was.

"Are you sure you don't mind staying with the baby?"

"Of course not."

"But are you sure?" Elizabeth persisted. "It seems a shame."

"I'm happy to read."

"Well, all right, if you're sure," said Elizabeth, backing away toward the water. "If he cries, give him the juice in the bottle with the blue cap."

Lark watched Elizabeth run into the water, where Tom hoisted her on his shoulders. The wasps flew about, attracted to the garbage cans and to the people. To protect herself from them, Lark put on a sunhat and sunglasses and draped towels around her back and arms and knees. She drew her knees under her chin and sat hunched with her book before her. She felt like Donna Bird.

Lark had only to move her eyes, without moving her head, to see the baby. He was asleep on the white towel. His back moved in and out as he breathed. One or two wasps alighted on the white netting and crawled about.

One wasp was particularly methodical. She watched it crawl down from the highest point of the net tent and make its way along the edge of the netting at sand level. It crawled into the toe of Elizabeth's sandal and upon emerging at the heel found that the edge of the netting had been caught up by the buckle. The wasp slipped through the gap and into the tent. She watched it walk across the towel toward the baby's foot. Just before it reached the foot, she brought her book down on it and crushed it through the netting. The parasol and net construction collapsed, and the baby woke up crying. Elizabeth hurried from the water to comfort him, and when Tom and Jean-Claude came out and stood over her, dripping, Lark said, "Please, Tom, get me off this beach," and back at the house she told Tom she wanted to leave France, because of the wasps.

He laughed and gave her a hug. "Let's go to Vienne and buy you a swimsuit, instead," he said.

In the store in Vienne, Tom stood outside the changing room reading a book while Lark tried on suits.

Then they all went on to eat nine courses on the terrace of a three-star restaurant.

"This is once-in-a-lifetime," said Tom, patting his wallet in his pocket. "Let's drink to grants that enable poor academics and thinkers to taste the good things." Then suddenly Tom pulled a dark red scarf out of his coat pocket. It was not in any kind of wrapping, just loose. "A present for Lark," he said. He held the scarf by one corner and dangled it in front of her.

"When did you get that?" Lark asked.

"It's lovely," said Elizabeth.

"When you were trying on your swimsuit," Tom said.

Lark reached out for the scarf. Tom jerked it back, laughing. "Say please," he said. And when she did not, he put the scarf back in his pocket. The red corner poked out, and it looked as if it were meant for him.

Back at the house Lark lay awake. Tom's coat, with the scarf in its pocket, was across the back of the chair.

"You shoplifted the scarf, didn't you?" Lark said to Tom.

Tom laughed. He was furious. When he had finished laughing, he turned over and went to sleep.

When Lark returned from the bakery, she heard Tom and Elizabeth talking. Elizabeth held a postcard in her hand. "My sister is coming," she told Tom. "If you stay until next week, you'll meet her."

"Is she as beautiful as you?" Tom asked.

Elizabeth looked uncomfortable. "More beautiful," she replied, and she looked to see where Lark was. "Tom, here's Lark with the rolls." Elizabeth ran over to Lark and led her to the table.

Jean-Claude was walking around the terrace, inspecting the grapevines and smiling off into the blue sky. He stood on a small rock pile. When he stepped back off the stones, he kicked over one of the beer bottles.

"Good grief," he said. The bottle broke and several drowned wasps spilled onto the terrace. Then Jean-Claude went around the terrace collecting the other nine bottles. He lined them up in a row.

"Who on earth had the smart idea to put these everywhere?" He was angry. They all knew that Lark had done it.

"I wanted them to get into the bottles rather than have them bother us," Lark said.

"How stupid," Jean-Claude said. "They're attracting every wasp in the area, it's like sending out invitations to a party." He made a rude noise and emptied all the bottles and put them in the garbage can, shaking his head the whole time.

"She meant well," Elizabeth said. "It could even be argued that it was a good idea. Original."

Tom laughed. "You just have to learn to live with minor nuisances like wasps," he told Lark.

Lark handed over the rolls and went inside. She leant against the sink and watched them talking. Tom had broken his roll and was spreading it with butter and Elizabeth's home-made fig jam.

They started talking about the goodness of simple food.

"Mussels, I love them, but I'm allergic," Tom said.

A wasp landed on the piece of bread he held in his hand. It stuck in the jam.

"I ate them twice before I realized what they did to me."

Elizabeth smiled at her baby, nodding at Tom's story. Jean-Claude was reading the paper.

Tom gestured with his piece of bread. "I thought I was dying. I even wanted to die. Agony."

"I can't wear wool next to my skin," said Elizabeth.

The wasp was thoroughly coated in jam and was no longer moving.

"Maybe the mussels were rotten both times, and I'm not really allergic," said Tom. "But I'm not game to try them again to find out."

He opened his mouth to eat his bread and jam, but decided to finish his story. "Every time we go to a restaurant, it's *moules* this and *moules* that. Delicious. But I can't eat 'em. It's hard."

Lark leant forward over the sink. "Tom," she said quietly, "you'll die if you eat that piece of bread."

Tom laughed at her silliness and looked at Elizabeth for support. He put the slab of bread and butter and jam, with the wasp, in his mouth and chewed. Lark waited for him to notice the difference in texture and spit it all out. He swallowed. She waited for him to cry out and start to die.

Nothing happened.

Tom looked at her. "What's the matter with you, Lark? If that's your idea of a joke, it isn't very funny."

"I don't joke. There was a wasp in your jam. You ate it." She was shouting at him.

"Nonsense," said Tom, frowning and shaking his head. He apologized to Elizabeth and Jean-Claude for her behavior.

"It might interest you to know that I'm pregnant," Lark shouted.

Tom laughed. "Aha. So that's it. That's what's the matter with you. Come here, Larkie, and gimme a kiss."

Lark stayed by the sink. Tom stayed sitting in his chair outside at the breakfast table, smiling and saying, "Well, well."

"And there's something else I want to tell you," Lark continued.

Elizabeth went in to Lark and put her arms around her.

"That's wonderful news," she said, and brought Lark out to Tom.

A wasp that had been circling around the table seemed to be pushed off its course by the arrival of Elizabeth and Lark. It flew straight at Tom and landed on his collar. It crawled onto his neck. Lark screamed. Tom had felt the movement and clapped his hand to his neck. The wasp stung him.

Tom's neck and face swelled, and they rushed him to the doctor. The doctor told Tom he was allergic to the sting and the reaction would be much worse if he were stung again. He advised caution as far as wasps were concerned.

Tom was unable to talk for several days. He stayed in bed and was terrified the whole time that he was going to die. Lark took care of him as if he were an invalid. After Tom had his voice back, he said that if Lark had not screamed, it would not have happened.

Tom and Lark left France as soon as Tom felt he could travel, taking the train to the airport and leaving the car for Jean-Claude to return to Madame Comet. When the photographs Tom had taken arrived in New York bringing cathedral towers, the Romanesque doorway, the gargoyles, the village parade they had happened upon, Lark saw that neither she nor Tom was in any of them. There was no evidence that they had even been in France.

# V

Lark and Tom were waiting for a reporter from *The New York Times* who was to interview them for an article on the alternative life styles being forged by the new generation. Their baby, a few months old, was asleep.

"I don't want to see a reporter," said Lark. "It's ridiculous, you and I talking about life styles. We can't even talk to each other."

"Never give up a chance to use the press," said Tom, having already agreed to the interview.

After the interview he was going out to march against American involvement in Vietnam. "You ought to come, too."

Lark shook her head. "I'll stay with the baby."

"It'd do you good," said Tom. "All you do is brood. You take no action at all. It's good for babies to march, too."

The doorbell rang and Lark brought the reporter in. She was a young woman, slight, possibly only five feet tall, with long, straight brown hair that fell over her face every time she leant forward. She wore a cotton skirt and a T-shirt and carried a backpack over one shoulder.

Lark invited her to sit down. The reporter looked around and chose to perch on the edge of the armchair, resting her backpack at her feet. She crossed her tiny, thin ankles and smiled at them both. "I'm Greta." She bent down to take a writing pad from her pack, her hair falling forward over half her face. With one finger she hooked her hair behind her ear. She took a fountain pen from her pocket, uncapped it, crossed one leg over the other, pad resting on her knee, pen poised. She could have been a high school student on assignment for the school newspaper. Lark thought that she must have looked like this Greta when she first met Tom.

"Would you like tea, or beer?" Lark offered. "Of the latter we have Australian or Philippine, and of the former we have Darjeeling, Yerba Maté, or camomile."

The reporter chose Darjeeling, and while Lark was in the kitchen Greta noted the types of tea in her pad. "Tea is so complex," she said to Tom. "Not many Americans appreciate that. They just give you a warm cup of water with any old tea bag beside it in the saucer." She pulled a face. "Barbaric."

"That's why I married someone who could brew a good cup of chah." Tom's voice was now jolly.

"Traveling is a way of life for you both, I gather."

"We've been everywhere," said Tom.

"All I want to do is travel. I want to be a foreign correspondent. I can't wait to get away." As Greta spoke, she watched her reflection in the French doors, rather like Donna Bird contemplating herself in the reflecting surfaces on the *Avis Maris*. "Of course, I only do light articles like this for the money. I am really a political analyst, and on the weekends, an activist."

"The world needs people like you," said Tom. Lark could hear that he sounded bored, that he was not in the mood for this encounter with the press, which sat there in the form of a very young woman in a T-shirt.

Lark bore in the teapot covered by her mother's tea cozy, and knelt down to set the tray on the coffee table, which, having legs the height of a coffee can, was extremely low. Then she sat cross-legged on the floor on a large cushion covered with an Indian fabric while she poured the tea.

"Lovely touch," said Greta, noting the tea cozy. She smiled at them both again.

"It's all very simple really," said Lark, her voice high-pitched, almost a squeak. She was gripping the teapot with both hands, as if to throttle it.

"We haven't spent a lot of time or money decorating. We have kept everything very simple," said Tom mechanically, without enthusiasm, rocking rather too vigorously in the bentwood rocker. "We value people over things. We trust our real friends to accept us like this." He waved his arms around. "Most of our furniture is secondhand or else we devised it ourselves."

"I didn't devise anything," said Lark. "He did it all. He is particularly good with wood, anything wood he can handle."

Tom took the tray off the coffee table and placed it on the floor so that he could turn the table over to show how simply it had been made. "I saw the other day that the price of rocking chairs like this has doubled since we bought it, which means ours is a bargain, after all. It's as good as second-hand." Tom told the reporter that the rocker was Lark's chair, which she sat in by the balcony to read, write, and feed the baby. "And just plain brood, eh, Lark?" He laughed and rocked back and forth. "The chair you're sitting in, Greta, is actually my chair. We found it on the street and brought it up, gave it a clean and threw a sheet over it, and *voilà*." He leant forward and punched the arm of the chair. Greta drew away from his pounding fist, still smiling and laughing a little. "And we'll have to buy a few other things new, like flatware. But we'll get it the next time we go to Europe, for half the price. We would have got it this last time, but our trip was cut short." He paused. "Wasps."

"Wasps?" asked Greta.

"Yup, they got me on the neck."

"What happened?"

Lark saw that Tom was talking himself into this interview. The wasp incident was about to become another story, and Greta was going to ask all the right questions to bring the story forth.

"I thought I was going to die. It was the second time in my life I thought I'd die. The first time was when I discovered I was allergic to mussels. Not too many people have been twice on the verge of death before they're thirty."

"I certainly haven't been," said Greta. "But then, I still have several years to go, so there's still time."

"And Larkie here was in the kitchen putting tea cozies on teapots, safe as houses. Tell her about the bookshelves, Larkie. Crude but comic. Go on, Lark, show her how the marble rolls." Lark took the marble and let it roll across the floor of the living room. "Isn't it comic," said Tom, annoyed that Lark was not speaking, "the way the sloping floor of this dear old apartment makes the bookshelves, which I just hammered together, look as if they might keel right over?" Tom said they were much more interested in ideas than in possessions. He said the thing contained was much more important than the container. Those bookshelves could produce anything of current relevance in the three worlds. "Four worlds, rather," he said. "Mustn't forget the aboriginal and dispossessed persons of the planet. I'm on my way out to demonstrate against our involvement in Vietnam." He went on to give his views on Vietnam, American policy in Latin America and the Caribbean, disarmament and nuclear proliferation, civil rights and education, and again Lark had to marvel at his fluency, at his quickness. He could present his views persuasively and intelligently.

"There's so much to read, to keep up with," Tom was saying. "We took speed reading, to get through it all."

"That's pretty bourgeois," Greta asked. "Kennedy used speed reading."

Tom looked angry. He stood up and walked to the window, his hands in his pockets.

Lark leant forward and touched Greta's sleeve. "I read *The Secret Sharer* using the speed-reading technique I paid a hundred and fifty dollars for, and only recently did I find out that its theme relates to *Doppelgänger* rather than swimming. You might like to know, also, that I hate marching and demonstrating. And I have a second-rate mind."

"That's all nonsense," said Tom, jovial again, coming alive as if he were making an entrance in a play. He walked over to Lark and plucked her from Greta's arm.

Greta nodded. "Tell me something about your life."

"I left home, traversed half the world, and have now settled down, with my baby. That is essential, the rest is episode."

"I'm always going to travel," Greta said. "I never want to settle down and become a stodgy bourgeois."

"Some people think that it can take great courage not to keep moving and traveling, to stay still in one place for a while," Lark said.

Tom had fallen silent. He seemed not to be listening.

"That won't happen to me, I hope. There's a whole world out there that has to be changed."

"Sometimes traveling can be a form of weakness," Lark went on, to this young woman who would not hear her. "To put down some roots, and to make friends, that can be a brave thing to do, for some people."

"Don't you care about the state of the world?" cried Greta. "Look at the Middle East, look at Latin America, look at what the rich hooligans running this country are doing to ordinary people."

"I know," said Lark. "You are right."

"Don't you want to do anything to save the world, to change things?"

"Some people are able to do more than others," said Lark. "Some can contribute more, often because of something in their past, some quirk of personality, and I am grateful to them. Tom is one." Tom grunted from where he was standing. "I hope you are one of them, too."

Greta shook her head impatiently. "Everyone should be doing

something. Do you realize that any day, any moment, someone, anyone, any odd group, could put together a nuclear bomb and carry it into Manhattan in a backpack?" She gave her own pack a kick. "As small as that. A suitcase. We've come a long way since Little Boy and Fat Boy and Hiroshima and Nagasaki. The cheapest, most effective delivery system you could think of— carry your own bomb in and put it where you want. That would be the end of the world, of any roots you might have put down."

"I know," said Lark.

"I don't know how you can stand New York. Far too much noise. Sirens, radios, car horns, people yelling at one another. It's like World War Three in your own backyard. The price postindustrial society willingly pays for its pleasures. If you're going to be staid and stodgy and settled and sit and put down roots, you might as well go home to where you came from. I hear the weather's good." From the street came the squeal of brakes, longer, louder than usual, followed by a crash. They all ran to the balcony.

"You see, far too much noise," said Greta. "It's not natural or healthy."

A white car had run into a green station wagon parked on the corner opposite. A man jumped out of the white car and started running away from the crash, across the road in front of the apartment, trying to get away, almost knocking down two girls roller-skating. Five police cars and three taxicabs were suddenly on the street, with uniformed and plainclothesmen pouring out. The two girls continued to skate. The fleeing man, seeing his path blocked in one direction, turned and ran back, under the balcony. One policeman had drawn his gun and was taking aim. The girls skated calmly in the line of fire.

"They're going to shoot the children." Lark, looking down on it all, a spectator, unable to help, tried to will the girls out of the way. If she screamed, it would make the situation worse. The children would be distracted and look up. The fugitive spread his arms wide, like a child imitating an airplane, but kept running. A second policeman was now blocking his path. The girls seemed to skate in slow motion, almost stationary. The first policeman's gun remained raised and aimed. Lark waited to hear the gunshots and to witness the death of a child.

The fleeing man careered into the policeman blocking his way. The two of them fell to the pavement. Then a dozen men were on top of him. One was kicking him in the ribs. He lay face-down, his hands handcuffed behind his back. Blood was running onto the sidewalk. The police rolled him over. The skin on his forehead had split open. The two girls skated up to have a closer look. Several policemen were going through the white car, cutting up the upholstery, tearing out the seats and throwing them onto the street. They hurled things out of the trunk. The green station wagon had been spun around and rested on the sidewalk, under a tree. One of its tires had been knocked off and was rolling through the traffic. A city ambulance turned up.

The fugitive had been lain across the trunk of a cab. His blood ran out onto the yellow paint. The ambulance attendant bandaged his head, and he was driven off. The two girls skated over to the blood on the sidewalk. They stood still for a moment, looking down at the red puddle, then took out tissues and dipped them in the blood.

The police cars left, the yellow cabs left, the police drove the white car off. One policeman waited with the wrecked green station wagon.

"They kicked him," said Lark.

"I can use this for a feature on New York life," said Greta.

"Drugs, probably," said Tom.

"Probably had a good kick coming to him," said Greta. "Those children could have been killed. Someone could have been in that station wagon or on the sidewalk."

"But the man was already lying on the ground when he was kicked," said Lark.

"Police brutality," said Tom. "That's what they're like, all the time, the police."

They drew back. "I'm going to have to make tracks," said Tom. "The demonstration won't wait for me."

Greta asked if there was anything else they would like to tell her. Tom related briefly the story of the phone tap. "Actually the government likes to have critics in the middle class. Dissension and criticism serve to legitimize a government, don't forget that. The antigovernment demonstration itself demonstrates that the government is the power." He looked at his watch.

Greta got up to go. "You know how I found you, don't you? Someone at the paper remembered seeing your wedding on television and said it was a brilliant piece of theater. So I thought you would be just the right people for this article. People are simply doing things differently these days, from weddings to childbirth to furnishing a home and preparing food. I'm sorry we haven't had time to speak about the wedding. But I can view the tape at the television station."

"If it's unorthodox living you want, you should talk to Manfred Bird, my mentor. Professor Manfred Bird? But he's off in the field, on some island in the South Pacific. He almost went to jail for theft and smuggling. Maybe he was set up. But they let him off. Good government connections. The Birds led a crazy life for years, long before it became fashionable. His apartment is something else." He looked at Lark. "Great guy, Manfred Bird."

"If it's theater you want, I'll give you theater," Lark burst out at Tom. "It is because of me that Manfred Bird was investigated. I told the authorities in Tacoma. I thought they didn't want to listen to me. I thought there were bombs in those boxes on the ship, but it was really his smuggled art works. It's his own daughter's doing. One of her jokes. Were you in on it, too? Educating me? Forcing me to make a spectacle of myself?

Donna Bird told me there were bombs. She is the one who really destroyed her father, not me."

"Why didn't you tell me this before?" said Tom.

"I loved you. I was afraid of making you angry," said Lark. "I wanted you to love me."

"All you want is love." Tom was standing up, his teacup in his hand, breathing heavily. "That's all you're interested in."

"Most people want love," Lark shouted back at him.

"Not the way you want it. Love is all you want." He looked all around him, as if he had lost something. He looked down at the teacup and saucer, then hurled them against the bookshelves, which swayed back and forth. The shattering sounded surprisingly trivial, slight.

"Do you, did you, love me?"

"Don't you know yet that that kind of question has no meaning?" Tom said.

Greta edged to the door. "I should be going."

Lark, still talking, led her back into the room. "I actually tried to set fire to the *Avis Maris*, I actually put a flame to the bedding, thinking I was possibly saving the world. I was even prepared to die." Lark gave Greta a shake. "Take notes. You want to see how people do things these days? I'll show you how marriages end." She kept hold of the sleeve of Greta's T-shirt.

"Now that's crazy," said Tom. "Setting fire to a ship." He was frowning, angry, and seemed to be looking around for something to throw or push around. His hands were clenching and unclenching, his eyes were darting from one object to the next.

"You had better leave. For good, I mean. I don't want to be married to you. For God's sake, leave. What a terrible error we made."

Tom was suddenly calm. He smiled, shrugged. "Well, well, well. It has taken you long enough." To Greta he said, "Ever since I've known her, I've been trying to get her to stand on her own two feet. I was wondering just what it would take, how far

I would have to go, how long it would take, for her to take some kind of action, do something." He looked at his watch, as if it would tell him exactly how long it had taken. "If you can wait a moment," he said to Greta, "I'll just throw a few things together, and I'll leave with you." To Lark he said, "You've got to admit, you don't know everything, but you know a lot now. Lesson number four complete. It's called standing on your own two feet." To Greta he said, "You see, sometimes an outside source of activation energy is needed to get a reaction started."

Greta, smiling, looking pale and frightened, looked dubiously at Tom then at Lark, who was still grasping her T-shirt. "Far out. You both planned that, didn't you? Another brilliant piece of theater."

Tom appeared with an overnight bag in which he had thrown a few clothes. He was also carrying the carving knife.

"Jesus," gasped Greta, trying to free herself from Lark and get to the door.

Tom strode over to the old armchair and turned it upside down with a thud. He slashed the underside of the chair, then reached into the seat, pulling out the stuffing. Then he cut up the seat cushion and the arms.

"That Russian," he said.

"I get it," Greta said, still nervous. "The performance isn't over yet. Okay. What Russian?"

"The one who came one night, to the party."

"That was months ago," said Lark. "Over a year."

"He was sent, it just dawned on me."

"Sent?" Greta echoed.

"Here."

"Why?"

Lark turned away from Tom, who was still attacking the chair.

"I was just thinking," Tom said finally, "that that Russian

must have planted a microphone in this chair. He didn't move from it all night."

The upholstery of the chair was spread over the floor.

Tom straightened up and threw the knife down. "Listen," he said jovially, seeing the appalled expression on Greta's face, "think of the kind of surveillance that's been going on in this country. You know they photograph demonstrations and then enlarge the faces and catalogue them and put them on file." He kicked at the chair stuffing. "It's not completely off the wall to look for a hidden microphone. And I am considered a troublemaker, I'm known as a critic of society. There's that phone tap I told you about."

He went to the typewriter and took out the sheet of paper he had been working on. "Outline for a manifesto," he explained to the reporter. He gave Lark a pat. "So long. Welcome to the real world."

Greta thanked Lark for her time. "Brilliant," she said to Tom as they left the apartment.

"You see," said Tom, "Jung didn't take his concept of the collective unconscious far enough." They were on the landing waiting for the elevator. "I maintain that we carry with us the memory of the single cell state and that everything we do is part of our drive to return to that primitive state. We constantly seek to break down the boundaries of complex structures. Look at the inevitability of nuclear war. Look at the sexual act itself. Look at Rigoletto. Verdi knew it. So did Einstein."

"That's truly brilliant," said Greta. "But haven't you heard that Darwin's evolution is no longer tenable, that we didn't crawl out of the primordial sludge, that life on earth was brought in on cosmic dust?"

"It was my ancestor who discovered the cell nucleus," said Tom in reply. "And he observed Brownian movement, the irregular zigzag of particles suspended in a fluid, the result of collisions between the particles and the fluid molecules, which are in constant thermal motion."

Lark watched Tom and Greta walk along the sidewalk beneath her balcony, past the wrecked station wagon. Tom gesturing as usual, Greta looking up at him, nodding, smiling, eager.

The doorbell rang. Lark, standing amid the fragments of the armchair, hesitated, then walked slowly to open it. Solomon Blank stood there.

"I've run away," he said, his voice high, tense, his face gray and pinched. "I just drove all the way. Now they've wrecked my car." He stepped into the apartment and leant against Lark, holding on to her. "I needed you."

Lark led him into the living room. He walked right through the remains of the chair and the shards of cup and saucer to the balcony. "I had just arrived from Chicago. I drove nonstop. I was trying to get the courage to ring your bell. I'd gone for a long walk. When I came back, my car was totaled."

Lark made fresh tea, which Solomon drank one cup after another, swaying in the rocking chair. He seemed to be in shock. Lark sat on the cushion on the floor. "So that green station wagon was actually yours? It was an accident. I saw it happen just now."

But Solomon did not seem to care. "We know the same things, you and I," he said. "The ocean, the rocks. I want to stay with you. I can't stand being inland. I just got in the car and pointed east and drove." He lay down on the floor, next to Lark, his head in her lap. "Take care of me," he said, reaching up and stroking Lark's cheek. The white stuffing from the armchair frothed around him. He looked like an angel at play in heaven.

Lark said nothing. She looked around at the chaos of the room. "Go home," she finally said. "To your wife and the baby."

"I'm not happy there. And I love you. I must stay with you."

Lark stroked his forehead. "It'll be all right," she murmured. "You'll feel better soon."

Solomon kissed her hand, then he closed his eyes and seemed to sleep. Lark sat and watched him. When he opened his eyes,

Lark reached for the phone. "Tell me your number," and she dialed Champaign-Urbana.

"I don't want to go home," grumbled Solomon.

Lark passed the phone to Solomon. Then, easing out from under his head, she left the room and lay on her bed, while Solomon talked at length to Amanda. Half an hour later, he came and lay on the bed next to her.

"I'm sorry, Lark. I can't stay. She's hysterical. She wants me back. She doesn't care about the car. I'm sorry. She says she still loves me."

"You're lucky."

"I'm sorry. It's you I must turn away from. Forgive me." Solomon propped himself on one elbow and looked down at Lark.

"It was your idea. I didn't ask you to come."

"I have to go back, but I never want to lose you. You are one of the most important people in my life." Solomon started kissing Lark, making love to her.

Lark rolled away from him and stood up. "I'll call the travel agent. You can leave right now."

"I love you. Will you give me a rain check? In case I'm ever free in the future?"

Lark dialed the agent. "Mavis? Can you reserve a place on the next plane out of La Guardia for Chicago?"

"I'm sorry, Lark," said Solomon. "But Amanda can't manage without me. She's very dependent. I see that now. She's not strong like you."

At the door Lark stepped back from his kiss. "Perhaps you should take her something from New York. A present. You can get it at the airport."

As she closed the door, the baby woke up and began to cry. For a moment Lark rested her head against the door, then went in to her little girl. "You woke up," she said softly, taking the soft, happy baby in her arms and kissing her.

In the space of a baby's afternoon nap, Lark had separated from her husband and rejected a lover.

Solomon Blank wrote: "Mother died today, or maybe tomorrow—the dateline, you know. My mother, not yours. We're going back to live in her house and start afresh. Think of us on that cliff, that beach, that rock shelf. Family life is at a really interesting stage. Little Hugo seems to be doubling his knowledge every day. When asked how old he is, he says, 'Almost two,' but he pronounces it 'oh-mose two.' It was good to see you in New York."

Greta telephoned. "I'll read you what I've written about your life style," she said, "in case there are mistakes. I treated your fight as theater. It was very good. I kind of reviewed it." And she read out the piece, ending with, "'They are now settled smugly in New York City.'"

"Smugly?" Lark was astonished. "Smug?"

"You don't like smugly?" the reporter said. "I'll change it to snugly. That's easy. One letter. 'They are now settled snugly.'"

"You realize we don't live together now. We don't have a life style, anymore."

Greta laughed delightedly. "I know you staged that fight for my benefit. I know a joke when I see one."

Mrs. Watter wrote: "My native garden is doing very well. The bacon-and-egg plant, the sarsaparilla, and flannel flowers are flourishing. The Susans are unsteady. The jacaranda is out and it happens also to be the year for the flame-tree to blossom. The red next to the purple of the jacaranda brings tears to my eyes.

"Which brings me to your father. I'm afraid we have lost him. There has been no news. Perhaps you've heard something. The letter from the shipping company was the first I heard of it. They said the ship stopped at some island and some of their

cargo disappeared or was mislaid. They said they hoped to re-
cover it and there would be no charge. I wrote to them saying I
hadn't shipped anything. He'll be back, I thought, all in good
time. I'd been away for a week, up the coast on a little holiday. I
managed to collect a few more specimens from the bush for my
native garden. He wasn't here when I came back. The box, that
project of his, had disappeared from the basement. I thought
he'd gone off in a huff because I went away. He doesn't like
being left. But I thought it was time he stood on his own two
feet, a man his age in a pet because his wife of twenty-seven
years went away for a few days on her first holiday in years. I
had had enough.

"I didn't think he'd actually do something. He never has before. The shipping company sent me a copy of the bill of lading.
It was for a big box, C.O.D., to New York. Among his papers
under the mattress I found a clipping about a penniless Australian athlete who had himself shipped home C.O.D. from
London in a wooden crate because he couldn't afford the ticket
home. But he shipped himself by air, not sea. That project of
your father's was certainly big enough to hold a man. Perhaps
he packed himself in it, along with supplies, food, drink, a cardigan in case it turned cold. He did say it would be cheaper,
when he went, didn't he? Well, that's what he must have
meant. And now he has been lost or mislaid, or maybe even
stolen. Sometimes freight is stolen. I am quite upset about it. I
don't know what to tell the authorities. It, or he, was insured
for quite a lot. The bill of lading said household effects. The
shipping company said I would get the insurance if they didn't
find the crate.

"Perhaps you will hear something. The whole thing was con-
signed to you. I had noticed that there were holes along the sides
of the box, but I thought it was for decoration or a mistake, so I
said nothing about it. He hates to be criticized. And remember
that lock. It was on the inside. Perhaps you will hear some-

thing. There's no news at this end. Perhaps he escaped and is wandering on some island and is happy. Too, before I left on my holiday he said to tell you, you have made your own way in this tricky world. You have done it all yourself. There has not been much help from us, I am aware."